Great Grisly Hall

By

Charles Lea

Dedicated to my wife Pippa for all her support and love during the writing of this book, my daughter Evie, and Lucy Thomas for reading all the drafts and providing feedback and Dylan, my four-legged friend, for taking me on walks where I could gain ideas and inspiration.

Thanks to all the children who come and participate in my creative writing workshops and their parents and families who bring them.

Part One

Chapter One

The long-term residents of Great Grisly Hall loved staying there.

People will never see this stately, old house from the road or on the train. Any planes fly too high above it for any passenger to spy its many roofs.

There are no electricity cables in sight, just acre upon acre of farm land and, at this time of the year, all the colours of the flowers, crops and trees returning from their winter break. Only the tall, steeple of St Hilda's church, nestled behind a clump of trees and residing in the small, nearby village of Little Grisly broke nature's panorama.

Sometimes, every couple of years or so, a walker or two might stray off the very beaten track and come across the Hall and its ancient, medieval splendour and gaze in wonder, asking if they had entered a time slip and were living in the times of Merrie old England. For one reason or another no map showed Great Grisly Hall. Perhaps the walkers thought they had got lost. Staring at the old building they would realise that without the sound of a car or a plane there was nothing modern from our century or even that of the last.

Time stood still at Great Grisly Hall.

Or so it seemed.

The owner of the Hall, whoever that was, must have simply loved the perfect stillness of the Hall and its grounds, the unkept fields and the old water mill lying next to the stream which also went past the village.

Everywhere there was stillness.

Everywhere there was quietness.

The owner of the Hall must not have minded how decrepit it had now become. Purple, overgrown wisteria grew out of the walls of the Hall and mixed with green other weeds which climbed out of the roof and gutter. A red rooftile or five were missing from its rooftops but no one seemed to mind.

Certainly, the owner did not mind, whoever that was.

Small, square mullioned windows dotted its dark honeyed walls. But there was no-one to look inside and discover just what went on at the Hall.

None of the many tourists who came, each day, to Little Grisly, knew about the Hall.

The Hall looked pretty much like it did, one hundred, two hundred, even four hundred years ago except now it just looked a bit wear worn. Quite wear worn indeed. It needed a lot of work on it. Lots of work and a big dollop of love too.

Was it that the owner did not care about it? Those very few who came before Great Grisly Hall would wonder whether the Hall had just been left to decay on its own, abandoned. Even the owner's family emblem, a knight's helmet and a horn, used for hunting, on top of a shield, situated above the front door to the Hall, was breaking up and falling apart.

To the outside world, nothing seemed to happen at Great Grisly Hall.

And that's how its long-term residents loved it. Just as it was, in the age of yesteryear and, preferably, with no new visitors coming anywhere near it.

You might say that they loved living in Great Grisly Hall.

Except, of course, that they were no longer alive at all.

Chapter Two

For centuries, on their eighteenth birthday, when Great Grisly Hall was full of the living, as well as the dead, the eldest child of the head of the family was told its darkest secrets and further told not to tell anyone else about them. One day they would be called to try and put an end to all the family's problems.

These secrets were:

1. That the last Earl of Huntshire, who used to live at Great Grisly Hall, had made a deal with the Devil himself and had been given a magical chain which could summon up the dead and make them obey him;
2. The Earl tried to break the deal and the Devil cursed him. The last Earl was swiftly taken to hell, only to return to the land of the living on a full moon where he and his two sons, and their marauding steeds, would tear havoc and tragedy on all who came before them and take them down to hell forever;
3. Great Grisly Hall itself became a home, not only for the family, but also for the spirits of those who had committed some terrible crime but, for one reason or another, were too good for hell, but not good enough for heaven.
4. The family, usually the head of the house and his eldest, became guides to these spirits to try and help them move either upstairs to Heaven, or sometimes downstairs to hell.
5. Only the head of the house and his eldest were told of the location of the magic chain, for it was hidden somewhere for safekeeping as it was told that the Devil would one day want it back.
6. Almost four hundred years ago, a young witch tried to steal the chain and gain its power. Although she was hanged till dead, legend told that one day she would return to look for it.

Every person told the family secrets was overawed by the very notion of such things ever happening in the place they loved to play in as a child. As soon as they were told of the ghastly secrets, their childhood fondness for the place was over. For some the enormity of the secrets was too much for them. Every generation had two duties: firstly, to help all the extra residents go either upstairs or downstairs. Once they had accomplished that the curse would be over, and the last Earl would stop his moonlit meanderings. Secondly, they would have to stop the chain from being found for the chain was so powerful that many, including the witch and the Devil, would seek it.

About one hundred years ago, the last of the living family had moved out, leaving Great Grisly Hall to the souls of the dead.

And grisly was a very fitting word for this place. Whilst the Hall looked pleasant, some of the people who lived and died there were rather unpleasant and some of them had died rather unpleasantly too.

The descendants of the last Earl hoped that no -one would ever find the Hall and stumble on it's dark secrets and past.

One fine spring day when the sun was out and there was only one dark cloud in the distance, someone new found Great Grisly Hall.

Primula Percy, and always called Prim, lived in Little Grisly which was, as the birds flew, only about half a mile from the Hall. Her parents, her grandparents and all her forefathers and mothers had, she was told, lived in and around Little Grisly. Prim was tall for her eleven years with strawberry blonde straight hair in a bob cut with a thin, freckled face and a small slightly upturned nose. An ever-present hair clip stopped her hair from covering her green eyes. The colour of her hair and freckles were inherited from her Dad, her nose and eyes from her Mum. People in the village would often tell her that she had an "interesting face" but Prim did not think she was interesting at all. Her parents would often accuse her of just being dreamy. To them, being dreamy was not a good thing to be.

She knew that both her Mum and Dad were clever because she had found lots of certificates hidden in the bottom of a drawer in the bureau desk in their living room, above the Post Office and village shop which they ran. Certificates for a degree in law for Dad and one for Mum in Fine Art and diplomas in Post Office management for both. She had also found photographs of her parents before she was born: playing sport or just hanging out with friends, laughing. Prim could not recognise where these photos were taken, but it was not in Little Grisly. Hidden underneath from these, she had found the school photograph of herself when she was seven. Prim hated that photograph, her Mum had given her pig tails that day in school and, not only did her hair look dreadful, Prim's face was one of anger as if she was a spoilt child, which Prim was not.

There were no photographs on the walls of any family members. Prim could well remember her grandparents on her Dad's side even though they had died when she was young. It would have been nice to have had a photograph of them on one of the walls to remember them by.

There were no photographs on the walls from holidays abroad or at home in England. This was because they never went away at all. They simply stayed in Little Grisly with the only exception being when her parents had to take Prim to her primary school, three miles away, in Longborough. Both of her parents had thought about home schooling but realised this meant they would have to teach her lots of subjects and they did not have the time with all the work in their beloved Post Office shop.

They never really left the village to go shopping. Instead they were reliant on deliveries from the local superstore. Prim's parents were not the most adventurous of eaters and neither of them liked to cook and so, for meals, Prim was only used to tinned food: potatoes; carrots; peas and meatballs, occasionally some tinned soup or something to stick in the microwave and, for pudding, treacle pudding and custard, both tinned too. Sometimes they would just give her sandwiches which they sold from their shop. Even the food at her school was nicer.

She longed to own and run a Hotel, even if she had never stayed in one. She wanted to travel the world and visit all the greatest Hotels and then start her own one which would be the most important, most beautiful, most successful and professional Hotel ever. In her bedroom, she would study her world globe avidly looking at all the places she could visit and where she could locate her dream Hotel.

That was until her Dad took the globe away. There was no need to leave Little Grisly to find a job he would say. She would take over the family business of the Post Office and shop. He had built a toy one in her bedroom, so she could play at being the Post Master behind the counter.

When Prim had gone through the drawer in the lounge, she had also found photographs of her Auntie Rosemary. She had disappeared when Prim was only about three or four but she still just about remembered her, the kind, joking face and, sometimes her parents would mention her, but only when they were angry.

Aside from the disappearance of her Auntie Rosemary some eight or so years beforehand, nothing remotely interesting had ever happened to the family.

Little Grisly was a sleepy village and not much ever happened there at all. Mum and Dad worked in the shop every day from early on to late except for Sundays when it would close at lunchtime. Prim had a great deal of time on her hands by herself.

Prim did not have any friends. With Longborough Primary School being quite far away she never saw the other children outside of school. She never had any birthday parties and, consequently, was never invited to any herself.

No other child lived in Little Grisly. Her parents never made any arrangements for her to play with anyone.

Little Grisly was rather pretty in a charming old-fashioned sort of way with its narrow roads and ancient looking houses and therefore lots of tourists would come and visit. They would come and take photographs, visit the local pub which was called "The Swinging Witch", admire the ancient history of St Hilda's, call into the small teahouse and then buy some postcards from the Post Office and send them to their friends across the world. Prim's parents were always busy.

Most of these visitors were old, retired people. There was hardly anyone her age that came to visit Little Grisly. Any child that did so always looked bored and grumpy and would never say anything to Prim.

There was nothing to do inside the village. No children's play area, no youth centre, nothing. To make matters worse her Dad had laid down some very serious rules to Prim:

1. To always, always be good and tell the truth;
2. To never, ever leave the village and wander out into the fields or even further;
3. To play only in the pub car park, which was down the slight hill from the Post Office, and to try and avoid any parking cars or coaches of tourists.

The said car park, belonging to the Swinging Witch pub, was, as can well be imagined, not the greatest place to play in the world but it was the greatest place to play in Little Grisly. That was because it was the only place to play. In one corner was a little cover for smokers to have a chat and a drag, in another corner were the bins and, regularly as clockwork, Mr Tanner, the owner, would empty out all the bottles of beer and lemonade and coke at around 10.30 each morning which gave the car park the permanent smell of stale ale.

In another corner, almost now hidden by weeds and an overgrowing weeping willow, from the house next door, was situated an old, very old, dirty and battered cream coloured Ford Escort. Despite its appearance, Prim longed to play in it just like the children would play in Chitty Chitty Bang Bang in Mr Coggin's breakers yard and escape into one of her dream worlds but it was locked. Prim looked at the Escort and it looked like the Escort looked back to her, it's headlights looking sad and forlorn that it could no longer play itself, its tyres deflated as if it knew there was nothing to look forward too, waiting for the day it would be taken to the scrap heap. How it must have longed to have driven around the roads surrounding Little Grisly, even as far as Longborough, perhaps even further than that. How Prim longed to take it for a drive and see something and somewhere different.

Sometimes, in the afternoons, Mr Tanner would come out with a bottle of coke and a straw for Prim.

She was always grateful when he did this but, in truth, a pub carpark was hardly an awe inspiring, imaginative place to play even for someone imaginative as Prim, especially so when huge, white coaches would drive in quickly and park to let all the new tourists off to explore.

Once, late last summer, she decided to have a closer look at St Hilda's. It was an old church, built of the local stone blocks that had a warm yellow tinge and reminded Prim of shortbread but not enough to put her off eating them when she could. She ventured into the churchyard, normally she would not even think to go there, not because of her Dad's rules but because it was just a little too eerie for her. The churchyard was mostly covered with the graves of the dead, long dead and not so long dead, their graves stones sticking out of the ground at all angles, here and there a stone statue of an angel standing over someone's tomb and looking sorrowful. Some of the older tombs, usually the bigger ones where many dead could be buried, looked like they had holes in between them and the ground, as if the dead were watching, and waiting. Even in the daytime, the place gave Prim the creeps.

On the day she visited the churchyard a whole pack of tourists where being given a guided tour. Being nice tourists, a few of them had, after noticing Prim underneath a Yew tree, gently pushed her to the front so she could listen to what the guide had to say.

She wished they hadn't.

They were all told about the age of the church: some of it was built well over a thousand years ago. That was amazing if you liked the history of churches. They were told about the fire of four hundred years ago and how parts of the church was rebuilt including sticking a spire on its top which housed the bells. That was not really that interesting. They were then told about the legend of the last Earl of Huntshire who had died centuries ago and, despite being buried in the family crypt below the church itself, was known to haunt the fields surrounding Little Grisly at night time when there was a full moon. The guide mentioned an old ruin of a house called Great Grisly Hall where he had lived but was not exactly sure as to where it was located.

Many of the tourists had gasped when they heard the tale. They gasped even more when they heard that he would take anyone that he met on his way, back to hell where his own soul had been cast.

Some of the tourists had also laughed excitedly when they heard this, perhaps because they were scared at the very thought of such happenings going on in the night time. But to Prim this was no laughing matter. She decided she would never go out into the fields at night time around Little Grisly. She began to realise why her Dad had given her that rule about only playing in the pub car park. Perhaps grown-ups were as sensible as they kept on saying they were.

If only Prim could explore far off places. She was always curious at school and imagining what life would be like somewhere in the rain forest or in a big city. And, of course, in her Hotel.

Not a Post Office.

She rather missed playing with other children. She was always imagining what life would be like if she had some friends. She rather wished she could play with other children and explore all around Little Grisly.

But only, of course, in the day time and certainly not when the moon was full.

The thing with Prim was that although she would dream of having friends and going to far off places: she wasn't sure how she could deal with the reality of having any friends or leaving Little Grisly. Perhaps it was best to just have such ideas in one's head.

Things were about to change.

One day, at the start of the Easter holidays, her imagination or whatever it was that does these sorts of things, brought her not one, not two but three new friends. At first, she was shy, and a little bit jealous of these three who were not just friends but brother and sisters but after only a very short time she realised that they loved her very much and she started to have many adventures and play lots of games in the pub car park.

The first and the eldest was dark haired Amy who, whilst being fun, was also the sensible one and always clever, considerate and careful.

Sadie was second was the same age as Prim. She acted a bit like Prim herself but was also quite wild like her wavy blonde hair and liked to come up with really, silly saying and ideas for things to do. She also liked to liken things to death or mention morbid things all the time. Sadie was certainly not shy in talking or doing.

The last one, and the youngest, was Lockie who was about eight years old and the only boy in the gang. He too was wild, again like his blonde hair, and extremely brave and would often get them all into trouble, that is, if it wasn't for Amy. Clever Amy.

They were always thinking of new games to play.

This was probably a reason why people said Prim had an interesting face. Perhaps they were being polite. Maybe they meant that Prim looked to be a million miles away. Despite her desire to travel further afield that Little Grisly, Prim became adamant that you did not have to travel half that far and that there was enough stuff going on in Little Grisly to last a lifetime when you had three good friends.

And then one day, she found Great Grisly Hall, not that she initially realised it was Great Grisly Hall.

The day she accidentally found the Hall was one of the most special of her life.

As per usual all four of them had been playing in the pub car park. Amy had heard a noise by the bins and turning around saw a crafty old fox nosing around some plastic bin bags. Of course, Lockie decided to run straight at the fox with no fear for his, or the girls' safety.

Silly Lockie.

The fox, frightened, ran out of the car park and behind a tall, overgrown hedge.

"Poor fox," cried Sadie. "He was only looking for food."

Considerate Sadie.

"Perhaps he was looking for some chickens to kill for his tea."

Not so considerate Sadie continued.

"Let's follow him," replied Amy. "Perhaps, we can find where he lives and drop some food off to him to eat."

Kind Amy.

Now normally, Prim would not have done anything of the sort in terms of following the fox especially if it meant leaving Little Grisly. Although she wanted to see the outside world, she was worried what her Dad might say to her when he found out she had left the pub carpark. Her Dad loved his rules and he loved nothing better than to make more of them.

"Are you chicken?" goaded Lockie.

"I hope not, otherwise the fox will eat me," and Prim was happy with her clever answer.

"I think you don't want to go down the path because your scared," Lockie continued.

"Only scared of getting into trouble, my parents will kill me when they find out."

"They will not find out, we are just going down this path, Prim," reassured Amy.

"Come on, you must get bored playing here Prim, a pub car park, I'd sooner play in that church with all those dead bodies." Sadie said backing Amy up.

Prim shuddered at the thought of playing there but thought some more and realised they were all right. She never did anything naughty at school either and despite never getting into any trouble, she also realised that she was not terribly exciting and perhaps she should be. Running a hotel had to be exciting and she should really get some experience of being excited before she opened one.

She agreed, although, she was still quite a bit nervous of going down the path and breaking the rules.

All four of them sprinted and followed the fox down past the hedge and onto a very rough path which ran next to the little, narrow stream and out of the village. All the while Prim kept on thinking that she was going too far out of her comfort zone and about how much trouble she would get into.

But it will only be for a few minutes.

What harm could happen in a few minutes, especially with friends?

Down the path they went with Lockie, leading way ahead in the front, seemingly still seeing the feral fox. Following the stream, they careered to the left past fields enclosed by wild, thick and shaggy hedges, a glade of yew trees mixed with old oak and then back into the open countryside.

Has anyone been down this path for years? Centuries?

The path became narrower here, and the wild flowers and plants, which had started to shoot back up after their hibernation, were already making access quite uncomfortable.

Thank God it's not summer, it would be impossible to walk down here.

In the fields, besides the hedges, they could see a carpet of bluebells growing ever tall in the spring sun, in another field daisies, *millions of them*, wild and gorgeous. Closer by and the aroma of wild garlic dominated whilst below thick nettles sprouted along the side eager to sting anyone who came close. Spiky, green gorse with its yellow petals and slight coconut scent grew in between the hedges and in some of the fields, a cherry blossom tree or three, already their lovely coloured leaves dropping to the ground and mixing with spring's other produce.

Prim had only seen such life in the hedgerows when driving quickly by in the car to school. She simply loved her first time experiencing everything it had to offer, and she was happy. For now, she had forgotten her initial nerves.

They came to the junction of what seemed like another, even tighter path but the brambles had pretty much closed it from access already and Lockie and the others continued down the main one.

15

All these paths around Little Grisly I never knew before.

Finally, as if all the paths led to it, Prim saw the back of the Hall. At first, she thought it to be a mirage or just something seen in the corner of her eye, but it was there, and the more she looked the more she saw of its roofs, its walls, windows and its gardens.

By now the fox was probably miles away and the chase had been long forgotten by Prim and her friends, even Lockie. They all stood facing the back of the Hall at an old wooden gate and looked around at the surrounding, dishevelled garden. Prim turned completely around too and could see the gorgeous view of green fields stretching out until the horizon with only the very tip of the spire of St Hilda's to show where she had come from. What an amazing place she was now at.

How did I ever not know about here?

And, of course, she remembered why she did ever not know, because of the rules.

Sadie and Lockie wanted to play at the Hall instead of the pub car park and this also reminded Prim that she was breaking one of the rules set by her parents. She thought it best to go straight back home.

"Nonsense," said Sadie as opened the gate and ran into the garden. Mischievous Sadie.

"We could play here for years, for ever and not get bored," Lockie joined in as he lifted both arms and pretended to be a plane. Funny Lockie.

"But the people who live in this house might call the police if they see us here." Prim explained. "We can't just go and play anywhere we like."

Amy, Sadie and Lockie all looked at each other.

"No-one lives here Prim," Amy said, "Look around, no-one could live in such a higgedly piggedly mess."

Prim did look around and could clearly see all the weeds, the unkept grass not to mention a few broken windows. Amy was probably right. Clever, clever Amy.

"But my Mum and Dad," Prim insisted, "I can only play in the car park."

"They won't know Prim. Mr Tanner has done his jobs in the car park for the day. No – one will ever find out we are here and not there," Sadie persuaded. Daring Sadie. "And if he does find out and says something, we'll kill him quick."

"Don't worry Prim," assured Amy, "We will leave here before the Post Office closes and before it gets dark. And we certainly will not kill Mr Tanner."

On that promise, Prim, reluctantly at first, agreed.

Within a day or two, the Hall became the only place they would play during the Easter holidays.

At first, they only played outside but one of them, Prim could not remember who, had found that a back door was open and soon they began to explore the entire Hall: the kitchens; the empty bedrooms; the massive hall; a small ballroom and a library still containing dust covered first editions of centuries old books; only the attic rooms were apparently locked and so they had pretty much the whole Hall to themselves.

Prim realised that she absolutely adored the Hall and wished that one day she could own and live in it herself with her family and her three best friends.

It would make a great Hotel.

They played some wonderful games which she made up. In one Prim was Queen Elizabeth I, Sadie was Mary, Queen of Scots, Lockie was Sir Francis Drake and Amy was William Shakespeare. At the start of such games they tried to be nice but Lockie thought it was much better to try and chop people's heads off and the games ended with everyone chasing and shouting at each other. In another, the three girls were the "Suffra-Jet" gang who threatened real girl power

17

against Lord Lockie if he refused them equal rights, which, in the end, he gave them but then went to play war in the corner by himself.

Of course, it wasn't all what Prim wanted to play, Sadie hated playing all these old-fashioned games. She had heard about all the modern things in life and wanted to play dance school where she was the dance teacher and the others were the students competing in local, regional and national finals but Lockie hated that and wanted to be a robot sent to destroy all girl dancers. Amy didn't mind being in dance school if it was only ballet they were dancing.

On the third day of playing at the Hall, they ventured out around the front and onto the main drive and there, announcing the place to all visitors, was a sign, its words almost faded away:

Great Grisly Hall

Private

Prim was a little worried when she saw this. Firstly, it brought it all home that they really shouldn't be playing there. Secondly and despite her living in a tiny village called Grisly, she just could not understand why someone would call their house it. Grisly meant gruesome and ghastly which was horrid, why would it be called that? Unless of course, it was gruesome and ghastly.

Then she remembered what the guide had said at St Hilda's, that the last Earl used to live there. She had wondered whether it could have been the same place but hadn't given it too much thought before.

Prim went from a little worried to quite a bit worried. She looked back at the Hall to see if it was mocking her for being so stupid.

Thankfully for Prim there was Amy who advised her that, for starters, she ought to realise the place was private, but it hadn't stopped her playing there for almost half the week and secondly, that there was nothing gruesome, ghastly or indeed grisly about the Hall at all, just like her pretty, tiny village. Prim agreed with her and decided to put any fears, and the tale about the last Earl of Huntshire to bed. She really was a clever Amy.

But the more they played and the more noise they made, the more the long- time residents of the Hall became a little restless and unnerved.

What had happened to the stillness, what had happened to the quietness of their Hall?

At first some of them thought it was very nice to have Prim playing in the grounds but what would happen if anymore of the living people came? What would happen if a grown up arrived and liked the look of the hall? What if they tried to change it?

The long-term residents were very worried themselves.

Perhaps it was time for Prim to stop playing in the hall.

They decided to hold a meeting to discuss what to do.

Chapter Three

The long-term residents met in the main hall to decide Prim's fate.

They loved "living" inside Great Grisly Hall and some were a little more determined to keep it just as it was.

The main hall was a massive room, the biggest in the entire building and was where Prim usually played. Its ceiling went almost up to the roof and an enormous, once elegant, wide dark wooden staircase led to the upstairs rooms. Close by was the fireplace in which you could park a small school bus inside. It must have been able to burn a whole, huge tree at once. Indeed, the iron pokers were the size of swords themselves. The only thing wooden by the fire place now was a small, and low, three-legged stool on the hearth. In the middle of this room was situated a very long, dark brown table – wooden again and once highly varnished- and it could sit at least forty people in it without getting squashed and this was where the long-term residents sat to make their decision. Not that there was forty of them, more like ten. All over the walls were huge paintings of some of the people who had lived there, centuries before. Between and above the paintings were equally large mullioned windows allowing fresh light into the hall. For some reason or another white sheets' had been placed over the paintings. The residents were unhappy at this as some of them featured in the paintings and they liked to be reminded of themselves when they were handsome or beautiful and alive, but, today, there were more pressing matters to discuss.

Now the long-term residents did not always see eye to eye with each other, some days there would be massive rows and fights between them. But on a matter as important and yet delicate as this they would at least all speak cordially to each other. Well, at least, at first.

Nine of the residents sat around the top of the table. As usual in these matters only the most outspoken were heard. At the top of the table sat the 14th Lord Le Grise, close by and to his left sat Lieutenant Peregrine Carruthers RN, to his right, Lady Elizabeth Riche and next to her, Barnaby Grudge who was dressed in the khaki green uniform of the British Army during World War One, except that it was covered, almost completely, in mud and blood, his blood.

As usual, it was these last two that were the most outspoken. Not only that but they were the most argumentative and feared residents at the Hall.

They and the rest of the residents, apart from one, gathered closely so as not to miss a word of the talk.

"What is our position regarding this living girl who has invaded our space?" announced le Grise showing that he was in charge. "Should she stay or be removed and, if so, how?"

One of the other residents challenged him, "She's just a child playing innocently. Like Harry and you don't mind him."

"I can live with Harry what! After all these years."

"A thousand times and more I have told you, you old fool," Barnaby Grudge cried, "You don't live at all. How many more centuries will it take for you to learn that? I for one am quite happy to make sure this little painful juvenile doesn't live anymore. Oh, to just have peace and rest around here once more."

Peregrine now joined the debate, "You have been restless in peace for a hundred years Barnaby, you should be used to the fact that we are left well alone and be grateful. Would you rather pop upstairs permanently?"

"We are all restless here," Grudge answered back quickly, "And I am quite sure some of you would love for me to go to heaven or hell and leave all you posh nobs alone. I see how you look at me, wondering how I got to stay here when my portrait isn't on one of these four walls, when my family is not of well to do stock. Well I love it here too and have just as much right as you to stay here as well. She, that chat a box girl, does not. How did she find us?"

"Enough of this stupid conversation," Lady Elizabeth said in her cool and clipped manner. It always paid to listen to Lady Elizabeth, she was clever. "As much as I agree with Barnaby that she has no place here, may I suggest we do something that ghosts are meant to be good at."

The other residents looked at each other and puzzled as to what Lady Elizabeth meant.

All eyes watched her as she settled herself properly in her seat, causing a tiny hint of her lavender scent to waft from her mainly maroon red dress and thick white Tudor ruff and into the air. "We scare her! Scare her away and she will never come back."

Barnaby Grudge looked at Lady Elizabeth and laughed. "You're losing your mind as well as your bottle milady. I would have thought killing a girl posed no problem to you. Want to move up to heaven, do we?"

She stared seriously at Barnaby for a moment or two. *What did idiots like him know?*

"It's hardly likely she would come back and stay with us at the Hall, after all she is just an innocent, unlike ourselves," Peregrine added.

"Thank you, sir," Lady Elizabeth said, "I am aware, after almost five hundred years of the rules and no, Private Grudge, I am not losing my bottle, instead I am using my brain. If we killed her then all sorts of people would come looking for her, things would change for the worse and all this would be lost."

And there was a lot of nodding in agreement by what she said.

"So, killing her is out of the question then," le Grise said. "Good news I say. So, we scare her off and never see her again. Now, I don't think anyone of us has any practice in scaring people."

"Well I think it will not be too hard to scare off a little girl," laughed Peregrine.

It was agreed, and they voted that the first option would be to scare her off. The second option, if that did not work, would be to kill her.

Hidden behind the giant fireplace the missing resident listened and was sad. Harry was the same age as Prim and wanted desperately to play with her.

It seemed to him that he was not allowed any friends. This was God's way of punishing him for what he did all those years ago, almost four hundred years ago to a girl who looked rather like Prim.

He didn't want her to be scared away. But he certainly did not want her killed. He could not let that happen, not again.

Back at the meeting of the other residents, it was decided that Barnaby Grudge would be responsible for scaring Prim away.

As the other residents left the meeting, Lady Elizabeth thought to herself. She was sure Prim looked like someone but just could not remember who. Someone with a connection to Great Grisly Hall. She looked up to the covered paintings and wondered.

Barnaby Grudge, 1900 to 1917

It is safe to say that Barnaby Grudge and his family lived up to their surname.

Not only did they hold grudges against everyone, they also held grudges amongst themselves.

For example, Barnaby hated his elder brother simply because he was older and possibly thought of as being more important to his parents. At the same time, his elder brother hated him for being the baby of the family and therefore was possibly more spoilt than he was.

Of course, this was relatively speaking as the Grudge family were not very well off, in fact they were very well poor and there was not much spoiling to be done especially by a mother who held a grudge against both her children for (a) mothering them in her tummy and (b) for them being young and male because in those days you didn't get much for being a woman and, as a consequence, she was regarded as the least important member of the family. If one of them had been a girl then she could have helped with all the washing and cooking, but two boys were simply not interested or willing in doing such domestic chores. Boys didn't do such stuff.

Barnaby's Dad also held so much of a grudge against his two boys for being young and with their future ahead of them that he had long left the house and had moved away with another, and much younger, woman.

Ma Grudge held a grudge against Pa Grudge and, given that there was probably another Grudge family now somewhere else, a grudge against them too.

The Grudge family, well Barnaby's family, lived in Little Grisly. As soon as he was nineteen years old, Barnaby joined up with the British army to fight in World War One or the Great War as it was known then. He wasn't being patriotic. He could not care for his King or country. He left because he could not stand his family, hated Little Grisly and wanted a new opportunity to grumble at something. It was if he held a grudge against life itself.

Now in the army, Barnaby realised that there was one thing he detested more than his family.

Authority. He simply hated being ordered about, by anybody.

Naturally, he didn't take well to orders from those in charge, especially from officers who were only a few years older than him.

He wouldn't take orders from his stupid elder brother so why would he take them from some posh, fresh faced rich boy? Especially one posh, fresh faced man called Lieutenant Brandon who became his platoon commander once training had finished.

Barnaby had accepted, albeit unwillingly, the orders from the massively strong Sergeant Major but only because he was massively strong.

But Brandon was not massively strong and was only an officer and therefore higher up the chain of command than Barnaby because he was rich and had gone to a very well to do school. Barnaby hated him.

The only thing or person stopping Barnaby from killing Lieutenant Brandon or from being court martialled for not obeying orders was Sergeant Hampson and guess what, he was massively strong too. He was also rather kind, but Barnaby saw this as a type of weakness but was never going to argue with a man whose arms were the size of his own legs.

On the fateful evening, near to the village of Arras in northern France, Brandon, Hampson and their thirty or so soldiers were poised ready to leave their trench and attack by cover of darkness the nearest German trench which was only about 20 feet away. Thick was the mist on that night, thick was the cigarette smoke of every soldier. It was only natural that everyone was nervous, well all except one. Barnaby was angry, angry at Brandon, the Generals in charge of the army, the British government, the world and especially his Mum for making him be here at this point despite he, himself, joining up by himself. There was always someone to blame. He cursed and cursed and when one of his brother soldiers said out a prayer loudly rather than in his head, Barnaby spat and cursed. *If God was still around why would everyone be fighting? If God was still around why is my life terrible?*

And the first whistle blew, and they gathered by the ladders.

The second whistle blew, and they cocked their guns.

The third whistle blew and up went the first soldier closely followed by the second and so on.

Despite the darkness, the Germans' were ready and prepared for such an attack and their bullets cracked past like lightning and into the British soldiers.

Soon it was Barnaby's turn and, thinking that Sergeant Hampson had already gone up he stalled and refused to climb up the rickety ladder and into no man's land.

Hampson, however, was leading the rear guard and having been used to Barnaby's antics was watching quite closely.

"Get up that ladder sharpish," he yelled at the top of his voice with such power that Barnaby thought the sound waves had helped push him up the ladder.

He climbed up quickly expecting a bullet to hit him within reaching the top.

He was lucky for now but was frantic.

Looking around for the first time he saw the state of what this land had become: smashed stone walls; a tree already with its leaves lost for autumn but now with its branches burning and just mud, long had the grass been scorched away from this one pleasant field. He could see shadows of his fellow soldiers running towards the German trench, sometimes illuminated by the close explosions here and there, some soldiers hiding behind whatever there was to hide behind shouting at each other whilst others screamed and lay down on the floor. There was a lot of other soldiers on the floor not moving at all and for an instant he did not think that they were dead, they had been alive only moments ago. Across no man's land came the heavy rattle of artillery fire and from that the gross realisation that he was being shot at with orange beams snapping past his body and thankfully not in it.

Immediately he bent down and ran to the closest wall. One of the soldiers in his platoon, who had climbed up behind him, was running side by side.

But Barnaby began to tire and, losing his balance a little, decided quickly to fall onto the wet ground.

It was just as well for the other soldier, just a young man like Barnaby, took one then two then three in the chest and face and, due to the motion of the bullets, seemed to fly backwards without a single scream such was the shock and quickness that his life was taken away from him.

Barnaby cursed, cursed his brother for not being there too and cursed his Dad for not being rich enough to make him an officer.

But crawling slowly through the mud to hide behind the relative safety of the wall who did he meet – Brandon himself. Brandon helped him to sit up and motioned Barnaby to put his rifle down for a moment and passed him his small, opened silver flask. Barnaby grabbed the flask and swigged the liquid down quickly, whisky! He had never tasted it before but knew its smell. It burned his mouth but then warmed his chest.

"I've seen a weak position in the German trench," shouted Brandon, the noise of all the guns and screams almost blocking out his instructions to Barnaby. "If I can get there and take out the machine gunner then it will be easier for the rest of us to storm the trench. Follow me out from behind this wall and aim your gun towards the left of the machine gun and cover me," he ordered.

Barnaby appeared to accept the order, smiled and stood up on his knees facing the wall.

"1, 2, 3." Brandon cried before running off, firing his rifle and running straight at the German machine gun.

Barnaby looked through a crack in the wall. The German bullets grew in their intensity as Brandon got closer to their trench.

I hate taking orders, sod him.

Through the crack in the wall, he aimed his rifle and shot once but could not see the effect of the bullet. He quickly reloaded, aimed and fired and saw the bullet hit Brandon in the back causing him to fall and take another bullet in the face from the German trench.

Barnaby turned around, sighed with relief and rested. He took another but longer swig of the whisky from the flask Brandon had left and felt good.

A few moments later and the wall took a direct hit. Initially, Barnaby re-joined most of his platoon in the big parade ground in the sky until he was court martialled out of heaven and sentenced to reside at Great Grisly Hall for the murder of Lieutenant Brandon until he had changed his attitude.

Of course, he argued that war was murder, but his submissions fell onto deaf ears.

They never found all his body.

Chapter Four

Prim rose early and opened the curtains to see a new lovely sunny day being born and was happy.

April showers, no way today.

Her parents, as usual, had risen even earlier and were working downstairs in the Post Office shop but had left, as usual, some breakfast out for her.

Where shall I go today? And she laughed, there was only one place to go, who was she kidding?

Dressed, she left the house and walked down the high street. For a moment she paused beside the house that used to belong to poor old Mrs Pilkington and for a second remembered her strange dream, her very, very strange dream about Mrs Pilkington the other night and the coincidence that happened before carrying on down towards the Swinging Witch pub and onto the path where she had followed the fox some days beforehand and onto Great Grisly Hall where she had arranged to meet Amy, Sadie and Lockie for a good play.

Small little blue flowers now grew on top of the stinging nettles making them entice and rivalling the bluebells not that Prim really noticed. She was too busy thinking of what games she could play with her best friends. Today she wanted to be in the modern era. A princess, no a Queen, no someone with actual real power.

Prime minister.

Prime minister Percy.

Prime minister Primula Percy

The alliteration of her name to the top job in the country pleased her. It must be written in the stars that, one day, she would become the leader of the United Kingdom.

She began to list words beginning with 'p' that could describe her:

Pretty; plain; powerful; petulant; peculiar; painful; problem and popular.

And to make her feel better she picked out her favourites:

Pretty; powerful and popular.

But then she thought of the words that really described her:

Powerless, plain, painful, peculiar and a big problem. Then she remembered her Dad's plans for her career.

Plain, Prim the Postie.

Post Master Primula Percy.

It was time to change the subject and, spying the roofs of Great Grisly Hall, she thought about her gang and who they could play.

Admiral Amy the assured.

Amiable Amy the admirable admiral.

Lord Lockie of London.

Laughing Lord Lockie.

Senator Sadie of Sweden.

Sweet and strange Sadie.

The three of them met her half way, by the stream and for the rest of the journey argued and pleaded with Prim as to who they should be.

Archangel Amy.

Super Sadie.

Loveable, lucky Lockie.

Sadie would not play at all until she had become supreme senator of the cemetery but Lockie goaded her by saying it reminded him of something he had heard about called chicken supreme, and he ran around Sadie doing a chicken impression until Amy warned him that the wily fox from earlier in the week might hear and try to eat him this time.

Snobby Sadie.

Naughty Lockie.

Sensible Amy.

Arriving at the Hall, they decided that the best place to play was in the main hall, surely that was a very good setting for a Prime Minister to rule especially around the very long and wooden table which could seat all the members of her cabinet at Number Ten, Downing Street, London. Prim stared around the great hall and up at the still covered portraits. *Who are behind the white sheets?* She thought about this for a second before reminding herself that they must be, had to be, former Prime Ministers themselves.

Barnaby Grudge watched Prim enter the hall from the safety of the balcony where the minstrels once played their music for the owners of Great Grisly Hall and their guests. He had watched her odd movements and chatting as if someone else was with her and thought her more than curious, she was a proper weirdo and girls in his day did not or should not behave in such a way. He hadn't given up his life in the Great War for girls like her. She needed taking down a peg or two.

Still, he grinned and looked at the windows bringing dazzling light into hall. *Wait until she is playing well and then let the scaring begin.*

Prim began play by pushing more money into education and the health service. Amy became her education expert advisor, but Sadie argued that the best thing for everyone would be to have longer holidays and no homework as that would help the teachers considerably.

Amy decided to take over the health service and the first thing she banned was sweets and all other sugary stuff. Prim, Lockie and Sadie all argued against her, ban sweets? Who would vote for that?

Lockie pressed Prim for more money to increase the size of his army so he could not only defend the Hall but also go on to attack all enemies and make the country great again.

The three girls were none too keen on this and so Lockie went off to fight the enemy by the fireplace on his own.

Prim was now onto deciding foreign policy and was playing at being polite to all the local countries by organising a ball inside the Hall. She was now busy greeting all these countries leaders by the main front door which led into the hall.

In her head was the most beautiful, melodic music and she began to dance.

Barnaby Grudge knew it was time. A single cloud had flown in front of the sun and, where once there was brilliance, there was now just a dim light and, instead of the sun's warming beams, there was just coldness.

Little girls should be seen and not heard

Little girls should run away when scared

Little girls should hide in their bed

Or little girls will end up dead

Yes, Barnaby Grudge hated little girls, and, in his mind, he was the best person to scare this little girl away and what was more he would enjoy scaring her off too although part of him wanted to kill her. Perhaps by scaring her too hard she could fall and break her neck.

He would take his time with this strange girl, not just appear and run at her shouting but slowly build up the pressure on her, make her shake in her boots before the coup de grace when she should scream, run away and never be seen again.

Primula was certainly a million miles away in thought as she danced around the main hall.

Unseen, Barnaby decided to walk very firmly, very slowly down the grand wooden staircase. Surely, she would look up and hear that something was coming down the stairs to frighten or even kill her.

Step by loud slow step came Barnaby Grudge but Prim did not hear anything; so far into her imagination was she, dancing and discussing politics with one world leader after another, bringing peace to the earth.

Barnaby reached the middle of the stairs and stared at her. If her hearing was so bad then he would have to try another sense, sight.

Little girls who are so weird

Of Barnaby Grudge, they should well fear

For one look of his face will fill them with dread

And little girls will end up dead.

He appeared in his full form of his dark, green, battered muddy and bloody uniform, his pasty white freckled face and short carrot hair. Surely, she would notice him in the corner of her eye as he got closer and smell the dreadful stench of the disease infected trench and the odour of death?

He began his descent towards her again but just as he was about to put another foot down the big front door creaked open and a voice, a posh clear voice, clearly belonging to a boy, called loudly.

"Hello, is there somebody here?"

Prim awoke from her play in shock and immediately looked towards the door. The owners of the house were back. *Quick get out of here before they see us and call the police.*

And Prim ran towards the back door, followed by the other three, into the courtyard and away into the fields and to Little Grisly without once turning back and without once seeing Barnaby Grudge.

Barnaby Grudge also fled up the stairs. *Who was coming into the Hall? Was it a whole family of the living?* He went into one of the bedrooms whose window looked onto the driveway but could not see any car or any other type of carriage.

Perhaps the child who had entered the house had seen him and fled? But then it slowly dawned on him, there was no child. There was no-one. He had been tricked.

Outside the front door Harry hid to prevent the other long-term residents from seeing him.

He had stopped them scaring Prim away. In his mind, there was a massive difference between someone living and someone dead scaring a person away and he was very happy and smiled.

Primula's Strange Dream

Old Mrs Pilkington, who only lived a few doors down from the Post Office, was always nice to Prim to the extent that her father used to say to her, "Stop being so nice to Prim."

She would always give her sweets bought from the Post Office, literally right under Prim's Dad's nose. Unknown to him she would pass them to Prim when he was not looking. She was a kind old soul who lived alone and always took the time to stop and speak to Prim and ask her how she was when Prim walked past her house on the way back from the pub car park.

One night, just before the Easter holidays, when Prim was asleep, Mrs Pilkington came to her in a dream.

Prim was playing, by herself of course, but in a field she had never been into before. It was a hot summer's day and she was traipsing around it looking for honey as if she was Pooh bear. She knew there would be honey somewhere as there were bees' flying all around the field and, as she got closer, she could see that there were lots of them around the yew tree which stood in a corner of the field.

As she smacked her lips with the delicious thought of lovely, gorgeous honey slipping down her mouth, throat and into her belly, she failed to notice something else walking alongside her.

Suddenly she realised the presence close by and could hear footsteps to her right-hand side. Turning quickly in case there was someone evil to hand, she saw that it was not. In fact, it was a lovely collie cocker dog, with a gorgeous fluffy black and white coat, a lovely smiling face and darling ears.

The dog looked up at her and asked, "I hope you are not going to have all that honey for yourself?"

"How do you know I am going to have the honey?" Prim responded as if she had never thought of such a thing. A talking dog, of course, was most common in a dream.

"It tempts everyone in your family Primula Percy. Has done for centuries. We see it all the time."

We, who is we?

And she looked back down at the dog and now he was accompanied by a neat, young fox who was also smiling. Prim thought he looked just like the fox they had chased from the car park of the Swinging Witch.

"You will need some help getting high up to the bees' nest to take their honey," explained the fox. "How will you get close?"

"I will climb the tree," guessed Prim making things up as she went along, and she tried to lift and float in the air as she had done in many other dreams but, sadly, in this one, she could not.

"You will probably need my help," said another voice. Prim turned to her left and saw that there was now a piebald horse walking alongside the fox, the dog and herself.

"Crikey," Prim cried, "What sort of animal is going to come next? I hope it won't be a lion or a tiger? Or even a big brown bear."

"Not everyone can come into this field Prim," advised the dog, "Only special people like you, but you can bring others in, if you like."

Without warning the day turned to a full night and the sky blackened inside a second and everywhere was dark and quite a bit cooler.

Prim turned to the animals', but they had disappeared, and she was alone and felt scared. Most of the moon was behind a thick, white cloud and she wondered whether it was a full moon or not and whether she would soon hear the horse of the last Earl of Huntshire, galloping towards her.

Thoughts of honey disappeared.

In the distance, however, she could see a figure by the gate to the entrance to the field and, instinctively, feeling that it was friendly, ran towards it.

It was old Mrs Pilkington.

"Oh, Mrs P, I am so happy to see you here," explained Prim.

"Are you dear?" Mrs Pilkington asked in a confused manner, "I don't really know where here is."

She turned to Prim and her eyes looked deep into Prim's. She was shivering.

"I am cold Prim, cold and lonely. I don't want to be cold and lonely anymore. Can you help?"

Prim wasn't sure what to do. If Mrs Pilkington did not know where "here" was then they could not be close to their homes in Little Grisly. Then she remembered what the dog had said to her.

"Why don't you come into this field with me, Mrs Pilkington? Then you will not be alone."

"Oh, thank you dear, you are kind to me. I saw the other field across the way and did not want to go into that one."

Prim opened the gate and Mrs Pilkington entered the field and for a little while they walked together in the complete darkness, and stillness, of the night.

Just as suddenly as night had fallen, the white, misty, cloud came away from hiding the moon and there was light, great illumination, and it seemed to take over the whole sky and the land, it seemed to suck everything inside it, Mrs Pilkington included, everything except for Prim.

"You have such a lovely smile sweet Prim," she could hear Mrs Pilkington say followed by a muffled conversation which sounded like it was in the distance, "Andrew, is that you?"

The brilliant white light disappeared, and Prim woke up in her bed, shaking, panting, sweating and, strangely, tasting honey in her mouth.

That was a very strange dream, too real for my liking.

It took ages for her to fall back asleep. She wasn't sure whether she wanted to fall back into the same dream. But when she did wake up in the morning, she was absolutely shattered and did not want to get up and go to school.

Later that day, when Prim arrived back from school her Mum had popped up from the Post Office and was writing a card on the kitchen table. She stopped writing when she saw Prim and beckoned her over.

"Prim I have some terrible news for you. Please sit down."

Prim sat down immediately, she did not want to have to wait and mull over what the bad news could have been.

"You know Mrs Pilkington, down the road? Of course, you do. I am sorry to have to tell you Prim that she died in her sleep last night. She was a nice lady. I know she was always kind to you."

Prim did not know what to say. She had never really experienced a death before, her grandparents died when she was a toddler, and did not know how to act or react. Instead she saw the card her Mum was writing on the table.

"What is that?" Prim asked.

"It's a card to go on a wreath for Mrs P's family, Prim. This is what I have written.

"Sympathy to the family."

That was all.

"Will she be with Andrew now Mum?"

"How do you know about Andrew, Prim? Did she mention him to you?"

"I'm not sure," Prim lied.

"He was her husband but died a long time ago, way before you were born."

"Are they together in heaven now?"

"Oh Prim, you are stupid. One day you will learn that there is no such thing."

It wasn't so long after this dream that Amy, Sadie and Lockie arrived.

Chapter Five

The long-term residents knew straight away that Harry was the reason their plan to scare Prim away had failed. Ironically, some of them had said, that to protect her he had scared her away himself.

Harry was upset. He hadn't meant to scare her away, just stop Barnaby Grudge from scaring her, or worse.

Prim was at home and, now that the shock of almost bumping into the owners of the house had gone, was soundly and roundly bored. She guessed and accepted that the owners of Great Grisly Hall had come back and that it was their house, but she simply loved playing there with her friends.

She looked out of the window, she had only been playing there less than a week but it was the best place around here she had ever found. She certainly did not want to go back to the pub car park. She had had quite enough of her old home-made games such as miss the bus, bump the bus or pretending that the coaches were space ships carrying alien warriors who wanted to take over the village.

There were four problems to these games played in the pub carpark even with Amy, Sadie and Lockie to play with her:

1. Mr Tanner, the pub landlord, would often shout at her to be careful when the coaches arrived;
2. There was a real threat that she could get run over and injured;
3. Only a few of the visitors looked like aliens and not one of them wanted to play with her and
4. The games were absolutely rubbish.

Of course, with the village being surrounded by fields and woods there were lots of other places she could play. Prior to Amy, Sadie and Lockie and before finding the Hall, she had longed to play in these places, make a den and pretend she was Boudicca and await the Roman legions and attack them.

Maybe now she had ventured as far as the Hall, she would be brave enough to just go and play in the woods. Lockie had loved the idea of playing war against the Romans when she had mentioned it to the gang, but Amy and Sadie were less than happy to play it for more than half an hour.

Besides in the woods it was cold in the shade of the spring sun.

Soon all four of them had decided that the best place to play would be back at Great Grisly Hall.

Prim suggested to the others that if there was a boy staying there then maybe they could play with him too. After all, he could be lonely himself. The others looked at each other to disagree but, nevertheless, it was decided that the four friends would return to Great Grisly Hall.

Chapter Six

Lord le Grise, the 14th Baron of Great Grisly Hall, was as happy as a bunny in spring. The sun was shining well, and he could sit on his favourite stone seat in the garden and relax. He loved spring and summer when the days were light and warm, and flowers grew wild in this garden.

He had just made his weekly visit to St Hilda's church and had laid out some of these flowers where his wife and children were buried. His strength was beginning to wane, but he would always pay a visit to his family.

Sadly, the flowers that he picked were, although still beautiful, more weeds than planted, organised flowers and he gazed over at the wildness of the garden.

Oh, how it would be even lovelier if someone could do some gardening.

How he remembered this garden, in his own life time, all laid out and cut clean. An English country garden it had been, and he had been proud of it.

How he also longed for a new book to read. He had read all the books in his library at least ten times and his favourite books a lot more. Some of the newer residents had told him of more modern authors such as Poe or Dickens and he longed to read such up to date books rather than all the old stuff. He was sure that the world had changed, even a little, since his much loved but crumbling at the spine, Encyclopaedia Britannica had been published in 1810.

But at least the world where he resided was quiet. He enjoyed silence but, in fact, he was a little upset that the little girl had been scared away, how he missed the sound of a child playing. How he missed his own children now up in heaven. It was now almost two hundred years since he had last seen them.

Then he had been Lord of this Hall, the master of all he could see with servants and maids and all his three children being very obedient to him, especially his two daughters. How different it was now. Here and probably in heaven everyone was equal, he had initially tried to push that, as a previous Lord of the Hall, he should oversee all the residents', but the others were having none of it. Certainly, Barnaby Grudge was not going to take orders from an old codger like Lord le Grise when he arrived at the hall almost a century later.

When would he see his girls again? How he longed to see them. If only Miss Rose could really help him. She was due to return soon, she must help him get to see his children. To be reunited at last. He would double his efforts to get his move upstairs. *Oh, if only Miss Rose can help. She is terrible at her job.* But his Lordship knew it wasn't just her fault. *Why have I not learnt my lesson? I could be up there right now.*

He was thinking more and more about going to heaven now that Prim had arrived at Great Grisly Hall though. She reminded him of his daughters, she looked familiar but there was also something else about Prim and her antics. Something he had remembered when he was her age. *Could it be?*

His thoughts were broken by a twig being broken across the very unkept garden and towards the path that lay close to the stream and which led to Little Grisly.

"What, what, what?" He muttered to himself, thinking it was probably an animal.

No harm in an animal.

But, of course, it was not. It was Prim herself, and her gang, they weren't being noisy, instead they were being careful not to be seen.

But, of course, they weren't very good at not being seen. Grise saw the young girl quite easily from his seated position.

Oh, bumble bees! The others will not be happy.

Quickly he looked up and behind him to see if any other of the residents were watching. No-one seemed to be around.

Some of those others wanted her dead especially Barnaby Grudge but his Lordship couldn't let another innocent child die.

He had to act before the others heard or saw her. He had to frighten her off himself. Standing up he walked as quickly as his aged legs could towards the gate where Prim was heading to. He could scare her off, he was old Lord le Grise who used to rule this house and all the land around it. He would save the day. For everyone.

Prim looked up into the marvellous blue sky and wondered how it must feel to fly like a bird and look down on the hall and the village and all the little people scurrying around like ants.

She had never flown in a plane before and wondered whether she would have a head for heights and wondered still whether she would have a head for heights even as a bird.

Because of looking up she never noticed the garden gate open by itself and she walked right on and into the garden.

Poor Lord Le Grise stood holding the gate and was sad. She should have seen the gate open by itself and have ran away. *Why did I even open it?* He should have held it firmly shut instead.

He would have to try harder. He would have to show himself as a body to her just like Barnaby did and, for good measure, make some sort of scary groaning noise too. That would surely frighten her away.

Prim looked through and up at all the windows to see if she could see anyone inside the Hall. There was no-one. Quickly, she ran to the front of the Hall, but there were no cars parked in the long drive and the front door was shut tight.

The owners must have come and gone again.

Maybe they were having afternoon tea in Little Grisly, perhaps even buying postcards in the Post Office.

Grise followed her to the centre of the garden where the old sundial was situated and where Prim was now running around ducking and diving, playing and laughing and looking for the others in a game of hide and seek.

Don't make too much noise for your own sake, he groaned and concentrating his hardest he squeezed his eyes and tried to appear so Prim could see him.

Poor Lord le Grise, he was not very strong anymore, and here his apparition lasted only for about a second, like a flash, and no more and his groaning was almost as if his voice was on mute.

He fell onto the grass exhausted. His shade was too old now, too weak to show for long and he sighed as he rested.

At that moment Prim, who had still been running around the bush, fell over and came a tumbling head first right onto poor old Lord le Grise, her hands landing right on his chest.

Ooh, it's terribly cold here.

She looked up into the sky to see if the rain cloud had arrived and whose shadow had landed where she had fallen.

But there was no cloud over her, and within an instant Prim got up and was surrounded by Amy, Sadie and Lockie who had come to see if she was okay.

Lord le Grise retired back to his stone bench, he had failed.

It was time to try and move upstairs.

The 14th Lord le Grise, 1753 to 1832

Fitzwilliam Launcelot Percy, 14th Baron of Great Grisly Hall, and owner of over two thousand acres of prime farm land was a proud member of the landed gentry.

First born and educated at Eton he lived a precious life at the Hall or at his property in London and although his title was relatively minor compared to all the Dukes. Earls and Viscounts that he went to school with he was happy with his lot: rather unknown to many but making a fine income from his land. He simply loved Great Grisly Hall even if he had to deal with the curse caused by the last Earl but, in those days, there wasn't as much trouble with the "other" residents and no-one had come looking for the chain for almost two hundred years.

He could have been a member of Parliament for Longborough and help run the country, but such responsibility meant staying away from his beloved Hall where he could reign supreme himself and undertake his favourite sports of hunting, shooting, fishing and reading. There wasn't much to Lord le Grise apart from these hobbies, apart from, of course, guiding the others either upstairs or downstairs.

Despite such an education, his friends all agreed that he was not the cleverest of garden peas.

There wasn't very much work for him to do either for he employed an estate manager to do everything for him: sort out all the income, speak to the farmers and all that.

Of course, there was one other very important job he and his ancestors had to do: make sure he had a son to inherit the estate rather than just daughters who would be married off to other rich landowners who would then take the land from him. The family jewels would be lost forever if that happened.

But the family jewels could not be lost forever.
Most definitely they should not be lost forever.

One summer's day he had met a very fine lady, certainly the most beautiful he had ever seen and the kindest and amusing. It took a while for her kindness and sense of humour to come out as they courted however, as she was extremely shy and lacking in confidence.

Her name was Miranda de Lancey.

Some of le Grise's friends told him he was punching well above his weight and that he would have to propose marriage to her very quickly otherwise one of those Dukes or Earls would woo her away to their estate.

Some of Grise's more intelligent friends suggested that there must be a reason why she had not already been married to one of those Dukes and Earls and that her shyness and lack of confidence was probably the result of something or other.

One of Grise's knowledgeable friends finally was able to explain the reason she had not already married a Duke nor an Earl and why she lacked confidence.

Her brother.

The stories le Grise was told about this sibling had made his blood boil, his face redden, and his hair go white.

Her brother was simply the most arrogant insufferable bully in England at that time and there were many stories of how he had mistreated people badly or caused them to lose their fortunes, so he could continue to gamble, hunt and drink without so much concern for anyone else.

But although he had made so much money from the despair of others he was not very good at keeping it. Most of it was squandered on wagers and drink and good food.

At least, the brother knew of his best asset which was almost priceless.

His sister. Now that both their parents were dead, he was responsible for her.

The brother was also wise to the fact that his own reputation had decreased her value to him, but she was still worth something from marriage to a Lord and a small estate or a cash payment would be awarded to him for agreeing to the marriage.

Le Grise was smitten with Miranda and she too upon him. She was nothing like her brother and Le Grise sometimes wondered whether they had the same parents. Very soon they had both fallen in unconditional love.

Miranda however still loved and respected her brother no matter what his reputation had been.

Le Grise had a dilemma to face, either stop seeing Miranda because of her brother and the disgrace he could put upon his own family or accept that love was stronger than anything else.

He chose his love for Miranda.

Miranda's brother chose for himself a nice, and rather large, house with some farmland to earn a living off not too many miles from Great Grisly Hall as his pay for agreeing to the marriage.

Some of Le Grise's close friends warned him that he could face ruin with his prospective brother in law. Openly Le Grise said that he was only marrying Miranda and not her brother. Secretly, however, he knew something would have to be done.

He had friends in the East India Company that could give her brother a good income and a nice house with servants somewhere in India. Miranda's brother laughed at such a proposal but then seriously asked for more than just money. The hand of Grise's only sister in marriage. Without this, there could be no marriage to Miranda.

Grise's good friends warned him that if he died without children then the estate of Great Grisly Hall would fall into the hands of Miranda's brother.

There was only one thing to do. The honourable and most noble way of doing things in his time.

He offered Miranda's brother a duel, and in this instance, to the death.

Miranda's brother accepted but on the strict condition that should he win, he would be allowed to marry Grise's sister and therefore gain Great Grisly Hall.

No one else was told.

The date and time agreed, Miranda's brother prepared by inspecting his duelling sword, a rapier. He was highly trained, skilled and experienced with it.

Le Grise knew he had been stupid to offer him a duel. He knew he would lose, he was out of shape and was not as practised or as hot blooded as Miranda's brother.

The brother knew the outcome of the duel. He would marry, inherit the estate and be rich beyond his previous wildest dreams. Even better he could still sell off Miranda and make more money off her. Stupid Lord le Grise he laughed, he clearly wasn't the cleverest in town.

He was still laughing to himself as he walked up the lonely hill about a mile west of Great Grisly Hall, far away from the village.

Le Grise is a fool alright. Today will be the eve of a new beginning.

The last thing Miranda's brother heard was a branch of a tree bend backwards. He never heard the shot, and nothing was ever heard from him again.

Grise married Miranda and had one son, who became the 15th Lord le Grise, and two daughters just as beautiful as their mother.

Le Grise never told Miranda about her brother. She had always thought that he accepted the offer to go to India and was not really surprised that he had never kept in contact.

When Le Grise fell terminally ill, many prayers were said for him to rise into the kingdom of heaven. Secretly, however, he knew he was going nowhere near that place.

He was right for whilst his body was buried in the family crypt inside St Hilda's, his soul remained at the Hall.

Chapter Seven

Harry had been watching the events in the garden with Prim and Lord le Grise and had laughed until he realised what Grise had been up to. Despite being dead for longer than his lordship he could still show himself easily and he had to scare Prim off before she was seen by the others.

But before he could think of what to do a hand fell firmly into his right shoulder.

"Don't even think about it boy! We've all been watching. Now get in here."

Barnaby Grudge pulled Harry into the main hall where most of the others were sitting around the long table.

"I told you we should have killed her." Grudge roared looking for the other long-term residents to agree.

"We can't just do that, think about the consequences," Peregrine Carruthers replied.

"She will keep coming back until we kill her."

"And if you kill her you will never be allowed upstairs."

"I've got no chance of getting upstairs anyway, not by myself nor with Miss Rose. Besides I like it down here, I can be like a lord," and with this statement Barnaby sat regally at the top of the long table.

"Be like a Lord can you? You are a fake," said Lady Elizabeth Riche entering into the conversation.

Barnaby Grudge was shocked.

"No need to be so horrible to me. I'm just saying how it is."

"Well, you are a cause of 'how this is'. Your attempt to scare her off was dreadful, simply dreadful."

"I had a go, that stupid child, Harry, got in the way."

"That child scared her off more than you did," Lord le Grise countered as he walked into the main hall. He looked at where Barnaby Grudge was sitting and was appalled.

"Well I say we kill her. I couldn't care less about going upstairs, I might bump into my family if I did and that's not a very inviting thought," Barnaby grumbled.

"I would have thought that most of your family would be in hell," joked Peregrine, but no-one laughed, and everyone ignored him.

"The law officers, what do you call them, the police, will find her and that will bring people, living people and people are problems, our whole time here could be ruined," said Lord le Grise, "What do you think Harry?"

It was now Harry's time to be shocked. The grown-ups were allowing him to speak and give his opinion. For the hundreds of years, he had been dead they had never asked for his opinion. He was just an eleven-year old boy.

"I think she should just be left to play on her own. She is an innocent, unlike us," he said nervously.

Lady Elizabeth Riche could see this debate was going to take a long time and was not going her way. It was time for her to make the decision for the household. She stood up and the others looked to her.

"Oh Harry, I do not think so. Killing her at this time would be inappropriate but I am very much afraid that we need to scare her off again. Properly this time so much so that she never comes back again."

She stared at Barnaby dismissively, ruthlessly. She then looked around the whole of the table. Everyone, apart from Barnaby and Harry, nodded in agreement.

"Then I think it can be accepted. It is time for the old, red lady of Great Grisly Hall to appear. Or, shall I say, it is time that I used my head."

And with that she smiled as some of the others chuckled. She looked at Harry who began to look terrified.

"And Harry," she checked, "None of your tricks this time."

The whole time that the long-term residents of Great Grisly Hall had discussed what to do with her, Prim carried on playing outside but, eventually tiring of running in the warm sun, she crashed into the long grass and sighed contentedly.

"Eek, there could be dog poo on that grass," shouted Sadie.

"There hasn't been a dog around here for years I reckon," replied sensible Amy.

"Well it's a dead dog then," Sadie said sarcastically.

"I don't want to lie down in the sun," yelled Lockie, "That's what old people do, let's explore the Hall again."

"No, let's play hide and seek again?" Sadie said.

And, it was decided to play hide and seek inside the Hall. By now, the long-term residents had dispersed from their meeting to different parts of the Hall.

The thing about playing hide and seek in such a big house is that there were simply loads of places in which to hide although you could not really know the best places until you had hidden from the seeker lots and lots of times.

The other thing about playing hide and seek in such a big house was that it could takes ages to find someone, especially if you did not know where all the best places were.

Prim was on and counted to thirty in the main hall. Some of the long-term residents of Great Grisly Hall watched her as she finished counting and went on her search around the huge building.

Lady Elizabeth Riche watched her closely, hadn't she played such games when she had been that age? Then she shuddered at the memory of playing with her Henry. Those had been innocent times but a long, long time ago and, for a second, she was jealous that Prim was still young and care free. There could be no more fun and games for Lady Elizabeth and no more fun and games here for Prim. Openly she had told the others that Prim had to be simply scared away. In reality, she wanted Prim dead. Her leader, her mistress had warned her about a possible child coming to Great Grisly Hall and that it might just be best for everyone if the child was terminated.

Is Prim that child?

Does it matter?

Lady Elizabeth decided that Prim must die.

Prim was calling her friends saying that she could smell them and that she would soon find them. However, she was bluffing, and a minute or two later she had sprinted up the grand staircase and left the main hall in search of the three.

Lady Elizabeth followed her.

Despite the warning from Lady Elizabeth, Harry followed a few steps behind, invisible to all.

And Lord le Grise? Well, having heard Prim's game, he now realised who she could only be.

Lady Elizabeth Riche, 1515 to 1555

Lady Elizabeth Riche was a very slippery person, indeed her own father once said that she was as slippery as an eel and just as smelly. She was also as dangerous as an eel however, especially if you happened to be a member of her family.

People say that blood is thicker than water meaning that you keep on the side of your family first before all others. This certainly did not apply to Lady Elizabeth.

In fact, the only part of that saying which had any relevance to her was the word blood.

Lots of it, all spilt from the axeman's block.

Throughout history there have been trying times, difficult and dark days usually when there has been war, famine, disease and natural disasters. In Lady Elizabeth's England there was all that but an added problem: religion. Lady Elizabeth was born a Catholic like pretty much everyone else in England. So far so good.

But then two things happened:
1. Martin Luther and others kickstarted Protestantism as a religion and
2. King Henry VIII, the most famous King ever, was desperate to have a baby boy who would grow up and be king after him.

In those days many people did not think women could rule the country and his first wife Catherine of Aragon had only given him a little daughter called Mary. How could Henry get himself a son? Well to cut a long story short, (and a lot of heads at the same time), using the idea from Martin Luther, Henry became head of the new Church of England, divorced Catherine and married his mistress Anne Boleyn.

Those rich nobles who were keen to keep their heads and curry favour with the King changed from being Catholic to the new religion of the Church of England straight away.

Some Catholics such as Thomas More refused to switch sides. Their heads rolled.

All the nobles were made to sign a vow agreeing to follow Henry as head of the church. Lady Elizabeth's family were very rich and lived not far from Great Grisly Hall in their own very large house. The rich Riches' they were known as.

Her family were very loyal Catholics and did not want to change their religion. They believed that England would soon be invaded and that Princess Mary, Catherine of Aragon's daughter would be made Queen as she was still catholic.

Henry, through his advisors such as Thomas Cromwell, were threatening to chop people's heads off if they remained catholic, so openly all the Riches' signed the succession vow but secretly they were in league with Rome where the head of the Catholic Church lived. Many other families followed suit.

But it was also an open secret that the King had spies located around the country seeking information from people about others who still looked to Rome for their religion.

All thought this sorry state would end soon and religion and life would be back to normal. Of course, they were wrong, how else did Lady Elizabeth end up back at the Hall after her death?

The eldest son of the 6th Lord le Grise was a rather dashing and handsome chap who Lady Elizabeth had known since childhood. In secret, they had been young sweethearts and had long talked about marriage, how many children they would have and even what names they would be given to them all.

Henry Percy was named after King Henry and from about eleven years of age had been sent to boarding school and from there to Oxford University. Up to a year previous he had always come back for the holidays and galloped straight to Lady Elizabeth's home. He would always bring her a present or two, one of them was always lavender. Henry loved Lady Elizabeth wearing the lovely scent of lavender on her dresses and she wore it always, even when he was not there, to remind her of him.

She had always remained at home, had not met many men but even at the age of twenty she had received many expressions of interest from would be suitors however she had rejected them all, ready for Henry to return from his studies and then his travelling and marry her. She loved Great Grisly, it was a delightful place, and one she would like to live in as the next Lord's wife.

Henry did eventually return after his travelling, but, this time, did not visit her. Instead Lady Elizabeth and her family were invited to a ball at Great Grisly Hall.

She felt sure, that now that his studies and riding around were over, he would be given a role in running the family estate and with that he would need a family of his own meaning he would need a wife.

Her to be exactly.

She was almost right.

The ball was such an occasion. Families from as far afield as thirty miles had ridden to Great Grisly Hall and people had talked of it being the social engagement of the year.

Lady Elizabeth wore her finest deep red dress with a brand-new cream ruff around her neck. Her face was powdered white, as was the trend in those times, and she put on her sweetest fragrance, full of the lovely smelling lavender and spices which Henry just adored.

She was, and she knew that she was, the finest looking lady at the ball.

In Tudor times music and the arts were respected by the great and the good and it was a sign of true breeding if one could play an instrument as well as know how to dance to the many new songs that had been written in that time.

Lady Elizabeth safely knew all the songs played at court and, more importantly, how to dance correctly to each one.

She was so happy, perhaps, the happiest she had ever been.

However, as you can probably guess, the ball did not end up being the happiest for her. Her family had been well received by the Percy family and Henry had been very graceful with Lady Elizabeth and had commented on her dress and the fantastic aroma of lavender and exotic spices. She was sure this was to be the night that he would propose to marry her.

There was a large problem.

Henry introduced her to his fiancée, Lady Olivia Pole.

Etiquette amongst these very rich families meant that Lady Elizabeth could not show her shock, then horror then anger at this news and for a further three hours she played or rather acted as the good friend and neighbour to Henry and his future wife. She smiled and laughed but inside she could not have been hollower and wounded. Something left Lady Elizabeth that night.

At one-point Lady Olivia even mentioned that Henry's younger brother was now looking for a wife and that she would recommend Lady Elizabeth to him.

Insolent, presumptuous Lady Olivia. Who does she think she is?

For the next few days Lady Elizabeth stumbled around her home forgetting to eat or dress properly whilst her anger and depression set deeper into her mind.

She tried to make herself better thinking that she would indeed find someone else, but she knew she was just kidding herself. She had never really met any other gentlemen her age and some of her friends had ended up marrying men double their age or older. At least with Henry she knew someone that she trusted, and they could grow old together in love.

But all that had been ruined. Love meant nothing to her now.

She was at a loss and she dived further into her despair.

And then something happened. Less than two days later a man visited her house claiming to be a priest, a catholic priest, and that he had heard that the Riche family would want to celebrate mass. Lady Elizabeth's father, however, thought the man was a spy from King Henry's court and dismissed him with a boot to his round and vast bottom.

The last they heard was that the man would travel to Great Grisly Hall as they had already requested him to perform a mass for the family.

Lady Elizabeth was sure that the Pole family must be wanting to have the mass, Henry's family despite still being secret Catholics were not as devout as to call for a stranger to the local area to come to their Hall.

Perhaps the man was a priest after all.

By coincidence a day later one of the King's officers called around, he was an old friend of her fathers and that night they dined at the Riche family Hall. No mention of the previous visitor was discussed at dinner by any of the Riche family but on the morning after, Lady Elizabeth told the officer that there was a rumour that a priest had travelled to Great Grisly Hall.

The King's officer left within the hour with his troop of soldiers.

Lady Elizabeth guessed that within a few days the engagement would be off.

She was wrong.

A few days later came the news that Henry and the Pole family had been arrested and taken to London.

A few weeks later came the news that Henry, his fiancée and her parents had lost their heads.

Lady Elizabeth never married.

A few years after Henry VIII died his daughter, Queen Mary, tried to reverse the decline of Catholics in England. Despite secretly still being Catholic, Lady Elizabeth was accused with her family of being traitors due to the events over Henry and the Pole family.

For that offence, Lady Elizabeth and her remaining family went to the block themselves and Lady Elizabeth found herself back at Great Grisly Hall, the home of her loved one, as punishment.

As an extra punishment, the portrait of her once loved one, and that of Lady Olivia Pole, stood staring down at her each day from one of the walls of the great hall.

Henry, himself, was safe in heaven with Lady Olivia.

Chapter Eight

Amy, Sadie and Lockie were very good at hiding. Prim hoped they weren't all hiding together as that would be a bit unfair, almost like bullying. She could hear them laughing.

Just, where are they?

"I know where you are," she announced looking here and there, opening doors and tiny cubby holes but, again, she was lying and was beginning to get a little upset.

She reached the dark, second and top floor of Great Grisly Hall and had tried to keep quiet by tiptoeing up the wooden steps which, ungratefully, creaked on her every step. She had only been up here once before, surely the other three wouldn't hide up on this floor, but their voices seemed to be somewhere close.

It was a bit more than a little bit creepy and Prim was starting to lose her bottle.

The oval shaped windows on the landing were dirt ridden and the only drop of real light came from a small hole in the roof above.

Across the landing stood one closed door. She stopped to listen to hear the other three. *Are they in here? They better be.* There was only one way to find out. Slowly, again on tiptoe, she gently crossed the wooden floorboards which again, of course, groaned as if they had been asleep for centuries and bemoaned being woken up by some little child.

She paused at the door and, as if on impulse, turned the small brass door handle around and pushed the door open with some force but the complete blackness of inside the room shocked and knocked her back a few steps.

Prim paused for a little while so that her eyes could get used to what little light there was.

The room ahead was empty, just wooden floorboards, walls and ceiling but further on she could see the shadow of another door to another room. It was not an inviting sight.

Would Amy, Sadie and Lockie be in there? Had anyone been in there for years?

She certainly could not hear their voices anymore.

In fact, she had not noticed it before but by being still she realised the absolute quiet in the Hall, no birdsong nor anything else could be heard up there, just the sound of her breathing. She was panting fast, she didn't like being so high up in the Hall. She could feel her heart beating faster.

A cold chill ran down her entire body from head to feet.

She realised she was all alone up on the second floor.

If Amy, Sadie and Lockie had been up here, they were not up there now.

But something else was.

Her nostrils tickled, and she realised she could smell something she knew. Lavender.

How could such a smell be here? Perhaps lavender grew as a weed on the roof. Perhaps the owners had returned from afternoon tea in Little Grisly?

The others must have scarpered, there's friendship for you.

It was time to go back downstairs and get out of the house.

Quickly.

Just as she turned she heard a floorboard downstairs creak.

"Sadie, Amy, Lockie is that you?" Prim whispered hopefully.

But there was no reply. She tiptoed to the staircase ready to run as fast as she could, not just back into the hall but right outside the house itself and back into the pleasant sunshine towards Little Grisly.

Just before she did she thought she saw something red on the staircase, *I need glasses,* but as she looked again she saw the red Tudor dress of Lady Elizabeth Riche standing still, motionless, her white face looking directly at her. She wasn't smiling.

Prim's hands began to tremble and then her whole body did, her legs turned to jelly. She was cold. She knew she was in trouble.

The owners have returned. In strange clothes.

Prim's heart beating was now the only noise.

Lady Elizabeth continued to stare at Prim, saying nothing.

Prim stared at Lady Elizabeth, her mouth shaking in fear.

She was going to get a right telling off. Maybe even the police would be called? Maybe her parents would find out?

Prim knew that there was something else about this lady.

Where are Amy, Sadie and Lockie? I need them now.

Lady Elizabeth, without taking her eyes off Prim, began to glide silently up the rest of the stairs. There was still no noise.

The blood from Prim's face drained.

"Give me strength," yelled Prim and somehow, she found enough energy and ran into the dark, empty room across the landing and towards the far door. There had to be another staircase she could use.

But the other door was locked.

Prim tried and tried again to open it turning it one way and then the other, but it was no use.

"Oh, God, please," she howled and fell onto the floor against the door, crying.

Had she just dreamt that she had seen a lady in old fashioned clothes? Was the lady only messing about being angry?

But the lavender scent was now in the room behind her.

Prim looked up towards the open door and there standing in her way was Lady Elizabeth, standing upright and simply staring, again, straight at her, saying nothing.

Prim froze, unable to move.

There was nowhere for Prim to run to now.

Slowly, very slowly, Lady Elizabeth raised both her arms and placed her hands on both sides of her chin.

And Prim could see her smirk, ever so slightly.

What is she doing?

She lifted her hands and arms and to Prim's astonishment Lady Elizabeth's head lifted right up and into the air leaving cut grey arteries, veins and muscle showing in its wake.

This is surely a dream. But she knew it wasn't. She knew it wasn't a magic trick either.

Prim tried to scream, tried to shift her body up from the floor but it was a dead weight. Lady Elizabeth moved her head down, to her right side and held it by her hip. Finally, from her mouth, came rich, cruel mocking laughter.

And she began to march slowly towards Prim.

This is it, thought Prim as she closed her eyes, perhaps for the last time, losing consciousness.

But before Lady Elizabeth could take one step further, from behind Prim came the noise of a key in the lock of the door turning. The door creaked open inwards and Prim, still leaning against it, fell into the next room.

Chapter Nine

Harry, who was at the other end of the room in which Prim had now half entered, looked shocked at what he had just seen and the sight of her slumped and shaking on the floor and within a second had run over to help her.

"Get in here," he cried, and, like a balloon bursting, Prim came out of her slumber and tried to scramble herself backwards into the other room. Thankfully, Harry was able to grab hold of her left arm and drag her away from the nearing Lady Elizabeth who had stopped laughing demonically and was now placing her head back onto its rightful place. She certainly was not laughing now, more her face was one of awful anger.

But, by the time she was one body again the door to the other room had been shut and locked.

Prim lay on the wooden floor in the dark room recovering next to Harry who was physically tired as well after manifesting himself to pull her away. She did not know what to say and yet had so much to say. Who was her saviour? What about the woman in the next room?

"Who are you?" she gasped before remembering her manners and to say thank you.

"I'm Harry," replied Harry now fully visible and looking to Prim just like a normal boy.

He must be the owner's son from yesterday and for a second, she felt happier and safer. Prim introduced herself to Harry and he nodded.

A second later, however, and her thoughts focused on the headless, red dressed woman on the other side of the door.

"Her, what about her?"

"Don't worry, she won't come in here, she's not allowed," and Harry could visibly see the effect his words had on Prim. "None of us are."

Prim stared at the boy, he was handsome enough if you liked boys at the age of eleven years and he was about her age too, with short curly brown hair and enormous green eyes. But he too was dressed in olden clothes. A sky blue top and matching breeches which went down just past his knees.

Has a fancy-dress shop opened in Little Grisly?

Before she could think of this further, there was an almighty banging on the door which seemed to shake the whole room.

"Harry de Spencer, you know you are forbidden to go in there. Come out now or you'll be in trouble." It was Lady Elizabeth.

"Don't listen to her," whispered Harry to Prim, "she can't get me into trouble."

Prim looked at him studiously.

Why isn't he allowed in this room? Why isn't she?

She lifted herself up and looked around the room for the first time. In one corner was a wooden double bed with a grey dust cover over it. Close by was a wooden, strong looking wardrobe and chest of drawers, it was quite tidy. *Who slept in here?*

Looking for clues she eyed the other corner and there stood a tall dark figure covered in the same grey sheets that covered the bed. Prim shrieked. *There must be others in the room.* She recoiled back towards the door before remembering who or what was on the other side of it.

From the other side of the door came, "What are you doing to her? If you kill her I will let you off this offence."

"No," yelled Prim and she became almost paralysed again. Harry knelt beside her and motioned with his eyes and mouth that killing her was not going to happen but that wasn't the only thing Prim was concerned about. She pointed to the figure in the corner, "Him," she shouted.

Harry laughed and walked up to the figure and pulled the grey cover from over it. It was a coat stand. That was all.

"You are a right frightened rabbit," he said.

Prim was emotionally, all over the place. *Oh, how one day I would like to laugh at this.*

What a predicament. She was going to kill Amy, Sadie and Lockie. Where were they?

Bang, bang and bang went the door.

"If you don't come out then I will come in," boomed Lady Elizabeth.

"She wouldn't dare," whispered Harry.

Prim realised something, that the headless lady and Harry were sort of similar, he had said "us" before as in "none of us are" allowed in this room. Unless there were some fantastic special effects going around, it was obvious to Prim that the lady outside was a ghost.

And that meant Harry was too.

She felt her heart flutter and a cold sweat poured over her. This was too much for poor Primula Percy.

One second later and she fainted again.

Chapter Ten

Harry lifted Prim over to and onto the bed in the corner. She landed perfectly, and Harry elevated her feet and put two pillows by her side to stop her falling off it.

What was he going to do now?

The other long-term residents met in the hall whilst Prim was unconscious.

Firstly, they discussed Harry and what they should do to punish him for:

1. entering Miss Rose's own personal room when all the residents were completely banned from doing so; and

2. helping Prim out (again) when the other residents had already decided that she needed to be scared off (again).

Harry, who had come downstairs and into the main hall, admitted to hiding in Miss Rose's room but denied unlocking the door to let Prim inside as he simply did not have the key to open it. Lady Elizabeth was furious at his denial, after all, she had seen the door herself open and there, to pull Prim in, had been Harry.

But in truth, there was very little they could do to punish him, after all he was a ghost and was already being punished by being left at Great Grisly Hall.

They could, of course, explain everything to Miss Rose but that was pooh-poohed by most of them as then their whole plan to frighten and then kill Prim would come out and they would all be in trouble.

Lady Elizabeth and Barnaby Grudge did not care if they got into trouble with Miss Rose and told the group that Miss Rose was useless.

It was decided to leave Harry alone for now.

And Prim?

Well there were two camps. Firstly, there was the people who thought that by fainting Prim had been scared enough and that when she woke up she could leave and that she would never come back to the Hall again.

Asking Harry to explain things and warn her off would also help bring him back into the fold.

The second camp, which was basically Lady Elizabeth and Barnaby Grudge, however thought that now was the time to kill her and end the whole problem making it look like an accident, so no one would get the blame.

Barnaby Grudge suggested that she could trip down the stairs "accidentally".

In terms of voting it was 70/30 in favour of letting her out with a warning, a final warning but Barnaby Grudge, however, decided to wait and hide on the landing for when Prim came down the stairs, just in case a quick kill was needed.

About half an hour later, Peregrine walked down from the top floor.

"It sounds like she's stirring."

The first signs of the sky beginning to darken came from outside the Hall. Harry ran up as quick as he could and just in time as Prim just opened her eyes to see him enter the room.

Straight away she recoiled into the corner of the bed and away from him.

"You're a ghost, you're a ghost!" she yelled, "You're going to kill me with that woman."

Harry fumbled his response badly.

"I'm not, I mean I am, I mean I'm not going to kill you, I pulled you into this room, remember?"

Prim did not actually remember that, given that she had fainted, but it must have been a given that he had helped. All the same, though, she was facing a ghost, a dead person.

"But you are a ghost? A real one?"

"Yes, but I'm not frightening, at least I hope not."

Prim thought for a second or two. *What a situation to be in.*

"Okay, yes you're not frightening but that woman." The thought made Prim shiver visibly.

"I have been asked to help you leave here but, on the condition, that you never come back. That woman, Lady Elizabeth Riche, only meant to frighten you away."

"Only meant to frighten me? She did a very good job. I was sure she wanted to kill me."

"But you must promise never to come back otherwise," and Harry had to stop and think about this because he certainly did not want her to die but he also wanted to play with her and be her friend. "Otherwise they will kill you."

Prim choked at this, kill her? An innocent child? She wanted to leave and get out of the house as soon as possible. She wanted to find Amy, Sadie and Lockie. She knew it was getting late and that the light would be dimming outside and knew now was the right time to go. She would be in trouble with her parents if she was not home soon. But oh! Better to be alive and in trouble rather than dead.

Prim stood up and looked at Harry, she liked him but balancing things up would rather live than be killed by his friends.

"Lady Elizabeth will not be in the next room," said Harry truthfully but where would she be and where would the others be he did not know. All through his years at Great Grisly Hall he had not trusted her, from his very first meeting and to when he was brought back to reside here.

Happy as she could be with this news Prim walked out of the room, through the other, and onto the landing. She checked carefully for any sign of any other ghosts and walked down the wooden stairs slowly and carefully down the corridor and onto the main landing where the main hall was situated.

Apart from her and Harry there was not a soul to be seen.

I will never, ever come to Great Grisly Hall ever, ever, again.

She began walking down the main staircase, getting more confident the lower she came and the closer she got to the main door and out of the Hall.

She thought about Amy Sadie and Lockie. They could, at least, be with her now. *Why have they left me?*

I will never, ever come to Great Grisly Hall ever, ever, again.

She could see the sun's rays disappearing, and she wanted to desperately leave. She could see the open front door. She was getting closer to getting out.

I will never, ever come to Great Grisly Hall ever, ever, again.

Neither Prim nor Harry, who walked beside her, noticed Barnaby Grudge slowly walk down the staircase behind them.

Barnaby was not able to read Prim's thoughts about never coming back to the Hall but what could they do to him if he pushed her down the stairs? Nothing. This was his second chance to do something to this little pain in the backside girl. He wasn't going to mess things up this time.

It was worth it, the little goody two shoes slip of a girl, *serves her right for coming into their Hall, trespassing that's what she's done, breaking and entering, she's nothing but a criminal and needs punishment.*

Prim was almost half way down getting and feeling happier but still looking all around her in case the headless lady reappeared to chase her out for good.

I will never, ever come to Great Grisly Hall ever, ever, again.

A chill went down her spine again. Amy appeared by the open front door of the Hall and pointed up and behind Prim.

Prim quickly turned around just in time to see Barnaby push her with all the strength a ghost can muster with both arms down the stairs.

She shrieked and Harry who had been miles away in his sad thoughts at never seeing her again, turned and grabbed her by the left arm and tried to stop the fall.

It almost did but made her spin not just downwards but to the side and she landed two steps below. The pain was not immediate as the adrenaline of seeing the man in bloody green push her made her get up and run quickly down the remaining steps.

"Grab her," ordered Barnaby who chased her, his head now gone and determined to kill her.

Lady Elizabeth appeared from by the fireside where she had been watching, grabbed one of the iron fire pokers and went to strike Prim before she could get out of range.

"Stop," cried Harry, "Let her go she doesn't want to come back here."

"Too late," said Lady Elizabeth, grinning like a maniac, "She's better off dead to us now."

One of the other residents who hid by the door grabbed and held onto Prim.

"Let me go, I want to go," she screamed but the spectre was too strong for her.

Both Lady Elizabeth and Barnaby Grudge walked directly towards Prim.

Lady Elizabeth raised the metal poker high into the air ready to thrash it against Prim's skull. Everyone in the room focused on this very action as if it happened in slow motion.

Again, the open front door came to Prim's rescue.

No one had heard the car coming down the long drive, but they all saw its headlights and were blinded. It came to a halt quickly and the driver got out and ran inside.

"Stop this, stop this at once," the driver, a woman with amazing dyed bright red long hair, roared out and immediately, like a child caught with their hands in a teacher's handbag, Lady Elizabeth lowered her arm and dropped the poker and the other resident let go of Prim.

"What is going on in here?" The woman demanded before walking quickly up and kneeling to Prim to comfort her. "You all know the agreed rules not to kill anyone."

"Miss Rose, this is not what it looks like." Barnaby Grudge explained.

"This child has broken into our home and is a threat to us," Lady Elizabeth added. "There was no other alternative but to kill her."

"I don't believe any of you. Now leave me alone with the girl."

And with that order most of the long-term residents drifted off from the main hall, at once chattering and discussing what had happened and what would happen now that Miss Rose had returned. She was rubbish at her job, but they still had to accept her authority.

Barnaby Grudge and Lady Elizabeth moved to the end of the long table and whispered, something Prim could not hear, all the while staring at the woman.

"Be gone, I said," the woman shouted, and they realised that she really meant it and so drifted off towards the back door.

After they had left the Hall, the woman looked kindly down into Prim's face and began to stroke Prim's hair.

Prim stared at her and knew she was not a ghost. She knew immediately that the woman was not out to kill her. Despite the colour of her hair, there was something familiar about the woman, but Prim could not remember.

"You used to love your hair being stroked when you were younger Prim."

What? Prim stared closer at the woman. She was attractive, but it was her eyes, she had seen those before somewhere. It had to be.

"Oh, my dear, sweet Primula. I am your Aunt Rosemary."

And with that Rosemary, or Rose as everyone usually called her, gave Prim a kiss and hugged her lovingly.

Part Two

Chapter Eleven

All the long- term residents gathered in the outdoor courtyard close to the back door.

"You're in trouble now," Peregrine Carruthers mocked.

"We're all in trouble," advised Lord le Grise.

"It will put those two back at least another fifty years." Peregrine said, continuing his fun against Lady Elizabeth and Barnaby Grudge.

"What's another fifty years here when I've already been here almost five hundred?" Lady Elizabeth countered, and it sounded as if she could not care less.

"Don't you care?"

"I've long ceased caring about myself," she advised, coldly staring at him, "Besides is heaven all that good? I like it down here."

"Like it enough to kill a child? They should throw you in hell for this," judged Lord le Grise.

"I think that's what she wants, and I'm not joking this time," and Peregrine wasn't.

Lady Elizabeth did not answer the question completely. "I might as well say I'm going to be here until kingdom come, fat use Miss Rose is to us, she'll never get any of you upstairs. Useless like the rest of her family."

"You don't help yourself do you though? You could have been upstairs quite a while a go if you tried. It's almost as if hell has a special place waiting for you."

Lady Elizabeth walked over to Peregrine and stared directly into his face. Peregrine expected a tongue lashing but got something even worse. Silence. For about ten seconds she glared into his eyes without blinking. For Peregrine this was absolute torture, as if something powerful was emitting from them and he stood back from her.

Finally, she blinked, moved away and mysteriously said, "I know more about things than you do. I'm going for a walk whilst it's still light."

And she turned and walked off, alone.

From inside the Hall, Rose could just about hear the long-term residents talking. Lady Elizabeth and her view on heaven. That was no surprise really. More importantly, at least for now, was the mention of light and she checked her watch.

"Goodness Prim, we've got to get you back home before all hell breaks loose and my brother and your Mum find you're not at home."

Prim sat in her aunt's battered old car and just let the scenery pass her by, the cooling air from the open window reminding her that she had been quite close to dying. She was safe now and the awful prospect of what could have happened had begun to dawn on her. She had been lucky, really lucky to have escaped. *Thank God for Rose, my aunt, my long, lost aunt.*

How many years had it been since she last saw her? She had only been a toddler.

How did Rose know it was her then? Children change in their looks from being young to eleven years old.

Come to think about it, how did Rose know that I would get into trouble with Mum and Dad?

Come to think about it, what is Rosemary doing at Great Grisly Hall at all?

Questions needed to be answered. But, maybe, not today.

They drove into Little Grisly and into the car park of the Swinging Witch, where Rose stopped the car.

"Here's where I drop you off Prim. I cannot suddenly come back and say hello to your Dad as if nothing has happened. Promise me you won't say anything to your Mum and Dad about me?"

Prim nodded.

"You're still looking a bit pale, best get some sleep tonight, don't worry about those silly ghosts now I am here."

Prim took off her seatbelt and turned to her aunt.

"And tomorrow when you come back to the Hall I will explain everything and answer all your questions."

Prim smiled and got out the car before racing towards the door to the flat above the Post Office. She flew upstairs, took her shoes off and sped into the lounge, just in the nick of time as she heard footsteps come up the staircase towards the flat, the click of the front door and her parents came in, tired after their day at work.

Chapter Twelve

Surprisingly, Prim's parents were concerned with how she looked, and she was put to bed early with a bowl of tinned mushroom soup and a tepid glass of water from the tap.

After what had happened that day she was glad to slip under her trusted old and faded pink single duvet. Now that she was eleven she had asked her parents for a more grown up style perhaps not so pink or perhaps not pink at all but for tonight she was more than happy to cuddle it and her fading, fluffy black toy, Labrador called Rufus who, recently, had been receiving less attention that he had done over the years.

Just before lights out Amy, Sadie and Lockie all came in and apologised for the game of hide and seek and after only a minute they were all best of friends again. Prim had cause to thank Amy for warning her of the horrid, stinky green man who tried to push her down the stairs. But, for now, it was decided just to forget about the events of the day and the three of them left her and, presumably, went to bed themselves.

Prim was excited at going back to Great Grisly Hall the next day. She longed to take one of the photo albums from the bureau desk, in the lounge, and look at the old photos of Aunt Rosemary but that would surely give the game away to her parents.

She also wanted to see Harry again.

She should have thought about the events of the day, the grisly events at Great Grisly Hall where ghosts, yes, ghosts, had tried to kill her on at least two occasions if not three.

But, thankfully, she fell straight to sleep.

Prim dreamt that night. She possibly had many dreams but only one she could remember, there were times that she was awake but not for long and, just as she could see through the bottom of the curtains that dawn had arrived, she drifted off into a real full sleep and a real full dream.

She and Harry were playing and laughing out close to the Hall but somewhere Prim had not been to before. It was no longer spring in the dream, more like winter and a cold winter's day heading towards dusk, the dark clouds covered the whole of the sky and the shadow of evening was becoming ever gloomier especially with the stiff and heavy wind blustering through. It felt like any moody Sunday with the threat of school the next day.

Nevertheless, they had walked, strolled, ran, jogged, ambled and panted all the way from the Hall and down to the stream along a different path to the one that led to Little Grisly. Here, they found an old stone building, like a barn and the same colour as most of the buildings in the village, with a large wheel gently turning in the stream, it must have been a mill but, again, Prim had never seen it before. Anything could happen in a dream she thought as she tagged Harry and raced further towards the mill.

But Harry did not chase her, and Prim turned around and called him a party pooper. *Is he too afraid of the dark?*

Harry stood quite still, as if he had been glued to the spot, and looked up towards a large, and tall, old chestnut tree and there was no laughter and no smiling now. The wind was visibly shaking its lifeless branches.

He began to shake.

With fear.

"Harry what's wrong?" asked Prim seriously, realising that for whatever reason the game was over.

Harry could not talk and instead raised his left arm up and pointed to the tree, Prim watched how his arm shook as if the strong wind tugged at it.

"Harry," she repeated, "what's wrong?"

Harry answered almost silently, "The hanging tree," and, as he said this, his pointing arm shifted from the tree directly to Prim.

Behind him, Amy, Sadie and Lockie appeared but instead of making everything nice as friends would, they stood, and pointed at the tree, their faces looking towards Prim, mournful. A tear fell down Sadie's face.

Prim woke up shaking, feeling cold with a wet sweat upon her brow and convinced her dream was real. Although glad that it had ended, she spent the next half an hour breathing slowly, eventually convincing herself that it had been what it was, just a dream and thanking God that it was getting light outside. Thank God she had found Rufus too, hiding under the duvet but ready to give her some comfort.

Nevertheless, when she got up and went back to the Hall, she would ask Harry about the tree as soon as she saw him.

Chapter Thirteen

Despite their child looking ill, Prim's parents both went to work as usual the next morning. If they had known the reality that she had almost died at Great Grisly Hall then they would have told her off, grounded her and then gone to work. Heaven knows what they would think if they knew she had almost died due to ghosts.

What would they really say or do if they knew that Auntie Rosemary was back?

The thought of her Aunt initially trumped what had happened in her dream or almost being killed. Firstly, it was just a dream and secondly there was little chance of being killed today now that Rose was at the Hall.

Little chance of being killed today. Ha! That made Prim strangely smile.

There was very little in the house for breakfast but that did not worry Prim as she didn't need much to refuel her anyway. The Post Office sold sandwiches and Prim's breakfast was half an all-day breakfast sandwich of bacon, sausage and egg which had been left in the fridge. It tasted good, but probably only because she was so hungry.

Washed and dressed she ran out of the flat and almost straight into another coach load of tourists visiting the village. One of the tourists, an elderly woman, wanted the others to take her photograph with Prim but there could be no chance of that.

Ha, I don't think my Dad would like to see that picture. But these tourists would really love to see Great Grisly Hall.

She began to skip excitedly down the high street and into the car park of the Swinging Witch and caught the attention of Mr Tanner, the landlord, who stared hard at her before returning to emptying the bins from the night before.

Why is she so happy, just playing around here? And he promised that he would bring her a bottle of something later.

He didn't see her disappear behind the bushes and onto her way towards the path that led to Great Grisly Hall.

The day was getting warm at even that time of the morning and Prim knew she was happy, it wasn't every day she got to play with a real friend, an auntie no less as well.

Of course, Amy Sadie and Lockie joined her but they were still a bit sheepish after yesterday's events at the Hall and did not say or play much. Prim was also a little unhappy at their appearance in her dream but decided to say nothing about it.

Finally, as they came out onto the fields, near the Hall, Prim gathered them together and told them that they were her best friends and they soon all cheered up after hearing this.

Prim was astonished by how she had handled the situation and realised that by saying what she had said, she was growing up.

Growing up, nicely.

This made her happy too.

And with friends.

The very thought of having friends made her even more happy.

They all cantered the rest of the way to the Hall and Prim thought of a song to sing to put them into an even better mood.

All things dark and devious

All ghosts large and small

All things fierce and frightening

You'll find them at Great Grisly Hall.

Soon the Hall came into sights and even the roof of Rosemary's car could be seen.

My Aunt Rosemary. Aunt Rose.

The events of yesterday, almost getting killed and all that caper, were most definitely easing into the back of her mind. She had friends and her aunt after all now.

But as she continued towards the Hall without a care in the world Harry jumped out from behind a bramble bush, where the deeply covered, ancient, other path was, and stretched out his hands to make her stop.

She, and the others, almost fell over. Prim was about to learn that a good mood could be spoilt in only a few seconds, usually by a friend.

"Harry, you frightened the life out of me," she cried but then remembered her manners in that Harry had no life to squeeze out of him and after yesterday's events this was nothing. Further, Harry looked like he had been in the dream, all shaking and cold, which made Prim worried.

"Harry what's wrong?" she asked and realised she had said the same question to him in the dream last night.

"I've come to warn you about some of the others."

"Did they get told off?"

"What do you think?"

"Well they did try to kill me. I hate even thinking about what happened, it's so fresh in my memory, that headless woman and the army man."

"So why are you coming back then? Do you want trouble?"

Prim became upset at how Harry spoke to her, she had thought they would be friends and friends would never speak to each other like this. All the horrible bits from yesterday were coming back to the forefront of her mind.

But she knew he was right. Saying this to her meant he cared, and Prim liked this.

"I've come to see my Aunt. I've not seen her for such a long time."

"Your Aunt?" Harry said looking puzzled. "You mean Miss Rose? She's your aunt?"

"Yes, didn't she say?"

"No," and Harry had to think for more than a few seconds. "So, you are one of them too. I thought as much. You look just like," and he paused and decided to change the conversation a little, "that makes all the difference, you should have said, then the others wouldn't have tried to scare you."

"One of them what?"

"Them that look after us. Try and sort us out, you must know what I mean."

"Harry, I don't have the slightest idea what you are on about." Prim wanted to know more.

"You best speak to Miss Rose then, she knows everything." It did not look like Harry believed her for an instant.

Prim began to walk in the direction of the Hall, Harry followed her.

"And another thing, you were in my dream last night."

Harry smiled a little at this. Was this a sign of them being friends?

"Was I? Was I nice?"

"Yes, at the start. But then we walked up to an old mill and there was this tree."

Harry realised what she meant and stopped her from continuing. He went visibly whiter, even for a ghost.

"I know that tree, don't ever mention that tree."

"Don't be silly Harry, you can't possibly know about the what, where or who about my dream."

"I'm serious Prim. That tree, bad things happened at that tree. I'm worried now Prim."

"I remember your face in the dream, white like it is now. And you called the tree, the hanging tree. That wasn't very nice."

Prim looked at Harry for a response, but Harry had gone. It was the best thing, for Prim's sake, for him to do.

From being all happy a few moments ago, she wasn't very happy at all now.

Chapter Fourteen

Prim continued to walk towards the Hall. At least that was a simple thing to do. But everything else was starting to get on top of her. She could add upsetting Harry and then the thing about the dream and Harry's warning was very strange but, as she carried on thinking about things, she realised that everything was strange here, very strange.

Things aren't strange playing in the pub car park.

Though people must think I am strange playing there.

Was strange, ha!

And she thought about whether she should just stay playing outside the Swinging Witch and realised that, strange or not, deadly or not, coming here was much better. For all the talk of death and all the dead people who seemed to still hang around here, Prim felt alive.

This made her feel a lot better and she began to smile again.

Rather than go past and straight in through the main doors of Great Grisly, she stood looking at the old Hall from the garden, perhaps really for the first time, noticing mainly all the green weeds growing out from the roof and walls.

She thought she saw something or somebody in one of the windows and froze a little in the warm sun.

They're angry with me, they hate me. Harry was right. Is it wise to come back?

At that very moment none other than Rose herself appeared from the direction of the main drive carrying some hand-picked flowers of bluebells and marigolds in her hands.

"Good morning darling," she announced loudly and gave Prim another wonderful cuddle which lasted a few seconds more than it should. "Have these sweetie," she said as she gave Prim the flowers.

Prim smiled even more, no one had ever given her flowers before and she bundled them together into a bunch, like in the shops, but with her hands.

"I feel a bit, well, like I need to apologise and explain but I don't really know where to start Prim. I'm not very good at explaining things in fact I'm not terribly good at anything." Suddenly, Rose's early warmth blew away with the gentle breeze.

"Like keeping in touch?" Prim asked but immediately wishing she had not been so direct and rude to her aunt.

Rose blushed. "Err well, that's not exactly all my fault but quite a lot of other stuff is."

Prim put her arm around Rosemary's waist.

"Thank you Prim," said Rosemary, "I'm afraid my memories of you are not as good as they should be, you were only tiny when I left but you were always a cuddle monster which made me feel better, it's so nice to have another one after all these years."

"Why did you leave?"

"For work I suppose Prim, there's not much of it around the village unless you run the Post Office, the pub or one of the tea rooms."

They walked over to the stone seat overlooking the garden where Lord le Grise had been enjoying the sun yesterday and sat down, side by side.

Prim said, "You could have come back or at least written, even sent a post card. One day I would like to go on holiday and send someone a postcard."

"You've never been on holiday? Oh, how could my brother not take you on holiday."

Prim said nothing, it was Rose who needed to do the talking.

"I haven't exactly just been truthful about what I do and why I left. I just don't know where to start but you need to be told and understand."

Rose looked serious.

Prim felt her good mood waning even more than after she had spoken to Harry. *Why can't everyone be nice and happy, just for a day?*

"My job is a little different to most. And that's putting it mildly."

"What are you a doctor, dentist? A spy or a soldier?" Prim was only half joking.

"None of those Prim, my job would never be taught at school or found in the local job centre you see."

She looked at Prim carefully and decided to continue.

"I help people, people who are initially lost after something massive happens to them and I well guide them to a better place."

And she studied Prim's face to see if she was taking all this in.

"Like when they leave somewhere like home?" Prim asked, innocently.

"Just like that Prim, but you see I help when they leave home forever. When they die."

Rose paused now to see if Prim understood.

"Die? How can you help when people die?"

"Well I help them understand what has happened and guide them to where they will go, shall we say afterwards."

"What does happen to us when we die?"

"It's a good question darling, no that's the best question to ask, and not as simple to answer, you see, basically, your soul leaves your body and the basic idea is, as you probably know, it can go up to heaven or down to hell depending on how good you have been."

"Go on," urged Prim, suddenly feeling a little bit hot and knowing that she was turning red with the idea of death.

"Well a lot of people go into shock and cannot understand what has happened to them. My role is to counsel them and help them to their next port of call. I travel around the world doing this, but this place, Great Grisly Hall, is home."

Prim went red and knew why she was going red. She still had that memory of the dream about Mrs Pilkington.

Was that real?

"You can see ghosts?" she asked her Aunt.

"Yes, but not everyone can. I know you can, though Prim. This thing I do, you don't get qualifications to do it, it runs in the family, like it's in our blood. Has done for centuries."

Rose realised this was a lot to take in and so she lifted her arm and invited Prim to put her head down onto her lap. As soon as Prim did so, Rose stroked her hair. Prim could not remember anyone stroking her hair before and was, at first, reluctant, but then, in the furthest, remotest, part of her memory, there was a sensation Rose had caressed her hair when she was younger, and she was comforted.

"Tell me more," she asked refocusing, trying to take it all in but desperate to hear as much as possible. She was sure she really must have helped Mrs Pilkington now.

"Well, the whole process can take a few days or even weeks especially if it had been decided that they should go to hell, eternal damnation and all that."

"I don't think I would like that much," replied Prim as she looked up to Rosemary and glimpsed the roof of the Hall. "But what about ghosts or souls that stay? What about the ghosts here?"

"For some it is harder to accept that they have died. It's different for these, the residents of Great Grisly Hall. These are souls who did something very wicked when they were alive."

Now this is getting complicated.

"What with hell being such an awful place, they were sentenced to stay down on earth until they had learned their lesson. Only then can they go to heaven. If they don't they go to hell. Well that was the plan anyway. The hardest part of my job is trying to help them up the stairs, as we say, especially those who would like to go down the stairs instead. I simply cannot let them do that."

Prim had heard enough, she had too many questions to ask. "And they all have been wicked? All of them."

"Yes, each one of them did something very tragic and nasty in their lives. The Hall has been used as a sort of half- way house for souls for years."

Prim thought about this for a while.

"What even Harry?"

"Yes, Prim. Even Harry."

Chapter Fifteen

"He's just a boy. What nasty thing could he have done to make him stay here?"

"They, the ones upstairs only look at your overall record during your life. Harry died so young and they didn't have much to go on." Rose decided not to explain to Prim about the nasty thing he did and, thankfully, Prim had moved on.

"But he's just a child, like me."

"Yes, so they decided that he should spend some time down here thinking about what he did. Thing is, he's been here for almost four hundred years now."

Prim thought for a second about the fact that Harry was not exactly her age after all. *Four hundred years.*

"And why hasn't he gone upstairs as you call it?"

"He and the rest of them have to be good for a certain amount of time. They must show that they are sorry and / or do some sort of act to show that they will be good forever. If they can then off they go."

"That headless lady must be about five hundred years old."

"You've been learning about the Tudors in school haven't you? Indeed, she is but, trust me, others have left and gone. Some upstairs and some, well, downstairs."

Prim reflected at this thought. Some souls still went to hell. "Why don't they realise and be nice people? Surely most people would do that? It makes me think that these ones are still bad."

"Not all of them are bad now. Some of them like it here, it is a nice place to stay. A bit like a permanent retirement home. There is one other thing too."

And Rose paused.

"And what Auntie?"

"The truth is, well I'm not exactly very good at my job. Keep that to yourself of course though most of them here know that already as they do upstairs. Those above don't care about whether they like it here or not, they want them moved upstairs."

Prim stood up and stretched. "I'm sure you are good at your job Auntie," and she saw Rose smile, "What did you mean when you said this thing runs in the family?"

"Ha, well you could say we are born to do this."

Prim looked confused and began to gaze down into the garden and ponder.

Rose continued, "I don't really know how much to tell you Prim. I hope you can take all this in. You see our family, throughout the years, have been doing what I do. We have had some sort of connection with the dead for centuries."

Prim gasped. "And before you, who in the family did this job?"

"Your Grandad had the power to do this as did your great Grandad and for generations long before them."

"How did we get it, this power?"

"Well it wasn't for being nice I'm afraid Prim. You do know about this house, don't you? On second thoughts, no you wouldn't. I imagine your Dad has not told you a thing about this place."

Prim nodded. Rose knew her own brother.

"This house, Great Grisly Hall, is ours Prim."

Prim giggled nervously, *what a load of old cobblers.*

"It's true Prim, you have to believe me, I know we don't live here now but I bet you can understand why."

And she could understand why, and she could also feel that there was something about the Hall, something she couldn't quite put her finger on but that she knew her family had a connection with it.

"Well Prim, there has been a house here for almost a thousand years. Our surname, Percy, is an ancient name and some of our ancestors were very noble and well to do. The old family took over the Hall from another important family, the last head of which entered something he really should not have, something that cursed him and the Hall itself.

"Cursed?" Prim questioned before remembering the tale she heard of the last Earl. "But who could have cursed it? The devil?"

"Precisely Primula, precisely."

The Curse and how Great Grisly Hall got its name

In 1066 William the Conqueror defeated King Harold at the Battle of Hastings and became King William I of England. But he certainly could not take it easy and live, well, like a King. The people of England were not exactly happy that he had defeated Harold. The people of England would need to be ruled over harshly, sometimes using the sword again for good measure. In old London town, he built a huge white castle that became the Tower of London.

To gain control of the whole of the country he sent his trusted and loyal knights, who had fought with him at Hastings, to run different parts of the land. They were given great power in these areas as a thank you for supporting William invade England.

Ranulf le Grise was one of those knights and was soon made the 1st Earl of Huntshire. After rebuilding the church in the nearby village to praise God for their victory over Harold, and to hold a place to bury himself and his family, he set about building a home, a rather large one for his family and all his supporters.

Like many of the other knights, Ranulf ran his shire very well, usually with an iron rod, but soon the local people fell into respect for him and he began to treat them all better.

Grise is French for grey but there was nothing so grey about life at Grise Hall. The surrounding area had rich soil for growing crops and soon Ranulf himself became very rich. He paid some money to the King, as was his duty, but always had enough left over to make the Hall one of the finest in the land and, to show off his wealth, to hold the most sumptuous parties known.

For the next few centuries the Earls of Huntshire lived mainly in peace: yes, some sons went off to fight for King and country, either against the French or in the Middle East at the holy crusades. Each generation of le Grise was lucky to have a son who could take over the Earldom and through marriage, obtain other big houses, manors and land. In short, the le Grise family became richer and richer year by year.

But it could not continue.

In or around the year 1455 a new war started in England, the War of the Roses. This wasn't just two people hitting each other with a bunch of lovely smelling flowers. This was a bloody fight between two of the strongest and most important families in the country: The House of Lancaster on one side and the House of York on the other. The roses were their symbols, the red rose for Lancaster and the white rose for York.

Huntshire was nowhere near Lancashire and Yorkshire but that did not matter. The whole country was at war and it would last for over thirty years. Wars in those days always did seem to last a long time.

The eighteenth Earl of Huntshire, whose full name was Peregrine Xavier le Grise was, like his ancestors, a fighting man who loved to joust and play all sports. He was also an ambitious man with a plan to use the War of the Roses to further his own aims and that of his family.

He already had power. He wanted more.

He already had money. He wanted more.

He also had two sons, in their late teens, and a daughter aged thirteen. One of the sons, the eldest, of course would inherit the Earldom and Great Grise Hall as it was now known, for many of those ancestors had built further parts to it, making it quite large indeed.

The second son could be put to good use. He could be used to lead soldiers in the War of the Roses and in that way, the eighteenth Earl would be seen, at least to one side of the War, to be loyal.

Daughters, in those days, were not thought of that much as fighters. The best thing they were good for was to marry someone important, someone not just with money but power, prestige and influence. With a good marriage the eighteenth Earl could get himself well into the most significant and central families in the country. Perhaps, one day, his daughter's son would be King of England.

Now that was something to think about especially with the War of the Roses.

The Earl just had to pick the right side.

He sided with the House of Lancaster which was led by the current King, Henry VI. A lot of the King's followers had died at the Battle of St Albans, but the Earl was sure they could overturn the Yorkists. His second son became a knight in the King's army.

The fighting began again in 1459 and the Duke of York, the leader of the House of York, had to flee the country to save himself from death.

The Earl's plan was working, and his second son had distinguished himself well on the battlefield and the King favoured this son very highly. It was now time for the Earl to fashion a marriage between his daughter and the King's son, even though the young heir to the throne was only six years of age.

His grandson would be the King of England.

More money. More power.

Unfortunately for the Earl, the War of the Roses took a turn for the worse for the King. About a year later, at the Battle of Northampton, Henry VI was captured, and the Duke of York became the "Protector of England" and, what is more, became the heir to the throne.

The Earl was furious. As things currently stood, his grandson – who, of course, had yet to be born - was not going to be King.

Oh, and his second son, the brave soldier, loyal to the King, was killed at the battle.

The Earl mourned for a short while. He mourned for his son but mourned much more for the fact that his son, despite distinguishing himself at first, had probably not done enough to satisfy the families honour and show them to be worthy of sitting at the top table with the King.

He would have to bring his eldest son into battle, even if it meant him dying as well. After all, the Earl could always have more children. Well that was what he thought.

Things began to look promising again.

At the Battle of Wakefield, both the Duke of York and his second son were killed. The Earl congratulated himself on choosing the right victor and sticking to his guns. A party, one of greatest known in the rich history of parties at Great Grise Hall, was held.

Unfortunately, when everyone had recovered from such a party, they were told that the Duke's first son had been crowned King, Edward IV.

This was simply not on and the Earl was red with rage.

He and his eldest son, and their soldiers met up with others supporting the red rose to fight the so-called Edward IV at a place called Towton in 1461.

But the red rose was dead-headed, and King Edward IV won a resounding victory.

And defeat also came with a personal loss. The Earl's first born was killed in battle. The Earl was enraged. Who would inherit Great Grise Hall now?

Either he would have to have more male children, or he would have to marry his daughter off to someone friendly and rich who he could dominate and rule over. By now there was no chance of his daughter marrying Henry VI's son.

A message reached him. His daughter, now fifteen, had fallen in love with a young soldier, a family member of the great house of Northumberland, the Percy family.

The Percy family who belonged on the side of the white rose, of Edward IV.

All the Earl's planning was in tatters. He rode back to the Hall; how different the atmosphere was compared to the party not so long ago. He sat in the main hall, at the head of the long table, thinking how he could save himself, his position and the Hall. Once everyone else had gone to bed and there were only dying embers left in the giant fireplace and only one or two candles left lit to keep a little light, he shouted at the top of his voice, "I would do anything to save my Hall."

"Anything?" came a response from the darkness.

The Earl was shocked and thought he was imagining things. Still he responded, "Yes, anything, now stand before me so that I may see who I am talking to."

The huge fireplace shook and the there was a flash of brilliant, dazzling white light for less than a second. Once the Earl, who was almost blinded by the light, had recovered his vision he saw a strange, little old man, weak looking, his skin all drooped and pasty and with only a few grey hairs, sitting on a funny three-legged stool and staring straight at him with a slight smirk to his thin red lips. Immediately the Earl felt sick at the stench of something like rotten eggs and it took him a second or two to realise that the man was dressed from head to foot in black.

"You did say anything?" The old man asked again.

"Who are you?"

"You know who I am." And the old man grinned, "I can bring your boys back, so they can fight again in your war. Would you like that?"

The Earl nodded, that would be the answer to all his worries.

"But it will come at a price, do you know what I mean?"

The Earl knew exactly what the strange old man meant.

The Earl's soul.

There was no other option. The Earl nodded in agreement and the strange old man draw from a bag, not previously seen, a chain seemingly made entirely out of gold.

"Wear this and call for your sons, indeed you can call for anyone in heaven or hell and they will return for you and follow you. But remember, upon your death, your soul will be mine."

The strange old man disappeared leaving his stool with the chain hanging from it. The Earl placed the chain around his neck and called for his sons. Minutes later, from out of the shadows, they walked quietly towards him, and he was enthralled.

"My sons, my boys, I worship the floor you stand on. Only heaven knows how happy I am to see you again, here at Grise Hall."

He ran towards them and cuddled both at the same time, feeling their heart's beating again.

But the boys were less than happy, standing there emotionless.

"Why have you brought us back down to here?" The eldest asked sadly, "We have done you no ill."

The Earl, however, did not hear the question, such was his happiness now that his plans were back on track.

That night he went to bed a blissful man.

A few days later the Earl, his two sons and what was left of their small army rode north to help fight some of the families loyal to the House of York. The Earl's soldiers were wary of the fact that his two dead sons now rode again, seemingly alive but that was of no consequence to the Earl. Of consequence, was the Percy household and the one who had caught the eye and heart of his daughter.

This Percy would be punished with death, the Earl's boys would lead the House of Lancaster's armies to victory and his daughter would marry the King's son.

His grandson would be King.

But the clash did not go according to plan.

Both of his sons were killed again along with most of his soldiers. The Percy who had found favour with his daughter, was victorious.

The Earl was beside himself with anger and rage all the way back to Great Grise Hall. When he arrived, he remembered his gold chain and called for his two sons to return to him.

This time they did not return. Instead the strange, little old man appeared again and sat, again, on the funny three-legged chair.

"Where are my two sons? Why have they not returned to me?" The Earl ordered.

"The chain only permits you to call a soul back once. Your sons will never return to you."

"You never told me that," the Earl cried furiously. "Blast you for your trickery."

The strange, little old man said nothing but simply stared at the Earl.

"At least they are back in Heaven, away from his god forsaken place," The Earl said to himself.

"Your sons have not returned to heaven," answered the strange, little old man. "Once they die after being called by the chain wearer, they come to me."

"What?" the Earl erupted. "Damn you devil, you have cheated me."

And with that he lifted the chain from his neck and threw it to the floor.

"I would pick that up if I was you," the strange, little old man suggested, "we have work for you to do with it."

"No more," fumed the Earl bravely. "I will do no work for you, you trickster, our agreement is off. I will have no more part in it."

"This agreement stands, abide by it or you shall lose your life now and your soul and this house will be cursed."

Such was the anger which had boiled inside the Earl, he unleashed his sword and ran towards the seated strange, little old man.

The Earl never reached him. Instead, looking down he saw his own body lying still on the floor and suddenly he was falling, falling through the floor and into the earth, falling through rock, through magma, falling still further until, at last, he stopped.

In the shadows, away from the confrontation, the Earl's daughter watched and listened. She watched her father die, she watched the little, strange fellow disappear and she watched where the gold chain, the very thing that had helped cause their problems, had landed.

The Earl's soul had been cursed. Every time when the full moon shone in the night's sky he returned with his two sons and rode the fields and towns around Great Grise Hall looking for those stupid to be out on such nights and take them back down to hell and eternal misery.

The daughter of the Earl became engaged and soon married her beloved and they took over the Hall and its land. The Devil tried to take the Hall from them because of the Earl's actions but, after some, shall we say, intercessions from above, it was agreed that the Hall would become what it was now, a place for those souls not good enough for Heaven and not bad enough for hell. The daughter's husband became the 1st Baron, or Lord, le Grise and he and his eldest child became ghost guides to those who came to reside in the Hall. And the rest, as they say, is history.

The local people knew well of what had happened to the last Earl of Huntshire and the curse. They gave the Hall a new name, one that well reflected the terrible things that had gone on there and the real threat of meeting the ghastly Earl, and his two sons, on a dark night when the moon was full.

Great Grise Hall became Great Grisly Hall.

The name stuck and soon even the local village was eventually renamed Little Grisly too.

Only the removal of all the residents from the Hall would remove the curse including the threat of the Earl and his two sons.

According to legend, no-one knew, or at least no-one told anyone what had happened to the golden chain.

Perhaps time had forgotten all about it.

Or was it a family secret?

Chapter Sixteen

Rose allowed Prim some time to take all this in. She guessed correctly that any normal girl would have laughed it off or thought it incredibly silly to believe in such nonsense. But Prim was different, for one she had already encountered the ghosts who lived in the Hall and, secondly, she was, herself, a Percy. She was family. Rose decided to say more.

"At first our ancestors thought they could manage to live here with the ghosts, but soon more and more ghosts arrived. Anyway, eventually it became too much, and every member of our Percy family moved out and into Little Grisly. From such a great house, our family became the owners of a village shop and Post Office.

But the family still had a duty to the ghosts who have been made to come to the Hall. Me and our predecessors have tried so hard to push the residents upstairs and empty the house of them and the curse for good, but it has been no use. For even if we get one up the Devil is quick to bring someone new in. That's how Barnaby Grudge, the soldier, got here, even without having anything to do with the Hall. No, we are doomed to never have our house back. We now think the Devil will keep it this way until he has found his chain."

"Where is the chain? Surely we should destroy it?"

"Exactly, Prim, but we do not know where it is, from generation to generation of Percy, we no longer know. Thankfully, we do not think the Devil does either."

"The Devil himself still comes here?" Prim felt cold and scared at this very thought.

"Not personally Prim, an ambassador from hell comes to the Hall. They were meant to help us guide the residents to one place or another. For years there was an uneasy trust between our family and the representative of hell but recently," and Rose sighed loudly, "recently someone new has come up from there and all the trust has gone. She is very persuasive, slippery and tricky. I certainly do not want you to be with her alone. It seems she has a different agenda than all the others. It seems she is more concerned about finding the chain."

Prim wanted to change the subject away from the devil and this new ambassador.

"What about my parents? Do they have this power?"

"Here's where it gets messy. Your Dad did as it ran down our line of the family, but he always hated the idea of this job, refused to believe it at first when your Grandad told him and when he met his wife, your Mum, he positively refused to do it. Your Dad told your Mum and when she realised it was all true she forbade him from taking it on. He was all too happy about that."

"So, you took it on?"

"Yes, I had to due to the curse, but your Dad was intent on getting rid of any sign of the family history, so I was banned from home and well I imagine he lay down some rules on you."

Prim nodded. *Yes, some very strict and odd rules.*

"But the power to help these souls is always strongest in the eldest and as I've said I'm not really very good Prim. Truth is I need help."

"Help from who?" asked Prim as the truth dawned on her.

"Well family history says that when the eldest gives up their power it automatically goes to their eldest. It almost gives that one double the power. Yes, you Prim, you must be the strongest we've had for at least a century or two. You could be the guide the residents need."

"No this is all mad I certainly don't believe this. I don't feel different, well at least I don't think so."

"Oh, you are different Prim, special and your parents know it. What they probably don't know is that you have already helped someone across to the other-side, up the staircase as we say."

"No, I haven't," Prim said but she went bright red. She knew she had told a lie and she scratched her nose, wondering why it hadn't started to grow longer.

"You have Prim. Do you remember old Mrs Pilkington from down the road?"

"Yes."

"And do you remember being in a field and letting her in through the gate?"

Prim remembered her dream. *But surely it was only a dream?* But how did Rose know about it?

"Think it was just a dream Prim?" Rose asked, "Think again. That was you naturally helping a friend and neighbour up to heaven. She was very grateful."

"But I was dreaming, I woke up and I was in bed. How could a dream help someone like Mrs P?"

Rose looked at Prim and sighed, she didn't want to tell her the everything's about everything. "Yes, you are in bed, and yes Prim your body remains in that bed, but your spirit, well Prim, that leaves your body and goes to another place, only until you have helped the spirit out and then you safely travel back."

Prim felt sick. *An out of body experience!* She did not like the feeling nor the fact that she had experienced this and the thought that it could, would, happen again. Her whole body shuddered at this notion.

"Tell me, were you really, really tired when you awoke in the morning? As if you hadn't slept and had run a marathon instead?"

"Yes," Prim remembered, and Rose let her think for a few moments before continuing.

"I cannot guide these residents upwards Prim and that is why I brought you here to Great Grisly Hall."

"You brought me here to Great Grisly Hall?" Prim now laughed.

What a load of rubbish.

"Yes, Prim that is exactly what I said, with the help of others of course. Rest assured there is a lot more for me to tell you about but please understand one thing darling, we are going to need all the help we can, not just about sorting out all the residents but dealing with those from hell too, and you are probably the best weapon we have."

Chapter Seventeen

Prim and Rosemary spoke for a bit longer. Rose told Prim why her parents never ever left the village and Prim explained the rules her Dad had given her when she was young. Rose told Prim that her Dad had wanted to be a solicitor, a human rights lawyer. He even went to university but, upon his return, Prim's Grandad had told him about the curse. He had met Prim's Mum at college and they had amazing plans for their lives, but these were now all shattered.

In one way, Prim's Dad was angry that his own father hadn't told him when he was eighteen or even earlier, allowing him to dream of a future outside of Little Grisly all the while at university only to then take the dream away upon his return. In another way Prim's Dad thought the very idea of a curse to be so absurd to be untrue, that his Dad maybe going just a little funny in the head.

But in another way, Prim's Dad realised there was something, he knew there was something to all the talk, little things, childhood memories and friends, dreams and something in his subconscious and that is why he gave up on his future career and so did Prim's Mum. They took on the new family business of running the Post Office together.

Openly he rejected the curse and he certainly rejected his so-called role as a spirit guide. That was when Rose had to take over, especially after their father had died young. But that then led to fights and arguments between Rose and her brother before he, and his wife, told Rose that they could no longer tolerate her and her "job" any more and she was told to leave home and move in elsewhere in the village.

From that day on Prim's Dad rejected the world and put his plans for the future to the back of his mind. It was best to stay in simple Little Grisly. And when Prim was born they decided that she would need as much protection as possible, from the curse and her aunt. Prim was never to be told about the curse and Rose was told to leave Little Grisly for good.

"I'm sorry Prim about all this. I suppose you really shouldn't blame your Dad too, he just wants to protect you."

"Playing in a car park for years when all this here belongs to the family." Prim was serious too.

"I'm sure he would have told you one day Prim I just don't know when."

"And why didn't you tell Harry that I was your niece?"

Prim stared at Rose. There was some resemblance between them, particularly their freckles and the shape of their face.

"You haven't told Harry that I am your Auntie?"

Prim said nothing, but the blood drained from her face. *What was wrong in saying that?*

But there must have been something wrong. Rose moved to stand up.

"Oh God. I hope I can get to him before he sees the others. Thank goodness a lot of them aren't speaking to him now."

"Why?"

"Because then they will think that we are up to something, like trying to get them all out and up to heaven."

"But isn't that a good thing?"

"Yes, of course, but not necessarily Prim, you see there's two of them in that house who well aren't that bothered about heaven, you've met them, and they are sort of matey with the ambassador from hell. They would probably prefer to go to hell, although, of course, it is much nicer in Great Grisly Hall than down there. And, the thing is, I don't want this ambassador knowing about who you are just yet. Oh, they have probably guessed anyway. Best you go home now sweetie, I've told you a lot and I need to find Harry fast. Don't you worry though and come and see me tomorrow."

"Tomorrow is Sunday."

106

"Oh yes, I forgot about that. The Post Office will be closed for most of the day. Come back on Monday Prim, darling niece of mine."

"Will you be okay?"

"I'll be fine, just fine, and, put those flowers in water soon."

With that Rose gave her niece a quick, final cuddle and shooed her away. Prim left the grounds of Great Grisly Hall and every few seconds turned to look for Rose hoping that she could find Harry quickly.

There was a great deal to think about on the way back home. Where was she to start? The curse, the chain, her parents, the ambassador from hell and her supposed ability to help the dead not to mention her own soul leaving her body. There was a massive difference between nice Mrs Pilkington and these dead for centuries people. She knew she would get a headache just from all these questions let alone thinking about the answers.

Thankfully, Amy, Sadie and Lockie had been waiting for her down the pathway towards Little Grisly and Prim soon began to forget as they played all the way back home. Then one question appeared in her mind. If Rosemary knew about the dream with Mrs Pilkington, could she answer her other dream, the one with the hanging tree?

Chapter Eighteen

With no work the next day Prim's Dad, Peter Percy, would always pop to the Swinging Witch on a Saturday night for a few cheeky pints and to chat to his very good friend, the landlord, Mr Tanner.

This was his time to relax away from the Post Office and to have some "me" time. Mrs Percy, in a similar manner, would invite a couple of friends around to the flat and obviously look after Prim at the same time.

Mr Percy loved to make lists of all the things he would do that day and simply loved ticking all the tasks off, one by one. He simply hated something new happening in his life which meant adding something to the list. Anything new was unpredictable and meant worry and anxiety. Would he finish his list in time for bed, preferably tea-time?

He didn't write everything down as somethings were obvious. He would always have his breakfast, lunch and tea and nothing, no task could come before his eating, although, at lunch time he would sit in the back office and read certain bits of all the newspapers. Not the bad bits, he hated reading about that: wars; famine; global warming, that wasn't his type of reading. He preferred the happy stories, such as missing things like cats or dogs getting found by their owners.

He wouldn't put down that he had to go to the toilet too because that was an obvious task to do as well and, despite not liking things being unpredictable, he could not really account on a list as to how many times he might need to pay a visit, nor for how long.

The sort of things he would put down on his list would be work related such as open the shop, send passport applications off, order more postcards and so on. He liked to keep a tight ship and never, ever run out of anything in the shop. He liked life being one whole list to be ticked off.

His favourite addition to the list, on a Saturday, was to write that he was to go to the Swinging Witch in the evening.

The old, red brick pub had been built just over five hundred years ago but, according to Mr Tanner, it was just not traditional enough for all the many tourists who visited it. And so, consequently, the inside had been completely changed from being a real old pub to one that people thought looked like a real old pub complete with lots of fake farming tools, upside down horseshoes and pictures of old and odd-looking villagers.

A lot of the visitors to Little Grisly asked Mr Tanner why the pub was called the "Swinging Witch" and whether a real witch had lived there many years ago. They wanted to know why the witch was swinging. Some of the visitors asked whether the witch, not believing in last orders, still popped in for a pint.

Mr Tanner had heard the rumour or legend that once there had been a witch or two in Little Grisly and had put up a display in a corner for tourists to read about over a pint. If it kept people drinking in his pub then talk about witches was fine. To others who lived in Little Grisly, he said that such talk was absolute nonsense.

But privately, and especially when he was locking up the pub on his own at night, he was often a little bit scared of the thought that a witch might be about his bar, watching him from the shadows.

He would have to calm himself down on these occasions.

There is no such thing as ghosts and anyone who believes in them are stupid.

And he had to repeat this a few times just to get himself through the day and, especially at night.

Thank God he lived in sensible Little Grisly. Little Grisly was a very sensible place to live in. So regular was Mr Percy's attendance that Mr Tanner would have his usual pint of "Old Rat's Tail" ready for him. Of course, it wasn't really made from old rat's tails. In fact, it was rather a nice real ale, the nicest, most satisfying ale they served at the Swinging Witch.

And it was well known in the village that Mr Percy was a stickler for being regular, how he hated unpredictability and it would have been an absolute disaster if there was no pint of his favourite brew.

Thankfully there was and as Mr Percy entered, his pint was carefully placed onto the bar where he always sat. Curse anyone who would sit on his tall stool. Everything, absolutely everything had to be regular.

Mr Percy was a very regular chap and simply adored rules, especially the ones he had made up for his family.

The family was there to obey him, after all, he was head of a very famous and historic one and this village had grown thanks to the Percys. But in his mind, as well as being famous and historic, it was also very much crazy what with its supposed curse and ridiculous job of helping people to heaven.

What absolute nonsense. What twaddle.

Whoever had made up such a lie deserved a medal. After all, the lie had lasted through the centuries. But Mr Percy was wise and saw through it. He had to be the cleverest cookie in the whole Percy family biscuit tin.

It couldn't really be true.

And Great Grisly Hall? It must be just rubble now, after all, it had probably been over ten years or more since he had last looked at it. His sister believed in all that stuff about the curse but then she had believed in unicorns and fairies when she was younger.

She should have grown up. Stopped messing about, dying her hair pink and all stupid colours.

He was right glad she had gone when he had finally told her to leave Little Grisly, hopefully for good especially with Prim growing up. She would have been a terrible influence on their only child.

Rosemary was always day dreaming and playing and that was no way to grow up. Yes, he had played, he even had some imaginary friends, but only as a small boy and he had soon realised how stupid his family had been over the many years.

Thank God, he had realised this and become a Post Office Manager instead. Nice and steady and there would always be a demand for the Queen's post. Christmas, Easter, Mother's Day, Father's Day and the rest, in fact there seemed to be more special days each year which meant the they were earning nicely.

Soon, very soon his one daughter, Primula, would begin to learn the trade too and take over the business when she was ready, and he ready to retire.

But for now, she could have her play but of course there were rules to be obeyed, she was never to leave the village, that was the golden rule, unless she had to go to school where either he or his wife would drive her there and drive her back. In the holidays she could stay in the flat or play here in the pub car park, and that was it.

That was enough.

Especially with the thought that Rosemary would, or could, be not far away, living in Great Grisly Hall, playing at being a spirit guide or whatever she wanted to call herself. Never once did he ever think about himself going over and seeing if the old house was still standing up or to see if his sister was there.

What colour was Rosemary's hair now?

And Prim seemed to be turning into a good girl, good at school but not that clever that she would leave and go to university. No, she could take over the Post Office when she was ready and that was that.

The Percy's were a fine, distinguished family.

The Percy's had not lived at Great Grisly Hall for years.

And for Prim's own sake, he had to break the link between that place and his family. *There couldn't really be a curse, things like that were just the talk of legend or just idle gossip.*

Prim could count herself lucky that she had such a sensible father.

Little Grisly was a sensible place to live and standards had to be maintained.

But three sips of the lovely nectar and his nice safe world was shattered slightly when Mr Tanner asked innocently whether Prim had been playing at a friend's house on the basis that he had not seen her play in the pub car park for a few days.

"What do you mean? She can't have gone anywhere else."

"Well I haven't really seen her, and I've had quite a bit of work to do outside what with all the tourists and taking that clapped out old banger of a car to the scrap."

"You must be mistaken. I know she's going out in the morning and not coming back till late, you must have seen her."

Mr Percy suddenly thought less of Mr Tanner.

"And I tell you that I haven't, I mean I saw her the other day and a bit later I took her a soft drink, like I always do, but she wasn't there. Searched the whole place I did. Hardly a great place to play is it a pub car park. She must have found somewhere else to play."

Mr Percy began thinking even less of Mr Tanner than he had a few seconds beforehand. Mr Tanner was making him angry. Was his friend ill?

"I'll ask you not to pass comment on my family and its affairs."

But his anger wasn't really directed at Mr Tanner. Instead, Mr Percy had second guessed what Prim had been up to. Or, at least, where she might have gone to.

She was a Percy.

And the Percy's used to live at Great Grisly Hall.

He had to break the link between the Hall and his family.

112

He picked up his pint and drank the rest of it in one go. *Oh God.*

"Mr Tanner forgive me, I am very sorry for how I have just spoken to you and I am grateful for you to give Prim a drink now and then. Now, if you don't mind I'll have another drink, a straight whisky and another pint please."

Prim was in trouble.

Chapter Nineteen

In fact, Prim was in more trouble. Mrs Percy's friends had only stayed for an hour as they both had to be up early for a new coach load of tourists arriving very early the next morning.

Mrs Paterson ran the quaint tea shop with her husband and whilst much of her afternoon tea business took place, well, in the afternoon she also offered the same for tourists who would only be stopping for an hour in the morning.

Mrs Russell had to get up even earlier as she ran the bakers with her husband and had a large batch of scones to bake fresh ready for the tourists.

They hardly had time to finish one bottle of wine between them and Mrs Percy knew her husband would be angry if she had opened another bottle without it being drunk. There was a rule for that somewhere in the house.

With time on her hands she decided to put the first clothes wash on of the weekend. Prim was by now fast asleep and so, quietly Mrs Percy went about the flat sorting out whites from darks to bright colours and as she did so the little bit of wine made her a teeny bit happy and so she sang gently and danced a little too, all until she noticed a mark on one of Prim's multi coloured skirts.

She brought the skirt close to her eyes - it was green. Frantically she went through all of Prim's dirty clothes and there was more of the same stuff on almost all of them.

Green was not the colour of fashion that year, not that such things ever meant anything in Little Grisly.

The green was grass.

There's no grass in the pub car park, where could she have been?

Mr Percy would have to add something to his list for Sunday.

Chapter Twenty

Sunday, Sunday, Sunday.

The weather records were all being wrecked this year as day after day there was more sun, sun and sun but Prim, upon waking, knew today would be different from the last week due to her parents being off work.

No Great Grisly Hall today.

But there would also be no family outings to a zoo or ice cream factory on such a lovely day, no visits to see friends from school (not that she had any), no, there would be nothing. She longed to meet up with Rose, but she knew there was someone else she wanted to meet up with too.

Harry. He wasn't like the boys in school. There was something different about him, not just that he was a ghost. He was more refined, more interesting, and nice. He cared and that, to Prim, made him mature. Harry was a boy she could spend time with.

At least Amy, Sadie and Lockie would be about to help make the day fun.

She was not prepared for what was in store for her.

She shifted from her room and into the kitchen helping herself to some cereal. Mrs Percy was down in the shop for a few hours selling newspapers and last-minute bottles of milk and the like.

Her Dad sat on the opposite side of the kitchen table and watched her. He was not clever enough to be subtle or have sympathy for her. He just wanted answers.

The onslaught began before Prim had even put some corn flakes into her mouth.

"Tell me Prim," asked Mr Percy, without wishing her a good morning, "are there any green bushes or grass in the car park to the pub?"

Prim blushed at such a question so early in the morning, why in fact was her Dad talking to her at all? He loved there to be absolute silence in the morning especially at breakfast, so he could read the newspapers.

"I'm not too sure Dad," she replied, "I don't think so."

"I would have thought that by playing there every day this week that you would know perfectly well or are you in such a day dream that you could be anywhere?"

Oh God, I'm in trouble.

He must have spoken to Mr Tanner, he must have reported her absence to her Dad last night. But what did he mean about the green bushes or grass.

She was soon to find out.

"For your information, I can tell you Prim that there are no bushes, trees or grass in the Swinging Witch car park. So, explain to me how come all your dresses, skirts, and shorts all have grass stains on them?"

And he pointed to the laundry basket next to the washing machine, in the corner of the room. Prim gulped, she had remembered seeing grass on her favourite yellow summer dress but did not even think that it would matter.

"Explain Prim. How could you get grass on your clothes?"

It was time to come clean. Sort of.

"I hate playing in the car park there is absolutely nothing to do there."

"Rules are rules and are there to be obeyed, where have you been? Tell the truth now."

"Just for walks." Prim was buying time and trying to think of a convincing lie. She could not, simply could not, mention she had been to Great Grisly Hall.

"Walks where?"

"Along by the stream."

"How far down the stream? Have you come across an old Hall or mill?"

"What Hall?" This sounded rather feeble.

Mr Percy's eyes searched Prim's to see if she was lying but there was not enough evidence to hold her guilty, not that such a notion had ever stopped a parent from sentencing their child to a punishment before.

"The rules are for your own good and one day you will be thankful to me."

"But Dad I can't play in the car park anymore." Prim was being brave.

"Quiet girl, I would have thought someone with such imagination could play anywhere just like that sister of mine. You have embarrassed me in front of Mr Tanner and the other locals and me, the Post Master. They will surely be talking about us.

No, you say you can't play there and I'm saying you won't play there, you're barred, grounded as the Americans say, for two months. From now on when we go to work you will remain here in the flat."

And that, as they say, was that. He stared at her for a second to make sure his new rule had sunk in before he lifted his newspaper to read something nice about the Royal family.

Chapter Twenty-One

For the rest of the day Prim stayed in her room. She knew she would have done anyway today but banned from leaving the flat for two months? Never to go to Great Grisly Hall and see Rosemary? If only there was a way of telling her what had happened. Perhaps Rosemary would guess something was wrong and try and come and see her. If only Sadie, Amy and Lockie could run over to the Hall and pass on a message.

If only everything.

Prim felt very down and slumped onto her bed. She looked at her bookcase, but nothing took her fancy. Strangely her Dad had left on her bedside table a book entitled "The Post Office Family: Running a successful business with the Royal Mail" but that story didn't sound like it had a happy or interesting ending.

Only a few weeks ago she didn't have any friends at all, now she was effectively banned from seeing them. At least there was Rufus, looking sad and lonely himself with his head on her pillow. She picked him up and gave her oldest friend a cuddle.

On top of the bookcase, for the first time ever, were flowers, the wild flowers Rose had given her, now inside a vase she had found under the sink in the kitchen. Prim chuckled, her parents hadn't even noticed them, *surely they are evidence of me not playing in the car park?*

Of course, the flowers reminded her of Rose. And her time playing in Great Grisly Hall. And of Amy, Sadie and Lockie.

Where are Amy Sadie and Lockie?

Perhaps her bedroom was too small for all four of them to play in, perhaps they were at the Hall playing all the games they had played with her?

Perhaps they're playing with Harry.

She was green with envy.

Prim was simply left by herself in her room. She had heard her Mum come back from the shop downstairs and about an hour later lunch was put out by her door, a packet of Skips and a pack of cheese and tomato sandwiches which according to the best before date ran out that very day.

The afternoon was much like the morning only now and then she could hear that the TV was on and her parents were watching Miss Marple.

For tea she was served with corned beef hash, still in its plastic tray, direct from the microwave. She thought about Rose, her lovely aunt, and hoped she had stopped Harry telling the others about them being related.

Harry wouldn't say anything.

She thought about Rose and what she had said about the family and their powers to help people.

They're not exactly powers like a superhero are they?

She thought about how she could have an outer body experience and worried that one day her soul would not come back and wondered what her body would look like being dead. For a minute she lay there and pretended that she was.

She thought about Rose and what she had said about Mrs Pilkington, the old lady, and bringing Prim to the Hall.

She thought about Rose and how nice she was to her compared to her parents.

She was about to think of Rose again but fell asleep instead.

In her dream she was out in the open and found herself walking alongside the stream, by herself, looking for Amy, Sadie and Lockie. She knew where they were and that they had gone on ahead and without her and she thought she could hear their voices playing somewhere quite close by. Laughing, joking, singing. Close, but never that close.

She shivered and looked up at the grey, glum sky, *where had the summer gone?* It was cold and would surely be raining soon and as she looked down and wrapped herself up in her rain coat she noticed ahead, in the distance, that there was the mill she had seen in the previous dream and just to its side she could just about see Amy running about and laughing.

Prim ran towards her, called for her, but Amy did not respond and instead ran towards the other two who were now in sight. Prim ran to the mill, but they had disappeared, only to reappear lying down on the grass, all silent close by to the tree, the hanging tree.

At first Prim stopped running at the very thought about the tree but, looking up, caught a glimpse of something hanging from one of its strongest and tallest branches which intrigued her.

Did I just see a?

A foot, how bizarre.

And another foot, wait on they are attached to legs.

Prim's curiosity caused her to come closer and she noticed that the legs were attached to the body of a girl in a very old-fashioned dress.

The wind blew the body making it slowly sway from side to side causing an odd screeching sound as the rope noose turned on the branch.

The girl had been hanged from the tree by her neck.

Dread ran down Prim's body and caused her muscles to slow down and tighten as if she was running in slow motion.

But she had to look up.

Prim saw the girl, with golden, straight blonde hair the same colour as Prim's, the same length too, the closed eyes, the freckles on her face, the small nose, the closed eyes, the closed, dead eyes.

Prim froze. The sound of laughter and singing had all gone and she realised that Amy, Sadie and Lockie had disappeared. She wanted to throw up.

She was left all alone with the girl. Prim guessed that the girl was her.

Chapter Twenty-Two

Prim awoke sweating and quickly retching. It was dark, and she fumbled for the bedside light for what was only a second, but which felt like a minute.

From across her room there was a sound, almost like the noose against the tree.

What if the hanged girl is in here? Prim was confused now and closed her eyes as she found and turned the switch. Quickly opening them, expecting the worst, she scanned the room. Nothing. She checked again from ceiling to floor, window to door, nothing. She felt her heart beating fast and tried to calm herself down.

The sound came again from the window and without thinking she turned and opened the curtains swiftly expecting the girl to be staring at her, if not in the room but in the reflection, not just any girl but herself.

But it wasn't, instead it was the blind being moved by a gentle wind coming in from the open window and touching the wooden frame. Prim got up to make doubly sure this was the case before sitting back down again on her warm bed and breathing deeply. She could taste sick inside her mouth.

There was a strange smell inside her room, familiar but strange. Strange because she could not relate the smell to her room.

Panic set in again. Was it the girl? Was it her?

No, it was the corn beef hash by the bedroom door.

She checked the time, 2.33am, her tea would have been long cold and listening she could not hear the TV on anymore.

But she could not sleep, was her dream some omen of what was to happen to her? She tried to remember how old the girl looked to see how long she had left but then her conscience was telling her that it was a dream.

Just a dream silly and no need to panic, calm down Prim, calm down Prim.

Calm down.

And she did but then thought of how she would never see her Aunt again and Harry and the Hall.

And she wondered whether she was having an out of body experience in these dreams too. She knew that she was beginning to panic again and needed to relax.

She needed something to take her mind away from the dream and being grounded. There was only one thing to do, she reached over and picked up the book on the Royal Mail and began to read it.

Chapter One

The Royal Mail and your family: a first class posting to success.

She was soon asleep but thankfully she had steered her dreams away from the stream, the mill and the tree.

A few hours later her Dad came into her room and woke her up. It was Monday morning and, rather unnecessarily, he said.

"Remember, you're to stay in the flat for the rest of the week until school starts again is that clear?"

Prim half nodded in her half-asleep state.

"I'm locking the front door, so you can't get out, we'll be back at 7pm. If you need us ring us in the shop." He was still angry and with a tone that suggested he really didn't want her to call them.

With that he left but left noticing that Prim had begun to read the Royal Mail book.

Perhaps this event will bring Prim and me closer.

The door to the flat was indeed locked from the outside as Mr and Mrs Percy went downstairs to work for twelve long hours.

A few minutes later Prim got up, yawned and walked into the kitchen for breakfast. What could she do in here for the entire day? As she pondered this question and munched on her pickled onion monster munch she heard a creaking noise on the landing, as if someone had stood on the floorboards by the door, followed by the clatter of a key.

One of her parents must have returned.

For a minute Prim carried on eating but no-one other noise was heard, and her parents did not come into the kitchen nor call her name. Her curiosity got the better of her again and she went to check.

There was no one there in the landing or on the staircase.

There was no one except her, the staircase and the open front door.

The open front door.

Chapter Twenty-Three

How was the only question Prim could think of. She looked down the stairwell and listened, but she couldn't see or hear one of her parents. She could clearly remember that her Dad had locked the door however.

So how is the door now open?

Amy appeared on the landing.

"Come on Prim! Get dressed, we've got twelve hours before your parents finish work."

Prim was hesitant.

"Where's Sadie and Lockie?"

"Downstairs and playing outside, come on let's go to the Hall."

"I'm not supposed to."

"Come on Prim, really. You know you want to come, and we will look after you."

"But what about grass stains?"

"Put some darker clothes on then and now you're eleven you can always wash things yourself. Come on Prim it's the last week of the holidays."

Amy was very good at persuading people, clever Amy. For a second, she hesitated, but she knew her parents wouldn't come back up. She was good to go.

Prim dressed, finished off her breakfast and, after a reminder from Amy, brushed her teeth, before tiptoeing down the stairs and out towards Great Grisly Hall with her three friends.

It had only been two days or less since she had been there, but it felt like decades. As she strolled, breathing the air deeply and enjoying her freedom, she noticed that some of the wild flowers had, well, got wilder and the grass longer, which made her of course more careful where she walked and then there it was, the rooftops of the hall in the distance then as she got closer the first floor, the ground floor and the sight of Rose's old car.

This felt like home to her. She was happy. *Without the curse, this would be where I live.*

The front door of the Hall was open, but she could not find either Rose or any of the long-term residents of the hall around anywhere.

Amy, Sadie and Lockie wanted to play in the main hall as they felt it was a better place to play "Lords and Ladies" but Prim wished to sit on the stone garden bench where her and Rose had sat only a few days ago.

Maybe Harry will pass by.

Something strange was afoot: it was not just Amy who insisted that Prim play with them inside the Hall but also Sadie and Lockie, it was Lockie who tried to push, then physically pull her inside.

Prim was being strong, the Hall was not a great place to be inside especially on such a warm day and she was forthright in staying outside to wait for Harry or Rose, whatever she was doing, she surely would not be long. Besides, if Prim was going to run away from her grounding at home, she might as well be outside.

She sat on the bench and her immediate thoughts were on how pushy Amy and the others had been and occasionally she could see them outside and what seemed to be them spying on her. *What's wrong with them today?* Perhaps they were feeling guilty over not being around when Prim needed them. Once or twice she saw Amy wave urgently to her to come over to them, but Prim was having none of it.

Soon she began to forget about them, even ignore them and she closed her eyes and enjoyed the sun's warm rays on her face and thought that she better not get too much of a tan in case her Dad spotted it and realised she wasn't in her room all day. There was some

Sun tan lotion to be found in the bathroom cupboard. Not that it ever, ever got used.

She kept her eyes closed and listened to the very gentle sway of the trees, the occasional bird and the silence in between.

It's lovely being here. Imagine staying here if it was a Hotel. Imagine living here as if it was still our home.

She thought of all the fresh, wild flowers and raised her nose to smell them but deep down she knew she was doing this because ever so faintly she could smell something quite uncanny for the season of spring, dead flowers and even worse, rotten dead flowers.

At first, she thought it was just her imagination but, after she had cleaned her nose with her fingers, the putrid scent of decay became stronger.

What wild flowers die in spring?

Before she could answer she felt a shade on her face and quickly guessed a cloud had hidden the sun. *But there were no clouds a minute ago.* She felt cold reaching out onto her face, neck and arms and opened her eyes.

In front of her stood a small skinny woman of only about twenty years, possibly a late teenager, with jet black hair tied right back in a pony- tail with a white face not exactly ugly, but there was a certain something which Prim could not quite make out yet.

"Good morning Prim, mind if I sit down next to you?" The lady asked, smiling sweetly.

Chapter Twenty-Four

Prim was in shock and stared at the woman for what seemed an age before replying. Was she a live human or was she a ghost? She was dressed in modern clothes like a business suit in black that matched her hair but at the same time there was something completely unreal about her.

"I have heard so much about you," the lady squealed with delight and raising her voice at the end. "You're a right little sparkle around here I can tell you. Everyone thinks you're a star, are you like this in school?"

But before Prim could answer no, the lady carried on.

"I bet you are and such a beautiful girl too."

She was sitting right next to Prim now and their knees were touching, her smile was almost as wide as the sun.

She seemed lovely, even nicer than Rosemary but who was she? As she thought about this a slightly stronger breeze picked up and Prim inhaled the stench of the dead rotting flowers again.

The smell must come from the lady. Now Prim was used to a few of the girls and a few more of the boys being a bit stinky in school, especially in the afternoon, but she simply wasn't used to adults with body odour issues.

But Prim was a good girl and decided to ignore the smell, Amy would do the same of course although Sadie and Lockie would probably start laughing and holding their nose.

"Who are you?"

"How silly of me," replied the lady, "I'm Lilith, though most people call me Lily. I'm a friend of Rosemary's."

For an instant Prim thought that Rose must have made lots of friends in her travels but why would one of them come here? Did she know the family history and what Rose's job was?

"Where is Rosemary?"

"She's having a chat to those inside, you know what I mean," and again Lilith smiled at her and began to giggle. The giggling became infectious.

"What are they talking about?"

Prim realised that she must have sounded like a police officer asking these straight questions and liked this, besides, it wasn't being rude was it? Lilith was answering her questions.

"Just a bit of this and that. I expect you know anyway what is going to happen soon?"

"Yes, Auntie Rosemary did say something," Prim replied.

"Auntie Rosemary?" said Lilith and paused for thought. For a second, she went very serious in her look and nodded to herself.

"Is there something wrong?" Prim asked, fearing she had said something out of turn, that Rosemary was her aunt when Rose had told her not to.

The lines on Lilith's forehead melted and she was all smiles again.

"No, not at all, it's just I have not heard anyone call her Auntie before. Tell me, is she a good Auntie? I bet she is."

"I don't really know, I guess that she is, it's just I haven't seen her for years."

Prim was puzzled that a friend of Rose's would not know that she had left the family a long time ago. It was time to ask Lilith some more questions.

"Do you do the same job as Rosemary?"

"Sort of, although we have been, how would you say, only working together for a short while."

Prim felt reassured by this news. Lilith was one of us, on the same side. She just wasn't sure who or what was the other side. Rose would surely tell her.

Before she could think of something else to ask, it was time for Lilith to ask her questions.

"Have you ever thought about following Rosemary into the family business Prim?"

Prim had to think.

"I'm only eleven. I've haven't started big school yet."

"It's a safe job though Prim."

"It doesn't sound very safe, what working with dead people, you know, ghosts." Prim began to think the job at the Post Office sounded safer and saner.

"Well there is the job security, after all there is only one thing guaranteed in life."

Prim could only nod in agreement, but this was rather gruesome talk. She thought about Mrs Pilkington and the explanation by Rose about how she had helped her to the other side, the after-life, heaven.

She had never really thought about this as a job or a career.

Helping the dead.

What about working for the Royal Mail?

Only a few weeks before she had been thinking of being a writer.

Only last year she had been thinking of being a farmer of unicorns.

Lilith continued.

"Well, all the same, it is nice for your Dad to allow you here by yourself. After all, he wasn't so keen on doing Rosemary's job."

The thought of her Dad made Prim shudder more than the thought of any ghost, especially after what had happened only the day before. She would be in very big trouble if he found out.

"He doesn't know I am here," she answered.

"But how did you find this place, I mean, Rosemary has only just come back but the others inside tell me you have been coming for a short while now."

Prim wondered whether Lilith would be interested in her story of playing in the pub car park and chasing the fox with Amy, Sadie and Lockie but thought better of it. Lilith was a grown up and probably didn't care about childish behaviour.

"I just found it," she said, before adding, in a jokey manner, "but Rose thinks that she made me come here. I mean to say."

"Did she say that?" asked Lilith, coldly and she thought. "So, you're eleven. Have you been doing some, how shall we say, unlawful work experience at home? Has anyone recently died in the that vile, little village?"

Prim was hesitant to answer. Lilith could obviously find out and she would find out that Mrs Pilkington had passed only a short while ago. But why was she so rude about Little Grisly? That was a bit unfair. She thought for a moment and decided to tell the truth.

"Yes," she said, "Yes to all your questions, I think."

"So, you do have the gift to guide people too, just like all your ancestors, all the way back to the daughter of the last Earl."

Prim shuddered at the thought of the last Earl and the legend of him haunting the local area. Lilith noticed this.

"How does it feel to have an ancestor like the him Prim? How does it feel to have someone in your family who could bring back the dead?"

"I've not really thought about that so much; more how scary it would be to meet him in the dead of the night."

"Oh, you Percys," laughed Lilith, "surely bringing back the dead would be of much more interest to you. All you need to do is find the chain."

But Prim did not seem to be listening, she was too busy thinking about the Earl and the Devil.

"Prim, do you know where the chain is kept?"

Prim woke up from her day mare about the Earl. "No, I haven't a clue, probably buried with him, I suppose."

Lilith got the impression that Prim did not know much about the chain and changed the course of the conversation onto another subject.

"I hear you and Harry are good friends."

Prim didn't like to hear that other people had been talking about her, especially about her and a boy, even if it just sounded innocent.

"We've met," she said grudgingly. "He's hardly my best friend."

He probably is, or would it be Amy?

"It's nice to have a best friend Prim. Harry used to have one when he was alive. I imagine he thinks of you as her, after all you are very similar in appearance, a dead ringer for her as some people say. She is an ancestor of yours."

Prim thought about the girl in her dream, hanging from the tree.

That was me in that dream, wasn't it?

"I see that Auntie Rosemary has put covers on all the old paintings in the main hall. Shame that. Cannot see why she would do such a thing. Have you seen the paintings Prim?"

"No, they were covered up when I first came here."

"Why would Rosemary cover all the paintings before you arrived? Was she trying to hide something? What do you reckon Prim?"

Prim didn't know that Rose had covered the paintings.

"I don't know. Really, I don't know."

"Neither do I, but I will find out. Ask your aunt to show you the painting of Lady Angharad Percy."

And with that she stood up.

"Think it's about time I went," and she looked back at Prim and smiled once more, "I will be seeing you around young lady."

And she went off without giving Prim a chance to say goodbye. Within a few seconds, the smell of decomposing flowers had gone.

Amy and the others rushed up to her.

"Are you okay Prim?" they all seemed to say at once.

Prim wasn't so sure, the conversation with Lilith had started fine but it hadn't ended on a high note. Still she didn't have much experience in speaking to adults apart from her parents, terrible Mrs Davis her class teacher at school, Mr Tanner and other, usually elderly people in Little Grisly.

"Well, I think so," was all she could reply.

"We all think you should get home, Prim."

"I'm here to see Rose, my aunt, thank you very much."

And just saying that sentence caused Prim to realise two things: that could not keep her mouth shut about the fact that Rose was her aunt and; secondly that Lilith kept on calling Rose by her full name of Rosemary.

Would close friends say that?

"She's still busy," said Lockie, "talking to the residents."

As quick as a flash, he got a look from both Amy and Sadie.

"How do you know?" Prim asked.

"He doesn't," said Sadie rapidly.

"But we still think you should go back home, with us." Amy said, putting her arm around one of Prim's.

Prim wondered if she was going crazy.

No, I'm just going crazier.

"Okay, I will go home, if Rose was free then I am sure she would have come and said hello. Besides she told me that someone from hell was arriving at the Hall."

Just saying those words made Prim feel uncomfortable.

Do people really come from hell?

She almost did not see the other three stare at each other with Sadie raising her eyebrows and rolling her eyes but she pretended to blank it. It was time to head back and hope that her parents hadn't discovered that she was missing.

But on the way back Prim thought about lots of things but mainly about Amy, Sadie and Lockie.

My imagination must be boiling over with these three. Still better than a pub carpark though.

Chapter Twenty - Five

Prim's parents were still working downstairs when she arrived back and slowly, quietly, went upstairs. The main door and the door to her flat had been left open and ready for her to enter, despite her closing them on the way out that morning.

Strange.

And stranger still, as she took off her shoes in the hallway, she heard the door lock itself from the outside.

Doors cannot lock themselves. Can they?

But she decided to leave this question for now and went straight away into her bedroom and checked for grass stains on her clothes. *Sensible Amy was right to tell me to wear dark clothes.*

Those three had gone for the day and Prim decided that she would have to read a bit more about the Post Office from her book but in truth, although she read the first page in the chapter about ordering birthday and other cards, it did not fill her with excitement.

Your life is excitement now Prim.

And although she sort of read the book, she turned the pages just in case there was a picture or something remotely interesting, her mind was on Great Grisly Hall and her meeting with the strange, smelly woman.

Don't be rude Prim, just because she is smelly doesn't mean she is bad.

But she did stink.

Now she was home and safe she thought about the chain and where it could possibly be. At home she was not frightened of the Earl, she would only think about him if she ever was out in the dark when there was a full moon and she would never do something stupid like that.

Maybe she was right about the chain being buried inside the Church.

Maybe she could go and find it.

But what would I do with it?

The door to the flat opened and gave her a little fright but, of course, it was only her parents and, like in the morning, her Dad was happy to see her leafing through the Post Office book.

"I should have grounded you months ago," was his attempt to be funny. But no-one laughed.

Nevertheless, they all had tea together, tinned meatballs with tinned potatoes, and Dad explained to her a lot more about running a Post Office and how rewarding it was. He explained his plan about finding someone to take some new photographs of Little Grisly, so he could make some postcards to sell inside the shop. He was mightily pleased with his plan.

Prim noticed that her Mum was slightly less interested in the plan than she was.

Prim yawned.

"Sorry Dad, but I think just being in the flat all day has made me tired."

"I thought we could all sit on the sofa and watch the telly together." Dad replied.

This wasn't a suggestion, this was an order. Not a horrible order of course, but there wasn't any room for argument or even a suggestion of doing something else. She would have to grin and bear it.

It wasn't that she hated her parents, far from it, it wasn't that she thought she was too cool to hang around them, far, far from it. It was just she really did have a lot on her mind and because of what they would watch.

Prim's Dad hated watching the news or anything that could show what the world today was like. He just didn't want to know. Instead, they would watch reruns of older programmes, from about twenty years ago, light hearted quizzes mainly and the odd detective series with his favourite actors. None of it wasn't child friendly but none of it was aimed for children either.

The best Prim could hope for would be to fall asleep as soon as she could and slope off to bed.

On some nights she would pretend that she had fallen asleep just to get out of watching TV. Sometimes she wondered whether had Dad put on all the rubbish TV just to get her asleep.

He probably had a list: have tea, put TV on, feet up, have cup of tea, Prim fall asleep, watch more TV but now in peace.

Well, if she was right with that theory, she wasn't going to let her Dad down and, about thirty minutes later she closed her eyes and turned over to allow her parents realise that she was in the land of nod.

Her Mum gently nudged her and told her to brush her teeth and go to bed and with a "Night, night," off she went, smiling to herself as she left the room.

But in fact, she was tired and, after brushing her teeth and putting her PJs' on, she fell asleep within minutes.

Chapter Twenty – Six

Prim found herself by the stream and was sorely tempted to have a paddle. She chucked off her shoes and dipped her left toe into the churning water, it was freezing but she put her foot fully in and gasped all the same, waiting for the shock and the pain of the coldness to disappear.

What did you expect, the water is going to be cold in winter!

Once it did, she put her right foot fully in as well and she went through the same process of enduring the sheer artic hell before smiling. She had overcome the pain barrier and was happy.

And she paddled gently through the stream, it wasn't deep but occasionally there was a dip and her knees were now wet, but she did not mind.

She did mind the stones on the water's bed even when a green one caused her left leg to slip making her yelp. She was still happy.

The mill was close by and the water wheel was turning gently and inside she could hear the mill stone grinding the wheat and she longed to have a look.

Getting out of the stream she patted her legs down, *any deeper and I could have been swimming,* and searched and found the doorway. It was a lot noisier inside and right in the middle sat the large, stationary mill stone and, just on top of it, the moving stone turning, thanks to the power of the stream and controlled by some basic arrangement involving what could only be a brake to stop it working. But there was no wheat to grind and she looked around for some to try out, but the mill was empty except for some old farming tools such as some spades and a fork.

For a moment she thought about putting a spade between the two stones to see what would happen, but she thought better of herself and decided to leave before she was tempted once more.

And as she walked out she saw the tree, the hanging tree, and she shuddered and tried to avoid staring up at it in case she saw the blonde hair of the girl but before she could she saw something else. Not blonde hair, dark hair. Long, black hair.

Attached to a body, swinging in the breeze.

Not someone else up there!

Prim was mesmerised and had to look closer.

And she ran towards the tree, she did not know why she ran, because the body was not going anywhere. It was just swinging from the rope, the rope attached to the neck of some poor unfortunate.

And although she knew she was being morbid, Prim wanted to see the face, because she could guess who the face belonged to.

And she was right, running right up to the tree, she could see Lilith's lifeless face.

What has she got to do with all this stuff.

There was no time for her to think any more, for one of Lilith's shoes fell and hit Prim, quite heavily, on her head.

Prim woke up.

Like in the first dream about the hanging tree, she was scared, shocked and sweating. She guessed her right hand had slapped her whilst she had been asleep, and her cheek was just a little tender.

Just a dream Prim. Only a dream.

Just a dream.

But she had also had a dream about Mrs Pilkington, and that had turned out to be real.

Or had it?

There was no way for certain that it had happened, she couldn't call heaven to ask if she could speak to Mrs P. She only had

Rose's word for it. But that counted, somehow, she did believe that that dream had been real. *Why am I dreaming these dreams?*

She began to wonder whether the dream she had just had, and the dream from other night were true too. Certainly, she saw a girl who looked remarkably like her and Lilith had told her that there was one such girl who was very similar in looks.

How she could she see someone who she had never seen before in a dream?

And she had seen Lilith, herself, hanged and dead.

My head is trying to tell me something.

At least it wasn't me swinging from that tree.

And she felt a chill so much that, although still a little bit sweaty, she wrapped the duvet around her for warmth.

She lay and thought for a bit, desperate to make sense of things, desperate to calm down and desperate not to fall asleep too quickly in case she found herself in the same dream. She found Rufus and stroked him and decided to think about owning a real dog.

When she did finally fall back asleep she knew what she wanted to do the next day, certainly go to Great Grisly Hall, but on the way, pop into St Hilda's. She needed to figure things out, she wasn't too sure what answers the church could give her, but it would be a start.

Chapter Twenty-Seven

Amy, Sadie and Lockie were eager for Prim to play when she awoke. Her parents had long gone to work downstairs in the Post Office by the time she had got up and the front door was already wide open.

"Come on Prim," said Amy, "let's go to the Hall and play and we can see Rose."

"Yes, we can play Prime Minister Prim Percy," added Sadie.

They are keen to get me to the Hall today.

But Prim was adamant.

"Yes, we can go to the Hall, but first I want to have a look around St Hilda's church."

"What do you want to have a look around that dump for?" Lockie suggested in a clear way that there was nothing to see.

"It's just full of the dead Prim, don't you hang around with enough of them at the Hall?" Sadie asked.

"I've lived my whole life in Little Grisly and yet I cannot recall having ever been into it before. I'm interested now, I might learn something about my family history."

"Rose can tell you about your family history Prim," advised Amy, "just ask her when we get to the Hall."

"I will only be ten minutes or so there, that is all. Are you going to come with me or are you scared yourselves?"

And she picked up her light coat and walked out onto the landing and looked down in case her parents were about before shutting the door firmly and tiptoeing down the stairs.

"Yes agreed, we'll come," said Amy chasing after her, as if she was being forced, and they all left and went silently down the stairs and out into Little Grisly.

"What happens if someone sees you Prim and tells your parents? You'll get into real trouble then." Lockie said.

"Maybe your Dad will tie you up and throw you in the family crypt. With all the dead people." Sadie guessed.

"Maybe not," said Amy quickly defending Prim, "but Prim we do have to be careful, you cannot be seen by people who may tell your parents."

And, of course, she was right, clever Amy.

It was probably a bit too early for tourists to visit the Church, and Prim could see that the front door was firmly shut without having to try and open it. Disappointed, she decided to walk around and study the stone gravestones, eager to check on the names of those buried there to see if any shared her surname. There were some very old stones dotted around almost all the churchyard. Some seemed as old as the church itself but were bent and at angles to each other, some clearly had chunks missing from them, some had fallen completely over, and it was almost impossible to read the older ones names because of weathering or because the letters were covered in yellow lichen.

She could see the dates of their deaths, some twentieth century, a lot from the Victorian period and, in some parts of the churchyard, a lot older, here and there were people born in the 1600's and that was a long time ago. Prim couldn't think what life must have been like in those days, and, for a second or two, could not imagine what people were like.

But, of course, she then remembered Harry.

Oh, and Lady Elizabeth.

Forget her, think about Harry.

But where are all the Percys'?

Come to think about it where have my three friends go to?

She looked around and could see them in part of the graveyard under an old, gnarled and bent tree. As soon as they saw her come over they ran across.

"I think you might find the name Percy over there Prim," directed Amy, pointing to a section where there seemed to be new graves, "let's have a look."

"What's in that area where you have come from?" Prim asked.

"No-thing in particular," replied Amy, "just more graves of other, unimportant people."

"Just some villagers from years back, not the great and good Percy family eh Prim?" Lockie said smiling.

Are they hiding something from me? Am I that stupid?

But she went to look in the area suggested by Amy and she was correct, here was where some of her, later, ancestors were buried. She saw her Grandparents headstone and what must have been her great grandparents too.

She only had a vague recollection of her Dad's parents. There were no flowers left around their grave, she had seen flowers dotted around the churchyard on others, but not here.

They've been here all this time and I have done nothing.

Prim was upset with herself for not looking after their grave.

Surely my Dad would take care of it?

She heard footsteps behind her and she turned around not knowing what to expect. It was an old lady, about the same age as old Mrs Pilkington, dressed in a light blue jumper, white blouse and long brown skirt. Only for the reason she looked tanned and had a twinkle in her eye, Prim realised she was facing someone alive as opposed to most of the people she now hung around with.

Nevertheless, Prim was anxious that she would get caught out and the old lady would tell her Dad.

"You have to be careful in the graveyard my dear, watch out."

"Why," answered Prim quickly, "do ghosts haunt it?"

And the old lady laughed gently, "No dearie, you might trip either on a stone or on the broken path."

Prim went red with embarrassment. Most people, even outside a church, did not talk or even think about ghosts.

"Are you from the village?" Prim asked as she had never seen her before.

"No, I'm from Longborough but I come and look after the church for the Vicar, whole load of tourists coming today, and they will probably need someone to show them around the place," and she looked up at the steeple and around, "there's a lot of history about this place, and, if you like, ghosts too, if you believe in that sort of thing."

Prim did not answer whether she believed in ghosts at first, though she did want to ask as many questions about the Earl as she could.

"Would it be possible to have a look around inside the Church before everyone comes?"

"Of course, you can, I'm just about to get it ready, but I can show you around bits of it whilst I do."

Prim was grateful, there's one thing being in a Hall with lots of dead people but quite another being in a Church. They seemed built to be scary, to put people off from popping in for a prayer. To have someone with her, someone alive and who knew the history of the place was fantastic, to have someone not from Little Grisly, just the bonus too.

"You know there has been a church on this land for about fourteen hundred years and there is evidence that before that this place was a site of pagan ceremony," the old lady said as they walked back towards the porch and the front door.

And she knelt and reached under a heavy but faded brown rug which lay at the foot of the door and pulled out a long, iron key.

"Don't tell anyone I let you see where it is kept."

And Prim smiled to confirm her secret was safe.

The door was opened, and the old lady led Prim inside.

Prim's eyes widened. She couldn't believe she had never stepped foot in the place before.

Was I ever christened?

It wasn't a large church, like the one she had driven passed in Longborough and it smelt a little damp as she walked in, with that smell of oldness which she really could not describe any better.

"Here, inside this building, the people of Little Grisly have come every Sunday for over a thousand years." The old lady, in respect to the place, was now whispering.

And Prim wondered at the residents of Great Grisly Hall and how they must have come here when they were alive.

Perhaps they still come now that they are dead.

There were stone arches on either side of the main room or nave and leading to the altar at the other end. Prim could see a step leading up to it. In the middle lay the dark wooden pews of seats for the worshippers to sit on. Above the altar and along the sides of the nave were beautiful, seemingly age-old stained-glass windows which let in gorgeous light infused with reds, greens and yellows.

"They don't get many actually coming to pray anymore but a lot of people over a thousand years can leave a memory or two."

Now, she must be talking about ghosts.

"What do you mean?" Prim asked.

"Look around, for example all the marble monuments attached to the walls, they've been built in the memory of a lot of the people who used to come and here and worship, some are hundreds of years old."

I am paranoid about ghosts! There are other things in life you know.

"And of course, there are remnants of the fire from hundreds of years ago, see the blackened walls, all fire damaged. The Lords le Grise had to rebuild a lot of the church, starting with the great window behind the altar and a spire, with its top pointing all the way to heaven."

Prim went to study the white memorial stones on the walls as the lady started dusting by the font at the back of the church. Despite it being warm already outside, it was cold within, especially on the left-hand side of the church, away from the sun's rays coming through the stained windows on the other side.

A bit too cold.

Prim shivered as she stood by a large ornate metal and wooden trolley pushed up to one side of the wall. The lady looked up and saw her.

"Not frightened are you, I thought children liked being frightened."

"No, just cold," replied Prim obviously telling the truth.

But the old lady smiled as if Prim was lying but still came over to be by her side.

"Look at the names of some of the families," she said, "some of these families can still be traced around Little Grisly and beyond."

"What about the Percys? The Lords of Grisly Hall. Don't they have any memorials here?"

Again, the old lady laughed.

"Well of course they do, that family was, a very special family indeed."

What do you mean, was?

"They have a whole floor to themselves," the old lady continued, "downstairs in the crypt, that's where most of them are buried There look, there is the door to the crypt."

And she pointed to a curtain close by to the altar on the left.

Prim stared, and she could see above the curtain a smaller stone version of Grise family emblem, of the knight's helmet and the hunting horn over a shield. Of course, she knew they were buried in the crypt.

"How many are there of them?"

"No idea, I don't ever go down there, no-one does, have you heard of the tale about the Earl, the last Earl of Huntshire who used to live at the old Great Grisly Hall?"

Prim wanted to hear another person's take on the legend and so lied.

"No, please tell."

And the old lady put down her duster and began.

"Well I don't know that much, and it's all really only made up, but the story goes that he made a deal with the Devil and now he rides on the nights of a full moon looking to take people with him to hell."

She knows the same as what I have been told.

"Most children tremble when I tell them that story young lady, but not you. You must be very sensible not to believe in all that sort of stuff. For one, the last Earl himself is buried down the stairs in the crypt himself and so how could someone who is now in hell be buried in a church?"

And she looked to Prim for an answer, but Prim just shrugged.

"Buried, it is said underneath a stone statue of a skeleton, a full sized one too. Not that I will go down and have a look, that's just a little bit too much for me."

147

Prim decided there and then that she would not go any closer to the door leading to her family's crypt.

"Do you not believe in ghosts?" she asked.

"Not really my dear, but you never do really know do you, sometimes when I am here on my own, it often goes all silent, as if time itself stands still and I often think I can see shadows lurking in corners or a voice echoing from somewhere hidden," and she composed herself and continued, "but I guess, at my age, it's just my sight and my hearing."

And as soon as she said this, the light from the sun outside must have become hidden and the church went dark and colder.

It was time to leave and head to Great Grisly Hall.

Prim thanked the old lady and left the church, grateful that it was a lot warmer outside and that the sun was about to reveal itself from behind the only dark cloud in the sky. She hadn't really learned that much from visiting St Hilda's but in a way she was glad she did.

Chapter Twenty - Eight

Amy, Sadie and Lockie were to be found were they had been before, but now sitting around a grave under the old, bent tree. Prim wondered a little about herself with having those three for friends, but they were glad to see her come out of the church and they jumped up and walked towards her.

"Can we get to the Hall now?" Lockie asked showing how glad he really was.

"Did you find anything of interest Prim?" asked Amy nicely.

"Did you find any dead bodies, that came alive and chased you around the place?" asked Sadie, not so nicely.

Prim answered only Amy and told her that there was not much in there but that she was happy that she had finally been to have a look.

On they travelled to Great Grisly Hall, careful not to let anyone see them in case Prim's Dad was told that she was not exactly living by his rules.

They ran quickly through the pub carpark and onto the path that lead to the Hall. The other three were not their usual playful selves on the way and Prim wondered about them and worried.

Why are they being so strange today to me?

Are they jealous that Rose is here and is a real friend?

But she did not try and please them or try to make them laugh. There were more important things to do, she simply had to speak to Rose for one. Find out if she was okay, if Harry had been stopped from telling the others, and whether Lilith was still there.

I really shouldn't have gone for a look in the church this morning. I should have just come here.

And as she got closer to the Hall she really did think she should have come straight to the Hall.

For, on the unkept lawn facing the back door to the Hall, where Lord le Grise had sat in silent contemplation, where Prim had met Lilith only the day before, there was Rose and Lilith and they seemed far from being friendly to one another.

They were arguing, loudly. Prim crept to the gate and rather than open it, she crouched down and listened in.

"What were you doing?" It was Rose who was shouting angrily.

Prim felt the rage in Rose's voice.

"Just getting to know your niece, Rosemary or shall I call you Auntie Rose." Lilith did not sound ruffled at all, even with Rosemary looking like she was about to erupt.

"You shouldn't have spoken to her without my permission," Rose demanded.

Lilith laughed.

"And very likely it would be that you would give me permission to speak to her. I was just trying to find out why she was coming here in the first place, Rosemary. She, your niece, daughter of your sensible brother who refuses her to come here! I think I should be told just why you have brought Prim to this Hall."

"My niece has every right to come here if she chooses."

Rose and Lilith were now standing face to face with each other.

Prim gently and quietly pulled open the gate and slowly snuck into the garden, hiding behind one of the many overgrown bushes.

"But you didn't introduce her to all the residents here as your niece, did you? Why was that Rosemary?"

Rose paused to think of an answer to that question.

"Thankfully Lady Elizabeth recognised the resemblance between the two of you and an old ancestor of yours, you know which one I mean." Lilith explained.

Prim listened well. *Old ancestor? She must mean the girl hanging in the tree. Lady Angharad.*

"The residents do not need to know everything do they Lily? Are you quite sure you tell them everything you are supposed to? Or perhaps, how shall we say, tell them the absolute truth?" Rose countered.

"Ha, I know your game Rosemary and it's not fair. Two against one, you two against me. That's bullying that is."

It was Rose's time to laugh now.

Lilith continued.

"So, this was your plan to get all these sad shadows up to heaven double quick before I could get here? Well what's that term people use nowadays? I'm going to have to be a party pooper and spoil your family plans."

It was time for Prim to become involved.

"What is going on?" she wailed, almost crying.

Both Rose and Lilith turned in shock to see her.

"She's the one I told you about Prim. The ambassador from hell, literally from hell. Who would use any trick just to get her way and find out information."

"She said she was your friend."

"She's no friend of mine, or anyone's, she's evil, that's why she ended up in hell."

Hell? Lilith is the one from hell?

Lilith was standing straight and facing Prim, her face long shorn of a smile.

"I heard that the others in there tried to scare you away but were foiled. That will not happen with me little girl, and I won't be scaring you away. There is only one thing I have in mind for you."

Lilith, still standing still, was changing. Her face whitened but where there was once a sparkle to her cheeks and eyes: they seemed to drain as if moisture and life sapped away causing her face to wrinkle into a yellow pallor. Her hair, once yet black, greyed from the roots down her long mane. Her lips once rich red staled to a pale pink, her eyes darkened until they were black, lifeless.

A stiff breeze had suddenly come up from behind her making her long hair seem to fly up around her face, the wind blew in the direction of Prim making her breathe in the reek of the dead flowers.

"Yes, look at me Prim," Lilith ordered, "this is what years of death does to you, years of being in hell thanks to your family, years of waiting for my time to come back. And now I am here, your stupid sister and your wet self will have no chance against me."

Prim expected something to happen, a blast of thunder or Lilith simply to attack her.

But Lilith walked away, back into the Hall.

Chapter Twenty-Nine

Prim was scared, even though Lilith had walked away. She was frightened. She had never been as frightened in her life as much as now. There was something terrible about her, she did not need to have come back from hell to make her terrifying. Prim believed what she had said, she knew Lilith meant it.

How nice had she been to her when they first met? But that was just Lilith being clever, to get information from Prim.

And I gave it to her, saying Rose was my aunt.

Will I ever learn?

Prim did not know what to do. Not even the sun's rays could warm her cold body from the thought of what Lilith wanted to do to her. She didn't need to say what she wanted to do, it was obvious. Now, the last few days of being with real ghosts felt like nothing. Now, it all seemed real and that she was, truly, in danger.

Rose hastened towards her to comfort her.

She's not saying anything though.

And Prim thought that was telling because, she was sure, normally an adult would say something along the lines that Lilith was all talk and was messing about. But Rose did not say those things at all. Perhaps Rose wasn't used to comforting children, perhaps Prim had high hopes for how she would like to be treated by adults, especially her parents, perhaps Rose said nothing, as she could do nothing.

Nothing about Lilith.

"What is going to happen?" Prim asked, wanting a conversation, wanting to know what was going to happen to her.

"She is after the chain Prim, she's always been after the chain, it's why she went to hell in the first place."

"The chain is definitely real?"

"Yes, well we think so, but it was enough to send Lilith to the gallows all those years ago."

Prim remembered her dream.

"I dreamt she was hanged, it was a nightmare."

"Yes, when I heard that you had spoken to her, the thought did cross my mind that you would," replied Rose, rather mysteriously.

Prim thought about the conversation they had just had with Lilith.

Conversation? Argument.

"She mentioned an ancestor, is she the one I dreamt about?"

"Yes, it is Prim, and she looks the very same as you, do you not think?"

"I don't know, I have only ever seen her in a dream."

"Trust me, when you see her painting, you will see the resemblance."

"Is that why you put covers over the paintings?"

"Yes it is clever girl, but we need to think about stopping Lilith, that is the first priority."

"Do you know where the chain is?"

"No Prim, I don't, I don't think anyone really knows, I can only guess the Earl's daughter hid it somewhere after he went down the stairs."

"I told her that it was probably in St Hilda's, buried with the Earl himself, but I was just making it up really. Still, it made me want to visit the church, I don't think I have ever been inside it before until today."

Rose paused to think and replied.

"I often thought it would be there too. Come on Prim, I think we need to find out for definite, let's go and search our family's crypt. I doubt she can enter a church so at least we will be safe."

Why did I open my mouth again? I don't want to go back to the church let alone go into the crypt.

Ghosts are one thing. But dead bodies.

And off they went, first to Rose's car to get some tools and then back down the path towards the village, hopefully away from danger. As they walked, Prim thought too about something nagging her brain.

How did Rose know what I looked like if she has been away for years?

And so, she asked her aunt about this directly.

And she got a direct answer.

"Because I've been watching you Prim. From afar, of course."

Prim almost choked. *What?*

Lilith's Story

Lilith or Lily Cook's family had not always run the new Twisted Owl tavern in Little Grisly. For some time, they had been, well cooks, but in the early years of Henry VIII they had taken over the tavern and generation to generation had run it. In fact, they had done more than that, they even brewed their own beer for the many locals, farmhands to the local squires, and their beer was well thought of as well as being well drunk.

As the eldest of four her family were keen for her to work in the tavern and, once married, take over the family business and ensure, by having children, that the tavern would remain in their family for centuries to come. In those days there was no guarantee that her three siblings, a brother and two sisters would survive childhood.

There was no school for her to go to. Instead, from the earliest age, she had worked in the Twisted Owl, cleaning the tables and floors, washing the cups which the men used to drink out of and, when she was not doing that, listen to their tales.

Sure enough, after a couple of pints of homemade ale, there would be quite a few tales told inside the tavern, some she was sure were true, some exaggerated through drink and some made up completely. Some of the stories she had heard more than twenty times, but it never stopped the teller of the tale from repeating it again.

She was not interested in the stories about farming the land around Little Grisly, what interest did she have in that? No, she was more interested in the tales of life away from her little village, usually by some travelling trader or even by of the Percy's themselves as even they would sometimes pop in for an ale.

She heard tales about London and the world, about expensive rocks called diamonds and other unbelievable items such as gold. She heard of the things the Percy's bought each other and for themselves: land; horses and jewellery.

She wanted to be able to buy such goods. She wanted to travel the world.

But how was an inn-keepers daughter going to do that?

She also heard tales about the Percy's, that despite their riches, they were cursed due to the wrong doing of the last Earl of Huntshire, how the devil had given him a chain, a magical and golden chain which could summon the dead, how the devil had tricked him and how he now, despite being dead for hundreds of years, still rode out with his two sons, on a full mooned night, searching for souls to take back down to hell.

All inside the tavern knew about this curse and all believed it to be true. They all knew some story or another of the Earl taking someone they knew downstairs, as they called it. Lilith was fascinated by talk of the golden chain.

All, on a full mooned night, would be careful how they went home after a few ales inside them. They certainly did not want to become another lost soul confined to the fire pits of hell.

Her father, eager to keep everyone drinking, would change the subject to other news, local and around the country, but more often, to keep in with the morbid subject of curses and death, this would turn to the rise of witches.

Lilith loved to hear the tales of these enchanted women and thought about them as being powerful, strong, certainly more than a match for any man.

She heard how one witch in the north had been seen talking to a strange man and, a day later had presented another woman with flowers taken from a field. On the very next day that woman had died. The locals knew the witch was working with the devil and had killed the woman on purpose.

She heard how another witch had been caught whispering something, they never found out what, to herself. A few days later and the sheep in the nearby fields all caught some disease and died.

For their witchcraft both had been killed, as had many others, by burning or by hanging.

157

One day something strange happened to Lilith. As she was cleaning the outside of the tavern, a hen, well known for walking about and clucking away around Little Grisly, came up to her and bit her ankle.

It hurt, it hurt a lot and she screamed in pain.

"Curse you hen, I might have you killed so I can bite you back," she muttered to herself before going back to her work.

No-one heard what she had said.

A few hours later, inside the Twisted Owl, one of the regulars came in with the hen. It was dead and looked like it had been attacked by another animal. The other locals gasped when they saw what had happened.

The local presented the dead hen to Lilith's mother, for the family's supper.

Lilith knew she was a witch.

And she liked it.

She thought she could make her powers to good use, she could gain riches for herself and get herself out of Little Grisly. Where could she start? What would make her all powerful that people would be too scared to challenge her?

The chain, of course. The golden chain of the last Earl. Even if it wasn't magical, it would surely be worth a lot of money. Enough money to leave Little Grisly forever.

She would have to find it and use it.

But just where was it?

Lilith thought for a time. If the Percy's had it, then it must be under lock and key. Surely one of them could have recovered it and raised their own army of the dead? But none of them had. So, she guessed, not all of them knew its location. Would it be inside the Great Grisly Hall itself? Surely that would be too easy, and surely too could servants and guests try and find it as well.

No, the chain had to be located somewhere else.

Think Lilith, think.

Of course, the most logical place the chain could be kept would be around the body of the last Earl himself, buried deep inside the village church.

There was only one thing for it. She would have to break into the Percy family crypt and, it would have to be at night.

Witch or no witch, this frightened her.

"I must be brave, I must be brave. I must have the chain. I must have the chain," she muttered to herself, so no-one could hear.

The next morning as she walked through the village to collect food for that night's dinner she came upon an old, short, beggar all dressed in black, one she had never seen before in Little Grisly, sitting on a three-legged small stool.

"Can you spare anything for an old man," the beggar mumbled.

Lilith looked around to see if there was anyone else about. She may be a witch, but she certainly did not want people to think she was a witch just yet and speaking to strange people was a tell-tale that she was.

No-one else was about.

Nevertheless, she was straight to the point.

"Get lost beggar, I have earned this food for my table."

She wasn't ready for his response.

"And I hear you wish to earn something more, something greater, don't you my dear?"

"What do you mean?"

"A chain, the chain, the chain of the Earl of Huntshire."

"What do you know of such a chain?"

"It used to be mine and now I want it back."

She stared at him properly for the first time. This man did not look like he owned anything, least of all a fantastic, magical chain.

Perhaps he had been drinking some of the waste ale left at the back of the tavern in an old bucket?

But then something dawned on her and she stared again at the beggar, this time more closely realising his eyes were as black as his clothes and showing no life.

"Who are you?" she asked.

"You know who I am my dear, and I know you want the chain, my chain. Do you know where it is?"

"It's in the church, buried with the man."

"I thought so too. You must help me get back my chain and, if you do, I will give you the riches you deserve, the riches you have dreamed about."

"Will you help me in the church?"

"I cannot enter such grounds as a church my dear, you must realise that?"

"But how do I get into the crypt? It will be locked. And the Earl, there is a full moon tonight."

"Ha, yes of course," the beggar laughed, "The Earl, I will stand him down for this night. And if I get my chain back I might end his curse once and for all."

The beggar was smiling now and continued. "The church verger drinks in your tavern does he not? I understand he keeps the keys inside his pocket. You must get him drunk, take his keys and enter the crypt. The full moonlight will illuminate your journey, that, and a candle from inside the church. Go my dear and tonight retrieve my chain."

Lilith did not need to get the Verger drunk, as he already was, and his keys were easy to snatch from his body, especially when he passed out and her Dad and a few of the regulars laid him onto a bench near to the fireplace. In fact, the keys almost fell out of his pocket.

It was also easy for her to take them and leave the tavern for she regularly left during the night for various reasons and, besides, her Father was with his closest friends and drinking well too.

It was a full mooned night, and no-one was going to be about outside. What better place to be than inside the Twisted Owl, safe from the Earl and his sons.

Lilith was not afraid, she had the Devil on her side, *what better means of protection,* and, strangely, despite the task in hand, the night was calm, and the moon lit the churchyard well. There would be no Earl tonight, the Devil had promised her that and she trusted him. After all, she was doing a job for him, he had to protect her.

She did not even mind if one of the spirits that haunted the graveyard came up and warned her off. A spirit was nothing to her, it was just the shade of some stupid peasant who had lived their whole life in god forsaken Little Grisly.

Dare they come and attack me! When I have the chain, I shall command them to rise. They would be fools to try and stop me.

And she did not encounter any spirit and she believed that they were all too frightened to try and scare her, she was, after all, employed by the Devil.

There were only three keys and the largest one was obviously for the front door and it turned handsomely and without a problem anti clockwise and Lilith was able to open the round ring pull attached to the heavy wooden door.

It creaked open slowly and all she could see ahead was darkness. For a second she thought something, or someone would come from out of this gloom and prevent her from entering and she waited.

She realised how stupid she was and that nothing was going to come out, not the living nor the dead. Not even the stupid Percys alive or dead would confront her.

She walked in with her eyes adapting to the dark just a little. The Devil was right, and she looked around, close to her, for the nearest candle and holder and chuckled.

I'm doing this, I am really doing this.

And I will be rewarded.

She found a candle, there were always quite a few in a church, and lit it causing a small blaze of light to surround her, making the rest of the nave dimmer. She walked up the nave towards the altar, fingering the keys, deciding which one would fit the door that would lead down to where the Percys where all buried.

Including the Earl. But she wasn't scared of him. He wouldn't be troubling her tonight.

She had been promised that.

And so, she arrived at the crypt door and as she stopped walking along the stone floor there was a silence she had never experienced before, certainly there had never been such silence in the Twisted Owl, and she felt the coolness of the church.

This is easy.

She placed the candle and its holder down to the side of the door giving her enough light to see what she was doing and examined the other two keys which she had taken from the Verger.

Neither of them looked like it would fit the lock, but she tried anyway but they did not work.

I cannot be trying properly.

And she used both hands and, individually, tried each key once more.

Again, they did not work and so she shook the door and turned the handle in a vain attempt to see if it wasn't locked in the first place. But it was and the once calm of the church was broken.

Damn this, it must open.

And she rattled the door with all her strength, but the door was strong. It had to be, of course, it protected the dead Percys from the ordinary people, like her.

I am not ordinary.

Exhausted she pulled herself away from the door and, in doing so, knocked the candle holder onto the chancel floor, close to the altar, and which was covered in a light, and dry, carpet.

The carpet took the candles flames and they spread quickly and far, up towards the altar, burning its cloth cover and reaching towards its surrounding wooden frame.

Within a few seconds the smoke had become unbearable and Lilith, now coughing, realised that she was not going to uncover the chain on this night and she ran. Just as she reached the front door she turned and saw the stone font in the corner and realised there was water, holy water, she could use to try and put out the flames.

She looked back towards the altar and saw the ensuing inferno and realised that the font water would not even stop an inch of the fire.

And she remembered who she was now working with and decided that she was not even going to try and put out the fire.

She left and shut the front door, thankfully, for her, still with the wretched keys.

The Verger can have these back.

And despite her failure she smiled, laughed even and she ran back towards the Twisted Owl before anyone would notice the fire and see that she must have been its cause.

Indeed, by the time the first folk of Little Grisly had stirred and calls had been made to save St Hilda's, Lilith was in her bedroom, the keys back with the still sleeping, now snoring, Verger.

Her clothes smelt from the smoke and, exhausted, she ran back towards the church with all the other villagers. There was a heavy fire and she could hear and see the stained glassed windows break in the heat of the blaze. But she wasn't going to help, she just wanted people to think her clothes were smoky because she was watching the fire with them. Besides, she was already thinking of the chain and how she could find it. In her mind she hadn't really failed.

Next time she would search around Great Grisly Hall itself. Perhaps it was there instead. And she laughed again at the thought of that building going on fire as well.

From behind her, the little beggar watched her and the near destruction of one of the houses of his old enemy. Despite not finding the chain, he was pleased with Lilith.

Lilith was going to find the chain he was sure.

And Lilith would also meet someone at Great Grisly Hall who Prim now knew.

Chapter Thirty

"What do you mean you have been watching me?" Prim probed as they marched towards Little Grisly and St Hilda's.

"Sorry Prim, but like I said, as well as going around the world on this job, I also work at the Hall, and that, shall we say, has given me chance to watch you grow up."

Prim was dumbfounded, for all these years her aunt had been close to her, close enough to spy on her.

She didn't like the idea of being spied on.

"But I couldn't just jump out on you Prim and say hello, your Dad would have gone ballistic," Rose continued, getting out of breath with the quickness of their walk.

"And what about you knowing that I would have a dream about Lilith? How could you know that?" Prim asked moving on.

"We all have had those dreams Prim, I suppose even your Dad. It must be evolution over the centuries or something, but when we become the age to guide spirits out of the Hall and elsewhere, we have had dreams about the hanging tree, well if you can call them dreams."

"Yes, your right," agreed Prim, "they are nightmares, and so you have had the same dreams, of the hanging tree and the girl who looks like me and Lilith hanging down and dead?"

"Not Lilith Prim, but certainly the Lady Angharad, none of us have ever realised why we have them though, so I cannot explain it that well at all."

And Prim did think and realised that they could not have had identical dreams as Amy, Sadie and Lockie were in hers. They couldn't have been in Rose's. She thought about Harry and wondered whether he had been in Rose's dreams too and perhaps he had been in countless members of the Percy family's dreams.

Prim became jealous and thought of something else to change the subject.

"How did you hear that I had spoken to her before?"

"What do you mean Prim?"

"You said that you had heard that I had met her when I told you about my nightmare at the hanging tree."

"Did I?" replied Rose thinking that Prim was one of those people that listened and remembered everything. Thankfully for Rose, they arrived at the Swinging Witch car park.

"Enough for now Prim, let's keep a low profile, I certainly do not want to be seen here."

And within a minute they were in the churchyard of St Hilda's.

Prim thought that St Hilda's and all other churches were not exactly child friendly places even for someone like herself who was about to go to big school.

They were more like child scary places with their cold dark naves and shadowy recesses, memorials to the dead and not to mention the dead themselves buried inside and out. Prim thought about this and how she had met quite a few ghosts in her life time in only the last few days. *Enough ghosts to last a lifetime.*

Prim thought about what they were about to do and wondered how long a lifetime she would have herself.

Are we really going to try and find the chain inside the crypt of this church, where all those people are buried?

Her face went a white stony shade and her hand became visibly shaking which was noticed by Rose who held it and smiled at her.

What on earth am I doing? I didn't like this place this morning and now we are going to creep around the coffins and find some chain.

166

Thank God, at least, it isn't night time.

The main door to St Hilda's was still open and a few tourists were looking around and marvelling at the otherworldliness of a building which could trace itself to almost a millennium.

Indeed, as they entered the church there was a group of about eight being given a talk by the old lady who Prim had spoken to earlier, on the finer points of Saxon and Norman church architecture.

But not even the fact that there were a few more people around the place could alter Prim's worries. Despite the coolness of the stone building, she could feel herself getting hot, despite its serenity, she was anxious.

Prim and Rose sat in one of the pews as if they were deep in prayer and took in the aroma of burning frankincense mixed with the stench of damp. Prim did not want to prolong their work in hand any longer, but the old lady was taking the group around slowly, looking and discussing seemingly minute points of interest, *when would their tour end?*

Rose accidentally kicked the bag of tools which caused a little metallic echo around the church. Prim turned quickly towards the old lady to see if she had noticed and was now looking at them to see what they had done, but she did not stir from her talk.

Prim thought about the need for the tools and shuddered. *Are we really going to open someone's coffin? The Earl's coffin?*

To soothe her rising fear, she was taken in by the old lady's talk and listened and learned: about the stone font where just about everyone else in Little Grisly had been baptised for centuries; about the magnificently coloured stained-glass window above the altar which replaced the older one after it had been smashed completely due to the fire four hundred or so years previous. Within the window, the old lady advised the group, with a hint of irony stood not only Jesus Christ, but the Lord le Grise who paid for the repairs. Some of the group chuckled.

Prim looked at this window carefully and recognised where Lord le Grise was standing. It was the tree by the mill and the stream in her two dreams, the tree Harry had warned her against visiting, the hanging tree. There was a yellow glow to the window as if the window maker wanted to show that the place was sunny and warm. *What was so special about that place? A place where people were hanged?*

There were too many coincidences.

She looked away from the tree and the mill and the stream and looked into the eyes of Jesus, who seemed to be staring down at her as if he had something to say. *He must be telling me to get out of here! What am I doing here about to enter the crypt? Am I angering him? But surely, I am helping?*

Prim wasn't sure.

And inside the crypt were the dead. Prim was nervous, very nervous. Dead bodies! Yes of course they would be inside coffins but coffins frightened Prim too. That was all she knew, all she needed to know that was down there.

What if there was something else? The last Earl himself. What if he moved about there in the day time ready to leave in the night? What if he took her straight to hell for entering his crypt?

Prim just needed to know, now. The more her mind thought of what they were going to do, the more it repulsed her, frightened her, worried her.

She listened again to the old lady and noted how she said nothing about the curse however, but Prim did not need to be told anything about that. She could give that talk to these tourists. Perhaps if she did now, then they would all scurry off to their coach and drive away from Little Grisly as fast as possible.

A few minutes later and the group continued their tour in the churchyard and that sound of absolute silence was left within and from outside, for no noise could pierce through the old stone walls.

Prim could hear and feel her heart beating faster.

168

"How are we going to get downstairs? She whispered, as if someone might hear her, "the door will surely be locked."

"Easy," replied Rose, "We are family," and she searched her jacket pocket and pulled out a large key, "let's do this."

"Aren't you a little bit frightened Rose?"

"Just a bit," Rose said, smiling.

But it was a nervous smile.

Chapter Thirty - One

Prim followed Rose forward towards the altar and over to the left. Here, behind the organ was a large, old blue velvet curtain which draped to the floor. Rose pulled it across to reveal a wide, double wooden door.

For a moment Prim hoped the key would not fit but it turned well without a problem and Rose opened the right-hand door outwards revealing a small landing with stone steps leading downwards. To the right, on the inside wall was a light switch. Rose turned it and the staircase was illuminated poorly. Both, Rose leading, walked onto the landing and Prim closed the curtain and shut the door as neither wanted the old lady to think the church was being robbed and the police be called.

This was it then. Prim could smell more dampness here meaning downstairs would be wet, *but just how wet*? How could she explain wet trainers to her parents? What if the crypt was completely flooded?

What if? But there was no more time to think for Rose had begun the quiet and slow descent, the smell of dampness and now also rotten wood becoming stronger as they trod down the wide steps towards the crypt. She had never heard her heart pulsate as strongly.

Rotten wood.

Rotten coffins.

Rotten, dead, decomposing bodies.

Again, the thoughts of a few moments ago inside the church came down on her fast, if only she was still inside the church, that was like a child's play school compared to what she was surely about to enter.

They reached the bottom and all she could see was the dark, no windows gave light to this room of the dead. They paused and could hear not a drip of water coming from inside the crypt but as if someone had left a tap on.

170

"A tiny brook runs through the crypt, on its way to the stream, it can sometimes be a little wet," Rose murmured before turning the one solitary light in the room on.

Prim fell back in shocked terror. Not even the thought, the worry of what she was going to see down here prepared her for the actuality of what was here.

Inside the chamber were stone walls, huge grey stone bricks leading upwards into an arched ceiling, about fifteen-foot-high and up there it was dimly lit and full of shadows. But it was inside the walls which was what caught Prim's attention. Niches or alcoves, three to a column and two foot, maybe three-foot-high and certainly long in length and width and, resting inside all, or many of them, lay giant wooden coffins, the coffins Prim dreaded, coffins with the dead inside, grey lifeless fetid faces and bodies.

Covered in cobwebs, apart from the ones close to the ground, which were sodden by the natural course of the brook, they lay proud within their resting places, some still with their metal handles and the family crest on their sides, some without after an age of decay, some regular sized and shaped but Prim could see at least two that were grand, tall too, as if they were double decker coffins and fitted for two.

Prim did not really want to look closely but, at the same time, had to look closely and noticed that some were close to falling apart and she shuddered at the thought of one breaking up in front of her, or even as she walked past and falling on top of her.

Had any of them collapsed onto the ground already? Was it only the brook she could smell, or maybe the smell of the brook and the stench of putrefaction.

Rose walked into the centre of the crypt. *She's brave or crazy.*

"Don't worry Prim, I can remember my first time coming down here. Nothing has changed though," and she thought for a second, "imagine coming down here with just a lit torch? Now that would be freaky," and her voice slightly echoed around the room.

But still Prim did not enter. *What does she mean by nothing has moved? Should something be moving down here?*

"These are most of your ancestors, well about five hundred years of them. Don't worry they don't bite their own."

Prim popped her head around, then her body and finally her legs and feet.

"Over there," murmured Rose pointing, "Are the remains of the early Earls although some and their families were buried still in France. On the other side are the most recent ones from about two hundred years ago."

Prim walked and stood close to Rose. The whole of the basement of the church was a crypt to her family. It was huge. *There must be over a hundred of them, buried down here.*

"Is there only one door out of here?" Prim asked.

"Yes, don't worry I still have the key, and don't worry Prim they don't turn into zombies and attack, we as family actually have a right to be here."

"What to search a grave?"

"I'm not pretending its nice Prim, you won't have to do it, I just needed some company. Even for me, working with the dead, this place can be spooky. Come on let's see and then we can be out of here. He's over there in that other room."

They walked past the solid stone columns which must have kept the church standing for all these years and over to the next room inside the crypt, away from the solitary light and the tiny brook of flowing water.

Rose stopped on the way and pointed to one of the coffins in a stone niche in the wall, about head height.

"You have met that one before Prim," she said jokingly, "inside you will find what's left of Lady Elizabeth Riche herself."

Prim recoiled as she realised how close she was to such a monster and wondered whether she was wearing her red dress and ruff inside the coffin.

I bet it doesn't smell of lavender in there anymore.

And she didn't want to think about such a thing anymore and almost retched at the idea. Prim began to think back to last week and wished she was just playing in the pub car park again. It had been Amy, Sadie and Lockie who had made her find Great Grisly Hall and who had started all of this.

Where are they now? They hadn't even made it to inside of the Church, a bit like earlier in the day. *Why do they always disappear at moments like this?*

She thought about all the other residents she had met at Great Grisly Hall and she wondered about Harry and the thought about him being nice and friendly, handsome even and yet probably in one of these wooden boxes, all decayed into dust, dead for centuries.

She really was going to be sick.

And what about the girl that she looked like, Lady Angharad, the one in the dream. She thought about what she would look like now inside one of the coffins and wanted to know which coffin it was and then thought better of herself, thinking all the time that this was what she would look like in a few hundred years.

She could feel the sick rising into her throat.

She didn't have time to think about this anymore however, there was work to be done. Rose pulled a long torch from her bag and gave it Prim who lit it. She shone it around this end of the crypt and noticed the different shape and size of coffins stacked up. Some looked worn away and she shied away from them, some had holes in the side and she shied away from them too. *I hope no-one is looking out at us from inside them?*

"Shine the torch this way Prim," whispered Rose as she looked in the bag again and lifted a short metal crowbar out.

173

But through one error or another, Rose dropped the bar from out of her hands and it clattered and clanged loudly onto the stone floor.

Prim crouched down and searched the coffins with the torch again in case one of the dead had woken up and decided to find out who was making all this noise.

Rose was looking up towards the church itself waiting to see if the noise had been heard by the old lady. She waited and counted down to ten but there was no response.

Who would think about coming down here? The brave or the stupid.

"Help pick the crow bar up Prim."

Prim saw it by her feet and lifted the heavy bar up, feeling the wetness on the floor. *Thank God it's not flooded, or I would really be in trouble with my parents.*

She handed it to Rose and they walked a few more steps towards the right-hand corner of the room. Prim shone the torch revealing the tomb of the last Earl of Huntshire, the cursed Earl himself.

He was not buried on a shelf like the others. Instead his grave stood proud as a single, large yellow stoned tomb, a cuboid and looking like a huge chest fridge, resting on the floor and covered, completely covered, by different sized wooden crosses.

"We might be in a church Prim," Rose explained quietly, "but no-one was taking any chances what with the curse. As you can see they went to town."

Indeed, there were also at least seven huge wooden and metal crucifixes surrounding it.

"Shine the light here, I'm going to try and lift the lid."

Prim did as she was told but gulped at the same time. The whole notion of what they were in there for came suddenly home to her. This was no dream.

She shone the torch directly at the tomb and, in the light, she saw, under the crosses, something sticking out.

She screamed.

It was a foot, the bones of a foot at least.

And a bony leg.

He had risen, and this is where he lay after a night riding the neighbourhood.

Rose came over quickly and took the torch before it dropped out of the shaking Prim's hands and, at the same time, looked to see what Prim could.

"It's a statue, Prim, crikey, you had me going for a second." Rose sighed and breathed deeply. "Someone, years ago, built a skeleton above the tomb, as if it needed to be made more frightening."

And with that, Rose continued about her business, as if all this was a daily job for her. Prim did not want to join the family business if it were. A post worker would be much more enjoyable and relaxed than this.

She wished for something to stop them continuing, even if it meant not finding the chain.

In another setting the rushing of the water would be relaxing but not here, the movement seemed to echo against the walls. How she longed to be able to leave the crypt as fast as the water could.

Rose began to stick the crow bar between the tomb and its cover but as she did, Prim guessed she heard something else other than rushing water.

Am I mistaken?

And she cupped her ear to listen carefully. "Shush," she whispered to Rose who was just about to try and yank the lid off as much as she could and they both heard the crypt door leading to the church itself creak shut.

Without moving a muscle, they waited to hear footsteps coming down the stone steps. Prim imagined the person taking their steps gently in case they slipped and all the time feeling her heart race even faster.

Who could it be?

The old lady?

The police?

Oh God, not my Dad.

But all they could hear was the water.

Did I, we, just imagine that noise? Did someone merely open the door look down the stairs and decide better to stay on ground level?

And she felt a little bit better with this thought, although she wanted to join them and get the hell out of the crypt as soon as she could. She certainly did not want to get caught.

Rose waited for a minute or two to see, and hear, if the person had gone before restarting the plan to remove the lid of the Earl's tomb.

But even though no footsteps were heard Prim felt something, not something touching her but something else.

Something watching her.

A presence.

Rose felt it too.

Prim spun around, guessing that there was nothing there.

But in the shadowy light she could make out the outline form of a tall and aged man, staring at her.

"There is no need to search in there," ordered a voice, a male voice and Rose immediately knew who it was.

"Lord le Grise, how did you know we were here?"

Chapter Thirty-Two

"You are looking for the chain and people always start by looking here." And with that his full body was shown and he walked towards them.

Prim darted quickly behind Rose, even though she could sense that he was not like the others, in other words that he wasn't out to kill her.

"No fear here, Prim," Rose said smiling, "May I introduce the 14th Lord le Grise, my lord I believe you have met my niece Primula before."

His Lordship stretched and looked at himself, he was now almost real like a human being again.

"Yes of course, please do not feel ill at ease with me child," he said kindly with a smile, "and forgive me what with the noise of the door, I thought it would be better than just appearing out of nowhere."

He stretched again. Prim thought he was going to shake her hand and she hoped that he didn't.

"I have met you before Prim, but I can scarce say you will remember, I opened the gate to you the other day and tried to warn you off from coming to the Hall when you were playing outside. Only with good intentions mind. I didn't know who you were then."

"I am sorry," said Prim nervously as if she was meeting and talking to a normal living person, "But I do not remember meeting you, sorry."

"Think none of it, these days I can hardly muster myself to be seen at the Hall, but here, in this invidious place, when I am close, I can always appear much easier."

"Close by to what?" Prim asked relaxing quickly.

His Lordship pointed to the other side of the very room they stood in.

"That box on the left at the top, the long one, that's me, well, was me, I suppose."

Prim tensed up again. *Here I am talking to someone and their dead body is just there.*

But she looked and saw his coffin and, nestled on the ground, close by, some dead flowers.

"Close by to my girls, my boy and dear wife, oh dear God how I miss them, how I hate coming here but come I still do," he groaned sadly. "As for the chain, it is not where you seek it."

"Where is it then?" Prim and Rose both asked in unison as his Lordship leant against a wall.

"I don't know to be honest. We, the Lords le Grise and our eldest sons were stopped from being told the precise secrets of our family after the witch Lilith tried to find the chain. And now she is back, to find the it again."

"Surely, you should have been told," Rose questioned. "I, myself do not know anything which I should really know. Prim's Dad knows a bit, of course, but he dismissed it all as idle rubbish."

"Your father," said his Lordship to Prim, "would not be the first to dismiss the curse of our family, although history will say that they understood very well, in the end, when they had to."

My Dad knows all this?

His Lordship turned to Rose, "And you Rose, not knowing everything certainly makes your job harder. We were not told the exact whereabouts of the chain to protect us from her. But we were told she would always come back one day from the pits of hell to try and find it again. Presumably with the Devil's blessing, after all, it belongs to him."

"But our curse. We still have our role in helping those to find Heaven." Rose said blushing at her last sentence for his Lordship knew that she wasn't the best in that 'role'. "The chain and the curse is all the same as far as I am concerned."

"The chain which the last Earl took from the Devil was the source of our curse, that is true Rose. But the curse is separate from the chain itself. You still need to guide people to the afterlife Rose, preferably upstairs but, if they are comfortable with it, downstairs. And now you must also find the chain and destroy it. It is the destruction of the chain which is most important now."

"But how can we destroy it if we do not know where it is?" Prim asked.

"Clues, in the house, perhaps even here. As my descendants I can tell you."

Both Rose and Prim fixed their glances at his Lordship and listened intently.

"All I was told was that there is a clue in one or two of the paintings in the main hall. Find the right painting and find the clue. It was also suggested there was a similar clue here in St Hilda's but I have certainly not worked it out."

"But there are over fifty paintings in the main hall, I know I put covers over all of them." Rose said.

"I know you did, wasn't exactly sure why you did that to be honest." Lord le Grise waited for an explanation.

"I put covers on the paintings, so Lady Elizabeth Riche would not notice the similarities between Primula here and the Lady Angharad. If she did then she would have realised that they must be related."

"Yes," agreed his Lordship, "it is true that they are very alike. But the truth is out now and so we can take down the covers and look for the clue. Well, when I say we, I mean you two. Prim, I want you to do your very best to help me finally go upstairs and be with my family. I am ready. Will you help me?"

Prim was unsure, and it must have showed.

"You will know what to do, trust me," his Lordship promised, "and besides Rose, you will not have to look at all the paintings. Only those painted at the time of when Lilith tried to find and steal the chain need to be looked at, and there is someone who might just be able to help you."

"Who?" Rose naturally asked, waiting for his Lordship to answer.

"Harry," Prim replied.

Chapter Thirty-Three

"Yes, Harry is that person Rose," Lord le Grise continued, "not that he really knows anything himself, but he can help I am sure of it. You must find the clue, find the chain and somehow destroy it before Lilith finds it. Trust me, it must be destroyed, if you find it, Lilith will kill to take it from you."

"But if we cannot possibly find it, what chance does she have?"

"She has a chance Prim, and a chance we cannot risk of her finding it. She was bad enough when she was alive, now she has been in hell for centuries, I don't think God can even help us. And that is where you, both of you come in."

Prim looked at Rose who seemed to understand what he was saying.

"Lilith has been talking about the chain being buried here but when she finds out it is not she will make a bee line for me. She will think I will know it's exact whereabouts. She will put pressure on me."

"But what can she do, forgive me, but you are already dead." Prim said, realising quickly that she sounded quite glib in making such a statement.

"True, Prim, true, and I do not need to be here, in this damp house of the dead, to realise that. But she is powerful, persuasive, and she will blackmail me. She will threaten, if she finds the chain, to bring my wife, my daughters, my son back down from heaven and kill them forcing them forever to hell. She could bring me back from the dead and then kill me, so I will never see my family ever again."

Lord le Grise looked over to where he and his family were buried and began to sob.

Poor man, if only I could put my arm around him.

And she did, and she could.

"But all this has made me, and some of the others think. The old order should have changed a long time ago and I should have done my best to make it upstairs years ago. But now I want to, I need to." His Lordship was now pleading. "If Lilith can be defeated, the chain destroyed, and all the remaining souls moved out, then the curse will be broken forever, you two must help us, your family. It is your duty."

Prim thought about this. *Wasn't it his duty some years ago to have tried to break the curse?* But how could she argue with someone so distraught?

Rose was thinking too. "Suppose we work out the clue and the chain is buried here? Why do you not think it is here?"

"For years people have looked here for the chain, but it never was. Now she has come back from hell it won't take long for her to realise it is not here. We have waited for her return. I was told by my father and I told my son as well and so it has continued down to the present day."

Prim and Rose looked at each other.

"Now you Prim have caused a right hurricane inside the Hall I can tell you. Lilith is paranoid. She thinks someone in the family must know the chain's location. She thinks, well you know what she thinks of you, I was there, unseen when you had your recent discussion in the garden. Be aware, she has her cronies in us residents, Lady Elizabeth for one, and that detestable soldier, Barnaby Grudge. When I was alive, Lady Elizabeth Riche tried to scare me into telling her where the chain was kept, thank God I did not know, but Lilith for sure, will feel she can get an answer from me."

It was no surprise for Prim as to who Lilith's main supporters were.

"If she finds the chain then she means to raise an army of the dead from heaven and hell and take over, well I suppose she could take over the world as we know it. It is what the Devil told her centuries ago. Now she is back on earth I imagine her plans are just the same."

Rose interrupted, "If one of her soldiers dies they go straight to hell, so the devil is happy, and she can always summon another poor soul back to life. What chance do the living have against that?"

But his Lordships thoughts were broken by something. He sniffed and sniffed again.

"Lavender," he whispered, "and from somewhere close, in the churchyard."

"Are you sure?" Prim asked.

"Without doubt, there is a little air hole high up in the wall, and my sense of smell has never waned."

That meant only one thing.

She must be here on Lilith's orders to find the chain.

It was time to leave. Both Rose and Prim knew what they had to do.

Lord le Grise walked over to his family and knelt in prayer quickly before fading away.

Chapter Thirty-Four

Prim and Rose gathered their things and ran through the crypt, careful not to slip on the wet stone floor and, most importantly for Prim, not to slip and fall onto one of the old coffins which, she was sure, would collapse and she would end up, literally staring at one of her ancestors.

Don't let it be Angharad.

And she thought about Harry, not one of her ancestors, but he had to be buried here, and she wanted to forget about what the remains of Harry looked like too.

I would like to bury that thought, thank you very much.

And she needed to because there were pressing matters to deal with, not the chain for now, but the old lady upstairs in the church, and worse, Lady Elizabeth Riche, somewhere about too.

Rose turned off the light in the crypt and they tiptoed as quietly as they possibly could up the steps, Prim holding onto the unlit torch as tightly as possible in case she dropped it.

What could the old lady say? This is our family's crypt.

But she hadn't told the old lady that before and wondered whether she would call the police and that Prim would be arrested and what her Dad's face would look like if, no when, he found out.

Especially as she would be with Rose.

If only I had thought of all this beforehand.

Probably a good thing I didn't.

Rose, as softly as anyone could push open a heavy, old wooden door, tried to but it creaked, loudly, echoing inside the Church and surely the game was up. They would be caught.

Could we possibly try and run? There was no chance she could catch both of us. Probably no chance that she could catch us at all.

But then what about Lady Elizabeth?

Rose paused to listen but there was nothing again, just like when the crow bar fell onto the floor down in the crypt. Not even a cry of shock or terror from anyone. She pushed the door open, so they could walk out and, looking around the church and seeing no-one was about, shut the crypt door firmly and locked it.

"Now, no-one will know what we were up to," she exclaimed, happily.

"Can the Lady Elizabeth come into the church?" questioned Prim, reminding Rose that she would be about, somewhere.

"I suppose so, she is buried here, and she has never been to hell, but I can't smell her, can you?"

"No, what do you think she could do to us."

"Not much Prim, apart from throw her head at us."

Prim laughed at such a suggestion, sometimes, in certain situations humour was in short supply but very much needed.

I'd kick her head as far as possible away too.

She looked at the stained-glass window above the altar again and thought about it smashing with her Ladyship's head. His Lordship, the one in the window looked upon Prim in an appalled manner at her very thought.

Perhaps no breaking of this window will take place today.

And she avoided his Lordship's face and studied the background again, of the mill, the stream and that tree and the sunshine that glimmered around it.

By now Rose had been looking out of the keyhole of the front door to the church but could not see Lady Elizabeth.

"I don't think she is here anymore Prim, I cannot smell her, and she is a smelly lady, in the nicest sense."

186

Prim awoke from studying the window and walked towards Rose who now held up a little card.

We are out for lunch, back at 2pm.

And that was the reason the old lady hadn't made any sort of fuss or called the police after all the noise down in the crypt. That was one less worry for Prim at least.

"Sit down Prim," said Rose, sitting down herself, and Prim duly obliged.

"You know I appreciate that you have gone through a lot over the last week and a bit. Knowledge and experience no other eleven-year-old would ever get to see or feel."

Prim just nodded, knowing more was to come.

"The stuff you have heard, learnt and seen is usually only passed onto people when they reach eighteen and even then, some, if not all, are unsteady about it, some don't believe it, some don't want to believe it. But you? You've taken everything very well."

Prim blushed and could not help herself from smiling. She couldn't remember the last time someone had said something nice to her.

"And at the same time," Rose continued, "without your parents knowing."

"I don't know about that Rose," it was time for Prim to come clean, "they found grass on my clothes and I'm grounded. Banned from leaving the flat. I'll be in double trouble if they found out."

"Yes, I know about that," replied Rose mysteriously, "but they don't actually know what you know or actually know what you have been up to."

And Prim tried to remember if she had told Rose about being caught before but could swear that she hadn't. In fact, now was a good time to ask Rose about her front door opening all by itself but Rose was too quick and carried on.

"What this shows Prim, well what I think it shows, is how strong a guide you are."

Prim could not blush any redder than she already was but still she pretended not to blush at all.

"When his Lordship said he wanted to go up, he looked at you not me. I imagine some of the others want to get clear of what is going on Prim, I believe you have the ability to help them all."

"I've only done it once," replied Prim, realising that she now admitted to helping dear old Mrs P.

"And you are eleven, no-one else your age ever did anything like that, you are a natural. I told you before I sent for you and you didn't believe me. You must realise Prim that I did, and I am glad I did too."

Prim nodded.

"You are an eleven-year-old with a fantastic ability but at the same time we are now in a war situation, no-one has ever really had to face Lilith like we must do. It's going to take some doing and without you I don't believe we could do it."

"Thank you," was all Prim could muster.

"But whilst I believe we can do it Prim, the question is, do you?"

Prim didn't know what to think or to say. She wanted to nod and say yes I do but she was unsure.

In fact, she did nod and did say, "yes, I am sure," but it wasn't very convincing, and Rose realised this.

"Come on Prim then," she said, "we've got work to do and guess what night it is tonight?"

Prim did not know, she was too busy thinking about whether she had the belief.

"It's a full moon Prim."

And they stood up and walked out of St Hilda's.

Not too far away, over the road and out of the churchyard stood Lady Elizabeth watching. Of importance to her was whether they were carrying anything like a chain. She had seen them walk in with a bag of tools, but they didn't seem to be carrying an extra load.

It was time to tell Lilith and she scurried off back to Great Grisly Hall.

Except Lilith wasn't there.

Chapter Thirty-Five

The Swinging Witch, for obvious reasons, was not called that the last time Lilith entered it. She looked up at the sign, itself hanging, and grimaced.

The painting of the witch looked nothing like her, instead the witch looked like she had light hair like that Angharad Percy. *Maybe my stupid parents, in saintly heaven, had been too embarrassed to have their own daughter on their own pub sign. Who cares really!* Certainly, all that was a long time ago and a lot had happened since then. Now she was back, and she was certainly certain that she would succeed this time in her quest.

The Lords le Grise, or whatever was left of them, were pretty much weak now compared to four hundred years ago, their main guardian, Rose, was feeble and looked for support from an eleven-year-old who, according to Lady Elizabeth Riche, was prone to fainting or just collapsing at the thought of anything terrible.

The odds of Lilith achieving her goal were very good now, far better than all those years ago. But still she wanted to leave nothing to chance, she wanted to know all about Prim's father and what he knew about the last Earl's chain, the curse and what his own daughter was up to at Great Grisly Hall. In the seventeenth century village gossip could be found in the village pub, why would now be so different? Rather than go direct to him she would find out as much as she could from the locals.

She stood outside and looked and stared at the pub, it still had a thatched roof and the small windows on the first floor where she had lived. *Ha where I had lived, living in Little Grisly was not living, it was just existing.* She had always wanted something better than this, but her parents could not have provided it for her, nor could she in any lawful way, what could the landlords daughter do to raise herself up into higher social circles? Nothing.

She remembered being told about the curse of Great Grisly Hall. At first it was just a legend to her, none of that was real, just a load of old nonsense from the drunken locals or the vicar to scare the children from exploring at night time, just another poor effort to

190

stop people like her moving on in the world and trying to better themselves.

But one evening they had found the body of young Luke somewhere down in one of the fields. She and the rest of the young folk of Little Grisly had known that he had been out and about stealing his lordships pigs and when they heard the news they ran to where a crowd had already gathered.

Some of the villagers thought that he must have been caught by his Lordship's game keeper, who was meant to protect the land and animals belonging to Great Grisly Hall. But other villagers said it could not have been him: he was still drinking in the Twisted Owl and it was likely that he could not walk five yards let alone manage to find his way to this field.

One of the other, older villagers, who arrived later than everyone else, pointed up to the moon and ordered everyone to return to Little Grisly quickly. It was not the gamekeeper he confirmed, and it was likely no pigs had been stolen either. On the way back, he explained the curse of Great Grisly Hall to all those present who did not know. Even those who did know about it listened, and they nodded in agreement. In their minds it was true. Everyone apart from one person was petrified.

Lilith was enthralled. She still wasn't sure whether it was all true but the very idea, not of the last Earl and his curse of riding the fields of Little Grisly looking for the lost and lonely with his two sons, but of the chain, the magical chain which had the power to bring back the dead was simply irresistible. Finding the chain could mean finding her way of Little Grisly, horrid, boring Little Grisly.

It was only later, in hell, when she finally found Luke did he confirm what had happened that awful dreadful night.

He had been out looking to steal a pig, as he had done so many times before and was well experienced in doing so. He knew the Lordship's Gamekeeper was in the Twisted Owl and was not likely to leave until very late and very drunk. The gamekeeper would always visit the pub on a full moon, better to stay in the village and not venture out on such a night he would say.

191

Luke knew the reason why but like Lilith too he had felt it was just a stupid tale, in his case, to stop people stealing the farm animals especially when there was drinking to be done instead. But Luke had never made it to the farm.

Guided by the full moonlight, he had crept along the ancient path from outside the tavern and alongside the stream until he reached the fork of two paths and took the left hand one which led direct to the le Grise's own farm, close to the Hall.

He heard it first, thought it must be his Lordship galloping back from gambling at one of his friend's houses. He soon realised however that there was more than just one horse, three of them in fact. He heard the neighing of one of the horses, but it was not the usual sound he was accustomed to, the horse was screaming, screaming as if possessed.

By the Devil.

He realised that the horses were coming towards him and fast, faster than any horse he could think of, faster than any horse could do in real life, faster than any living horse. He heard the yells, the yells of the riders, all men, screaming like their steeds, laughing loudly, crying coldly.

As if possessed by the devil.

Then he saw them. He knew who they were. Quickly he had ran to the nearest tree to hide behind thinking that they must be after another poor soul. But they were after his. He tried to run back down the path towards the woods and Little Grisly, but they were soon upon him. The screams of the men and the horses were deafening. He turned and fell backwards and the three horses ground to a halt immediately.

In the full moonlight, Luke had looked up and saw the wide grin and bulging red eyes of the Earl himself, his long blonde hair seemingly alive due to the steady wind. Despite running and being hot and covered in sweat, Luke felt a shot of cold down his entire body before it became like a dead weight.

He had pointed up and screamed himself, his eyes transfixed with fear at the sight of the Earl before realising, that despite screaming the loudest he had ever done, he could not hear his own voice. He was feeling that he was being pulled, pulled away from himself, pulled by some great strength and, as if something strange had popped, he looked behind and there was his body, his arm still pointing, his eyes still wide open.

And that was how the villagers found him the next morning.

Yes, the curse was true, and the Earl and his sons truly stalked the village on a full moon, truly terrifying the villagers and removing their soul to hell for eternity.

And yet they called the pub the Swinging Witch! Not the "Unearthly Earl or Lethal Lord or something similar, no that would never happen with her family and all those who lived in Little Grisly being so far up the backside of the Percys'.

Lilith had enough of thinking about the past. It was time to sort out her future. The Earl was not her problem, finding the chain was.

Above the door was a sign which stated: Mr L C Tanner, Licensee.

Chapter Thirty-Six

She opened the wooden front door to the Swinging Witch and walked in for the first time in almost four hundred years. Gone was the smokiness from the large fireplace which used to be situated on the left-hand side. Gone was the smell of the farmhands, their coats caked in mud, sweat and sometimes blood. Gone too were the rats who searched for titbits of food.

Gone, especially for Lilith, were her parents.

She stood a while, maybe even just a few seconds and took the room in. The bar was still in the same place, the fireplace now had a new copper chimney breast gleaming over it. She opened her nostrils and smelt that drink, *what was it called, coffee* and finally the faint smell of beer. She looked at the walls and saw paintings and the new paintings called photographs strewn across haphazardly showing drinkers from after her time.

She continued to stand there for a while taking all this before she noticed the others inside, all now looking at her. She didn't look like the type of lady who would come into the pub during the daytime and she certainly did not look like the normal sort of tourist to Little Grisly.

"Afternoon," announced Mr Tanner from behind the bar, "are we waiting for others?"

As if she had woken up from a dream, Lilith suddenly shook with shock, looked at him and regained her composure.

"Are you the owner of the Swinging Witch?" she asked walking up towards the bar and ignoring his question.

"I am indeed, and may I offer you a handsome welcome to our hostelry," Mr Tanner was smooth talking now, "will it be a table for two?"

Lilith was not used to sitting down in pubs and having lunch. It had been a very long time since she had eaten any food and so the question from the innocent Mr Tanner did not mean anything to her. But, of course, she was here to find out information about the village

194

and the Percy family and she knew that it was always better to pretend to be nice rather than start out all nasty. That never got people very far at all.

She nodded in agreement and, to confuse things for poor Mr Tanner, she walked directly to the bar and sat on one of the high stools.

"It's been a very long time since I was last here, what ales do you brew?"

"Begging your pardon my lady, but I have been the owner of the Swinging Witch for quite a number of years, quite a few years, I would imagine, longer than you were born," and Mr Tanner was smiling in a very friendly way, "are you sure you have been here before?"

"Oh, yes," replied Lilith, smiling back but in a less friendly manner, "but it was, as I said before, a long time ago."

Her response puzzled Mr Tanner and had made the other, few patrons on the Swinging Witch take notice of her and her clothes.

She's certainly an odd one a few of them thought. *Still the world is an odd place these days but sooner she comes, the sooner she will go back to wherever she comes from.* Certainly, Mr Tanner thought this too but there was also something interesting about this young woman, he had never seen her before, but his old sixth sense told him that maybe she had been here before. It was strange and strange too was the odour he could smell on her, like dead flowers at a funeral. *These city types were odd, odd, odd.*

"How long have you been the owner of the Swinging Witch?" she enquired getting back to the whole point of visiting the place.

"Twenty-seven years," Mr Tanner replied proudly.

"You must have seen many comings and goings in that time?"

195

"Sure, but not as much as you would living in the city. It's mostly all tourists these days, they come from far afield to eat here and visit our village. They say it hasn't changed how it looks for hundreds of years."

One of the patrons loudly smirked at what Mr Tanner had said, probably about the boast on how good the food was at the Swinging Witch. *Deep fried food will never win any awards.*

"I'll vouch for those who say it hasn't changed. It hasn't really changed a bit," and Lilith laughed, "and how is everything at Great Grisly Hall?"

It was safe to say that Mr Tanner was not expecting this new visitor to ask such a question. No visitor ever asked about the Hall for the precise reason that they did not know anything about it. That was how his good friend, Mr Percy had wanted it to be for a long time as had his Dad before him too. *Who is this woman, what's her purpose here? Is she a historian? Does she want to buy the Hall and do it up?*

Much as Mr Tanner liked Mr Percy he could not help thinking how helpful it would be to have Great Grisly Hall all looking grand again, perhaps as a Hotel and how that would probably increase the number of people who came into his pub.

"Okay, I suppose," was the awful answer. He really did not know what to say, "it's still there."

"Still there," cried Lilith in mock amazement, "you make it sound as if it is crumbling down."

"Well it is, I suppose."

"And what about the great Percy family? Do they no longer live and thrive there?"

"Ha," came the sound from a man who was now obviously listening to this conversation.

Mr Tanner stared at the man before continuing, "No, they don't live there anymore although they do still live and work in the village. Are you a historian or something, or a journalist?"

"You could say history is my game Mr Tanner, but it is the present that concerns me, especially about Great Grisly Hall."

He smiled at her response. *She does want to buy the Hall.* This could mean more business at the Swinging Witch. He could overcome the now powerful stench if this lady meant business.

"Fire away," he announced beaming broadly, "I will give you as much information as I can."

She had him, she didn't know exactly how, but he had been very easy to come around to her way.

"The current Lord le Grise," she asked knowingly, "what exactly does he do in Little Grisly?"

And with such a question the man who had laughed quietly beforehand could take no more and laughed out loud.

"Lord le Grise, Lord le Grise," was all he could say as tears came down his face and he doubled up in amusement.

Lilith looked and waited for him to calm down.

"He's no longer a Lord, I can tell you," the man said, "the nearest he now gets to the Queen of England is to put her face on an envelope."

Lilith did not understand, and her face showed it.

"He's a postman, he runs the Post Office, just like his Dad and he was a Lord too wasn't he?"

Mr Tanner stepped in.

"Now, now, there is no need for sarcasm in my pub," and he turned back to Lilith hoping that the man would soon leave them alone again, "but it is true, they left the Hall years ago and now just run the Post Office."

What sort of family would run a post office after running Great Grisly Hall? Surely, he had his pride, and that of his family to maintain? And the curse? Did he not care about the curse anymore?

197

"I have heard that there is a curse upon the Hall, is that why he no longer lives there, with his family?"

"I am not entirely sure to be honest," replied Mr Tanner, "he would be the best one to ask himself."

"Of course, there is a curse," the man in the corner said as he re-joined the conversation, "all the villagers know about it and some of us tell the visitors as well. It is legend."

"Do go on," ordered Lilith gently to the man. *Now we are getting somewhere.*

"They say there was some pact with the Devil and of course, the Devil always wins in such deals."

"He does indeed," whispered Lilith to herself but audible for all to hear.

"It was one of the old Lords, the Earls, centuries ago. Now they say, come the full moon, that he and his two sons ride out and take any that they can find back to hell."

And with that statement he lifted his pint glass, downed what was left and indicated to Mr Tanner to pour him another. A second later, he indicated that he would buy a drink for the young lady now in the bar and talking to him.

"Oh, thank you," she said politely, "I'll have the same as he."

Waiting for her pint to be poured she continued her fact-finding mission. "But why would the Devil simply put a curse on someone, surely they must have done something wicked to deserve it?"

The man and Mr Tanner both looked at each other. They did not have a clue.

"And I have heard about a chain, legend says it is a magical chain, powerful but that it has been lost."

"I'm afraid you have lost me there, Miss," advised Mr Tanner passing her the pint of Rat's Tails and he stared at the man who nodded in agreement.

"There might be something about the chain in your display in the corner," the man advised. He was now standing too close to Lilith and she could smell beer and nicotine on him very well.

Mr Tanner was not sure who smelt the worse between the two of them.

"We've had that display up for a few years now," said Mr Tanner, "a lot of the tourists were interested in knowing why the pub was called the Swinging Witch."

And so did she, well, she wanted to know what people now thought about it. She was, in a little way, slightly chuffed that, four hundred years later, they had a display in her memory and she went over to read it.

In fact, the display was about not just her but also about the curse too. *Why did the owner of the pub fake ignorance of it when he clearly knew about it?*

But Mr Tanner was not her concern, she wanted to know what people thought of the curse.

There was very little to read, just the usual on the Earl and a sentence on angering the Devil, but nothing on the chain and its power.

Perhaps the chain has been forgotten in the passage of time?

She turned to read the rest of the display, about herself. It read:

In this pub lived a wretched disciple of the devil

An idiot child

199

Who tried, and succeeded in making the villagers think, she was a witch

And, consequently, she was hanged.

Now she resides with the Devil,

Forever, in damnable Hell.

Lilith was incensed and enraged. *How dare they call me an idiot?* She was a witch. *Is this how the villagers and tourists now see me? A joke?*

There would be payback time soon.

Find the chain Lilith, then reek your revenge on them all.

And with this thought she calmed down, composed herself and went back to the bar noticing that the man, who had bought her the beer, had gone outside.

"Did that answer your questions?" Mr Tanner asked.

"Fairly useless," she replied as she decided to neck her beer quickly. "Who wrote such rubbish."

Mr Tanner stared in disbelief as it took her only three large sips to drink the whole pint.

"Careful Miss," he whispered, "but the display was written by none other than Mr Percy himself, upon my insistence, and he told me that was all that he knew about the whole thing. And mark his words, not mine, for he told me he believed it all to be a load of old rubbish as well and said he wanted no-one else to speak to him about it."

"Then I will say no more about it myself," said Lilith soothingly, for she now had the information for which she came in. *The chain, and pretty much the curse, was now just an old legend, no – one believed it to be true, especially, and most importantly, the current Lord le Grise. And if he did not know where it was, then neither would his stupid sister nor his stupid daughter, Prim!*

They are the idiots.

But there is at least one person who should know its whereabouts.

"I must take my leave, thank you and please thank the man for this drink, it is certainly a much nicer drink than the ones I had the last time I was here."

Not for the first time in this conversation Mr Tanner was confused. Still, he did not want to annoy or anger her. If she was going to buy Great Grisly Hall, then she was to be a friend.

"A good day to you Miss, please do come back and we can chat again, and please, say nothing of what I have said to Mr Percy."

She smiled and walked out of the pub.

Mr Tanner remembered that the Swinging Witch would be closed on the following night and was just about to tell the lady, but she had truly gone.

The man who had bought her a drink watched her walk off, as he finished off his cigarette.

"Fancy another drink Miss?"

"No, thank you," she laughed, "I'll buy you a pint the next time I am in."

And she walked off.

The next time! The Swinging Witch is named after me! The next time that man sees me I will be all powerful.

Now, to find that chain.

PART THREE

Chapter Thirty-Seven

Strangely, why am I so happy thought Prim as she and Rose marched back along the path to Great Grisly Hall.

I am always happy when I walk to the Hall, only to feel down when I have met someone. Is it wrong to feel like this? We have a clue and if we are quick and discover it we could end all this now.

All this now! What was all this? A curse, the dead still residing at Great Grisly, a witch wanting an all-powerful chain: this was what was going on right now.

I should not be happy, I should not be happy, but how should I feel? Am I forgetting something?

Prim now knew that there was a very real chance of her death and a very real chance that Lilith would succeed and that could, no would, mean terrible things for all and not just in Little Grisly.

And yet she was beginning to not care anymore for her own personal safety. Perhaps hanging around with dead people made her unafraid. She certainly did not fear the uncertainty of death and what came after, after all, she had proof enough of what did.

She began to think of the bad things, how she might die, how Lilith could kill her, about Lady Elizabeth and Barnaby Grudge, they would delight themselves at killing her.

Maybe it was not the fear of death but how she would die.

Could die!

And what about the Earl himself? Imagine meeting with him and his sons in the dead of night?

The dead, the dead. Everything is about the dead.

I am not going to die, we are going to succeed. We are going to find this chain, stop Lilith, end the curse and live happily ever after.

But how are we going to succeed really? What good am I in all this?

Prim was no longer feeling so happy. Perhaps play acting at running a Post Office was safer.

She looked up and noticed that the sky was no longer as blue as it had been. More and more clouds were beginning to hang around, grey clouds, full of rain.

As they turned into the garden of Great Grisly Hall, Rose spied Prim's worried face.

"Come on Prim, I'm relying on your young and eager eyes to spot this clue, I'm sure we'll find it with you on board."

And with that Prim felt happy again. Had a cloud moved a little out of the way allowing a little bit more sunlight brighten their path?

The hall of Great Grisly looked empty but Prim could sense that some of the residents were about, but it did not faze her at first, she had come from a damp crypt after all and had had plenty of experiences of hanging around with the dead to last a lifetime.

A lifetime? Ha, I do not know whether to laugh or cry.

Just get on with it Prim. Get this done quickly and it will soon all be over.

Come on Prim, there's work to be done.

But what will Lilith make of us taking down the covers?

Rose left Prim alone in the Hall for a moment allowing Prim to stand in the middle, close to the long table, and, slowly, spin around looking at all the cloaked paintings. This was going to take some time, there was so many of them.

All these times playing here, and I never really thought of them at all.

She stopped directly in front of the largest painting and wondered who could be behind the covers. It would surely have to be someone important to have been painted at twice, no, three times their normal size.

Suddenly her thoughts turned elsewhere as a sudden shot of cold air went down her spine.

Please be Harry, or his Lordship.

"You have a nerve coming back here little girl. Perhaps even a death wish."

It was, of course, Barnaby Grudge.

Prim turned around and saw him, materialised. It gave her a shock.

"Scared at the sight of me eh? You should be scared to death little girl," he warned.

Quick Prim, what should I say?

"I'm not afraid of you, I'm not afraid of any ghost anymore."

Prim wondered whether she would be believed. She scarcely believed it herself.

"Perhaps you need a little bit more persuasion." And Barnaby pushed his head forward so that his nose was inches from Prim's face.

Oh, the stench, the stench of the dead, of blood and the mud from the war.

Prim thought she was going to throw up, but she was determined to show this bully she was strong.

And so, they faced off for a few more seconds, seconds which felt, to Prim, like minutes, neither of them saying anything.

Thank God for Rose, who now returned carrying a long ladder which, due to its size, meant that it clattered and bumped into the wall, the door and the staircase.

"Ah, are you two getting on well together?" she asked sarcastically.

Barnaby did not understand and, instead, went for the metaphoric jugular. "I don't have to pretend to be nice to you anymore. Now Lilith is here I can do what I want. Why don't you and your family pack it in and stay in the village?"

"Is that some sort of rhetorical question Barnaby?" asked Rose, knowing full well that he would not know what she meant. Prim smiled, she had done a bit of this sort of thing in school.

"Questions should come later, after actions. I could kill both of you and Lilith will be well pleased with me."

"Oh Barnaby," Rose continued to tease, "Valentine's day was a few months ago now," but then she decided on a different tack, "you know to her you are just some silly lackey, someone to help her do her dirty work. She will discard you once you have served your purpose. You do realise that upstairs is a lot nicer than down the stairs, why don't you just let us help you."

"Enough, enough," he roared back at her, "if heaven is so nice let me help you there." Barnaby charged at her in as close a body as a ghost could leaving Rose with the only choice but to swing the long ladder in his direction causing him to shudder backwards and away.

"Save it Barnaby," she ordered. Prim never expected Rose to be so commanding. It certainly worried Barnaby who retreated, still growling with his face.

"Ignore him Prim, his anger will turn to the objects we are about to reveal," and coming close to Prim, Rose whispered, "he hates all these paintings of all the old owners and their families. He thinks now they are all dead, everyone is equal and so there should be either no paintings at all or that he should have one. You should have seen him the day I hung all these covers up, laughing and clapping he was. Neither of us made friends with the other residents on that day."

And with that explanation Rose lifted the ladder and plonked it against the wall close by to the staircase.

"I think it will be easier if you pull the covers off the paintings Prim, don't worry about nasty Barnaby Grudge, I will hold onto the ladder darling."

Chapter Thirty-Eight

Prim climbed up the ladder and was now in the middle of about four paintings. She looked down at Rose and across the Hall to where the largest painting was hung.

That has to the Earl, the last Earl, it must be.

"Sometime today would be nice Prim," said Rose, again being sarcastic, "it will be time to get you back to the flat in about an hour and a half."

Prim began to pull the cover off the first painting.

"Easy Prim, do you want them to fall on my head?"

Oh God, can I not get anything right? Come on Prim, uncovering a painting is nothing compared to what you have done today.

And with some delicacy, she lifted the cover off the first painting to reveal who lay behind it.

It took her a while to realise who it was, she was sure she recognised the face, but this person was elegant and well dressed and handsome and young.

It's the 14th Lord le Grise.

And, as is to the confirm who it was, his ghost stood watching her from beside the long table, Harry, looking sheepish, behind him. His Lordship smiled weakly, glad to see his portrait.

Perhaps he can at least give us a clue as to which paintings to look at?

But he did not and, with a grumbling sort of noise from Rose, Prim continued her job.

For a while there were several paintings of people that Prim did not recognise, nor did Rose say anything about them. Tudor, Puritan, Restoration, Georgian, Victorian, Prim was able to guess their time quite correctly, and she was also correct in guessing that when their time had come, they had all departed upwards. Men, former Lords of Great Grisly Hall, women, boys and girls, Prim began to understand that not all her ancestors were bad.

Prim and Rose shifted the ladder together onto another wall and the search began again.

Two paintings in, she came across another familiar face. It was a shock at first, for she had to get very close to the portrait to remove the cover which had become stuck on the other side of the frame, and, as the cover fell, her eye turned and realised she was staring at Lady Elizabeth Riche.

Again, as if to emphasise this, the Lady herself, became present inside the Hall. Indeed, unlike Lord le Grise, this portrait was very similar to the one she knew and, consequently, she almost fell off the ladder, recoiling in fear.

The Lady herself was none too pleased at this lack of respect. After all, she had been one of the most famed beauties of her time. How dare a little, stupid girl, object to her portrait.

"Quick Prim," called Rose noticing her Ladyship's shadow, "lift the cover of the next one, there to the right of you."

Prim did as she was told, at the same time realising that Lady Elizabeth was drifting towards Rose, her face now in anger but then, in an instant, in mourning, for the painting Prim had just uncovered was none other than her childhood sweetheart Henry Percy, as his name adorned the bottom of the frame.

There was no love lost between the Lady Elizabeth and Barnaby Grudge.

"Ah, young love, is there not a finer feeling than young love," he laughed even though it was unlikely that he ever felt a pang of positive feeling towards anyone.

Prim noticed that Lady Elizabeth did not reply immediately.

He's certainly hit a bone there, hasn't he?

The threat of them both having an argument brought out the rest of the residents and they all stood, a little distant, and just a little hesitant, from Barnaby and Lady Elizabeth, towards the main entrance to the Hall. None of them laughed at his joke.

The Lady Elizabeth turned to him, stared and said with a low voice, "I paid the ultimate sacrifice for young love and do not regret it, what did you do Mr Grudge, what did you do to end up here, in a house above your station?"

"I fought for my country, I did," Barnaby quickly replied, "more than most of you lot, still sticking around in those paintings like you are important, well none of you are important now, Miss Rose should take all the paintings down and burn them."

"For your country did you say?" There was no delay in responding now from her Ladyship, "you hated your country, you hated your fellow man, you were a coward, you shot your leader in the back, you're still a coward now, I've already told Lilith not to trust you."

"How dare you question my loyalty to her, I did more in my lifetime than you ever did in yours, oh, which dress to wear for my darling, oh, I must put on my lovely lavender for my future husband."

"You only work for her out of spite for everyone else, I promise Mr Barnaby Grudge, that when the chain is found, and if Lilith could ever marry your soul up to your body again, that then, when you are not looking, I will kill you, personally, and I will rejoice in seeing you go down to hell."

"There's nothing wrong with hell, that's why you are on her side too you hypocrite." Barnaby retorted, his voice getting louder, and angrier.

"Do not even dare think you can understand me or my reasons," Lady Elizabeth's voice gained volume as well, "you are not clever enough to think properly for yourself, if you did, you would have gone upstairs years ago."

"Unlike you, still here five hundred years later."

"Enough," and it was Rose who was now screaming at them both, her voice sounding as if it hurt her throat. "This is still my family's house, and you both know the rules, Lilith or no Lilith. Now get out of here and calm down the pair of you."

There was to be no messing about with Rose when she was in this sort of mood and, whilst both were surprised at the strength of Rose's order, they both accepted it for they departed quickly, and separately from the hall.

So, they're talking about the chain and its powers, we better had find it and quick.

And with that, she carried on her job, careful not to annoy Rose.

Chapter Thirty-Nine

Finally, they moved the ladders to the final wall, the wall holding the largest painting.

Keeping the best until last thought Prim, herself being sarcastic.

Climbing up to the top of the ladder, she slowly turned and once more saw Harry watching her nervously.

Of course, what Lord le Grise told us, Harry would know something. Perhaps he cannot just shout it out because the other residents will tell Lady Elizabeth Riche or Barnaby Grudge.

Or even Lilith herself.

Where was the witch anyway? Surely, she must be around somewhere.

She uncovered the first portrait on the wall, someone she didn't know but whose eyes appeared kind. Prim looked around the Hall to see if this lady's ghost still resided there. But of course, kind people would not be still here. They would be up in heaven.

And she thought about Harry and why he was still down here. Would she just ask him direct?

Just before she went to pass the painting's cover to Rose, Prim noticed something about it, the background. It was set on a cold, grey day, down by the stream, near the mill, as if in her dream and, just to the left of centre was, the hanging tree.

A deep, cold shudder blew down her back as she studied the painting hard, the lady's eyes now seemed to mock her, *yes Primula Percy, this place really does exist.*

And the tree, the whole landscape was just like it was in her dream, except here, in the painting, the tree looked like it was shining very brightly in the sun.

"Found anything?" Rose said, breaking the moment.

"Err, I'm not sure, look at this."

Rose checked the ladder was safe and walked into the centre of the hall to look.

"Don't recognise her sweetie, she must have been a good one."

"Look at the background."

Rose nodded, "The old mill down by the river, of course. I doubt it looks like that now, it must all be over grown like the rest of this place. I've never been there myself, though it's not really far away at all."

"How do you know where it is then?"

Rose stopped to think.

"After I had a dream about it. A dream just like yours."

What? Rose has had the same dream as me. What does that mean?

This is hard to take in.

"Let's speak about it later Prim. But be warned, most of the paintings on this wall, have the same background. Do you want me to uncover the rest?"

Prim nodded to say no.

"Come on then Prim, let's get this done."

All the while, Harry, patiently, waited.

The next two paintings were of the same size and had the same background of the hanging tree but from a slightly different angle and, of course, a different sitter, who Prim did not recognise but, from the clothes, guessed it had been painted at the same time.

Literally the same time, given the grey sky yet the sun lighting the tree. Why paint all the portraits on a miserable looking day? If I was the artist, it would have been a lovely summer's day.

213

For some reason or another, she peered down at Harry, who, from waiting patiently and quietly before, had now become nervous, and, ghost or no ghost, Prim thought she could detect his face going all red as if he was embarrassed.

She smiled at him in an act of reassurance, but she knew the reason for his mood change.

His painting was next.

But even though, she knew it was, his face was still a little bit of a shock for her. The artist had painted him nicely, dare she say it, and she wouldn't, more handsome than he was and she had to turn twice to compare the painting and the real, albeit ghost Harry to compare.

Why make Harry so much more good looking than he is yet set the scene so gloomily? Why use the same scene repeatedly? Could they not have painted a background of the Hall itself? Miserable weather but a gleaming tree, a gleaming hanging tree.

She turned again, to smile at Harry but, due to his nerves and embarrassment, he had disappeared, presumably out of the Hall itself.

Rose signalled that she was becoming impatient. Prim could see that some of the residents had come over to Rose to see what they were up to.

There were two more paintings left. One the size of all the others, the remaining one, the largest in the entire hall.

Prim knew it could only be the Earl, the last Earl, the man who had caused all this trouble for her and for her ancestors. She had heard so much about him and was intrigued as to what he looked like, but still, she would rather just leave him alone, as she would wish he would if ever they came across each other on a moonlit night.

She chose the smaller of the paintings to uncover expecting to see another elderly ancestor.

But there was not an old lady or gentleman in the painting.

It was almost as if she was looking into a mirror and it made Prim almost fall off the ladder again and onto Rose.

It was Angharad. Behind her was the same setting as with Harry's painting.

Prim stared at her hard. She looked at her nose, slightly upturned, her freckles, her strawberry blonde hair, her green eyes.

How could I have seen her so perfectly in my dream? We are like twin sisters. And she is in front of the mill and tree. And Rose had the same dream too.

"Stop admiring yourself Prim," chuckled Rose gently, "I should have warned you about that painting, sorry. One painting left, take your time with this big one, do you need me to tell you which of our esteemed ancestors is behind the sheet?"

"No," Prim said, smiling weakly as she came down the ladder, so it could be placed directly to the left of the last painting, "what are the residents asking?"

"They want to know why we are taking the covers down now, they are quite in the dark about what exactly is going on Prim, but a lot of them have never wanted to move away from Great Grisly Hall as quickly as they do now. I and the former guardians of the Hall have spent centuries trying to get some of these to move, and now they want to go up to heaven as quick as you like."

"What are we going to do?"

"One thing at a time, get the cover off this big boy, and then we are going to have to find that clue to where the chain is. Lord le Grise is scared witless of Lilith. We'll talk about that in a bit and about our dreams too. First things first though, I want to get out of here."

Prim scaled the ladder to take down the cover on the Earl's painting. As the first cover came off she noticed how ornate, and large, the gold painted wooden frame was around it, this was the painting, after all, of an Earl.

The cover slipped off easily and fell to the ground without a problem not that Prim was looking. She was now mesmerised by the Earl and his face.

She had been expecting some monster to appear but instead the man before her was someone who looked familiar. It was the eyes she noticed at first, they were not the fierce eyes you would expect from someone who haunts the fields of Little Grisly looking to take the innocent to hell. Instead they were kind and warm. She remembered a photograph she had found in a drawer of her Dad and imagined that the Earl must have been the same age as her Dad when both painting and picture were taken.

Their age was not the only similarity. Underneath the Earl's large, black hat were strands of blonde hair, the same colour as her father's. They even had the same build.

But no chain. Instead, slung over one shoulder was a cord and attached to it was a hunting horn, not a metal one, but one from an animal. She had seen that horn before, it was part of the family crest.

This could almost be my Dad in fancy dress. But where is he standing in the picture?

Prim looked around and behind the Earl. For the first time, on this wall, thought Prim, they had decided on a different location for the painting, but, again, there was no Great Grisly Hall, Little Grisly or anything known and important to show in the picture.

I would have my painting with Great Grisly behind me.

If she ever had herself painted she meant. Then she laughed.

And I will never get my painting with the Post Office behind me.

She concentrated on the Earl's painting and stared at the stream and the tiny building behind it, probably not possible to see from standing on the floor of the Hall. It was a small mill using the stream to grind wheat into flour.

What is so special about a stream and a mill to this family?

216

And it dawned on her, this painting and all the others on this side of the Hall, they all had a background of a mill, a stream, and, standing close to the Earl, a small sapling of a tree.

That's it, the background in the Earl's portrait is the same scene as the others, only a few hundred years before. Before the hanging tree grew. Before painters decided to make it look like the sun was shining on it. But what is so special about this place?

She scanned the whole of the painting and to her surprise there was someone else in it, a young girl, almost hidden under his robes. It could only have been his daughter, the artist had showed her smiling, as if she was happy to be standing next to a man who, for centuries had been judged to be a demon.

But as she continued to look at the daughter and the Earl, she, and Rose below her, felt two shooting beams cut through them causing the hairs on the back of their necks to rise.

She quickly glanced at the Earl's eyes one more time before turning around to face Lilith. Despite his reputation, his eyes were always going to be more attractive than hers.

Chapter Forty

"Spring cleaning, I think not," Lilith said, starting the bout.

Prim searched the hall and noticed that the eyes in all the paintings seemed to be watching her, waiting for her response.

"And were we spring cleaning at that church too?" Lilith continued.

Prim and Rose kept quiet.

"My source says you went down into the crypt to have a look at your old relatives and perhaps to look for something too. You know what I mean don't you? The chain, the chain that he wore until he lost his bottle," and she pointed to the last Earl, clearly she did not scare easily.

Prim looked around the hall at the remaining residents who were eager to hear the next instalment of the battle between Lilith and the Percys'. Tellingly, she could not see neither Lord le Grise nor Harry.

Still Rose and Prim did not say anything.

"But you didn't find it, did you? If you did one of you would be wearing it, using its power," and for a moment Lilith became lost in a dream about the chain and what it could do.

She woke up from her moment of fancy and smiled. "On second thoughts, you would not dare to use it, you could not dream of what it could do and what it could do for you. Besides which it is not yours anyway to use, your ancestor had the chance but threw it away, and threw the chain quite literally away too," and she was back pointing at the Earl's painting again, "that little madam, his daughter, it must have been her, she was quick to hide it, but it is rightfully mine and my master's."

"You are not fit to wear the chain Lilith," countered Rose, her anger clearly building up, "no-one should, it must be destroyed so that people like you, and your master, never have the chance to use it."

218

"So, it is fine for the Percys and their forebears to have it but not me, a simple girl, the daughter of the local brewer and innkeeper?"

"You are more than that now Lilith," replied Rose, hating to admit to her that Lilith was very potent. "It has been used once and the consequences of that have echoed in our family for generations. It should be destroyed before any more harm is done with it."

"That's a bit rich from your family when the Earl tried to use it to help win a civil war."

"And we learnt from that never to use it again. It is evil."

"Is it? It can be whatever the wearer wants it to be. Raising an army of the dead could make the world a safer place, stop war, make peace. You would like that wouldn't you?"

"Not when the owner is the Devil," Prim started, "raising an army is hardly a sign of peace."

"We can keep the peace Prim and have the power too. Why don't you join me now and be a part of something special from the start?"

"Not when I have my strength I will not," Prim countered, "do you want to be cursed like the Earl because I certainly don't."

"The Earl, ha, he was stupid, he thought he could handle it, but he was weak, and weakness never gets you anywhere Prim. I'd say remember that as a life lesson, but you will not get much chance to appreciate it."

Now it was Rose's turn to fight Lilith with words.

"You'll have to find it first Lilith, how are you going to do that?"

"Oh, I will find it. The only reason it has not been found for years has been that no-one has searched properly for it. We know it's not buried with the Earl, and we have been searching high and low in this Hall, including your room Rose, but we will find it."

Rose was enraged. *They must have just been in there.* And she saw the Lady Elizabeth smile.

"Besides which," Lilith resumed, "I know someone, perhaps I know two people, who should have a clue to where it is hidden."

Prim knew exactly who she was talking about.

But where is it? And where are they?

Come to think about it, I know she thinks Lord le Grise will know its location, but who is the other?

She doesn't think Harry knows does she?

Does he?

"Yes Prim," said Lilith, "It is like I can almost read your mind. Harry is the other person I think knows its whereabouts. I made him look for it inside the Hall almost four hundred years ago, but he could not find it, or he said he could not find it. Consequently, I was hanged and so was that girl, the one who looked like you."

And she pointed to Angharad's portrait.

"Still would I be one to let a little problem like that simmer for all those centuries?" and she smiled, and Prim knew that Lilith was the exact person to let such a problem boil for all those centuries.

"I did think you and your family would know more about it, perhaps you are all liars too like young Harry. Still it seems your Dad has given up on Great Grisly Hall."

"My Dad," screamed Prim, "what do you know about my Dad?"

"Oh, my dear Prim, have I touched a nerve, the secrets of Great Grisly were passed down generation to generation. Either your father is an exceptional liar as well, or he does not know anything about the chain. As a matter of fact, I think the latter, but I can always change my mind, in fact, I could change my mind about what I think Miss Rose knows too."

Prim saw Rose look uncomfortable but knew she did not know anything more than she did.

And now I will be off," stated Lilith, "it's time to find that old head of your family and squeeze the answer out of him. And if I cannot get any information out of him, I will squeeze a few more from your pathetic family and Harry."

Smiling again, she walked off closely followed by Lady Elizabeth and Barnaby Grudge.

Chapter Forty-One

Prim was very happy to leave Great Grisly Hall with Rose, so she could get home before her parents finished work but was worried for Lord le Grise and, of course, her aunt.

> *At least his Lordship is already dead. It's my aunt who I really care about.*

Rose had told Prim that there were other places for his Lordship to hide besides in the crypt next to his family and himself. He would not dare go in there for fear that Lady Elizabeth would come in and try and either drag him back or drag the answer to where the chain lay from him.

Rose knew her Ladyship could not do the latter but was worried that he might reveal as much as he knew which would be enough to give Lilith a head start in finding the chain.

But Rose was adamant. "They will not find him tonight Prim, I am sure he will be fine but tomorrow we must help him, and the others get their move upstairs. It's not going to be easy Prim, they have all been reluctant to go beforehand and, as you already know, my skills are not the best. And, of course, we need to find the chain."

Prim was determined not to waste time by going home, that was giving Lilith a definite head start. "I shouldn't be going home now Rose. I don't care about my Dad finding out, for the greater good, wouldn't it be better if he did find out?"

"Prim," advised Rose, "we need you back here tomorrow. And you can only come back tomorrow if your Mum and Dad don't know that you have been here today. No, go and get some sleep. I doubt Lilith would ever dare come around to your flat."

"But what if we, I mean I, mentioned Lilith to him?"

"I don't think he knows who she is, and he would know where you had been. Think Prim, think."

Prim did think.

"But what about you? You can't stay at the Hall tonight Aunt Rose, she might do something terrible to you."

Rose smiled, "Thanks for that warning Prim. Yes, I am very sure she, or her two stooges, would very much like to disturb me tonight and that is putting it gently."

"So where will you go?"

"Somewhere she will not think about looking. Nowhere important, meaningful or exciting. Just somewhere, close by to you actually but no-one should come looking for me."

"Where is it?" Prim asked.

"I won't be telling you that sweetie, after all, I don't want anyone or no-one coming looking for me. Just tonight Prim, have a think about what you looked at today with those paintings, sometimes thinking is better than action. When you can tomorrow, get out of the house and meet me at the church, we can then go back to Great Grisly Hall together."

And that made Prim think even more, about how she was able to get out of the house that morning. As she did so, Amy, Sadie and Lockie arrived.

"Just how Rose, am I meant to get out of the house tomorrow morning when I am grounded, and the door is supposed to be locked?"

"The same as you did today, magic!"

And with that, Rose stopped walking and waved goodbye to her niece.

Chapter Forty - Two

Prim thought about this magic as she entered through the main door along with Amy, Sadie and Lockie. She could hear both her Mum and Dad chatting to a customer in the shop and guessed from their tone that they were happy. If they had found out that she had, somehow, escaped, they would have hit the roof and there would have been no politeness to anyone, even to customers at their beloved shop.

Taking her shoes off to avoid any obvious stomping up the stairs she tiptoed upwards.

I am going upstairs myself, crikey if Heaven is like this place.

And the door to her flat was already open for her and she looked about in case something else strange occurred before going in and closing it ever so quietly.

You've seen lot stranger things Prim. What is a magical door to you now?

And as she pondered this point she heard the bolt locking itself from the outside.

Incredible.

But she did not feel scared and she walked into her bedroom and checked her dress, socks and shoes for anymore tell-tale grass stains.

None.

It was now 6pm and Prim realised that she hadn't eaten and that, if her parents realised that she hadn't, she would get into trouble.

In fact, she thought, it would be handy to show signs of pretending to have been in the flat all day.

Quickly she moved to the kitchen, opened the fridge door and devoured what was her lunch, a cheese and pickle brown sandwich from her parent's shop. She checked the date, it ran out that very day but still tasted good, although, Prim thought as usual, that anything tastes good when you are hungry.

She thought about the book, about how to run a Post Office and she found it and fingered a few more pages and learnt a little more about running one and decided to tell her parents that she had played at running a Post Office all day. Clever Prim.

Amy would be impressed. She's usually the clever one.

Where exactly have they gone? They were all here a minute ago.

She thought that playing at running a Post Office at the age of eleven was a little too immature but then, she thought more, what would her parents know about what eleven-year old girls played or, for that matter, anything, apart from running their beloved Post Office.

A few moments later and her parents arrived back, happy and, after seeing that Prim had been in the flat all day, even happier.

Prim's Dad was in a very happy mood. He had been asked out to the Swinging Witch by Mr Tanner himself. That was an honour he thought, to be invited out by the landlord of his favourite pub, even if he was already his friend.

Tea was, as usual, a quick affair but, this time, they all had same, ham tagliatelle, direct from the microwave. Prim, of course, had to find room in her tiny belly for that and her sandwich starter. She thought she was going to burst but simply could not let her parents realise that she had only just had lunch.

"I see you have been reading more of that book I gave you on running a Post Office," her Dad stated as he finished his pasta.

Prim could only eat her food in one setting: dead slow and would not dare speak as she was chewing.

"I am glad of that," Dad continued, "it is a wonderful job, meeting lots of different people from lots of different places, but all here in our wonderful village. I think, once school starts up again,

225

that perhaps you could do some work experience on a Saturday for us. What do you think mother?"

Prim's Mum was busy chewing as well but managed to quickly swallow some food quickly so to answer her husband.

"I don't think she is currently old enough dear, although she could soon be able to deliver newspapers for us."

"No harm her being with us on a Saturday, or even perhaps a Sunday too. After all she is family and she would learn off us, so she can take on the family business."

And with that statement, he stood up, kissed his wife but then stood in front of Prim.

"No matter how glad I am at your career choice to become a Post Office manager, you are still to stay inside this flat for the remainder of the holidays under lock and key. It will be the making of you, and you will one day thank me for it, believe me."

And with that largely unneeded remark, he picked up his keys and left the flat.

Prim thought for a bit.. Her Mum sat in contemplation, even though she had finished her tea.

"Mum, did you grow up wanting to run a Post Office?"

Prim's Mum still sat in silence and Prim wondered whether she had heard the question. She was about to ask it again, then thought better of herself when, almost inaudibly, her Mum replied.

"No."

Mr Percy, Prim's Dad walked to the Swinging Witch with his head held high, things were looking up. His daughter had begun to think seriously about taking over the family business of running the Post office and, in less than five minutes, he would be consuming his favourite tipple of Rat's Tail.

226

Just to be clear, he thought he would ask Mr Tanner about how often he would see Prim playing in the car park and he would explain to his old friend, why she would not be there for the rest of the Easter holidays.

He simply could not see what he was walking into and how it could affect him and his family.

Chapter Forty-Three

It was time for bed, even though it was only 8pm, still light and Prim was eleven years old. She was quite sure none of her school friends would go to bed at such an early hour, especially during the holidays but she had had enough of watching a documentary on train travel on the telly and decided she needed some me time anyway.

School friends? You mean people you go to school with.

But Prim had more important things to think about. It was one thing being all innocent in front of her parents and biting the bullet as her Dad proposed she work her way up to running the Post Office, and one to lie to them both about what she had been doing that day.

And what have I been up to today. None of my school "friends" would ever believe me. If they ever asked. And, if we had to write about what we did over the holidays, then Mrs Davis would think I had written the most fictional tall tale in the world.

But then Prim's doubts set in.

If I ever get the chance to get back to school, that is.

She changed the subject and thought for a bit about her Mum and that she knew Mum never wanted to be a Post Office manager. She knew her Dad did not either, it was all there to be seen in the photographs of when they were younger, the travelling and so on.

They could have done anything.

I can do anything.

I will do anything.

She looked at the book on post office management and yawned.

Just thinking about it makes me tired.

With that she got into her PJs and looked for a book to take her mind off everything to no avail.

She was beginning to fall asleep.

In the holidays some other children might go mountain biking, swimming, surfing, visiting Buckingham Palace or some other normal attraction.

She had visited a crypt, hung around some ghosts, searched for a clue, an important clue and had been threatened with bloody death by a maniac from hell.

Oh, my dear Aunt Rose. I do hope she is okay.

Prim was falling asleep.

What am I going to dream about tonight?

And she thought back about her day and worried, she had seen the hanging tree in so many paintings today, she had been in an old crypt surrounded by the dead, she had also been surrounded by the spirits of some of those dead people.

I'm going to dream about the hanging tree aren't I? With me, or Angharad, staring, staring with eyes wide open even though, she or me is dead.

The very thought of such a dream appalled her. It had frightened her enough the first time and she certainly did not want a second time. She knew that dreams could be based on something that had happened in the day, even though it could just be a teeny-weeny part of the day. But then she thought about how she could have had the dream in the first place, without ever having seen the hanging tree before.

I must keep awake tonight.

She knew, feeling clever, that she would, of course, fall asleep but she had to delay that eventuality and, if she could, think of something, do something that could end up being her dream. Not only had she seen the hanging tree but there was also the going on in the crypt too plus Lilith, her threats and the chain itself.

Surely, something bad is going to be in my dream tonight.

What could she think of? The book on running a Post office? Surely that would make her fall asleep. What about the door opening magically? No, that was also a bit spooky too. How about her tea? Perhaps she could pretend – it could not be a day dream as the day was now night – that she was an Italian chef who owned a restaurant in Little Grisly but then her thoughts turned to Little Grisly itself and led her down the path to Great Grisly Hall and onwards in the direction of the tree.

I think I am probably going to see that tree for real tomorrow.

I think that I should see that tree for real tomorrow.

I need to think of a clue to where the Earl's chain could be hidden. How did I forget that? How stupid can I be?

She was angry with herself but making herself calm she began to think back to all the paintings she had uncovered that day.

To start with this brought back her thinking of the hanging tree and her worry about her dream, or nightmare as it was likely to be.

Think Prim, think.

She thought about who the portraits were of: Harry; Angharad; the last Earl; the Lord le Grise that she knew, all the others that she did not. She thought of Lady Elizabeth Riche and could not get her out of her mind, her face, staring at the artist who painted her. She thought about the story of her and the man she loved, who spurned her.

This isn't the thing I need to be thinking of. Lady Elizabeth Riche is not a clue.

And she thought about the time that Lord le Grise had told her to think about: Harry's time and to make her relax as she lay in bed, she thought about playing with Harry, Amy, Sadie and Lockie in the garden of Great Grisly Hall, along the path and even in the car park to the Swinging Witch.

And, slowly, as she calmed herself down, became cosier in her bed, as the night became darker, with only the light of the full moon behind the curtains, she finally fell asleep. Sometime later, she began to dream.

Another Dream for Prim

Prim did not know where she was at first. She looked around to try and get her bearings and remembered that this was the field where she had met Mrs Pilkington.

She was alone, but for some reason she could tell that Amy, Sadie and Lockie where somewhere close for she could hear their voices at just a little distance away.

Her field was dry, it was a sunny day, more summer than spring, but the sky was not blue, more covered in an illuminous orange cloud giving a strange but not upsetting atmosphere.

She did not feel afraid; the others were close by.

What are they up to?

And she stopped her walk and listened carefully, so she could hear them all talking.

Or could she? She wasn't so sure, but she was still convinced that they were not far away, perhaps in the very next field and now she raised her nostrils to smell if they were having a barbecue, but she could not smell anything, not even the soft, fresh grass that she walked on, and for a second she smiled, thanking that she could not smell any cow pats or any other animals business and carried on her journey without a care in the world.

She skipped for a bit and despite wishing her good friends would stop and wait for her, she felt happy and began to sing a song she made up as she went along.

Cow pats and doggy mess

And other kinds of poo

All kinds of excrement

Remind me of you

Strangely, she could hear someone else, a male, singing her song.

How does that person know the words to my song?

And she looked around to see who was singing but could not see anyone but still she felt happy and wanted to sing a duet with whoever it was.

"You really should release that song," said the collie dog who she had dreamed of before and who strode next to her towards the other field, "it really is so catchy."

"Thank you," said Prim realising that she had met him before, "do you think it could get to Number One?"

"Oh, without a doubt," said the fox who now joined them on their quick walk towards the other field, "I would buy it."

These certainly were the most-polite animals Prim had ever encountered and, despite her dream, she felt terrible that she had eaten pig that very night. She decided not to mention this to any of the animals.

"Can you hear my friends, in the next field?" she asked, "I am trying to catch up with them."

"It is not your time Prim to reach that field, but there are others waiting for you at the gate who want to go there," said the collie, "rather a lot of them."

And suddenly, Prim was at the gate, the very same gate as in the dream with Mrs Pilkington.

But she was not there, nor were Amy, Sadie, Lockie or Rose amongst the people who waited by the gate and so she stared at them to see if she knew them.

She knew them all and, immediately, knew what her dream was about.

Standing at the front was Lord le Grise, behind him were six of the other residents of Great Grisly Hall including Peregrine.

"We're ready Prim, all of us are, finally," his Lordship stated wearily, "let us in please."

And Prim opened the gate, let them in and for a little while they walked in the field. His Lordship told Prim that it wasn't just that they now wanted to go upstairs, it was her strength as a guide that was helping them too.

But before she could think of a compliment in return, the world went brilliantly white.

"They never got to me you know Prim," said Lord le Grise and with that he winked and disappeared.

With his Lordship and the others gone, Prim was all alone in the field.

With seven of them gone, that only leaves three plus Lilith, the witch.

Anymore whilst I'm here. She laughed at her little thought.

But before she could look around, she heard a noise and began to wake up quickly. Her body seemed to become heavier and she felt like she was falling and then like she was being pulled away.

And she was awake.

She desperately wanted to get back into her dream and tried to fall back into a deep sleep, but, despite being completely worn out, it did not work.

She heard a banging again and was now wide awake.

It was her Dad, closing the front door to their flat, after coming back from the pub.

She heard him talking to her Mum, he was not whispering but her closed door hid a lot of the words from her.

All she could make out was that her Dad was not happy.

Thinking she was in more trouble, as if Mr Tanner had told that he had seen Prim around the village, she summoned up enough strength to lift her weary body up, snuck to her door and listened carefully.

234

Chapter Forty-Six

Thankfully, by the door, she could hear a lot better.

"I tell you it must be her, the one my Dad told me about," her Dad stated, "they always said she would come back again. And I thought it was a load of rubbish."

"You're just overreacting, you always do after a couple of pints," comforted Mum, "all that is a load of rubbish, your being paranoid."

"Tanner said she was acting all weird, mentioned that she had been to the pub before, don't you see, that is where the witch used to live, it must be her."

Prim's Mum was having none of it and changed her mood from nice to cold. "Snap out of it, all that stuff is rubbish and you're talking the same way. I bet if I had been in the pub tonight I would have come to a different conclusion. It's just some woman wanting to buy the Hall, now what's wrong with that? Certainly, there is more probability of someone wanting to do something with that pile than some dead witch returning from the grave. Pull yourself together."

"I need to see her, to see for my own eyes. I told Tanner that if she comes into the pub again to call me. Oh God, what if she comes into the Post Office tomorrow."

"Good I tell you, let her make an offer and buy the place. Then we can get out of running the Post Office, living in this cess pit and get out of Little Grisly."

Now Prim could not see what was going on, but she was sure she heard her Dad give a little squeal of surprise at his wife saying such things to him. There was a pause for sure, as he thought about his response.

"What? You know I can't do that."

"Why not? You told me all that stuff years ago and told me you thought it was rubbish, but we've had to put our lives on hold for years and for what? I didn't dream of becoming a Post Office

Manager when I was a child. I've got a degree in Art History for heaven's sake."

And with that reference to a child and becoming a Post Office manager, both parents looked at Prim's door to see if it was ajar and were thankful that it wasn't. All the same, they began to whisper.

"I want Prim to take over our business, why not?" Dad said.

"Why though? Even if that woman is neither of what you or Mr Tanner thinks she is, why not sell and get out of here. Your sister did, she escaped. Probably living the life now in London or somewhere a lot more interesting than here."

And with that reference to Rose, Prim, who was standing on her tiptoes still, fell a little backwards causing a slight thud on the carpet.

Both parents realised that Prim must be listening and whispered lower still.

"If that woman is who I think that woman is then my sister might be here too."

"Oh, go to bed, you must be drunk, do you want me to remind you of this conversation tomorrow morning? I think not. You've got it all wrong. I've never heard so much claptrap from anyone, even Prim."

"Thank God she is grounded," her Dad said, and he left the hallway, and went into the bathroom, turning on the light to see.

Prim stood still for a few seconds more to try and give the impression that she was not standing directly behind the door before, ever so gently, she headed back to her bed. Soon, she heard her parents turn the lights off and head to bed themselves.

Dad knows about Lilith. That woman must be her. It can't be anyone else.

Should I tell him the truth?

236

It sounds like he may believe me.

And Mum! She's not so keen on being a Post Office manager too. But that's nothing for now. Finding the clue to the chain is what matters now.

I hope I can get out of the flat tomorrow. Rose needs me.

Prim knew that was the most important thing to think about but, at the same time, her mind was buzzing about the conversation she had just heard. There had been so much to take in, not just about Lilith, but about her parents and their views on life in Little Grisly.

She thought and thought about this and thought that she would never fall back to sleep and was glad that she was thinking so deeply because she did not want to fall asleep again.

She thought about her earlier dream from that night and the similar one she had had a while ago and wondered if, when she returned to Great Grisly Hall, his Lordship and the others had all gone, as they called it, upstairs.

If only I can get out of the flat to get there.

But she was tired, helping his Lordship and the others had really taken it out of her.

She thought about Amy, Sadie and Lockie being in tonight's dream.

She thought she could hear a horse, or horses, whinnying in the distance, and perhaps another noise, like a shouting, but knew there were no horses around Little Grisly for miles around.

A few moments later she fell asleep.

Thankfully, her dreams were not as she had feared they would be, and, for the rest of the night, she slept soundly.

She would need it.

Harry Despencer 1635 to 1646

Harry Despencer was nine years old when his parents decided, with no notice given, that he should be sent to Great Grisly Hall to learn under the 7th Lord le Grise as a novice.

The English Civil War was raging and the Percy family, learning the lesson from the last Earl's attempts to curry favour with the King, were keeping well and truly out of everything.

Harry didn't want to go that was for sure, it wasn't because he would miss his Mum, she never had time for him, it wasn't because he would miss his Father, well he was never around anyway what with business in London, it was just he didn't want to go to there. His elder brothers had teased him about the legend that one of the old Earls rode around the estate at night looking for children to snatch and eat and obviously Harry was horrified.

His Nanny, who looked after him since he had been a baby and to whom Harry loved dearly, held him in her arms and kindly told that the legend was only there to make sure young children were safely tucked up in bed at night.

Nevertheless, moving away was devastating for Harry. His childhood was over, and he was to learn from the Lord le Grise on how to be a gentleman, to fight bloody battles and win, and to run an estate of land and make money.

He had imagined what Great Grisly Hall must look like what with the words "great" and "grisly" in it. A dark foreboding sky surrounded it. It would have two massive but dark windows as eyes and a huge front door as its mouth with fire raging from its lips and the thought of the Earl riding and searching for him, ready to eat him. Why was he being punished by his parents so badly?

Soon I will be dead

Soon I will be dead

And will my parents miss me?

Of course, the reality was different from his fears. At first, he thought that the coachman had dropped him off at the wrong Hall, there was no fire breathing house and the grounds, with the beautiful coloured flowers and bushes being tendered by scores of gardeners, were much too pretty for a demonic Earl to haunt.

Great Happy Hall was a better way of describing it.

There was something even better in store too for Harry too.

Lady Angharad Percy, niece of The Lord le Grise and roughly the same age as Harry. To Harry she was the most delightful person in the whole world, not that he had seen too many girls, and he was certainly too shy to tell her.

She was the same age as Harry and roughly the same height, with straight, strawberry blonde hair in a long bob and a small, slightly upturned nose surrounded by freckles.

Before Harry had arrived, she had been the only other child at the Hall, the Lord's children were all grown up. At first, she would tease him, a little boy lost inside a great Hall, sent away by his parents. How utterly horrible he must have been for his parents to do that to him.

Harry denied her taunts but, deep down, he knew Angharad was telling the truth. All the same he just did not wish to hear it and he would run away from her and the Hall and find somewhere that could be his.

On one such occasion he had run so quickly away from her that he almost fell into a small narrow stream, he could not run any further in that direction and, spotting a small wheel attached to a flour mill, ran towards it.

The sun was overbearingly hot, and Harry sat close by under the shade of a giant tree, the largest and strongest in the field and watched the wheel turn gently around as the mill workers quietly going about their work

Soon this was the place he would not just run to when Angharad was horrible but just where he would run to escape all his troubles. This was his place and he enjoyed sitting close or sometimes under the crown of the tree if the sun became too hot.

He imagined, especially when under the trees great canopy, that he could hear his family calling him, Harry.

Harry. Harry.

This was his home from home.

Angharad realised that her teasing had affected Harry and realised even more that without him she was just left alone in the Hall without anyone to play with. She too was ignored by the adults. She too felt alone at Great Grisly Hall.

One fine, spring morning she decided to follow Harry to wherever he was going.

Initially Harry was angry, then upset but it only needed one genuinely said word to turn the tide of their feelings.

Angharad said sorry. She had taken her feelings out on Harry, the one person she should have been friends with.

And after that they clicked.

Harry had to have lessons each day, but he longed to finish them, so he could go outside and play with Angharad. Soon they became close.

The saying little children should be seen and not heard was made for these two. They played up and down inside the Hall, outside by the stream, and sometimes in it, and then, to relax and get their breaths back, they would fall underneath the giant tree.

Their tree.

The children were not kept up to date in the affairs of the country especially in relation to the War and Lord le Grise was at pains to stop both Harry and Angharad from hearing anything from the outside world.

But soon, terrible news had come from Little Grisly for which everyone at Great Grisly Hall was talking about. A fire had started at the Church and it had been damaged badly. Lord le Grise had visited the church as soon as he heard of the disaster and came home looking very sad and angry.

Harry and Angharad decided to keep away from him for some time lest he would take out his anger upon them.

Upon Lord le Grise's instructions, a famous painter arrived at Great Grisly Hall to paint portraits of the family. Angharad wanted Harry to be in the painting too but Lord le Grise refused this but, to compromise, ordered the artist to paint Harry separately.

For some reason of his own, Lord le Grise ordered all the paintings would have the background of their tree, Angharad remembered her uncle stating they needed the light in their portraits.

Both Harry and Angharad loved having their portraits painted. They had pulled faces at each other and laughed until they almost cried and until the artist told them off, repeatedly for trying to ruin his work.

When both paintings were finished, Lord le Grise was most happy at the painter's work and paid him handsomely. But both Harry and Angharad had chuckled, at first due to looking at each other's faces in the paintings and at the curious shining light around the tree. Clearly the painter had gone overboard on the Lord's instructions.

Anyway, it was not up to them, they were mere children and they counted for nothing. Both paintings were hung up in the great hall and, for the next few weeks, both Harry and Angharad played inside the hall, often mocking their portraits.

Lord le Grise was at pains to stop their constant fooling and playing. This was no way for a gentleman to act and certainly for no niece of his either.

He was also at pains to stop their friendship. *What would happen if they started to fall in love? What would happen if they wanted to marry?* Was Harry the right sort of chap to marry his niece?

The current Lord le Grise had to do something and fast.

The painter, who travelled across England working for the richest and noblest families, knew everything that was going on in the country and was not afraid to discuss it with his Lordship and the children.

Outside, away from Great Grisly Hall, away from the bloodshed of war, something very odd, very scary was going on.

Witch hunts.

In the 17th century, although Christianity was by far the most practised religion throughout the land, there was a great panic with the very real threat that witches, loyal to the Devil, were trying to take over not just the land, but also the souls of everyone across the country.

Many people, women mainly, were accused of witchcraft and usually found themselves dead: killed by drowning, by being burnt at the stake or hanged from a strong tree.

Everyone was fearful of being accused of being a witch. You only had to be accused by one person for everyone else in the town or village to believe them. Soon you would be condemned.

Ghastly tales of witches and their powers spread across the country. Some members of these families believed they were witches. The painter told the family of a young man called Matthew Hopkins who was making a name for himself as the Witchfinder General. Once accused by Hopkins and there was very little that could be done. The person accused was usually condemned and hanged.

Lord le Grise had told the painter that witchcraft was nothing new and that he was to stop discussing all this gossip in front of Angharad and Harry, but the two children were transfixed with interest and fright. In fact, Lord le Grise was too. He was petrified of witches, having been told stories about them before bedtime as a child, and was determined to stop them or any talk of them happening whilst he was in charge of the Hall.

News of Matthew Hopkins work around the country spread quickly and many people feared acting, in any way differently from the norm, in case they were accused of witchcraft, or to give its name maleficium. One way of showing that you were not a witch was to accuse someone else of being one.

At this very time, in Little Grisly, a young woman of around eighteen years became known to the Percy family.

Her name was Lilith Cook.

She was normally a very good girl, according to most accounts, but one day she was found wandering about Great Grisly Hall. She was caught by a maid and charged with attempting to steal from the Percy family. Two days later the maid who worked within the Hall came down with a terrible illness and died.

The locals knew what had killed her. She had been cursed by Lilith. Lilith must be a witch.

She was brought before Lord le Grise, who oversaw justice in this part of the kingdom. She denied being a witch and that she was looking to steal something from the Hall.

Most people who attended court simply believed that she, as a witch, could magic herself anywhere she liked including inside Great Grisly to steal. One evening, Harry heard his Lordship tell his wife that he was sure Lilith was the one who had broken into St Hilda's and had caused the fire and that he knew what she was looking for inside Great Grisly Hall.

In court, Lilith had responded by saying that if she was a witch, which she denied, then why did she not make herself invisible, so no one could see her.

At home, Lord le Grise had told that he did not think the evidence was strong against her as a witch and that she had killed one of his maids. But, if he could find evidence to show that someone had let her inside the Hall, then she could be found guilty of stealing something or trying to steal and that would mean, at least, that she would go to prison. And his Lordship was desperate for her to do so.

Who could have let Lilith inside the Hall?

There was only one person.

Harry.

Surely this was the opportunity to remove Harry from Great Grisly Hall, to send him back to his family and to stop his friendship with Angharad.

Killing two birds with one stone.

The court hearing was postponed for a few weeks for evidence to be obtained against Lilith. For good measure, and to protect her from any of the locals who wished to take the law into their own hands, she was thrown into the dungeon below Great Grisly Hall.

A day later Harry was accused of helping Lilith into the Hall to steal.

Lord le Grise had hoped that all talk and threats of witches would be dropped immediately. No-one would think that Harry Despencer would be in league with a witch and, just because he had helped her in, no-one would, in their right mind, believe that she was a witch.

Sadly, not many people were in their right minds when claims of witchcraft were made. Instead of going along with his plan, the locals began to believe that Harry was a witch himself and if he was a witch, then who else in Great Grisly Hall was as well?

Angharad was devastated by the news that Harry must be a witch. She loved him like a brother, well a good brother and not a naughty, loud real brother. She could feel in her heart that Harry could, in time, be suitable as her husband.

Harry, of course, denied that he was a witch and told Angharad. His feelings for her began to increase. Once all this was sorted, and it would be, he would tell Angharad what his feelings were.

Lord le Grise was now in deep despair and, rather than simply remove Harry from his Hall and send him back home, had to place Harry into the dungeon too.

Lord le Grise thought and thought and thought. He would have to quell all the talk about Harry being a witch at the next court date. Perhaps he, as the local Judge, could nip everything in the bud, send Harry home and end this sorry matter.

But the locals had other plans. As the matter had taken place at Great Grisly Hall, they decided that he could not be trusted to be the Judge. Perhaps he was a witch himself.

A few days later there was a knock at Great Grisly Hall.

Matthew Hopkins, the Witchfinder General, had arrived with his gang. They were now in charge of the investigation.

Harry had never wished to be back home with his family so much than when he was placed into one of the tiny cells down in the dungeon of Great Grisly Hall. How could this have happened to him? What had he done to deserve this? Surely this was all a mistake?

But as the minutes turned to hours and finally to days his thoughts turned to survival. He was freezing cold; the cell was wet and his bed hard with no cover to cloak him and keep him warm. He could imagine what was going on upstairs, the warmth of the sun, the fires lit at night time, the fun, the food, the friendship. The sun certainly did not shine down in the dungeon and despite only being two floors below from the main hall, he felt as if he was in hell.

Surely Angharad would speak for him and Lord le Grise would relent, realise his mistake and bring him back upstairs.

But no-one came for him. Only the gaoler visited him with food or what was supposed to be food. It was disgusting, looked it, smelt it and finally tasted it for, as the day turned into days, he became so hungry he had to eat it.

And he wasn't exactly alone. Throughout his few days down there he was sure he could hear something breathing, sometimes a cough, sometimes a snore.

Of course, the inn keeper's daughter must be in a cell too.

Next door to be precise. They began to talk to each other. At first it was comforting, just to hear someone else close by was a real comfort but then Lilith started to ask some deep questions.

"Why would Lord le Grise believe you had let me into the Hall?"

"I don't know, someone must have said something, but I am sure he will see that I would not do something like that."

"Well he hasn't yet Harry, and it has been five long days now since you have been down here with me."

Harry could not really think of an answer to this. He had to keep up his hopes that Lord le Grise would change his mind, surely that would be the case?

"I would have thought that Lady Angharad would have spoken for you."

Harry could not really think of an answer to this too. Angharad must have said something on his behalf.

"Maybe she is hiding something," suggested Lilith. "Maybe she hasn't spoken on your behalf. Maybe it was her that let me in."

246

"No," cried Harry, "She would not do such a thing and even if she did, she would explain that to Lord le Grise."

"Are you stupid boy? Admit to helping me into the Hall? I am meant to be a witch; do you think she is stupid enough to admit helping a witch? If she did then she would be down here with me."

"And if you were a witch then you wouldn't need anyone to help you enter the house," said Harry proudly. He wasn't going to take being called stupid by anyone.

But there was no response. Harry waited for an age for Lilith to say something, but she did not. As his thoughts turned away from her, he began to think and then worry about what she had said. *Did Angharad really help Lilith? Does his Lordship know this and is trying to blame me?*

What had he done to deserve this?

Not long after, Harry could hear Lilith talking to someone else but there could not have been anyone else down in the dungeons. Was she muttering to herself like a witch would? He listened carefully. No, there was another woman talking to her, an older woman. *Who is it?*

Harry could not recognise her voice and yet from a few of words he could make out, the elder lady knew so much about the Hall.

She must be a Percy, where have they been hiding her?

The conversation stopped, and Harry sighed, trying to work out who Lilith was talking to had allowed him to stop thinking about his situation. *Was this woman going to help Lilith escape? Why else would she be down here?*

Harry felt something, the tiny hairs on the back of his shoulders and neck stood up in unison like a sway of flowers in the wind and he turned to the cell door to see if someone was there.

But he couldn't see anyone.

But he knew someone was there.

Harry smelt something.

Lavender.

He didn't know it at that time, but he had just had his first meeting with Lady Elizabeth.

A few hours later, Lilith started to ask Harry more questions.

"Do you know of the tale of the last Earl?"

"It's just a fairy tale to make sure children are in their beds at night."

"It most certainly is no fairy tale."

"How do you know?"

"I have seen the Earl and his two sons fly across the fields looking for someone else to drag down to hell with them."

"You must have been drinking some of that groggy ale your Dad makes."

"Oh, I think not Harry Despencer. It is a true tale but do not worry, the Earl won't come looking for you down here. No, it won't be the Earl who comes for you Harry, but the witchfinder and we all know what he likes to do."

Harry's body chilled even more than it was at the very thought of Matthew Hopkins and the Earl.

"Is there a painting of the Earl in the Hall?"

"Yes, there is one in the main hall." Harry replied not really knowing where the conversation was now going.

"And does the Earl wear a heavy gold chain around his neck?"

Harry had to think, he had walked past the painting every day but never really looked at it, to stare at the Earl, in Harry's mind, could encourage the Earl to pick on him in his dreams or, worse, to plan to take his soul to hell.

"I'm not sure," he said honestly, "possibly," he said a little dishonestly.

"And do you know where that chain is kept now?"

Harry thought for more than a second. Was this woman trying to steal the last Earl's chain?

"Answer me," Lilith now sounded angry.

"I have never seen it at all." Harry was telling the truth.

"Why does Lord le Grise never wear it? Is there going to be a special occasion soon when he could put it on?"

"I tell you I have never seen it before. Perhaps it is in his bedroom. Perhaps the lady you spoke to knows?"

It was Lilith's turn to pause and think. She was angry that Harry had been listening in to her conversation but even the century old shade did not know its whereabouts.

"What is so special about this chain?" asked Harry innocently.

"It has the power to bring back the dead and to command them to do whatever you want them to do. The Percys have had the chain for years but have not used it. Think of the power you could wield if you had the chain."

Harry did think about the power of the chain. If he had it now he could certainly escape from this cell. But his happiness was only short lived as he knew that he did not have the chain.

Lilith had given Harry some time to think about it and came up with a proposal.

"If you found the chain we could both be free of these charges. You would like that wouldn't you?"

"Of course, but how can I find the chain stuck here?"

"I could say that it wasn't you that helped me into the Hall."

Harry's heart was overjoyed with such news. If she said this to the court then he would surely be free.

"But I will need to say someone else let me in. Do you have anyone to suggest?"

He thought of the housemaids and servants.

But maybe Angharad had let Lilith into the Hall. He hoped not but it certainly would be believable that she could.

"You said Angharad could have done so. Do you think the court will believe us if you said it was her?"

"Brilliant Harry, I think they would certainly believe that could have done that. And, once you are released, find the chain, use it and rescue Angharad and myself."

And Harry smiled at his cleverness. Yes, he could save the day.

"It's a deal," he said quickly. "You have my word of honour as a gentleman."

"Good boy," said Lilith chuckling gently to herself. "And at the next court hearing I will say that it was Lady Angharad Percy herself who let me in."

She laughed quite a bit louder now in her cell.

Harry too was happy.

But for the days leading up to the next court hearing, Harry had become downcast. He had entered into an agreement with someone that everyone was calling a witch. Sure, he had brokered a deal to get himself off with the charge of being or assisting a witch, and of course, he wasn't at all, and he was sure that the court would believe Lilith.

But at what cost?

Angharad would now be blamed. In his head he went through all the scenarios of what could happen at court. Surely a judge and jury would not believe that she was a witch? They surely would not believe that she would let Lilith into the Hall so that something could be stolen. In fact, nothing had been stolen had it?

But things had moved on from there.

Lilith was being accused of witchcraft and anyone associated with a witch was believed to be a witch themselves.

And if they were found to be witches then they would be hanged.

I cannot let Angharad be hanged.

He had told Lilith that the deal was off, but she would have none of it. He had given her his word of honour. He told her that he would not search for the chain if he was released but, again, Lilith told him that they had entered a deal and that it was unbreakable. More importantly did he want Angharad to die?

In order to save his skin and that of his beloved Angharad he would have to go along with the plan and then find the chain, wherever it may be.

And so, they went to court and in front of the judge, the jury, Lord le Grise, Matthew Hopkins and the members of the public (and everyone from miles around came to hear what was going on), Lilith kept to her side of the deal.

To say that there was a shock was to put it mildly. First, there was a sort of quietness as people worked out just what Lilith had said. Then, there was murmuring as people asked each other what Lilith had said. Then, there was utter turmoil as the court erupted.

"We told you, those Percys were up to something."

"It's always the one you least suspect."

"I always knew it was her."

And Lord le Grise was crestfallen.

Lilith denied being a witch and Harry was thankful. She said that she wanted some money and so decided to steal from the Hall and that Lady Angharad had helped her because she was bored. She said she had nothing to do with the dead maid nor did she ever know her.

The jury only partly believed her.

They believed that Lady Angharad was her accomplice.

But that they were both witches.

Harry was found not guilty and left the dock.

The Judge sentenced Lilith and Lady Angharad to be hanged by their necks until dead.

Angharad had come to the court to support her best friend. Now she had been accused and found guilty of being a witch, all in the space of a few hours.

She was in shock herself and could not realise the full consequences of what was going to happen to her. People who attended the court said to their friends and families that she had a puzzled look to her face, but that was all.

It would only be later that she realised just what was going to happen to her.

Lilith, however, was under no illusions. Despite stating she wasn't a witch at court, she fully believed that she was.

The time to speak was now, the court room was full.

"Do you think hanging will rid you of us? Do you think that will be the end and then you can go back to home safely to your beds and sleep tight? Well you are wrong. Yes, I am a witch and I will be back, I will return to this hovel of a place, and sooner than you think. I will come back more powerful than anyone of you, more powerful than the King."

She was bold and provocative to the people in the court, but as she was led away she managed to pull away from her guards and have chance to whisper a few choice words into Harry's ear who sat with the rest of the baying public, his face, his body, disconsolate.

"Find the chain, before we are hanged, and use it to stop them. That is your part of the deal. That is, if you want to save your loved one."

Harry went back to the Hall with the rest of the Percy family, minus, of course, Angharad. For a time, his Lordship left Harry well alone, such was his grief at the thought of his niece being hanged.

There were only two days before that would take place.

Harry furiously searched the whole of the Hall, the top to bottom, east to west, bottom to top and back again, morning till night, dusk till dawn.

The chain could not be found and two days later both Lilith and Lady Angharad were hanged, from the hanging tree.

Harry was devastated. He could not forgive himself for the death of his beloved friend. It wasn't really his fault, it was Lilith's all along, but Harry felt that it should have been him that was hanged, even though he was innocent. He had failed Angharad, he had failed to find the chain and now she was gone, forever.

Every day he would walk past their portraits and remember the day they were painted, how they had smiled and laughed.

Those days were gone.

About a month later, Harry died. Some say he died of a broken heart. Others, worldlier wise, say he died from a plague, the same one that killed the maid who had found Lilith searching Great Grisly Hall. His death was a terrible one: slow; harrowing and painful. He believed this was just, given his role in the death of Angharad and he hoped to see her in heaven and apologise.

Poor Harry, those in charge of the great court house in the sky determined that he had been part of the plan to blame Lady Angharad. Some wanted him to go direct to hell, but others, thinking he was a little too young, decided that he should go back to the place where he had recently lived and spend some time, thinking about his actions. No-one thought it would take him four centuries or thereabouts to think it all through.

Chapter Forty-Seven

Prim's Dad left for work early that day, wanting to get himself thinking of something else rather than the possibility that the witch from centuries ago had returned. Working in a Post Office was harder than most people would think, and he set himself some big targets for the day.

If only I could live a bit closer to work, he manged to chuckle to himself as he walked down the stairs.

Prim had breakfast with her Mum and said nothing about what she had heard both her parents talking about last night. That would have been most unwise. Yes, the return of Lilith was a very bad thing, but Prim wanted her Mum to go to work as soon as possible so that she, Prim, could try and open the door and get to work down at Great Grisly Hall.

I have got to think of what it all means.

Quick, Prim, come on and think.

But as much as she wanted her Mum to go to work, it seemed her Mum did not really want to go herself. She sat there, at the kitchen table, staring into space and Prim wondered what she was thinking about.

It had to be about last night. Prim sensed there was something deep between Mum and Dad, a deep rift that was something she had not even thought about before. They had always been so at one with each other, always agreeing, always warning Prim off things. And now, it seemed, her Mum did not want to be working in a Post office in Little Grisly.

But for Prim, for now, this had to be placed to the back of her mind.

Mischievously, she told her Mum that she needed to go to the bathroom.

She didn't really but it got her Mum standing up and rushing out of the kitchen, to the bathroom to get ready for work.

255

Two minutes later and, "now remember you are grounded Prim, there's a massive coach load of tourists who have come up from London and we will be busy. There's corned beef in the fridge."

And with that she left the flat, locking the door. Prim thought that the mention of London had taken her Mum off into a different place, and maybe it had, but not enough to forget to lock the door.

Quickly, Prim got dressed herself and brushed her teeth and hair.

I hope it opens, I hope it opens.

She thought this for a bit, it became a bit of a mantra and she started to say it aloud.

"I hope it opens, I do hope it opens."

And she was ready and facing the door.

She tried it. It was locked.

Quickly she turned to jelly.

I cannot be in here all day with all the work we have to do against the witch.

How else can I get out? How did it happen yesterday?

And she thought and thought to no avail and she grabbed the door handle and tried to twist it around, so it would open but it would not and in the action of trying, she hurt her wrist.

If only Rose knew what a pickle I was in? If only I had her number. If only I had a mobile phone.

She walked around the hall of the flat for a bit and then returned to the door.

"Open," she ordered.

"Open sesame," she shouted.

"Open, NOW," she roared, desperately.

But it did not budge. Whatever had made it open before was not doing its job today.

Prim fell to the floor and felt that she was going to sob.

Stop it Prim, get up and think.

She got up, went into the kitchen and looked at the clock. It was still early, in fact, it was earlier than the time she had escaped yesterday by about twenty minutes.

Maybe the magic is on a timer?

And she smiled and began to calm down and crashed onto the sofa in the lounge and closed her eyes.

Don't fall asleep again Prim, you never know what will happen in your dreams.

And this made her think.

She thought about all the strange things that had happened since she had discovered Great Grisly Hall. She thought about the power, the strange power she supposedly had to guide the souls of the dead to heaven and with that she immediately thought about the dream from last night.

She was meant to be special, part of a special family, a special but cursed family who had played the devil and lost.

She did not want to dwell on that bit any longer and her mind drifted to the other dream she had been having, of the hanging tree and Angharad, who could have been her twin, they looked so alike.

This made Prim wince.

She thought of the place, by the mill and the stream, it was a real place. A place she had only visited in her dreams.

Strange that she had been to an actual place only in a dream, but her imagination could show it her just as perfectly as the paintings at Great Grisly Hall.

And it clicked.

What had Rose told her yesterday? She had had the same dream. And weren't they supposed to be a special family?

The clue is there Prim.

She was excited, and her heart began to beat faster. Was she getting closer to solving the riddle of where the chain had been hidden for all those years?

But where in the paintings could it be?

She searched her mind back to when she was looking at the paintings made at the same time, of Harry, Angharad and others, of the grand painting of the last Earl, what were they telling her?

The tree. It had to be the tree itself.

It had only been a small sapling when the grand painting of the last Earl and his daughter was painted. A few centuries later and it was tall, wide and strong, good enough to be a background in the paintings of all those who lived in the Hall at that time.

Good enough to hang Lilith and Angharad.

But how could the Earl have buried the chain somewhere near the tree? He was dead according to Rose, dead in the Hall.

It could not have walked there.

Prim thought some more, and then some more.

The clues, according to Lord le Grise, were all in the paintings.

And they were. Of course, they were. In the last Earl's painting was the final clue.

His daughter.

The one, who after his death and the deaths of her brothers had taken over the Hall. Hadn't Lilith mentioned that she had probably hidden the chain?

She would have known about the power of the chain, she would have seen what it had done to her father and brothers and hidden it somewhere safe. Not in Great Grisly Hall, that would be too obvious. But somewhere safe, on their land, and no one would suspect where.

The chain had to be hidden, or buried, under the tree.

She thought about the shining lights around the tree in the paintings of Harry and Angharad. But they were not lights.

Could they be the glistening of a gold chain?

Are these lights the clue Lord le Grise told me to find?

I must have cracked it. It must be true.

Prim was excited and danced around the room.

Prim's mind turned to Lilith and wondered if she had begun to work out the clue.

I've got to get to Great Grisly Hall, find Rose and get to the Hanging Tree quickly.

But how am I going to get out of the flat?

She didn't have to think about this for more than a second. She heard the bolt of the front door unlock and she ran to open it quickly.

There stood Amy, Sadie and Lockie, they must have run up the stairs but were not panting.

"Well that was good timing," said Prim, half joking.

From the look on all three of their faces, this was no time to be joking at all.

"Prim," cried Amy, "something's happened at Great Grisly Hall. You better come quick."

And Prim put on her shoes as fast as she could and followed them down the stairs as quietly as possible, half thinking about just what had happened.

The other half of her thinking was how her three friends could have possibly opened the bolt to the door to her flat.

What sort of magic was that? What exactly are my friends?

Chapter Forty-Eight

After checking that her parents were both in the shop and busy, Prim ran out and towards the Swinging Witch and onwards, with her three friends, along the path towards Great Grisly until she could run no more, and she was out of breath.

"What has happened?" Prim asked between breaths and bending over.

Lockie put his hand onto her back and gently patted it as if to help.

"Too much for one night," he said.

"Last night eight of the residents left the Hall. At first, we thought they had just hidden, especially as Lord le Grise was hiding. But it turned out that they have left forever, gone to heaven." Amy advised.

"Gone upstairs," said Sadie, "but you knew about that didn't you Prim."

Prim could only nod in agreement.

Amy continued her explanation. "Lilith is, as you can understand, absolutely furious. She, Barnaby and Lady Elizabeth searched everywhere for Lord le Grise."

"They know you were responsible for guiding them to heaven Prim." Lockie told her straight.

"Lilith is so after you," said Sadie in an even straighter way than Lockie, "she wants to kill you."

"But that is not all Prim," Amy said, "this morning Rose came just before to the Hall to look again at the paintings. She didn't know about Lord le Grise and the other residents."

But we were supposed to meet at St Hilda's.

And Amy paused and looked at Prim, who had now recovered her breath and was standing normally.

"Lilith, Barnaby and her ladyship ambushed her in the garden."

"Ambushed her? What do you mean?" Prim was now highly anxious, the blood from her face disappearing fast.

"Sorry Prim, but Lilith sees what happened with the others as an act of war. They took Rose, kidnapped her if you will and took her into Great Grisly Hall. With Lord le Grise and Harry gone, they think she is the only person who could possibly know where the chain is hidden."

"But she doesn't know," cried Prim, "unless she worked it out herself last night or this morning. Oh, why did she not wait for me. Come on we have got to rescue her."

"Steady Prim," Sadie warned, "if those three are strong enough to overpower Rose then they easily get hold of you. No offence."

Prim was angry, but knew Sadie was right. She fell onto the floor putting her hands to her face to try and cover her from the reality of it all.

Rose, my aunt Rose, what were they doing to her? Were they torturing her now? We must do something?

"Rose signalled for us to take you away from the Hall and to the mill and the hanging tree," Amy advised, "I think she may have had an idea about the chain but that was all she gave us."

Of course, that was the place to go to. Rose must have worked it out herself too. Find the chain Prim, find it quick.

And then what?

What exactly am I supposed to do with it?

"Come on," she told the three of them, "I think I know exactly where it is, we might need a spade or two but let's get there quick."

"There should be a spade in the mill, I am sure there is a least one," said Lockie.

And, from thinking about the conversation they had just had, rather than run to the hanging tree as they really needed to, there was something else Prim needed to know.

"How do you all know so much?"

"What do you mean?" Lockie said, looking at the other two. Presumably they all looked back at him, but Prim could only see him.

"How do you know all this has happened? All about Rose, all about Barnaby and Lady Elizabeth. I know you know about the others going upstairs because I, myself know that."

"Well," Amy began to say.

"And another thing," Prim was flowing now, "how come you have been able to open my blooming front door? You're just from my imagination, aren't you?"

And she stood there waiting for one of them to answer as it slowly dawned on her that they probably weren't from her imagination at all.

"We ought to get to where we are going Prim," said Sadie.

"I agree, but I think I have the right to know what is going on?"

It was Amy who explained.

"Prim, we've been your friends for only about a week or so, but it feels like we have been friends for ages," and the other two nodded in agreement, "we know you're an only child, and this has happened before, but do you really still think we are just imaginary friends?"

Without thinking Prim replied, "You mean you are not?"

Chapter Forty-Nine

"Come on we need to go, now," ordered Lockie to everyone but without anyone, listening.

He was right, of course, but Prim needed to know exactly who, or what her friends were. After all, friends were important and if unsure about whether they existed or not, then this, obviously, was a problem.

And she stood still, expecting a response.

"Well we are your friends Prim," said Sadie.

"But we're not imaginary, we are real," said Amy.

"But no-one else can see you, what exactly are you?" Prim replied and then it hit her.

In a world and place full of ghosts, what are three more?

"Okay Prim let me explain quickly," continued Amy, "we are, how shall I put it, friends or guardians, not from your mind but from above. We can be seen by you and Rose and your family but can, if needed, hide from the others, living and dead."

And Amy gave Prim a moment to think.

"It was Rose who asked us to come and and find you, and help you come out to Great Grisly Hall to help her," Sadie added.

So, Rose did summon me to the Hall.

"But we are your true friends, honest." Lockie confirmed quickly and rather impatiently. The other two nodded in agreement.

"So, I didn't imagine you." Prim was now in a state of shock.

For a second or two she was angry, angry because they hadn't become her friends naturally like people did in school.

They were placed here to help, help Rose, not me.

But then she realised that she had loved playing with them, especially before everything kicked off at Great Grisly Hall.

They might not be that real, but I do like them.

"And you're from above? Are you angels?"

"Yes," Amy replied sheepishly.

And Prim thought. *Guardian angels?*

And perhaps unfairly said, "you haven't exactly been around to help me all the time I have been here."

"Sorry Prim," Amy said, "we love you and we have kept our eye out for you as much as we possibly can. There are limits to what we can do. We can open doors and other things like living people do, but we are powerless against someone like Lilith."

Prim remembered the first time she had met Lilith on the lawn at Great Grisly Hall and that Amy and the others had looked concerned but had not done anything.

And they explained about opening the door to the flat with the bolt key and how they had taken it from the coats of her parents from inside the post office and put it back before they noticed.

And Prim remembered the door opening inside Great Grisly Hall when Lady Elizabeth was coming after her.

"We played hide and seek, and you all went missing, and the door, the locked door opened."

"That was us then Prim," said Amy, "Rose had given us the key to her room."

"But I almost died, why did you hide up there?"

"We knew Rose was coming back and we decided to get you out of the way of some of the residents. We didn't know exactly what Lady Elizabeth was going to do until she got up there," explained Lockie.

"And we couldn't let ourselves be seen or to help you Prim, otherwise it would be known you had help," explained Sadie before Prim could ask such a question.

"How long have you known Rose?" Prim decided to ask.

"We have been friends of the Percy family for a long time Prim, for four centuries, even with the 14th Lord le Grise when he was a boy," advised Sadie, "you could say it is our family's way of saying sorry."

Four centuries! And what was there to say sorry for?

"For what?" Prim asked.

But she was to get no answer.

"Sorry to dampen the party, but there is another thing we need to worry about," said Lockie.

"You are right," replied Prim, "we must get to the hanging tree as soon as."

"Not just that," said Lockie, "but we need to do it before dark, last night, if you did not see, was a full moon, as will tonight."

A full moon? Oh brilliant, the Earl and his sons. Wait, didn't I hear horses last night?

"That part of the legend is definitely true isn't it?" Prim asked just for confirmation.

"Oh, yes," confirmed Lockie in the most complete way he could, "very true, indeed. Now please let's get to the tree."

Chapter Fifty

Prim had a rollercoaster of emotions going on inside her, not only about the reality of Amy, Sadie and Lockie, as they walked, fast, towards the tree by the old mill which was located further down the stream from Little Grisly.

She was, at first, excited at arriving there, the place she had only seen in her dreams, the place in the paintings, the place she never really thought existed, but then, only a bit longer than a week ago, she did not realise Great Grisly Hall existed either.

She was excited as she was going on a search, a search for a missing chain. Not just missing for a day or a morning like a hair brush could be, but something that had been missing for centuries.

And what something it was too. If all the stories were true, and by now Prim believed them – why would she not after all the events that had happened over the holidays - then she was looking, going to find, a magical, powerful chain, belonging to none other than the Devil himself.

She was scared at the thought of the Devil and the power of the chain and the fact that there was another person, and her despicable friends, who also wanted the chain for themselves.

I must get to it first. I must.

Again, she wasn't quite sure what she would do with it if, when, she found it first. Perhaps she would have to use its full power just to stop Lilith. And this scared her some more, she wasn't used to doing anything new.

Find the chain belonging to the Devil before an evil witch does and then do something with it.

Destroy it.

It wasn't, especially the last bit, exactly the greatest plan in the world. Even Mrs Davis could plan a better lesson than that.

But it was the only plan, certainly she had to find it before Lilith did.

Or did she?

And now she became confused.

What if Lilith cannot find it, with Lord le Grise gone, she might never think where it is hidden. And if I find it for her?

Prim cringed at the thought of the joy of finding something, just for someone to take it away. And use it for the worst possible purposes. What Lilith probably wanted to do with it made some of the world's leaders' positively cuddly.

This is the Devil's work, and all sorts of situations and circumstances came into her head.

No, I must find it, it's about Rose now too.

And she could not stop thinking about her poor aunt and what must be happening to her. Would it not be best to try and rescue her first?

Amy and the other two had led her to a gap in a hedge where there was a stile she had to climb over. She was readily glad to climb it to momentarily forget everything she had been thinking about.

Just do it Prim.

And, of course, as soon as she landed into the next field, she began thinking of it all over again, especially about Rose and what they might be doing to her inside the Hall.

Stupid Devil, if he had not have lost his chain, none of this would ever have happened.

But then she thought better of herself to think things like that.

Soon they were half way across the grassy field and Prim could see the stream again, the same one that ambled past Little Grisly and which had previously meandered off from the path. They were getting close.

The field began to drop towards the stream, which now looked much more like a little river and there stood, as if it had been hiding, the old honey coloured mill, very unlike her dream and the paintings, now just a ruin without much of a roof.

If that is the old mill, where is the tree?

And suddenly, she realised that as she walked on a little raised bit of ground, a few hundred yards above the mill and the little river that she was about to walk almost underneath it, enough to take the shade from the bright sun from some of its leafing branches.

Because of this realisation, she jumped but, thankfully, did not say or squeal anything.

And she made to get out of the way of such a distinctly gruesome tree. Except, as she did move away from it, she noticed that it wasn't an ugly one, only its history was gruesome and ugly. For some reason it was loved by the last Earl, someone whose soul remained in these parts under a terrible curse, and where Lilith and Angharad had been horrifically hanged.

Prim realised there were lots of awful adjectives which could describe it.

The hanging tree for starters.

It had certainly grown bigger in the last few hundred years, taller, wider and wilder but, at the same time, Prim thought she could see the bough from her dream, the one that had hanged Angharad and Lilith.

She shivered, she hated looking at it, the tree, in real life facing her, staring at her and Prim, herself, could not take her eyes off it.

Lockie came up to her with two old rusty spades found inside the old Mill.

"Come on Prim and hurry. Rose needs us, let's find this chain."

And with the mention of her aunt, Prim woke up from the enchantment of the tree and set about for business.

Where exactly, in those paintings, were the shining lights, the guides to the chain, hopefully the guides to the chain, from the paintings?

She found where she thought it would probably be, close by and back under the shade of the tree, but in truth it was more guess work than any notion or theory and stuck the spade into the ground and was thankful that, despite the spring sun, it was still soft.

"Are you sure?" Lockie asked as he joined in, digging up the grass close by.

No, I am not sure. Perhaps the roots of this now giant tree cover the treasure.

"Yes, I am sure," she replied, "Amy and Sadie, go and keep a look out for Lilith and her friends."

And the girls did as they were ordered and Prim and Lockie continued to dig, not really knowing what they were doing.

But it wasn't Lilith who they only had to fear.

Chapter Fifty-One

Prim's Dad had not stopped thinking about the person, the woman, that Mr Tanner had described.

It had to be Lilith, of course it was her. She had returned.

The Post Office had been busy that morning, all the visitors would come in and buy postcards, stamps, write on them and drop them into the post box and, at the same time, speak to him and Mrs Percy and tell them how lucky they were to live in such a serene place as Little Grisly, that the big city was a bad place and that they would dearly swap working there or living in the ghastly suburbs with the Percy's.

He smiled, he always smiled, but he knew, that his wife was probably, in her mind only, accepting their offer to swap homes. A lot had changed in twenty-four hours.

Perhaps it would have been better if Mr Tanner had kept his stupid mouth shut!

But Prim's Dad knew, deep down, that he should know. It was, after all, his family's secret, their curse. The curse he had not believed, and, at first, laughed at - as if he had some special power or talent to make the dead go away - then worried about as his Dad had told him in no uncertain manner about it all, had taken him to Great Grisly Hall itself and introduced Lord le Grise to a rather shocked, and quickly white faced, twenty-one-year old young man.

How he could he dispute the curse now?

But, if he could not dispute the curse, should he carry on ignoring it as he had done for years?

For a time, he was angry, angry at his forefathers, angry at his father for bringing him up in such a terrible life, owners of a large stately home, but unable to live there due to the increasing number of other residents who refused to go to heaven or hell.

He was angry more over the idea that he had a duty to protect Great Grisly Hall and, one day, destroy its curse, take all the

271

other residents to where they belonged so that life could be happy again after centuries of sorrow.

As a teenager he had hopes of becoming a lawyer, and for a time, his Dad played along with his hopes and dreams, and he had left home for university, met his wife and, just as he thought life would take off, his Dad told him about everything he should have told him when he was eighteen, and despite trying his best to ignore it, not believe it, he simply had to come back to Little Grisly.

Just in case.

He had persuaded his wife, or so he thought, that he did not believe in the curse, and he had persuaded himself that a life working as a Post Office manager was one which was better than working as a lawyer, especially as a human rights lawyer in London.

But like, for most people, the next step after death is uncertain, he too was uncertain about whether the curse was real or not.

He just could not be sure, and this is how he and his family came to be in their position of complete uncertainty, living in limbo.

And, like others who had stopped taking themselves and their children to church on a Sunday morning, he believed the best thing to do would be to make sure, their baby daughter, Primula, would have absolutely nothing to do with neither the curse nor Great Grisly Hall itself.

But now the things his Dad had told him were coming about, the woman, the woman with the dark hair, the one they had feared would one day come back and search again for the Devil's chain had returned. Her look, her smell, that she had told Mr Tanner she had once lived there, and yet she was only about eighteen years old.

His Dad had told him that it was one thing to have the curse on Great Grisly, another to have a spectral Earl and his two dead sons patrol the area at the dead of night when the moon was round, but it would be quite an enormous another when the witch returned.

272

Something had to be done about that.

But what? What could I do? What had Dad told me? There was some clue kept at the Hall and made at the time the witch had last been there. But as if I would go back to that place, it must have fallen down by now.

His mind turned to his little sister Rosemary.

How old must she be now? Late twenties?

He thought about her and wondered if she knew that Lilith had returned, perhaps she was at Great Grisly Hall herself, perhaps she had taken control of all the family mayhem and there was nothing to worry about at all.

Perhaps not.

But what can I do?

I must protect Prim. Thank God she is grounded.

But then something made him doubt everything, made him think that perhaps Prim was involved too, the green grass on her clothes, Mr Tanner telling him he never saw her anymore in the pub carpark.

Like all good parents, he wanted not to just know or think she was upstairs, but to see with his bare eyes that she was.

I am a good parent, aren't I?

And with that, he closed his booth in the Post Office, picked up his keys, and bounded up the stairs leaving his wife to deal with all the customers by herself.

Tick Box number one: Prim is at home and reading her book on post office management.

But, something inside was already telling him that he was not going to tick that box.

273

Chapter Fifty-Two

Prim was absolutely exhausted and, looking down, had very little to show for it. She had barely scuffed the top soil and grass.

Is this the right tree even?

But she knew it was, of course it was.

Lockie was doing no better and this led to Prim wondering if angels ever tired in the same way as the living, but they couldn't really, could they?

As he continued his digging, and Prim thought he was humming a little song to himself, she stopped and looked up at the tree and closed her eyes and tried to think of all the paintings she had unravelled with Rose only yesterday.

For Rose's sake, come on Prim, think.

And slowly she went through all the paintings of this place, painted at the time of Harry and Angharad and Lilith.

Harder Prim.

And she looked for where the "shining" or glimmering had been and, at first, it dotted all around in her mind, as if it was poking fun at her and she had to open her eyes quickly as the lights were becoming too much for her mind to take.

And she thought back to when she had realised it all, realised that it was here.

No, not just under the tree but underneath the very branch that hanged the witch and poor Angharad.

Of course, Lilith had been hanged directly over the very thing she had been looking for.

They had been digging in the wrong place and she took her spade and skipped over to the spot directly under where, in her dream at least, the hangings had taken place.

This must be the place, surely all my forefathers must have dreamt the same as me and could have realised this.

Perhaps they didn't, as they didn't have to face the witch herself.

And she dug the spade into the grass and forgot her dream and the fact that centuries ago the feet of Angharad and Lilith had swayed only above where she now stood.

Lockie stopped digging in the first spot and went to join her.

Amy and Sadie looked and saw Prim digging hard and realised she was onto something and came over to watch.

Only a few seconds later and Prim's spade hit something hard.

Chapter Fifty-Three

"Quick Lockie," screamed Sadie, a little too loudly, "dig right by Prim."

"I'm just about to," he replied defensively, "give me a chance."

And he began to dig too and soon his spade was hitting a solid object too.

"It's definitely wooden," he advised as if he really knew.

"It must be a box and in it will be the chain, well done Prim," said Amy smiling.

"It might be another sort of box, maybe a box containing a dead body," advised Sadie.

Prim knew that she could be right.

"No, it can't be," said Lockie as he moved his spade around the deep object, "it's not big enough."

Prim and Lockie dug up the top soil from over the box and, finally, stuck both spades under it and wedged it up with all their strength.

"We've got it," cried Amy happily.

She had to be right, for a first glance at the dirty, soil covered box, about the size of a large shoe box, showed an emblem. Prim wiped the dirt from around it which revealed a knight's helmet and a horn over a shield and Prim knew it belonged to the le Grise family. There was also some writing, it looked likely to be in French, but Prim's knowledge was limited.

This must be it.

"There is a dead body somewhere around here," Sadie said, but no-one was really listening. Here was a wooden box with the crest of the le Grise family on it and everyone wanted to know what was inside.

Prim knelt on the floor, she didn't care about grass stains on her jeans today, this was far more important, and she slowly lifted the lid. It looked like there had once been a lock, but it had long since perished in the soil around it.

Inside was nothing but a red velvet bag and, finding the end, she lifted it up and out and placed it on the ground. It was heavy.

"I bet that hasn't seen the light of day for a long time," said Amy.

No-one challenged her for saying the absolute obvious.

"Come on Prim, open it," urged Lockie.

The top end was tied together with a thick, red rope which she undid, and she opened the bag apart.

It was there.

The chain, the golden chain.

And it gleamed, like in the paintings.

"For all these years, it was here, and no-one had found it apart from you Prim." Lockie stated.

"No-one needed to find it," replied Sadie.

"Pick it up Prim, come on," Lockie demanded.

But she didn't really want to do that, this was an evil thing, and she was close enough to it already thank you very much. Instead, she thought about the last person who had worn it, and what had happened to him. She didn't want to be a Queen or a leader of the country or the world, true, she could do with a few things, but she certainly did not need nor want a chain, made by the Devil, to help her achieve that.

And that very thought terrified her. Imagine putting it on and the Devil, himself, appeared, asking her to enter a deal with him.

Besides which, it looked was heavy and thick.

No, that was not going to happen, it didn't need to happen, and Prim did not want it to happen. Already though, she was feeling the power and lure of the chain, this object was enticing her to put it on, or was this just in her mind?

Destroy it Prim, like you have been told.

But how? Finding it was easy compared to thinking how to destroy it.

"No, I won't pick it up, we need to get rid of it."

And she stood up as if to take immediate action.

"Where?" asked Sadie.

"How?" asked Lockie.

"The water mill," said clever Amy, "if we could get it working we might crush the chain on the millstone."

"Come on then," ordered Prim, thinking this was all too easy, "let's get this done and rescue Rose."

But it did sound too easy, much too easy. The stillness in the wind meant that they did not realise they had company until the last moment, their excitement and concentration on wanting to see what was in the box had stopped them hearing or even sniffing that the aroma of lavender, the stench of rotten, dead flowers and whatever had stained Barnaby Grudge's green army uniform in battle.

Chapter Fifty-Four

It was he who ran and dived into the middle of them and took the precious chain, and its velvet bag and gave it to Lilith who stood with Lady Elizabeth by her side, without even a chance of a fight from Prim and the others who, at first, were in shock.

And they screamed.

Lilith's eyes gleamed with excitement. Barnaby stood in front of her just in case any of the four tried to steal it off her.

Prim heart sank, this was how she thought the day would end, but, in all hope, wished that it would not. Now the reality, the inevitability, was here she felt faint and sick and all her energy was zapped from her bones. It had been all too easy for Lilith to take the chain from them.

She felt that the first thing Lilith would do would be to destroy her and the rest of the Percy family.

However, Lilith turned to Amy, Sadie and Lockie.

"Well, what a lovely sunny morning to see my stupid brother and God-awful sisters after all these years. You have all grown a little but, I am glad to see, you never grew up to adulthood. All died of a plague I heard, and on the same day too."

They, my friends, have her as a sister?

"And so lovely of you not to come and visit me down in hell and then, to make matters worse, I can see that you came back to help this piddling, pathetic family protect something which isn't even theirs."

There was still silence from the four of them, Prim eyed the velvet bag, thinking of a chance to take whilst Lilith carried on talking. The others took their telling off from their long lost and older sister like they would have done hundreds of years ago.

Lilith carried on, "I can see you are all strong shades, able to use objects like a second spade to dig. Good on you. But you will see here that Private Barnaby Grudge and the Lady Elizabeth are also still strong too. So, don't try anything. You hear?"

Lilith turned her anger and excitement upon Prim.

"They might be strong, but there were eight weak souls last night that disappeared. But I suppose you know all about that don't you Primula."

Prim did a face as if she knew nothing about what she was going on about.

"Do not lie to me, I have your Aunt back at Great Grisly Hall and will do what I want with her. For a moment I thought it was her who had taken the others upstairs, but she is weak and, it seems you are not. I wonder what your Dad would say if he found out what you were up to?"

This wasn't the first time there was too much to take in for Prim, her poor Aunt and now her Dad. But if ever there was an excuse to tell her Dad what was going on, this was it. If only he could do something against these three.

"And you are such a clever girl, just like we discussed when we first met only a few days ago. Unlike stupid Rose, she is pathetic, we grilled her and realised she really didn't know, she couldn't even work it out. Now she is no good for anything. But you are, you could work it out, and so when you left home this morning, Barnaby followed you. You, my clever girl, led us here to the chain."

"It's not yours to have," yelled Prim, finding strength after hearing that her Aunt had been tortured.

"And neither is it yours," Lilith shouted back to her, "take her and tie her to the tree Barnaby then wait here on guard. I am sure you are used to that from your old days, make sure these three little tykes do not try and release her. Come, Lady Elizabeth, it is time to try the chain for the first time and bring you back."

Barnaby grabbed Prim as she was still listening with alarm to what Lilith had to say. Again, she screamed but she was still too weak to stop his arms lift her up and carry her to the tree.

Lady Elizabeth walked in front of the three to stop them from thinking about an immediate rescue attempt. Lilith placed her hand into a pocket and pulled out keys, Rose's keys.

"Look at the present Auntie Rosemary gave me Prim. Access to your whole family."

"Why don't you try and bring yourself back first?" Sadie shouted.

"Ha," joked Lilith, "you haven't forgotten where I still lie have you. Underneath the very tree where I was died, and next to the very thing I sought in my own lifetime. That was a very neat little trick by that Lord le Grise."

"You're afraid," said Lockie, "afraid it might not work so are using her as a guinea pig."

"Oh, you are such wonderful friends to dear Primula aren't you. Trying to side the Lady Elizabeth away from me. I do not really need to come alive again, my work is done on behalf of he who commands below the earth, he who soon will command upon the earth too."

But she did now look like she was thinking about becoming alive again.

"It will never happen, just like it didn't years ago," said sensible Amy.

"Yes, it will my little brother and sisters, and when I get back, I am going to get my first bit of revenge on the pitiful family who had me killed."

Lilith pointed to Prim who was now well tied up by Barnaby to the tree.

"Yes, Prim, I am going to hang you from the same branch as I was hanged from."

And with that, Barnaby Grudge laughed loudly.

Chapter Fifty-Five

Despite having a death sentence upon her, Prim was able to think clearly once Lilith and Lady Elizabeth had left. It was the others who had gone berserk at the news and who were running around lividly as Barnaby, angry for a different reason, pushed them away.

"Clear off," he cried, "she, Miss Lily will turn you into living children again and kill you, sending you to hell forever."

We have at least half an hour before they come back and then what? Lady Elizabeth will just be human again. What can we do in the meantime?

Before they hang me.

And the dream of Angharad came back to her and she felt a growing pain in her throat.

Come on Prim, you are not done yet.

Rose.

Rose must be on her own. How could Barnaby guard both of us?

How could Lilith be so stupid? Or was it that Rose was in such a bad way?

Poor, poor Rose. I've got to find out how she is.

Barnaby was busy fending off Sadie and Lockie, Amy, on the other hand, was trembling all by herself.

"Amy," Prim whispered, "come here."

Watching Barnaby carefully, she quietly walked over to Prim.

"Oh, Prim, I am so sorry, she is no sister of mine really. How could she do such things to your aunt?"

"Find Rose Amy, find out how she is, we need to know."

"Oi!" shouted Barnaby, "stay away from her or else."

"Or else what?" Amy said raising her chin in defiance, "will you kill us?"

And with that she winked and walked off in the direction of Great Grisly Hall.

"There's no point going to look for that stupid aunt of hers," shouted Barnaby, "she's in a right state, no good to help anyone."

"How do you know soldier," said Sadie defiantly, "you were outside Prim's house, hiding like a wimp."

Barnaby couldn't argue with that and it made Prim smile.

She saw Sadie and Lockie follow Amy back to the Hall but then Sadie took a different course, as if she was heading back to Little Grisly.

Don't follow the witch and Lady Elizabeth too closely.

"You all think you are clever, don't you, cleverer than me." Barnaby said to Prim, "you've all done nothing like I have done, but I tell you what Miss Percy, something you haven't done which we have, and that is die. Would you like me to tell you what happens when you die?"

Prim did not want to know but realised that he was not going to let that stop him.

The shadow of the tree was already making her feel cold.

As he began to talk to her about the Great War, she remembered something what Lilith had said.

"There were eight weak souls."

She also remembered that Amy had said the same,

But in her dream there had only been seven.

One of the long-term residents was still here.

Chapter Fifty-Six

Prim's Dad had skirted through the Swinging Witch car park as quietly and as quickly as possible to avoid bumping into his friend, Mr Tanner, who would have wondered what on earth he was up to, walking down towards the path and the stream.

He was now walking down a path he had not been along for some time and, although he walked fast (running was out of the question after years of inactivity) he was able to remember certain things such as trees and the hedgerow as he went along. Sensible shoes were another thought, especially as he wasn't wearing sensible shoes. In fact, he was quite happy to think about such things as shoes and the path to stop thinking about what he was going to do. But, he could not.

Prim has been coming here for days. She must have.

If that is the case, then what is different about today. She still comes back for her tea.

But what about Lilith. That is what is different about today.

And he wished he was fitter, so he could run, wished he was strong, so he could throw the witch back down the deepest hole which would hopefully reach hell.

There was no checklist of things to do today apart from find his daughter. And then sort out the witch.

Two things to do, and finding Prim is my number one priority.

I wish I had put on some sensible shoes.

He could feel his phone, deep in his back trouser pocket, vibrate. It had to be his wife, it could only be as she was the only person who had his number.

Sorry darling, but I'm not going to answer. I'll explain later.

If there is a later.

How many years had it been since he had come this way to visit Great Grisly Hall? True he had driven not too far away from it when he took Prim to school in Longborough, but he hadn't purposively headed anywhere near it for well over a decade, certainly before Prim had been born. Over the years how he hoped it would just become such a ruin that no upstanding ghost would ever want to live there, perhaps the curse would run its course and everything would be back to normal again.

The curse of being part of a, no being the head of an important family.

The curse of not doing anything about it for years.

And now the problems he had tried to forget, but really could not and had been simmering in his head, had stirred. No, they were bubbling up fast.

He heard birdsong and looking up he saw not the singer of such a delightful tune, but a large crow resting on a branch of a still empty tree. And, in the sky, he saw dark clouds rolling over the Hall itself.

The crow began its harsh caw and suddenly he realised that he could hear people coming from the other direction.

Voices, talking, and not so far away.

He had to hide. Somewhere. But where?

To his left was the hedgerow and to his right the stream.

He could hear them now, make out their voices, it was two women.

They were getting closer.

He decided to head back quickly and try not to make a sound.

What about that old oak I passed before?

And Prim's Dad legged it back, conscious that his running would make a noise but hoping, beyond hope, that they would not hear it above their conversation.

If only I was fitter.

If only I had sensible shoes on.

He found the tree and it was a good size to hide behind. His breathing, his heavy breathing was the problem now. He was so unfit. He had to calm down and so began to breathe deeply and, at the same time, wipe the sweat pouring freely from his brow.

What age was I the last time I was chased and had to hide? Fourteen years old?

As their voices got closer he knelt on all fours, able to move around the tree as they passed it. From here he could well see who they were.

And all his suspicions, were right.

The woman dressed in black, with the jet-black hair and white face, that was the description Mr Tanner had given him, it was also the description that had been handed down from generations of Percys.

It must be the witch.

And the other one, she was fainter.

It must be one of those rotten residents.

And it had to be, one of the only ones he could remember from his Dad's stories, the really evil one.

Lady Elizabeth Riche.

He held his breath for what seemed an age and they passed without seeing him, too busy in conversation, and all he could hear was something along the lines of "outside the church walls, but you must be inside it," and, "do you think I should too," but he could not tell who had said that and what it meant but, to emphasise their destination, the church bell rang four times to signal the time.

They disappeared around the corner, and he exhaled gratefully.

What on earth am I going to do?

And he nodded his head from left to right, deep in thought.

He needed help.

And he got it.

He suddenly realised someone was behind him.

Was it the witch, returning?

He turned and saw a young girl with fluffy blonde hair, and instantly he had the most amazing flashback to when he was a child and he had three friends who he used to play with but, with age, could not remember if they were real or imagined.

"Do you remember me Peter?" Sadie said smiling.

Chapter Fifty-Seven

Harry looked down on Rose's peaceful sleeping face. He had to do something, he knew that, but what was right?

Poor Rose.

Harry often thought that Rose was like a big sister to him. Seeing her tied up, seeing her being tortured, in her own room at the top of the house, was too much for him. Lilith had lit a torch and told Rose that she wanted her to feel what hell was like, that she would burn her and the damned house down if she didn't tell what she wanted to know.

Rose's intense shaking, her fear, her sweat, her gaunt eyes staring at the scorching flame had reminded Harry of his own torturous death.

But thankfully Rose lived.

Thankfully she had fainted with just the fear of the fire, before Lilith could, and would, have charred her.

Yes, she had screamed.

She could have screamed Great Grisly Hall down before it could have been burnt down.

But all was now fine, he had checked her arms and there only a reddening on her left arm. The threat of the torture had only lasted a few minutes and most of that was Lilith whispering to Rose, something Harry could not quite hear as he was keen not be felt by Lady Elizabeth or Barnaby Grudge.

He now had to get Rose up and help her get to Prim.

Last night he felt the urge to go upstairs. Surely he had paid his penance? He realised some of the other residents were heading that way and knew it was Prim who was luring them. It was not Rose who held that power in the Percy family, it was all Prim. He was amazed when he realised that all had gone with her and had left Great Grisly Hall forever. He was happy for her and happy for them too.

They had loved staying in their old home just as they done when they lived.

Yet he knew some of them had wanted the move away for an age, sad Lord le Grise had missed his family, especially his daughters, but it was only with the re-emergence of Lilith that they knew they must finally take the decision and leave their old home.

That and having Prim guide them to the gates. Rose could not have done that. But Prim, only eleven years old had helped remove some of the most stubborn residents, quickly.

And why hadn't he gone up?

Why didn't you go with them Harry?

But he could not answer his own question.

Perhaps.

Perhaps he wanted to help his friend, Prim.

Perhaps, she would need him.

He had known what Lilith would do when she found out that the others had gone upstairs, and he was correct. She had hit the roof, she had screamed louder than Rose had, she was livid and never had he seen someone so angry as her.

All night she and her two sidekicks had searched for Lord le Grise, it was he they really wanted. He would surely know or have some clue as to where the chain was kept. Lady Elizabeth had searched the crypt, but there was no sign of him.

Of course not, he was no longer a resident in this world.

Sensibly Harry decided to keep out of the way of the three of them but through hearing their conversation, realised they had thought he had gone up too.

And that could be a weapon against her and to help Prim.

That morning he had come over to the path that led to Little Grisly and had told Rose what had happened. She realised straight away that it had been Prim too and was pleased. Harry tried to stop Rose from coming anywhere near the Hall, that it was unwise to do so, but Rose needed to. She needed to look at the paintings again, something had stirred her mind as to where the chain might be.

She had also told him to hide, so no-one would know where he was. He had accepted this order and left Rose as she continued to the Hall but, secretly, he had followed her.

She did not make it that far, they had captured her easily in the garden and taken her to her room at the top of the Hall. Then Barnaby was told to go into Little Grisly.

When he had come back from spying on Prim he had told Lilith and her Ladyship where she was heading. For Lilith the picture of where the chain lay had been painted.

Harry hoped they were wrong.

But now, whilst away, he had to get Rose out of Great Grisly Hall.

Where to, he did not know, but anywhere was safer than there.

How softly she sleeps.

Harry knew, however, that he had to wake her up.

And somehow get her out through a locked door.

Chapter Fifty-Eight

Barnaby Grudge had seemingly forgotten to tell Prim what it was like to die. Instead he sat down on the other side of the tree to take a quick rest in front of the ever-warming sun. After all ghosts needed to relax too, he could not imagine being awake all the time.

Meanwhile Prim wondered how long she had been left, waiting.

Waiting for her death.

How long would it take Lilith and Lady Elizabeth to walk to the church in Little Grisly, perform whatever they had to and return? Surely it would take more than the half an hour they mentioned?

Rather than thinking about anything else but the fact that she was going to be hanged, Prim thought about it carefully. They had no rope, no ladders, so what were they going to do?

They might be bluffing.

I need to know about Rose, I need to know what they have done to her. Then, I need to tell my Dad.

"Different to me all this," said Barnaby, mysteriously, his eyes still closed.

"What do you mean?"

"I died in a war, the great war. Every day we would wonder whether it would be our last, whether we had an hour, half a day before we went over the top or were gassed or something. You never got used to it, but you learnt to live with it. And, when it happened, it was quick, I don't think I even felt a thing, though it was a century ago. Different for you."

"What on earth do you mean?" Prim asked but immediately regretted. She did not want to hear anything which this cruel man had to say.

"You'll be hanged, high by the neck and you know you are, the longer it takes for Miss Lilith and the Lady Elizabeth to come back the longer you must worry about it, you know, death."

"That's a nice thing to say to someone, isn't," Prim replied sarcastically and in a rather furious manner but what he had said, hit home.

"I'm not a nice person, I've already tried to kill you. Now you'll be hanged today just like a murderer."

"Except I'm not a murderer, am I?"

"But you are one of them, the Percys', rich and all that. That's enough for me."

"Do I look like someone rich? You saw where I live. I'm probably more like you and your family than the Percys of old."

Barnaby Grudge took exception to this statement.

"You don't know what you are talking about. Have you ever had it so bad? Scrimping and searching for food? Having to go and fight a war? You Percys."

"Can I be blamed for my family? You should only be blamed for what you do in life or applauded. What did you do Mr Grudge?"

"Shut it I say, I order you. Yes, your family is no longer what it was, and I say good, simple greed led to the downfall of the Percys. Who is going to applaud that?"

"That happened a long, long time ago, how can you blame me?"

Barnaby did not have a ready response to this. Prim realised she was getting to him. "Is Lilith's ambition to find the chain not about greed? Perhaps, Mr Grudge, you should also be thinking of going one way or the other, preferably, in my mind, up the stairs."

"Ha, I don't think so. Upstairs." And he laughed, nervously.

"Would you sooner go to hell? What could possibly be nice about that?"

"I have a purpose now," he boasted, "I almost said I had a purpose in life." But the chuckles were not loud or convincing.

"You may think you have a purpose but do you? Why didn't Lilith take you with her. Not to protect me but because she can't do anything with you. You can't be made human again, your body was never found. You may still be strong, but your shade is fading, your strength will not last forever."

"You're talking rubbish."

"Am I? Wait until she has started her army of the undead, and then where will you be?"

This did make Barnaby think, Lilith had promised to make him a General, but could a private in the army really be promoted so high and so quickly?

But Prim attentions were turned, she noticed something in the distance and had to double take. It was Sadie, and she was with someone.

I don't believe it, she's bringing my Dad.

And she smiled.

Chapter Fifty-Nine

By the time Harry had woken up Rose, Amy and Lockie had arrived too and thankfully they still had their set of keys to open her room.

Rose may have been awake, but she was in no fit state to do anything. She was short of breath, looked extremely tired and Harry did not know what to do.

Neither did Amy or Lockie to be honest but first things first, they had to introduce themselves to Harry who got a bit of a shock when he saw them enter the room.

"What, who are you?" he stammered in a loud way.

"We are Prim's friends, and Rose's too," said Amy quickly. She wanted Harry to understand straight away that they were not the enemy.

"But you are not alive, you are like me. Where have you come from and why are you here?"

"We are, we were from Little Grisly Master Harry, we remember you from all those years ago and over the years have seen you since."

"What nonsense, why would I not have seen you?" Harry cried searching for an answer as to what and how these two came to be here at Great Grisly Hall.

"I don't remember you from Little Grisly," announced Lockie, but he had only been a little toddler when his eldest sister had caused all the mayhem.

Amy shushed Lockie up, she didn't need his "help" when she was already trying to explain things.

"It is true, we lived in Little Grisly when Lilith," and she paused to make sure she was getting through to Harry, "our detested sister tried to find the chain and blamed Angharad too."

"She's your sister? Are you?" And Harry backed off from them.

"No Harry, not at all. Ask Rose, we are your friends. We were only young, or younger, then. When we died, we did not become just ghosts, we became helpers to the Percy family."

"Helpers?" questioned Harry, "heavenly helpers?"

Amy did not answer the question directly, "we can hide ourselves from ordinary, begging your pardon, ghosts, that is why we can be so helpful. We have been back down in Great Grisly Hall this time for over a week playing with Prim. We, err, helped Prim get into this room when she was being chased by Lady Elizabeth. You should remember that as you were hiding in this room already."

"Yeah, and we saw you looking at her in the hall, wanting to play, perhaps wanting to be her friend." Lockie suggested in quite an angry and ill-timed manner. It was clear he still had an issue with Harry over Angharad.

"Enough Lockie," pleaded Amy, "this is not the time," but it was obvious, by the way her cheeks could still go red, that she, herself, had a soft spot for Harry. "We are all singing from the same hymn sheet Master Harry, and we need to help not just Rose but Prim. Lilith and her gang have caught her and have plans to have her hanged, like Angharad, and from the old hanging tree."

Now this was enough to summon up Harry's real anger.

And his fear.

Despite his reservations about these two, he realised in the short space of time that he needed them on his side and that rescuing Prim was of paramount importance.

"We can't leave Rose here," he said.

"Yes, I agree, she must come with us," Amy replied.

Harry stared at Amy and Lockie and thought. He had received the blame for helping Prim by opening the door when she was being chased by the headless Lady Elizabeth and he could not fathom how it had opened. Now the answer was in front of him and he no longer had any reservations about the pair of them and he smiled.

Rose grunted, and it sounded like she agreed with everything said.

From across the fields, the bells of Little Grisly Church were ringing for 5pm.

Chapter Sixty

The sight of his daughter tied up to a tree, and not just any tree, angered Prim's Dad. It certainly made him forget he was wearing the wrong sort of shoes for this sort of trip.

It had also made him stop thinking about his childhood, how, in his mind, he had imagined three friends called Amy, Sadie and Lockie and how he had played with them in the fields around Little Grisly and in the garden at Great Grisly Hall.

Then he had only ventured once into the Hall itself and vowed that he never would again, for he had felt not just one, but many an unseen presence, around him. The portraits of old family members were most unsettling, and he believed that some of them were watching him as he walked past. He fled the Hall, out and back into the warmth of the sun and away from the cold of the dead and their shadows.

Those were the days when he hadn't yet been told about the residents, nor the curse, nor the fact that he was related to them all.

And upon his decision to not want to go back to the Hall the less he saw of his three friends until eventually they petered out of his mind.

Until now. And, of course, he had needed Sadie to explain what and who she and the others were and, of course, it had taken him more than a few seconds to realise and take on board that they were not figments of his imagination but real.

Walking onto the field he could see his daughter talking to a soldier and Sadie had explained to him who he was.

Prim's Dad felt like punching him, grappling him to the floor and giving him his mind for tying up his Prim.

Can I really punch a ghost?

I've never asked myself that question before.

He needed Sadie to guide him towards the tree without Barnaby realising what was going on.

Thankfully Prim could see what they were, obviously, trying to do and continued her conversation with Barnaby in a way that kept his gaze away from the oncoming rescuers. Sadie took Prim's Dad along the top of the field, close to the hedge and then downwards, directly to towards the tree, but with the cover of other, smaller trees, to hide him if necessary.

Slowly, they walked up to the hanging tree and all Prim's Dad could think about was what he should do when he got there.

Punch him for a start.

If I can punch him.

What if my arm goes right through him and it chops my arm off?

What am I going to do?

And he started to sweat a bit more at this thought.

I wish I had listened to my Dad a lot more when he told me about this place.

But his rage at Barnaby did not cease and soon they were close to the hanging tree and that was when, despite the fact they had been as quiet as they could possibly be, Barnaby turned around, as if stirred by his own sixth sense.

"Good God," roared Barnaby, "who the hell are you?"

But Prim's Dad did not respond.

He walked straight up to Barnaby.

And punched him hard in the face.

Barnaby went down like a sack of spuds.

So, you can punch ghosts!

And with that Prim's Dad controlled himself and ran to the tree and began to undo the rope that chained Prim to it.

"I don't think any living person has ever punched a ghost before," Sadie laughed as Prim and her Dad put their arms around each other.

For Prim this felt like it was the first time her Dad ever shown such love to her. But she was grateful. Grateful to see him, grateful to be rescued and grateful for him to be on her side. She didn't need to say anything to him, for it appeared in his face and eyes that he was happy and content just to be with her.

"You won't get away with this," shouted Barnaby as he began to lift himself up.

Prim looked at Barnaby and wondered whether he would attack her or her Dad. But, in truth, Barnaby looked well beaten. It was just talk now. He might be fine trying to push children down stairs but against another adult, he had no chance.

If only we could tie him up.

But you just cannot tie a ghost up, you can surprise one and hit them, but tying them up will just lead the ghost to drift away.

"Come on Dad, we need to find your sister," she whispered.

Her Dad's eyes enlarged as his suspicion that Rose was about was confirmed. He wanted to say something to Prim, something about everything, the whole situation they were now in, and why he had stopped them from doing anything about Great Grisly Hall.

Prim sensed this. "Don't worry Dad, now come on."

"The witch has gone into Little Grisly," Dad replied.

"I know, and she already has the chain."

The cheeks of her Dad's face drained at this news. Obviously, Sadie decided not to update her Dad fully.

"But we can still defeat her," Prim continued, "but we need our family to do it."

And they left for Great Grisly Hall.

A few moments later, a still shocked Barnaby Grudge left towards Little Grisly.

Chapter Sixty-One

Prim felt a lot better after being untied. She was now free and much more in command of her future. Whether that was in the short, medium or long term now depended more on her and not Lilith.

Better still she had her Dad, she was on the way to meeting up with Rose and Amy and Lockie and, if he wasn't hiding, Harry.

I'm with my Dad, my very own Dad.

Despite her best intentions, she made up a list of things that needed to be done, just like her Dad would. The first was to make sure her Aunt was fine, the second was to regroup and think about what they could do to stop Lilith.

And the third, the hardest of all, was to physically stop Lilith.

But at least she had a team to help her.

She looked up at her Dad, his face was energised by what was going on and she thought whether he was making a list of things to do too.

But he wasn't. He was back thinking about his childhood, trying to work out in his head about Sadie and the others. They had tried to get him to come back to Great Grisly Hall, telling him that it wasn't a bad place and was, in fact, a fantastic place to play games like hide and seek. As a parent he had begun to think about them again, they had never seemed real like the other children he used to play with in Little Grisly.

When there were other little children who lived in Little Grisly. Prim is the only child who lived in Little Grisly now.

And he guessed that they had enticed Prim to the Hall too.

He realised that they were not real or imagined, but guardians, they were there to protect him and now Prim. He was saddened that he had abandoned them as a child, ignored them and ignored his duty as a Percy to oversee Great Grisly Hall. After all, the Hall was his, somewhere there was the ancient deed that confirmed that he, or the family, owned it.

But at least he was here now, involved. What could he have done about this before? Would it have made a difference? He doubted it but was glad to be with his daughter and away from the Post Office.

This made him think of his wife, the Post Office would now be closed and so he checked his phone and found that he had eleven messages all from her.

She wasn't happy.

And she knew Prim wasn't in the flat too.

As they made the final journey up onto the meadows that stretched between the hanging tree and Great Grisly Hall, he began to text her, then stopped and decided to call her instead.

She knew where he was, had already guessed that Prim was there too. Without going into any detail at all, especially about how he found their daughter, he explained that Prim was fine and that they were just going to the Hall to check it out before coming back. He apologised, more than once, probably about thirty times, and despite his wife seemingly accepting his apology and explanation, knew that she did not believe him, she knew that it was unlikely he would be back for his tea even if it was microwavable chicken tikka masala.

But he had made the call, and although a further explanation would be needed later, he had ticked that box, and now he could now focus on what they were going to do next.

And there, as he caught sight of Great Grisly Hall, for the first time proper in years, coming down the garden, was his sister.

Chapter Sixty-Two

"Why do you always smell of lavender whilst I smell of dying flowers," Lilith asked Lady Elizabeth as she came out of the churchyard and back onto the road. But it wasn't a real question and Lilith was proud to see that Lady Elizabeth was now a breathing human again.

So, the chain does work.

"And your neck, I can see the line from the axeman but everything seems to be fine."

And she thought more about using it on herself.

A small bus drove passed them, and the passengers had all looked at the two strange looking ladies, one in period costume and the other all in black except for a large gold chain around her shoulders and probably wondered whether there was an amateur play being held, some lavish party in the village or whether Lilith was the Mayor of Little Grisly, as if such a post existed.

"Move out of the road, quick, you don't want to be killed this easily."

Lady Elizabeth did as she was told but still did not respond.

Lilith took one of her hands and placed it to the side of Lady Elizabeth's neck, and felt the beating of blood.

"Congratulations, your ladyship, as we can both see, the chain works perfectly after all these years in the dirt."

"Yes," was the only reply from her Ladyship.

She looked glum and stared straight ahead into the distance. Lilith realised that all the talk she had heard was correct about the chain, yes it had the power to raise the dead back to life, and yes, it also made the newly living obey her, but she did worry about whether the newly living would lose all their intelligence and knowledge.

She continued to look into her ladyship's eyes and wondered whether all the scheming would still be there.

"What are we to do now, your ladyship?"

"Kill the girl, kill her aunt."

"Are you quite happy to do that?"

Lady Elizabeth smiled and began to laugh a little.

And with that, Lilith knew that Lady Elizabeth was still the clever so and so she had always been.

But before she could herself smile at this news, Barnaby Grudge ran up to the pair of them, his face the absolute opposite of her ladyship.

If only he had intelligence.

"Why aren't you guarding the girl?"

"She has escaped, mam, with the help of her Dad. They're all going to the Hall now."

He was expecting Lilith to shout at him, to tell him off good and proper, and despite hating authority figures, despite having shot one dead, he was very much scared of her.

But she wasn't angry at all. In fact, she smiled.

She looked back at Little Grisly and noticed the church clock. It would soon be six.

"Then it is time for a show down, isn't it Barnaby Grudge," and she smartened his collar.

"And, for a show down, we will need a little army to help us and I think I know where to get one too."

"Yes, ma'am." Barnaby saluted, not quite sure about what she meant.

After only a few instructions, Lady Elizabeth and Barnaby walked off, back towards the churchyard.

Chapter Sixty-Three

It would be safe to say that Prim's Dad did not really show his emotions to many, if anyone at all on an ordinary day but today wasn't an ordinary day and the only thing he could do when he saw his sister for the first time in years was blub like a baby.

And obviously put his arms around her.

And she put her arms around him.

Prim then put her arms around both.

Amy, Sadie, Lockie and Harry just watched.

Prim was also very happy to see Harry and she felt like putting her arms around him too, but she then decided that was probably not the best thing to do right at this moment. Still she was glad to see her friend and he smiled back at her too.

Of course, she was happy to see that Rose looked well, she had worried about what had happened to her, but Rose brushed off any concerns.

"Enough," said Rose in a matter of fact sort of way. "We can carry this on later, we must discuss what we do next, now that Lilith has the chain."

Prim's Dad nodded, and they all went inside the Hall and sat around the long table where the residents used to meet up and decide how best to do things.

The place seemed empty without them.

"Very simply," said Prim, "we need to get that chain off Lilith."

"But how? Barnaby will have joined her by now, so that will be three adults against us," Rose replied.

"There's seven of us," Lockie interrupted in case Rose thought that children could not scrap it out with adults.

Prim's Dad had now not only been reconnected with his sister but also his other two childhood playmates and was intrigued.

"Do you three have any special anything that could give us an advantage?"

"We can hide ourselves from others, and lift, push and pull physical things and people like ghosts can but nothing else no, we merely help and guide," confirmed Amy.

"And what else can that chain do apart from bring the dead back to life," he continued.

"Nothing else, apart from those brought back to life will obey your every command." Rose replied.

"So, on that basis," and it was clear that Prim's Dad was taking control over the situation, something Prim liked, "Do you know I do not think it will be that hard to take it off her. Especially with you children."

And although he called them children, he clearly realised that they were hundreds of years old.

"Although we call her a witch, I think it is safe to say she doesn't actually have any magical powers," Prim's Dad continued.

"Well she can't ride on a broom stick, if that is what you mean," piped in Sadie.

"Good, then here's a plan, it's not a great plan and we will have to be quick as I guess she is on her way here right now. She sees us three in the Hall, and then one of the children sneaks up behind and steals the chain off her."

It really wasn't a great plan, it was dreadful actually, but at least it was devastatingly simple.

"She will know about Amy, Sadie and Lockie, so might think we are up to something if she cannot see them," advised Rose.

"But she doesn't know about Harry," said Prim happily. "She thinks he has gone upstairs and won't expect him to be here.

The six of us can face the three of them and Harry could try and steal it off her, we could also rush the three of them and cause havoc."

They all looked around at each other and agreed. All except Harry who stood shaking and staring away from the rest of them and out of a window towards the direction of Little Grisly.

"Are you with us Harry?" Rose asked.

"I don't know," he whispered back. He looked scared.

"Harry are you okay?" Prim asked, and she stood up and quickly went over to see if he was alright although she knew straight away that he was not.

"I don't know," and his shade kept on fading and then coming back again, "I feel like I am being called, I feel like I am being drawn to somewhere, somewhere I do not want to go to."

Prim grabbed his hand to somehow stop his shade from fading, their eyes met for a second but before anything could be said, he disappeared.

Prim was concerned and upset, she had always wanted to be his friend. But where had be gone, what was drawing him to where? Perhaps, he missed all the other residents now that they had gone. Perhaps all this was too much. Something was not right.

"I hope he comes back," said a shocked Sadie.

Prim did not respond but agreed, she knew he would not have disappeared because he was scared. Something had definitely happened to him.

"Well what now?" Prim's Dad said, "that element of surprise is truly gone."

"It's the three of us she will want," replied Prim thinking, "we represent the family that killed her, before she does anything else, she wants her vengeance on us. Hopefully this will side track her mind, then one of Amy, Sadie and Lockie can try take it off her."

No-one stood up and applauded this new plan.

But it was a plan, the only plan and they had to succeed.

No-one thought of what would happen if it didn't.

"When we get the chain off her, whoever does it, needs to run to the church and wait there. She will not be able to enter the church and that will give us some breathing space." Prim's Dad ordered.

"No," said Prim, "I imagine now that Lady Elizabeth is just as alive as us, and she can enter the church too. The best thing to do will be to destroy the chain."

"How?" asked her Dad.

"In the mill, by the stream. I have seen the millstone and that could easily break it up." She didn't tell anyone that she had only seen it in a dream.

"That's good thinking Prim," said Rose and she could see her brother agreeing.

"Okay," he said, "for now, let's set up a watch system so we can know early when they are coming."

And Amy, Sadie and Lockie all went out to watch for Lilith and her cronies.

The members of the Percy family sat around the table and waited.

Waiting was the worst thing of all before a battle.

It was just after 7pm when Amy, Sadie and Lockie came back into the Hall with news.

"Well, this is it," said Prim's Dad, clearing his throat and trying not to show that he was scared, "to our stations everyone and good luck."

"You better come outside and have a look," said Amy, "all of you should."

And Prim, her Dad and Rose walked out of the back door to the Hall.

There in front of them, standing in the garden, was not only Lilith, Lady Elizabeth and Barnaby Grudge but also ten others, all from the Percy family crypt, who clearly had been made living again. They all stared in the direction of the door, awaiting orders from Lilith.

Prim looked at the ten, initially she did not recognise any of them.

But then she did.

Two of them.

Standing, almost bent, behind Barnaby, was the 14th Lord le Grise.

And behind him was Harry.

Both very much alive and now under the control of the witch.

Chapter Sixty-Four

"I thought I might bring some of your family back for a party," laughed Lilith, "and they are here!"

Prim was gob struck.

She's raised Harry back to being alive?

And she wanted to cry a great deal. She wanted to call out his name.

"I've brought back to life some of the strongest and cleverest of your ancient clan, oh and Harry and the aged Lord le Grise too. I've brought back Harry Prim just to upset you, I can see you are trying to hold all yours tears in my dear. Of course, he deserves it for not keeping to his side of our agreement all those years ago. And I brought back Lord le Grise just to get my own back on him leaving me last night."

And Prim could now see that his Lordship looked even more sorry than the rest and she thought that he must have been mightily upset at leaving his family for this.

"You do not know what you are doing with that chain Lilith," shouted Rose, "you will get in all sorts of trouble, none of it is good for you."

"Ha-ha, I see you have woken up Rosemary, but you really sound as if you are still asleep. I know exactly what I am doing with this chain, thank you very much."

"What do you need them for? Couldn't you just let them rest in peace?" Prim's Dad shouted.

"No," replied Lilith instantly, teasing, "no, I couldn't help myself. I brought back Lady Elizabeth and well, I heard you were all reunited as a happy family, an extended family if you count the three little horror bags I had to call sisters and a brother, and I thought, well, I can have a family too. One that will do exactly what I say. Just like an army."

"But what was the point Lilith?" Rose asked as if she was dealing with someone sensible, "surely the very threat of the chain is enough."

"Have you always been so stupid Rose. I am here on behalf of my master, and he has a little job for me to do. Not only was I to find the chain but also to use it. What's the point of having something nice to wear and never wearing it?" And she stroked the chain gently.

"You'll never win," yelled Prim's Dad but it was a pointless thing to say, clearly Lilith had all the aces, and so she even ignored what he said.

"The point of bringing these dear members of your family back is to do a little job I want doing before I go on my global errand. Do you know what that is?"

Prim knew exactly what that little job was.

"Yes, I am going to hang the three members of the living Percy family, high on the hanging tree that did for me. I think it quite touching to have other members of your family do it, don't you? Oh, and when you are dead, I will bring you back alive and you can work for me."

Lilith was rather enjoying herself now, and was looking into the eyes of Prim, her Dad and Rose to see what their fear looked like. None of her little army did anything save for just staring ahead, awaiting instructions, all of course apart from Barnaby, and he wasn't really smiling as well. Prim wondered whether he resented the fact that Lilith had called them an army. Everyone knew Barnaby hated the army and what he had done to his superior.

But that was a side issue, a side issue to a massive main course of bother, and that was putting it extremely lightly.

Prim stared at Harry, hoping to see a trace of his own self, a sparkle in his eye, a wink to say, "I'm just pretending," but there was nothing.

"And what do you say about that, darlings?" Lilith asked, and waited for an answer, milking it and already thinking of an answer in response to their reply.

But, as if there had been some sort of communication of thought between Prim, her Dad and Rose, they ran.

All three of then ran back inside Great Grisly Hall.

So much for the plan to steal the chain from Prim.

"Prim," yelled her Dad, "get the hell out of here, get help," and he didn't have time to regret the word hell but bounded up the stairs making as much noise as possible.

Prim could hear Lilith roar, "Get them."

"Get yourself back to Little Grisly Prim, get that help. I'm going to divert them." Rose shouted.

"What help? We need to stay together and grab the chain."

"Everything has changed now that she has her little army, think of something, call the police, just go."

And Rose ran out of the front door to Great Grisly Hall and towards the drive where her car was still parked, shrieking and shouting.

Prim knew her aunt was right, and for now it was important to keep on running as fast as possible. Looking at some of the undead army, she knew she could outrun them easily, especially poor old Lord le Grise, except he wasn't poor anymore, in a way it really wasn't him.

But the one she did not want to run into the most was Harry, not just because he could probably run faster than she could but because it was just him. She knew she would try and cause him to react and not be a bad person but also knew that the chances of that were not slim, they were probably at absolute zero.

Rather than follow Rose, and she could hear her car start up, Prim wondered where she could run to, there was no point staying inside the Hall, they could just surround it easily and send in a search party to look for her.

They're going to find Dad first inside here.

But Prim needed to sort out her own survival especially as she heard some of Lilith's army scuffling inside the Hall. There was only two exits, the main door and the back door and both would now be covered by them.

But she was not going to go upstairs.

And she certainly wasn't going to get caught.

Running down a corridor of the Hall she could not remember going down before, she saw a mullioned window half way up the wall. It was too high to reach without some sort of help, but it had a latch type device to open it up.

It was her way out.

But how?

There was frantic footsteps getting closer to the corridor.

Prim spied a wooden chair covered in nothing but seemingly a century of dust and she ran to it and dragged it to under the window, quickly jumping on top of it.

She could just reach the latch, but she would have to lift herself up with her arms to climb out.

The footsteps had stopped as they reached their destination into the corridor.

About ten feet behind Prim.

She jumped to reach the latch.

She missed.

Her heart was beating heavy. She could not be caught so soon. Not again.

She jumped and nudged the latch.

She jumped and with all her might pushed the window open and lifted herself up, wishing all the time that she had chosen to do some active sports at school to make her fit and strong.

She still had not looked behind her but now the undead bearded man dressed in what could only be Victorian attire, had ran towards the window and grabbed her left leg.

He was strong.

But not as strong as a young girl who did not want to get caught again.

With her right leg she kicked out and her foot landed directly in his face causing him to fall back with a cry.

When was the last time he had a nose bleed?

Come on Prim. Move it.

And with that call to arms she lifted herself up onto the window ledge and without thinking or waiting for the man and any others who might come to try and grab her, she jumped.

The ground, another overgrown lawn, was lower than the floor in the Hall, and she fell about eight foot onto it, the long grass easing her fall somewhat, and she landed safely.

Good work Prim.

Now to get the hell out of here.

Looking around she saw a small path and realised, looking in the general direction it went, that it must head back towards the main path and towards Little Grisly. It was a risk, but she ran down it fast, glad that it was still light but wary that it was getting dark too.

This must be the path that joins up with the one I have walked down so many times.

This must lead back to Little Grisly.

But what if it did, and they were there waiting for her, knowing this would be exactly her move?

She wanted to turn back and look, she was getting a stitch, her heart was beating faster, and she was now sweating quite a bit.

There was no way she could hide silently now if she had to.

She had to keep on running. This wasn't some rubbish game in the school playground.

This was real.

And the threat of hanging was real.

She turned around to see whatever there was to see but there was nothing, only the path she had passed and that was that, until she turned around to the front and missed her footing and fell sharply to the right and into a little, shallow hole in the ground surrounded by a bramble bush.

So stupid.

She didn't feel the pain straight away, but knew it was going to come and so grimaced a face of pain as she put her hands onto her twisted right ankle, ready for the agony to arrive.

From her position on the floor she heard, or felt, footsteps running up from another path, the main path and guessed it was not far and that the paths were due to meet.

Prim froze. *God he must be fit to have got to here so quick.*

"This is where the path meets the one leading to the kitchen," she heard Harry say to someone Prim did not know, "stay here whilst I run down it and back to the Hall."

There was no noise from the other one. Prim turned herself into the smallest of balls inside the little hole and behind the bush, thankful that she had found somewhere to hide, but conscious that being found now was the end of everything.

Harry ran right past her. For a second, she thought his left eye had glimpsed her and she wondered whether he was going to attack her from behind, but the footsteps could still be heard going off in the direction of Great Grisly Hall.

She was getting her breath back and, although the pain in her ankle was terrible, as it also was in her right hand, she knew it wasn't a bad fall and that the pain would go away.

Thoughts turned back to planning her escape. There was an undead, that was the only way she could think of describing them, at the junction of the paths.

Could she outrun that one? Probably.

Did she want him or her to see her? No.

Could she stay hiding in this hole for ever? Possibly.

She wondered what her Dad and Aunt were up to.

She wondered how many of them were looking for her.

She needed to get back to Little Grisly.

As she thought her plans out footsteps came from the direction of Great Grisly Hall along the main path. Raising her head ever so slightly, Prim could see two others had arrived. One was Lady Elizabeth.

"Our mistress has work for us in Little Grisly," she told the one who had stood guard at the junction.

"What about the girl?"

"This work will bring the girl to us."

Chapter Sixty-Five

At first Prim's Dad had ran up the stairs as it was his normal default thing to do when people had last chased him, way back when he was at school. Normal people would run down the stairs when being chased but no-one would think to search up the stairs.

However, he was already thinking that it wasn't such a wise decision to have made for two or three of the undead army were now on the same floor looking for him. Would they look out of the windows and discover him on the roof of the Hall?

At least some of the undead were looking for him and not his daughter. Hopefully she would now be halfway to Little Grisly.

He hoped she had not got into his sister's car as that had started, skidded off and then, seemingly, driven around the driveway for about ten seconds before ending abruptly after hitting something. He had heard only one car door open and close.

He hoped that the longer it took Lilith and the others to find them, the more chance they would think the further he, Prim and Rose had gone.

Well at least Prim had gone, for he remembered all the noise he had made running up the stairs, hence the search party looking for him.

Like in a game of hide and seek when he was young, he kept very still.

This was a game of hide and seek he wanted all the hiders to win.

There was just one thing he could do to try and stop all this.

Slowly, and carefully, he used his fingers to reach for his mobile to text his wife.

Chapter Sixty-Six

There had been no time for Rose to put her seat belt on and start the car at the same time. There were no police to stop her and fine her for not wearing a seat belt, but she sure wished there was.

She was just about able to lock the doors before the first of the undead had run over and tried to open the door.

Is it a crime to run over someone who has already died?

Instantly she put the car in gear and skidded off in the direction of the long drive that led out onto the main road to Longborough but then saw another of Lilith's little army bearing down on her from that direction.

She couldn't run them over.

Or can I?

And she locked the wheel to the right and spun the car around.

What are you doing Rose? Get out of here. They won't mind if you hit them.

In fact, she did not need to hit one on purpose.

She hit one by accident. Thank God she did not know the man, but it must have hurt.

She got him in the left side of his body as her tiny car span around and it gave the car an enormous judder.

"Oh my God," she screamed as she noticed another two of the army standing still, waiting for her.

I bet you have never seen a car.

But she realised, as she span the car around again, that she needed to concentrate and get out of there fast.

As the car span it went past the exit to the drive again.

Come on Rose, go around again and take the exit.

But her old car wasn't taking subliminal orders lightly. She hadn't changed gear due to panicking and the car began to overheat.

Come on, come on.

One of her ancestors began to run towards the car. The other followed.

"Get out of the way," she roared and, as the car began to face the drive, she twisted the wheel around, hit another one of her forefathers and drove off, not in the direction of the way out, but into one of the fruit trees that lined the drive.

She only hit it at around ten miles per hour but without a seatbelt it gave her a real fright and a jolt forward too. She would be in pain soon and but needed to escape. She reversed the car out of the tree's trunk and ended up hitting the other one.

"Three down Rose, keep it up girl."

And then her car broke down.

In vain she tried to start it up again using the key, but the starter motor did not even register. She knew it should have gone into a garage months ago for a repair and that it had been living on borrowed time.

As I am now.

And she screamed as loud as she could possibly do so before realising screaming wasn't going to save her and she got out of the car and ran down the drive with her adrenaline fuelling her for the first fifty yards. She turned back and saw, by the car - her dead car – that Lilith, Barnaby, Lord le Grise had arrived and were all staring towards her.

That stare fuelled at least another fifty yards of running away.

Harry arrived and joined the pack.

"Prim's not on the path to Little Grisly," he explained.

"Then she must still be around here. Go, and you too Barnaby, go and catch Rose."

Without question Harry did, with Barnaby following behind.

Lilith, herself, was feeling rather exultant at the night so far.

Hunting for humans, what an excellent sport.

She knew they would all be captured soon, especially with her plan in Little Grisly.

Two of the three undead who had been hit by Rose's car were now standing up, sore but fine.

"Take the other one," she pointed at the undead still on the floor, "and take the long table from the main hall to the hanging tree, Lord le Grise will show you the way if you don't remember after all these years. And get some wood, we will need a fire too."

And they did her bidding.

Lilith thought back to when she had chosen her army. With the chain around her shoulders she had not cared about walking on open church land, hallowed land. Barnaby and Lady Elizabeth had simply waltzed down into the crypt and chosen eight of her new army entirely by random choice, like a child picking any of the sweets in the shop.

She did not really care who they were. They were Percys and all dispensable in the end. But, for now, they were doing an okay job. Only two did she choose for maximum effect and revenge.

She shouted towards Lord le Grise, "set up the tree for hanging, we will soon follow down."

And she smiled. Four people would be hanged by their necks tonight.

Chapter Sixty-Seven

Prim's Dad simply text:

"Call Police to Great Grisly Hall now."

And he followed it up with:

"Please x."

Thank God for mobile phones he thought as he saw that both messages had gone. His wife would soon see them and would immediately call the police.

How long will they take to get here? Twenty minutes from Longborough Police Station?

He realised he hadn't given his wife enough information to tell the police. They could be extremely busy tonight, but he would have to give them more, so they could prioritise and get all cars to Great Grisly Hall as soon as possible.

But what do I say?

Three people going to be hanged?

One of them is a child?

By ten, no thirteen, no eleven people who were dead but are now alive, one ghost and one, the boss, who has come from hell?

No-one is going to believe that.

He thought and thought of what he needed to say, thinking even more, as the clock was ticking, that his wife hadn't text him back yet.

What is she doing?

Is the TV on too loud?

Is she on the loo?

God, she could be ages.

And in his moment of panic he text:

"We are going to die, quick get help."

"From the police!"

"Not going to die by the police, need the police to rescue us."

He calmed a bit down and text:

"Tell the police there is an attempted murder of three people including a child."

And, as soon as he sent that he regretted it, He didn't want his wife to panic like he had just done. She would be there, all alone in the flat, and to get a text like that, about someone trying to kill her daughter.

And her husband.

He counted for ten seconds, then another thirty seconds, all the time calming himself down a little but then getting over anxious that she had not responded.

He listened to hear the others searching for him, where they in the room close by?

His phone rang. It was his wife.

Loudly, as he always had the volume at top setting even though no-one ever really called him.

On a still spring night, the noise could probably be heard across the fields to Little Grisly.

It was certainly loud enough to be heard inside the Hall.

Within a few seconds, two of his finders, had poked their heads out of the window and he had been found.

He didn't answer the call.

Chapter Sixty-Eight

Prim waited for a few minutes before deciding to follow, slowly, the group and head to Little Grisly. It must have been close to 8pm now with the light fading quickly and she preferred to be somewhere with lights on rather than on a dark path, surrounded by bushes and trees.

And people looking for her.

The air was chilled and fresh. From a pleasant spring day, dark and gloomy rain clouds had muscled in and taken over the sky. Prim knew it would rain soon.

Why had the others walked to Little Grisly? They mentioned work to do. Had Rose driven there? Had her Dad escaped from a window too and found a new route there through the woods?

She slowly crept onto the main path and firstly looked left towards Great Grisly Hall to see if anyone else was coming along. No-one. She looked to the right to see if anyone was coming back. No-one.

And so, she walked back to the village, half her mind wanted her to walk fast and the other half, run as fast as possible but her conscience was telling her not to listen to her mind as that would be a sure-fire way to get caught.

Soon she reached the straight bit of the path and could see, some distance away, the silhouettes of the three as they reached the bushes next door to the Swinging Witch.

Prim realised the best course of action would be to tell Mr Tanner what was happening, he would call the police and hopefully they could come down and arrest Lilith and take the chain off her. Lilith couldn't stop them could she?

She guessed she would also feel a lot safer in the company of others too.

She realised she was gaining on the three and with them turning right and into Little Grisly, she stopped and counted to ten in seconds before continuing, just in case it was a trap and they were waiting in the pub carpark.

Would any of this have ever happened if I carried on playing in the pub carpark?

Stop thinking like that Prim. Think of what you are going to do.

She decided to go straight into the pub to tell Mr Tanner and, after that, she would have to tell her Mum.

What on earth is she going to say?

She will kill me. And Dad.

As she edged closer to the trees around the carpark, she again stopped to listen in case anyone was talking. She wondered if anyone might be smoking in the designated area but, to her surprise, there was no-one.

No-one in the carpark.

And no-one in the pub.

There were no lights on and the doors were locked.

A sign on the front door read:

"Closed for one night, sorry for any convenience. Back open tomorrow."

What? How can a pub be closed?

And she banged on the front door just in case Mr Tanner was in the back but there was no answer.

She went back through the car park and onto the main road of Little Grisly in the direction of the Post Office and her home.

Mum must understand, she must.

And Prim was running now, the few street lights were coming on giving that eerie illumination of just before dark and some

324

people had put the lights on in their homes, and then, just around the corner, she could see the light coming from the lounge of her flat.

Mum's in, oh to be home, safe indoors.

What Prim needed was an ally, she could not know what was happening back at Great Grisly Hall, she didn't want to know either. She just knew that there was very little time to do a great amount of lots.

And just as she got close to the Post Office shop door and was about to go around the corner to door to the flat, she heard a little scream.

"Put something in her mouth you fool."

Prim knew that voice, it was Lady Elizabeth's.

She hid behind the small post van that was always parked up there at night time.

She knew what was going on. She realised that the others had come to kidnap her Mum.

Defiantly she looked around for a solid stick or even something more dangerous, was there something she could use inside the flat? She wasn't going to let them get away with it. She was angry.

She tried the van to see if it was open, it was locked.

The others came around the corner, Lady Elizabeth first and the other two holding Prim's Mum. Her hands were tied and there was something in her mouth.

Prim hoped whatever was in her mouth hadn't been in a coffin for about four hundred years lying beside a decaying corpse.

There were no solid sticks or anything remotely useful for attacking people outside.

Maybe there is something inside the flat.

And she remembered her Dad's old golf clubs, probably completely covered in dust too and situated in the downstairs locker.

The others went past her and the post van without looking. Prim winced at seeing her Mum's terrified face, but it made her the more determined to stop them.

She raced through the still opened back door and scrambled through the locker and found a club with an iron head.

This will come in handy.

And she smiled and ran out and charged down the street using the slight hill for momentum.

As soon as the others realised they were being chased, Prim let out a death defying, gurgling scream and it certainly shocked the two pushing her Mum along. Their hands were still holding onto her Mum as Prim raised the club over her head and thrashed it into the nearest one's head.

He went down. It must have been the one who had been looking for her with Harry.

Oh, my God, what have I done?

Lady Elizabeth went over and took hold of her Mum and let the other undead, a woman in her early thirties and with short, mousy hair which Prim recognised from being a style in the 1930s, come and wrestle with Prim.

Prim did not have time to even think that this lady was a relative of hers.

"Let go of my Mum!" she roared.

But she was still in shock from hurting someone and did not raise the club again in time. The woman used both her hands to grapple the club to try and take it off Prim who, of course, was equally trying to keep it and hit her.

The woman was strong and clever, she twisted one way in a feint and then, speedily, twisted the other way causing Prim to lose her grip in one and then her second hand. She had lost her weapon.

There was no time to mourn for it, the other began raising the club to hit Prim back.

"Run Prim, run, get out of here," her Mum managed to yell despite the rag in her mouth.

Ashamed, Prim ran down the street and away.

Ashamed as she was leaving her Mum.

"Put that down," shouted Lady Elizabeth to the undead woman, "we do not wish her to be injured. We want her to feel the full pain of being hanged." And she turned to Prim's Mum and said, "it lasts longer than having your head chopped off after all." And, naturally, she laughed for a moment.

"Now find the child," she roared at the woman who duly ran off following Prim.

The other who had been struck was getting himself back onto his feet. Blood trickled from his head and he was in some pain.

"Get up quick," Lady Elizabeth ordered, "and take hold of this prisoner."

Prim had only run down one street before deciding to hide behind a fence, close by to the Church. She reasoned that the chaser would be able to see her running and know where she was, as opposed to not seeing her and therefore not knowing where she had gone.

It worked. Or so it seemed.

The female undead stopped at the junction of the road and the church and looked around. A second or two later and the others and Prim's Mum had caught up.

"She's hiding somewhere close," said the female.

327

"There's not many places to hide in this dump and she wouldn't dare think about running towards Great Grisly."

"What about there in the Church, what about the crypt?" The other asked.

"She wouldn't dare hide in there, she's just a little cry baby, besides that's where we all came from. Carry on searching for her, I'll get some others to help you. We will take her Mum back to the hanging tree and get her strung up with her husband."

Prim was certain Lady Elizabeth knew that she was nearby and had only said those things to make her come out and either run or attack.

Now still and crouching she could feel her heart still beating fast.

Would they really hang my Mum?

Yes, I think they would.

But Prim was wise, she knew it best to keep still and let there be an air of mystery about where she was.

Maybe her Ladyship doesn't really know where I am. And I'm not going to make it easy.

She heard Lady Elizabeth, her Mum and the injured other walk off and the remaining one walk back up the road searching under cars and behind bins.

What am I going to do?

She thought about waiting for a bit where she was and then following the three and attacking Lady Elizabeth. The injured one wouldn't put up much of a fight and she was sure she could punch her Ladyship.

Listen to yourself Prim, you're no boxer.

But that was a good idea, attack when there wasn't many of the others about.

328

However, the female undead was slowly coming down the road and the three were still only ambling along thanks to the injury to the man.

Prim had to hide somewhere else.

Am I really going to do this?

And she did. She decided to go and hide in the church.

In the dark.

Just as it started to rain.

Chapter Sixty-Nine

Rose was not very fit and after the first one hundred yards began to flag. She thought about hiding in the long, tall, unkept grass and bushes that boarded the drive but by now Harry and Barnaby Grudge were in full sight.

How much further to the gate and onto the main road? Five hundred yards? No longer, it's such a long stupid drive.

Come on Rose, you must do this.

She said this in vain hope and soon the much fitter, and younger, if you did not count the year of their birth, two had caught her up.

Rose fell and cried. She did not feel that she was useless. Now, in her mind, she was useless.

Within ten minutes she was hauled inside Great Grisly Hall and standing in front of Lilith with her brother and surrounded by the others, including Harry and Barnaby Grudge, in the main Hall, two tall candles giving light in the dusk of the evening.

She crouched down on her knees for a few moments, desperate still to get her breath back.

"Two of the remaining four members of the Percy family," announced Lilith. I have to say you did not give much of a chase for us. I wonder how long it will be until we catch the brat."

But she received no response from the two who, instead, put their arms around each other in comfort. They were too tired to argue, too tired to play her games. But both could at least think that with Prim still free there had to be hope.

And that was the only hope they had.

"Oh, take the sad little souls to the hanging tree, but tell Lord le Grise to wait for me before he starts."

And she smiled at them both.

"Say goodbye to Great Grisly Hall, your family once owned it and now, I suppose it is mine."

"It is still ours," whispered Prim's Dad under his breath to Rose. His anger was coming back.

The others took them out leaving Lilith to herself in the main hall. For a few moments she looked up at all the paintings. She did not have to curse the people in the portraits anymore. They were all dead, well dead unless she had brought them back. Perhaps, she could bring the rest of them back just to spite them, to laugh at them as they had to obey her every command.

But what would be more fitting than to burn this whole place down to the ground.

No more Percys.

"Do you fancy a portrait of your own?"

Lilith turned around in shock at hearing another voice in the Hall. But she knew who it was, she had heard that voice many times in the last four centuries or so.

She wanted to answer back, argue and tell him that she could not think of anything worse than to have her own painting, especially sitting next to all the Percy family but she knew her place.

"No, master," was all she could say.

The little man sat on his three-legged chair by the huge, empty fireplace. Lilith could scarcely see him in the little light that she could muster but his presence was keenly, and coldly, felt.

"Ha, you can be proud, after all they were all proud, although some had nothing to be proud about. And you do. You have found my chain."

"Thank you master."

"And now you wish to burn this Hall down."

"Yes master."

"And yet you have not finished your job. Do not get carried away. Finish the task here and I will reward you. But there is much work to do afterwards."

Lilith knew that in his presence it paid to listen.

"And I see you have resurrected some of the old family, I like that especially with what you are about to do with the current members, you are a chip off the old block. But one thing, when you have finished, destroy all them and send them down to me."

"Thank you master."

And with that he disappeared. In his absence, Lilith resented calling anyone master. She knew what she was doing and didn't need to be micro managed.

She sat down on a chair around the long table. She would wait for news from Little Grisly.

It would not take long before the task here was finished.

Chapter Seventy

Trying to be ever so quiet Prim crept into the churchyard over the sodden low stone wall, careful not to slip and fall. It was already dark, there was no illumination from street lamps or the warm lights from inside homes here. Up above the large, grey clouds lay over most of the full moon so much so that Prim forgot about its meaning. Instead, looking up, she was glad that it was raining, the drops washing her face, hoping that its drops tinkling onto the ground would muffle her movements.

The difference between the rational and the irrational was confusing Prim.

Yes, ghosts exist, and I have met a fair few in the last week or two.

But she was still quite a bit scared of going into the church on her own. The old lady had told her about the shadows and sounds which she could not identify.

Still, she needed to survive, she needed to not get caught, she needed to hide and needed to keep dry. Now by the main door, she began to kneel to search for the key under the old and slightly damp matt but realised that she did not need it, the door was slightly ajar anyway with the large metal key still inside the lock.

For a second she winced at the notion that someone was inside, waiting for her. No-one would be inside on this night with innocent intentions. If they did then the lights to the church would be on, and Prim could see that they were not.

For another second she thought about the location of all the undead army but could not work out where they would all be, apart from, of course, looking around for her and the rest of her family.

But she needed to make a decision. The one member of the undead army she did know about would be close and getting closer and closer for each second Prim hesitated.

She decided to enter the church itself taking the key with her.

There can't be any of them in here. There can't.

The door to the church creaked open and although her eyes were becoming used to the dark, she would have welcomed some sort of light. As if to toy with her, she could just about make out the light switch, but she couldn't use it, could she?

No, you can't Prim.

And there was some light from beside the altar, to the left, near the crypt but it was weak, and Prim was not sure what or where it was.

Nevertheless, it helped cause shadows in the long nave, thankfully all standing still, or were they? She had to stand still herself and watch, and slowly, she could recognise bits she would not have seen a few moments ago.

There were the pews, the columns holding the church up, in the corner was the font and, as she walked in slowly, to the right, was the altar and pulpit.

Everything was in its place, but Prim was careful.

What if there really is someone in here already?

Waiting for me?

And what is that light?

What if Lilith comes back and brings back more from the dead?

And she listened carefully for the sound of breathing or rustling, and all she could hear were her internals going ten to the dozen.

From outside she heard the gate to the churchyard yank open.

This chaser does not give up easily. Did she hear me open the church door?

Perhaps I can just hide in one of the pews.

Prim wanted the chaser to come into the church, she wanted her to walk down the nave and then Prim could run out and lock her inside. With the door locked, Lilith would be unable to raise any more Percys into her new army.

But then Prim realised that a chaser did not have to chase under the cover of darkness. She could turn the light switch on if they wanted to.

She would have to go deeper into the Church, deeper into the ground.

With her eyes becoming well used to the dark, she noticed the source of the light. It was at the entrance to the crypt. The curtain was closed but the door leading down to it was open. *Of course, the front and crypt doors must have been opened by Lady Elizabeth, what does she care about locking up afterwards.*

Prim, keeping ever so silent, watched in case she saw any movement. She realised that Lady Elizabeth had probably also turned the light on when she, and Lilith, had raised some of the dead family members and turned them into an army.

And what would they know about saving electricity?

But she winced thinking of Harry and thought for a moment.

Is there anyone still down there?

But there couldn't be.

Whatever the answer, she was going to have to hide fast, she could hear the undead woman walking briskly towards the main door and Prim realised that she had left it slightly more open than she had found it, giving the game away as to where she was.

She had to hide. Quickly.

And it had to be in the crypt.

You've been there before Prim.

But only with Rose, and Lord le Grise.

But she also did not have time to think and she ran as sprightly as she could through the nave, up to the altar and to the left and, pausing ever so slightly, moved the curtain to one side and peered downwards.

Come on Prim.

The light was from the bulb inside the crypt and not the one from the small landing. She took a deep breath and began her descent, once more into the dank room of the dead.

As she did so she could hear the front door of the church groan open fully.

It was not entirely dark on the staircase, but she still walked downwards carefully. The undead woman would most likely look around the church on the ground floor first and she was right, for, as she reached half way down there was great illumination as the main church lights came on. Of course, the undead lady lived, whoever she was, during the time of electricity. And this light helped Prim. It would now be easier to continue her steps. Just as long as she didn't slip and make a noise.

And she could hear the tiny stream of water running through the crypt.

Step by slow step she descended. She needed to breathe, she needed to breathe deeper.

And yet she knew there was not much air downstairs.

And what air there was infused with the decay of the dead.

Finally, she entered the crypt.

Prim let her eyes search around. Now the place was a mess, there were empty, open coffins strewn over the floor, their former inhabitants now fighting on the side of Lilith.

Prim hated coffins, even if they were now empty. But she had to enter within and hide.

Nimbly, she tiptoed in between them, careful not to make a splashing sound in the water, careful not to peer too closely into any of the coffins to see if there was still a body inside.

From above, she could hear the curtain to the crypt door being pulled across.

She could hear footsteps coming down at a much faster pace than she went down and, so, she moved quickly into the other room, which included the remains of the last Earl, and his family. It was safer to be in a room full of the dead than in a room with an undead person.

She looked around for somewhere to hide, she would be easily found in the corners. If only she had hidden somewhere upstairs, behind the font or somewhere.

If only she had stayed playing in the pub car-park.

The only place to hide would be behind the great tomb of the last Earl himself. She passed all the wooden crosses left around the floor and saw a little recess right at the back of the stone sarcophagus. She did not really want to have to do this but there was no other choice.

She squeezed in and crouched down.

She could hear the woman searching around, this had been her home for so many years and yet it must have come as a shock to her when she was woken up in the employ of the witch.

And, thankfully, she did not have a torch.

Prim slowed her breathing, it was the only thing, apart from the water, that could be heard in this part of the crypt.

The stench of decomposition mixed with the wet, mouldy stone became unbearable.

The undead woman entered the room and stood still for a second or two. Prim crouched down as much as possible and closed her eyes. There was nothing she could now.

Please, please, please.

The woman began to walk around, Prim could only hear her, she did not want to open her eyes and peer around in case she made a noise. The woman was now looking at all the crosses on the floor and the great tomb itself.

In the throes of waiting for what seemed an age, Prim did open her eyes but managed to not move her head.

Breathing controlled.

Body not shaking.

Keep it up Prim.

Looking down, her eyes saw something close to her foot and prayed it was not part of the Earl himself. She wanted to kick it away.

The woman appeared to be satisfied and left the room. Prim waited for her to walk up the steps before moving from behind the tomb. She was sure that she had become stuck behind it.

Perhaps she thinks I was hiding by the door or behind the font and that I have escaped.

She heard footsteps going upwards and heard the door shut. It was safe. Thankfully she also left the light on.

She placed her hands on the stone tomb, it was moist, and used that to raise herself up. As she manoeuvred herself out she kicked the thing close to her foot and it shifted half out and half under the tomb.

Getting herself free she saw what it was.

A horn. A musical horn.

Not one made from metal but out of the horn of an animal.

Prim had seen one of these recently.

Where Prim?

The family emblem. And the painting of the last Earl. He had worn it slung over his shoulder and here it was now, with its leather sling attached too. She picked it up. It was obvious that it had not been used for a very long time and was partially covered in green mould.

She realised the exact location it had come from. From inside the Earl's tomb, lying by his side. Obviously the tomb was collapsing due to the moisture and age.

And the fact that he leaves this chamber when there is a full moon.

In the dim light, Prim realised she was now covered in the same green mould stuff too after being behind the tomb. It stank.

What do I do now Prim?

Do I wait and see if that woman is well and truly gone? Do I find someone in the village and call the police? Or do I simply go back to Great Grisly Hall myself and sort this out?

Prim decided to leave immediately. She was about to place the horn down onto the Earl's tomb, but something told her to take it. Just like the Earl she slung in over her shoulder and rubbed the horn itself clean with her clothes.

She moved into the first room of the crypt and was just about to walk up the stairs when she heard something stir from behind her.

Prim did a doubletake.

Haven't I just been in that room and there was no-one else in there.

Maybe I've sent something over and it's tumbled to the floor.

And there was a crack, like that of an old wooden door being opened. But it wasn't wood.

It was stone.

There was no secret doorway, she knew that.

Prim guessed what it was.

And it wasn't good.

From outside she could hear horses whinnying, it sounded like they were literally in the graveyard.

She heard the slight friction of stone upon stone once more and she waited, immobile, for it to stop.

And it was then that her sixth sense told her that something was now behind her.

It was time to leave. Fast.

But before she did, her intrigue took the better of her, and she turned around.

His portrait was like the real thing, hair, and clothes all the same. There was no burial shroud for him.

It was the eyes that were different, and the skeletal, wizened face. She had liked his eyes in the painting, but they had long departed and here they were red, brilliantly red like freshly drawn blood.

Prim was frozen, heavy, she could not move, her legs were like jelly. It was like that time when she was chased by Lady Elizabeth at Great Grisly Hall, but that was small fry to this.

Of all the things she was told, never be about on the night of a full moon. Oh, how she could tell people that the legend was true, all true. If ever she saw another living person again. The chances of that were now close to slim. In fact, there was no chance.

She was ready for the worst; the day had set her up for this.

The Earl stood and looked at her, his maddening eyes looking at her from top to bottom and then focusing onto her face.

Please let me live, please let me live.

"Are you a Percy?" His voice was dry, stern and orderly.

All Prim could do was nod slowly, once and then twice.

He looked at her shoulder and saw the horn. Prim knew she was in trouble, stealing the last Earl's horn, the last Earl who rode people direct to hell on a full moon night? And to say she was a Percy, the family he had waged a war with and lost his sons to.

But all he did was point to it and, she couldn't really tell, gently nod himself, all the while staring straight at her.

Prim remained unmoved, unable to move, almost unable to breath. She had to remember how to. Was she now dead? Was this the start of death?

Just as she was able to confirm she was still alive the bell above, in the clock tower, struck 9pm.

In the shock she fell to the ground, semiconscious and with her eyes firmly closed.

Without a sound the Earl left her alone.

Chapter Seventy-One

She must have lost conscious for a while for the next thing she heard was the half hour bell, not as loud as the hour one but enough to get her up, especially when it was chimed immediately above her, in the steeple.

When she realised she was resting on the rotten and damp green stone floor and quite close to at least one of the opened coffins, she stood up in a flash trying to remember everything that had happened. Thankfully she had not really hurt herself when she fell and all she could now really think about was the Earl. She searched around for him, but he had gone. Why had he not taken her to hell?

Perhaps it was too easy for him?

Perhaps it was because I was in a church?

Why did he ask if I was a Percy?

But she was thankful that he had left her, and she realised that she did not have time to think about things for too long and had to get going, back to either Great Grisly Hall or the hanging tree and careful not to bump into the Earl and his sons along the way.

Again, she was unsure as to what she was going to do when she got there but she had to be there all the same.

She bounded up the stairs, the woman chaser would have been long gone by now. Perhaps she had met the Earl herself and was now in hell. Prim felt sorry for her at this thought, it wasn't her fault, it was Lilith's. She also felt something else as she had run up the stone steps, through the still lit church and into the graveyard: the horn around her shoulder.

Perhaps the horn kept me safe.

Forget that for now Prim. Now run fast or walk slow and think what you are going to do?

Walk Prim, keep your energy.

No, run, what if my Dad and Aunt are caught too? Will they hang them?

Yes, they will. Come on Prim, they could be doing that now.

And so, she ran towards the pub, into the carpark and down onto the well-worn path leading to Great Grisly Hall.

Careful Prim, careful, they might be about. This is the quickest way to get to the Hall and.

But Prim, after all that had happened to her, was desperate to know what was going on her with family. She simply needed to know, she need to do something.

Trust my luck to get caught by one of them now.

Trust my luck to bump into the Earl again. I doubt he will be so pleasant the next time.

He wasn't that pleasant the first time.

The full moon guided her as she ran close to the stream, she was getting closer. Soon she would have the choice of going direct to Great Grisly Hall, and there were now two ways to get there, or go straight to the hanging tree, by the mill.

A minute or so later and the decision was made for her. Over to the right, and away from the Hall, she could see light, not the light of the moon but firelight. For a second she wondered if there was a party going on or something completely away from her task, but there could not be. The fire, or it seemed, as she got closer, fires, were in the direction of the field with the mill by the stream, the field containing the hanging tree.

A second later and she could see the mill, and there, just above it and despite the now relentless rain was a fire lit, another lit in front of the hanging tree, and another to show the path direct from there to Great Grisly Hall.

In between the fires and her, she could see little narrow silhouettes of people darting about.

This was the way to go.

Suddenly she felt a presence along the path. Goose bumps rapidly shot straight up her spine and she ducked to the left in a vain effort to avoid whoever it was.

But it was only Amy.

"Prim, are you okay? We feared the worst," and she looked at Prim, "you look the worst, oh, Prim, we've been searching for you, but no-one could find you."

Prim thought that after the day she had experienced she would not get frightened anymore, but this seemed to be the most frightening thing to have happened to her. Thank God she did not let out a shriek. Still, her heart was pounding after the shock.

How much more excitement and danger can my poor body take?

"Amy, I thought you were."

"A ghost?"

"No, one of them. Where have you been?"

"We've been with your family but there hasn't been much we could do, not with all of them. Do you know your Mum is here?"

Prim nodded.

"All three of them are by the tree, I'm afraid Rose and your Dad weren't they good at running away like you."

"Are they alive?" Prim realised the significance of what she had just said. Not many eleven years olds would have to ask the same question.

"Yes, sorry I should have told you that first. But Prim, they are going to hang them in the next ten minutes or so. Lilith is waiting on the ten chimes from the church clock."

"But what about me?"

"One of your ancestors came back and said you could not be found. Lilith thinks you are therefore around here, waiting to attack."

"Well I am around here."

"I know that's why I am here, some of her army are hidden, waiting for you. Let me take you a way to avoid them."

"There is someone else, some others, around here too," Prim told her.

"You mean the Earl, yes, I have felt his presence, but he has not shown himself yet around the hanging tree. Come on Prim, the clock is ticking."

"Amy, we need to take the chain off Lilith, we simply have to, can you three really help?" Prim needed the reassurance.

"It's what Sadie and Lockie are now trying to do, it's not going to be easy Prim."

"Nothing is," and with that Prim followed Amy through a not very easy route onto the field, through an already thick hedge and over an old drystone wall, careful, due to its age, not to push or kick some of its stone pieces onto the ground and make a noise at the same time.

Chapter Seventy-Two

The three fires in the field gave light to all those who needed to see. Prim hoped desperately that such activity would cause the local police to become suspicious that something strange was afoot, but the police never took an interest in the world of Little Grisly. Usually, not much ever happened there.

Getting closer, but under the cover of darkness, Prim could see what they were doing, and her heart missed a beat. In the tree were three of the undead, and they were tying ropes to the strongest branch which was about ten or eleven feet from the ground. Underneath them, some others were placing the large, long table from the Hall directly below.

Near to where they found the chain she could see Lilith and the chain, and it did gleam like in all the paintings. It wasn't really a difficult sort of clue once you had seen the chain in real life. Lilith, herself, looked radiant and Prim noticed, just a few feet away, that there was an old upturned rotten long casket left on the ground.

Lilith had made herself human again.

Now that is vanity for you.

Close by, and guarded, were her Mum, Dad and Rose, standing with their hands tied, trying to be still but shaking. Prim thought that she would not have the stomach to stand if she was condemned like the rest of her family was. Caught and guarded she would become a gibbering wreck.

But Prim also did not have the stomach to see her family be hanged, they had committed no offence, the only offence Lilith could offer was that they were the current members of a family that centuries ago had been a bit cruel and a heck of a lot greedy.

Did the Devil and his disciple, Lilith, not believe in redemption? Prim guessed not as she stood counting how many of Lilith's army she could see.

Including the witch, there were thirteen.

And she could only see, nine.

There was Lord le Grise by Lilith, there was Barnaby Grudge ordering members of the Percy family in making the nooses, he would be enjoying that, and Lady Elizabeth talking to Prim's family.

Except, Prim thought, she probably wasn't just talking to them but goading them, teasing them. Out of Barnaby and Lady Elizabeth it was her ladyship that Prim despised the most. And Prim also realised that her ladyship probably hated them all for being a Percy. Lady Elizabeth had wanted to be one, but, instead had taken some to the scaffold. What was four more members of the Percy family going to be killed to her?

Prim winced at this thought. One day, she hoped, she would look back at all this as if it was just a very long, very strange dream. In dreams she had remembered she had always been able to extract herself from strange and scary moments.

Will I extract myself from this one?

She felt a tugging on her right sleeve by Amy, turned to her and saw that she was pointing.

Someone was coming in close.

It was Harry and he had seen them both.

"Run Prim," whispered Amy, desperate not to make the others hear her.

Prim couldn't nor wouldn't, she wanted to Harry to realise what he was doing was wrong.

Harry wouldn't, couldn't seize me and take me to Lilith?

"Harry," she too whispered, "what have they done to you? We can make it better."

"You are to come with me," he replied sternly and without any of the warmth he had used when previously speaking to her. He grabbed and held her arms, tightly.

347

"Look into my eyes Harry, it's me, Prim, we are friends, remember?"

But he did not even think for a second. Instead he pulled her towards him so abruptly and powerfully that a tear dropped from Prim's eye. Harry must have seen that.

"Come with me," and he called for others, and out of the shadows, the three missing others came to help him. Over in the distance, Prim could see Lilith look at the commotion and smile.

Oh, what have I done? I've been caught without even a struggle. Is this it? Am I going to die now?

But Prim still had one chance.

"Amy," Prim said, "you have to do your bit."

"Yes," she replied, "but first."

And she took the horn and hid it inside Prim's coat.

"Best keep that hidden for a bit."

And Harry, puzzled, looked around to see who Prim was talking to.

Clever Amy.

Chapter Seventy-Three

Prim was taken to her family and she immediately embraced them.

"I'm sorry Mum," she said softly, "you never wanted a part in all this."

"None of us did," replied her Dad, "this is all my fault, to you all."

Barnaby Grudge stopped barking orders and came and stood by Prim and her family along with Harry to guard them. She was sure he was going to say something, but Lilith beat him to it.

"Well isn't this a lovely family reunion? The four surviving members of the Percy family altogether for the first time in years and, also for the last time."

And she paused to see the reaction on Prim and the others of her words, but she was searching in vain now, for at least three of the family were at rock bottom anyway.

Lilith smiled and continued, "well for the last time alive anyway. I don't think the police would be happy at finding four bodies in a field, so what better way to remove you than to give you rebirth as a soldier of Satan, in my army."

Prim was almost sick, she still had hope, she had to have hope but the notion of what they would do to her and the family was appalling.

Me as a dead body.

And working for her before being sent to hell.

"You're sick," yelled Prim's Mum thinking the same as her daughter.

"I know," replied Lilith laughing, "but I am in charge, and when you are in charge, everyone must obey, isn't that right Lady Elizabeth?"

And all Lady Elizabeth did was nod. If she had still just been a spirit, Prim knew she would have answered back alright, Lady Elizabeth was smarter than Lilith by a million miles, but power, obviously, to Lilith, was the most important factor to have. Lady Elizabeth could have been a well-used deputy, a free thinker, but Lilith had lost that now.

Perhaps that was her weakness.

"You Percys' were given the ultimate weapon, this chain," and she stroked it lovingly, "but you could not use it properly, you did not want to use it, didn't have the strength to use it. And that is why you suffered. Now someone else has the chain and knows how to use it. As you can see I have even used it on myself. Oh, what it is like to be able to breathe again, to feel my heart beating with excitement," and she realised that she was straying from the point, "I've been waiting for centuries for this, and now you will suffer."

"You're not strong enough," replied Prim, searching for sight of Amy, Sadie and Lockie, "you need others to do your business, well you've ruined one of them," and she pointed to Lady Elizabeth. "Will you destroy your other supporter?"

And Prim looked at Barnaby Grudge to see if he was moved.

But he wasn't.

"Sticking up for someone who has tried to kill you? Well what a pathetic young lady you are Prim, and, as you can see, my army have to obey my orders, any order that I give them, even to die for me, and your poor Harry, him to."

Lilith smiled at the talk of Harry for it was clear to her that Prim had an affection for him. Indeed, Prim turned to Harry for any sign that he understood what was being said, but it was no use. He was now under the curse of the chain.

"And tomorrow, I will start to make my big army, of all the souls of those who have died, and they will listen to only me."

"Do you need to do that?" Prim said, "what good would that be to anyone?"

"Oh, you are a clever girl, it will not be good for just anyone, but for me it will be divine."

"You're taking orders yourself from the Devil, you don't have to take them, he is just using you, can't you see that?"

And Prim could see that Barnaby liked that, he liked her having a go at authority, even respected her for saying it on her execution day. Maybe he was thinking that she was not that pathetic.

But Lilith had had enough.

"I cannot wait to see you as one of my soldiers, I will give you the worst of all the orders possible. But first, to show you how much I hate you, I won't hang you yet Primula. No, you can watch your family hang first. Take the other three and put them on the tree ready for my order."

"No," screamed Prim and she went to protect her family, but it was Harry who quickly pulled her away from them. Her Dad wrestled his guards but with their hands tied behind their backs there was little they could do.

It was their faces that told their fears.

And Prim's.

Harry tied her arms together and left Barnaby to stand guard behind her.

Where is Amy?

If anytime is a good time, with eight of the guards working on the tree, it is now.

Come on Amy.

But she, Sadie and Lockie were nowhere to be seen and very soon all the others had climbed off the tree and Prim's Dad, Mum and Rose stood trembling, trying to keep their balance on the long table, thick rope nooses around their necks. Four of the undead stood ready to kick or push the table from under their feet.

"Count to three Primula Percy and say goodbye to your family," Lilith sneered.

And that was when Prim saw Amy, Sadie and Lockie jump upon Lilith, who in her determination and excitement had completely forgotten about her younger siblings. Lockie continuously punched her belly, Sadie twisted her right arm and Amy began to pull the chain off her neck using her left hand and her other, smothering Lilith's mouth to stop her from shouting orders to her soldiers.

Clever Amy.

Prim could see her Dad beginning to shudder in his fear and she realised that he could slip from the table and hang himself.

Prim also felt her hands being untied and soon they were loose.

She looked around to see who her rescuer was. She smelt him first: dirt and blood and sweat.

It was Barnaby Grudge.

"Go on girl," he whispered, "and don't forget your horn."

Quickly she ran over to Lilith and she too tried to pull the chain from her shoulders, all the while her undead army, Lord le Gris, Harry and the rest, did nothing, they couldn't as they had no orders to do something with.

Just as they thought they had the chain off her, Lilith turned around quickly, causing Amy to stop being able to stifle her orders.

"Stop them," Lilith cried and four of the nearest came immediately over to throw the children off her.

Prim was thrown to the ground by Lady Elizabeth, she was very strong for someone who had been dead only hours ago and Prim, landing on her left side, felt pain around her left arm and waist. Harry came over to her and held her to the ground, again his face soulless, showing no emotion or character at all.

Lockie was grabbed and carried off by two of them and the other two were pushed away.

Lilith settled the chain upon her shoulders, looked up and looked like she was about to swiftly give the orders to hang the three, when suddenly Barnaby Grudge appeared and tried to punch Lilith in the face with his left hand and grab the chain in his right.

But it was too no avail. There were some strong soldiers in Lilith's army and they jumped down onto him and pulled him away and pushed him to the floor.

The chain was still around Lilith's shoulders.

"Barnaby Grudge," she said viciously getting her bearings but realising that she was still dominant, "I would not have suspected something like that from you. What is the meaning of this?"

"You are just like those from the great war. I hate authority, and you are the authority here," he replied. And he did not care.

"I will deal with you later," she said staring at Barnaby. "Where is the girl?"

"She is here," answered Harry.

"Bring her to me."

And as Harry began to try and lift her up and before any of the others came to help him, Prim realised exactly why her midriff was in pain. She had landed on the horn. Barnaby had only just told her not to forget the horn.

Perhaps?

With all her remaining strength, she stood up and pulled and pushed away from Harry, all the while using one hand to take the horn which she placed on to her lips and blew.

She was expecting a dreadful sound to emit from it, like that of a child blowing a trumpet, but it was a loud, almost thunderous ruckus, and then, her breath being short, it fell silent again.

Nothing happened.

"I said bring her to me," shouted Lilith and Harry and another went to collect her.

And just as Lilith was about to give the order to hang the three Percys in the tree, there came, from the direction of Great Grisly Hall, the sound of another horn.

Everyone stopped and looked in the direction it had come from.

The piercing sound of horses whinnying was heard and getting closer.

Fast.

"Look," gasped one of Lilith's army.

Horses galloped onto the field. Their shadows danced in the light caused by the burning fires.

The last Earl and his two sons dashed demonically towards the group, screaming.

Prim glanced at Lilith, whose eyes took on the most terrified state she had ever seen.

And Prim was worried too, for her and her family. Was the Earl about to take them all to hell?

But it was too late to think anymore as the Earl and his sons encircled the group causing Lilith's army into a pandemonium of panic, shouting and shrieking. The power of the chain to order the undead army appeared to be waning against the threat of the Earl and his curse.

"No," shouted Lilith at the top of her voice, and she gave the order to hang Prim's family, but no -one heard or obeyed.

Prim put her arm around Harry, who did nothing to stop her.

She saw the undead lady, who had searched for her in St Hilda's, be struck by the gaze of the Earl and then, for a second, come out of her body and realise what had happened to herself. Prim could see the frightened look in the woman's face as it dawned on her what was about to occur.

The woman cried before disappearing out of sight. Her body fell to the floor in a heap.

Two, three, then five more of them disappeared all the way to hell, their carcasses simply dumped onto the bare ground with not a jot of dignity.

They don't deserve this.

Prim saw Lord le Grise, poor Lord le Grise, as he too was struck but by one of the sons. He stood upright, as if waking up from a nightmare, and then look around at the sight around him.

"What am I doing here?"

And his soul departed too, his fleshy remains slumped into a lifeless clump.

Prim looked up at the tree and saw that her family was safe, still standing on the table, even her Dad had become more comfortable.

But she no time to think anymore. From behind she was grabbed, and she knew it was Lady Elizabeth from her lavender scent and from her dress and then from her face, her desperate, angry face.

"You have killed us all," her ladyship screamed, "if I die again then you will come with me."

And she meant it as she locked both her arms around Prim's waist, stopping Prim from wrestling with her own arms to try and escape.

Prim struggled and shook but her ladyship was strong, and she began to laugh like Lilith.

"Do not fight me Prim Percy, this is what you deserve for calling the Earl, this is your fault."

Prim was not going to just accept this. Instead she was going to fight this lying down and with her all her weight she pushed herself and Lady Elizabeth onto the drenched grass in an effort to try and escape.

It was her ladyship who landed first and for a moment she loosened her grip upon Prim who took the advantage and tried to scramble up and away. Lady Elizabeth grabbed her arm and pulled her back.

There was no time for talking now from her ladyship. This was the last roll of the dice for her. She clenched her teeth and pulled over her other arm to hold onto Prim.

But Prim had learnt what to do over the last few days. She certainly was not the spineless little child Lady Elizabeth thought she was. She kicked out and onto her ladyship's torso and, using her leg as a lever, pulled herself away and from the grasp of Lady Elizabeth's arms just at the right time for the Earl rode passed and stared down at her.

Lady Elizabeth did not have time to scream at the pain that Prim must have caused her. But scream she did for she knew what was to come. Her eyes turned to Prim's, they seemed to grow with the realisation that the end was due. Tormented and terrified her eyes became, her body shook, and her spirit was gone, broken and heading downwards leaving her still warm corpse on the ground, her eyes still seemingly still watching Prim.

By now there were not many left of Lilith's army and they would have run in all directions save for the Earl's sons rearing them around the tree like sheep.

Lilith, defiantly, tried to order for new soldiers to be born to try and defeat the Earl. Who was the Earl to her? Just a failure in the eyes of her master, and she was not.

She needed new recruits and she needed to leave urgently. If she had kept herself as just a spirit she could have hid but there was no point in looking back in hindsight.

She started to run back towards the path which would lead to Little Grisly. She would have to try and enter the crypt herself. Surely she could now she was human again. Perhaps Barnaby Grudge would realise his mistake and come back on side with her?

But it was too late to run or to call for more of her army. The Earl himself stopped and steadied his horse and faced her from about twenty yards. He pointed to the chain and charged at her, shrieking all the while before riding right towards her.

Lilith jumped out of the way and onto the ground herself, but the Earl had done his bit. Her sick soul was returning to hell.

"Help us take the chain off her Prim," cried Amy, "quick before she goes under otherwise the devil will have it again."

Prim ran to Lilith and saw that in her eyes she too, like Lady Elizabeth, was petrified. Amy and Prim grabbed the chain around her shoulders, but Lilith still would not let them take it even though she was shaking with fear. Prim's hands were close to Lilith's face, pulling at the chain, Prim thought she they would break the chain in two and she felt Lilith's breath wheezing, desperate to take in all the air in the world.

Lilith could do nothing, she was fading, weakening. Her hands slipped from holding onto the chain allowing Prim to quickly lift it over her head and away from her.

Something extraordinary happened.

Lilith began to cry.

"Don't let me go back down there. Not again."

Sadie and Lockie now joined their sister and Prim and knelt by Lilith's side.

But before any final things could be said to her, she fell limp to the floor. She had exhaled her last breath. Her soul had left for the final time.

Prim had the chain. Lilith was gone. They had won.

From behind they all heard a yelp.

Prim turned and saw Harry staring at her. His eyes flickered, and he began to shake.

"Prim," he called, "Prim, what has happened?" And his face showed his confusion. "What have I done?"

Prim ran to him, putting her hands onto his, trying to warm his freezing cold body. Their eyes met, Prim desperate for this moment to last but his pupils and face quickly dropped, his hands wilted, and he fell onto the muddy grass beneath him.

And Harry was gone too.

Prim would never forget that last picture of his face and fell onto her knees and began to sob.

How could this happen?

But she knew why.

How? Could I have done anything else? When?

But there were too many questions to ask and she was too sad, too tired to think of answering any of them.

And she realised there was still so much to do before she could begin to think about things.

She stood up and looked around her. From all the screaming and mayhem, only a few moments ago, there was an unbelievable, eerie stillness and she noticed that the rain had finally stopped. For all she knew it had stopped some time before.

All the undead army had left.

And suddenly out of the quietness came the gentle neigh of a horse to her left. Prim realised that the Earl and his two sons, still on their horses, were waiting for her. She looked around the rest of the field and saw that Amy, Sadie and Lockie still knelt around their sister's dead body. Above on the long table, her parents and aunt were still tied up, but that Barnaby Grudge was now untying them.

Barnaby Grudge. Without him what would have happened?

"Lady Percy," the Earl called, "you have made excellent work tonight, now you must finally break the curse that I brought upon this family and before the Devil takes revenge. One other thing stands in your way of future happiness."

And Prim knew what he meant.

"The chain, destroy the chain now, before it is too late, or you wish to test it upon yourself."

The Earl smiled, looked at his sons, and they rode off into the dark blanket of the night sky leaving Prim, her family, the three guardian angels, three burning fires and a lot of dead bodies strewn on the floor.

Her Mum, Dad and Aunt were now back safely on the ground and they all embraced.

Chapter Seventy-Four

Prim heeded the advice of the Earl and taking hold of the chain, for she was no longer scared to do so, she began to walk and then run to the old mill house by the stream. Rose and her parents followed.

Yes, she had defeated Lilith, but she knew the Devil was so very powerful. What could he do before she got to the mill? What must he be thinking of right now?

He must be livid.

I wonder whether he is here?

And she wondered and hoped that the old mill stone would help her crush the chain, after all she had only been to the mill in a dream beforehand. Of course, it wasn't a normal dream.

Will I ever have a normal dream again?

And she guessed that she probably would not until the curse had been ended. And that meant not only destroying the chain but somehow dealing with Barnaby Grudge, someone, who until recently, had been very keen on killing her.

She arrived at the mill and its door had now broken off its hinges and was just lying against the doorway. Prim simply pulled it back and let it drop firmly to the floor and she entered without hesitation into the immediate thick black tar of darkness. This was no crypt nor darkened room inside Great Grisly Hall, but, as soon as she had entered, she wondered whether something sinister could be lying in wait for her.

The devil himself, ready to snatch the chain off me when I least expect it to happen.

And she quickly turned a complete circle and there was no – one. Well no-one who could be seen. But by now she could hear and then see her Dad, panting hard, reach the doorway too.

He really was unfit. But thankfully, after what had just happened, at least he was still breathing as opposed to Lilith.

Thankfully too, his well underused phone had a torch light.

Together they checked the mill stone, it looked like it hadn't worked for centuries and that was probably true, but Prim placed the chain on top of the lower lying stone and it fitted between that and the top stone. All they needed to do was start it up.

Prim could hear the water in the stream flowing past but, checking through a small, narrow open window, saw that the water wheel was not turning.

What about the brake?

And she saw it, a large iron lever, it had to be the thing stopping the wheel from working and the mill stone from turning.

She put as much strength as she had left into turning it but to no use. Her Dad came over and they both pulled, once, twice and then three times and it budged, budged by making an awful screeching sound, but it was free, and she checked out of the window and the wheel began to turn.

And they realised that they had to get out of the way for the millstone did begin to turn and its effect upon the chain was clear and straight to the point. For all the magic contained within the chain, it was no match for good, hardworking stone, and its links seemingly burst as they broke up, some flying off from the millstone causing Prim to quickly move out of the way.

Within about thirty seconds Dad had pulled the brake back again and the millstone stopped.

"Check in between Prim, can you pull the pieces out."

And she did, well almost all of them for some had strayed deep inside the mill stone but there was no chance of her getting to them.

Both Prim and her Dad inspected the pieces they could find.

"Broken beyond repair," advised her Dad and she could only agree, "not even the Devil could repair that."

Together they collected the bits of chain and put them into their pockets.

"He could always make another chain," suggested Prim, feeling suddenly down after the high of defeating Lilith and destroying the chain.

"He better not, not around here," and her Dad smiled.

Leaving the mill with the pieces they saw Rose and Mum chatting half way across the field. They were getting to know each other, and Prim was happy.

Chapter Seventy-Five

They returned to the hanging tree and Barnaby Grudge and Amy, Sadie and Lockie had piled all the corpses up albeit rather unceremoniously and without a hint of decorum.

Prim decided not to look, it wasn't that she did not want to see Lilith or Lady Elizabeth, she did not want to see the body of her Harry. She could not even say to herself that he was in heaven, for he was not.

"Begging your pardon, ma'am," said Barnaby, and he looked directly at Prim, "we thought it best to tidy up so to speak, before anyone see's what has been going on."

And he looked to Prim for approval.

"Thank you Barnaby," she replied, "that is very thoughtful. How are you going to get them all back to St Hilda's?"

"Young Lockie says there is an old trolley outside the Church, it might take us a few journeys, but we reckon we will have all back to bed before sunrise."

"And what of Lilith?" Rose asked.

"We'll be burying her right here. That's the first job for me whilst her brother and sisters bring back the trolley. Is that good?"

"Yes," smiled Prim, "I think my family need to get back home for a bit but before we do, I have to thank you not just for what you are doing now but for your help tonight, I don't know what we would have done without you."

It looked like he was about to blush, but he had not gone completely soft in the head.

"I just used my loaf really and realised what I was getting into. Didn't sound so good to me in the end."

"Well we are glad," but before Prim could say more, Barnaby continued.

"If you do not mind Miss, I have a favour to ask."

And Prim knew what it was. And Barnaby did not have to ask any further for he knew she would help him, after all, not only would it help him, it would break the curse once and for all. Surely he had done enough to earn his trip upstairs.

"You get yourself back home then Miss. Don't go to bed too early though," and he looked around at the bodies, "we have got a job to do here first."

And he smiled.

With that, Prim, her family and Amy, Sadie and Lockie left Barnaby to bury Lilith back into the ground.

Feeling about, Prim realised she still had the horn around her shoulder and she patted it. Glad that she had wiped it clean before using it.

Chapter Seventy-Six

No-one really said anything on the way back. There was so much to say but no-one could work out the order in which to say it. They all realised, however, that they were a family again for the first time in years. They then all realised that they were a family close to breaking a curse, one that lived with them for centuries.

But they did not go back to their ancestral house. Instead they all went back to their home.

They passed the pub and saw Mr Tanner arrive back from his night out and, as one, all hid from him, behind a bush and waited for him to park up and go upstairs.

With the utmost respect to the man, now was not the time to talk to him about anything.

If ever the Olympics started hide and seek as a competition, us Percys would definitely win gold.

They said goodnight to Amy, Sadie and Lockie who left them at the church and walked up the slight hill towards the Post Office and home.

The three siblings stood in a line and watched as the Percy family walked away. Twice Prim stared back and waved.

And they waved back and smiled but Prim noticed that despite their victory, it was only half smiles that they gave.

Was there any better way to come home but to put the kettle on and make a cup of tea? It was Prim's Dad who made the tea and, as he did so, realised that none of his family had eaten for some time. Inside the fridge were three packs of microwaveable chicken tikka masala and nothing else.

Hardly the food to celebrate.

And he decided there and then to start buying and cooking proper food with fresh ingredients.

And, looking down to his rain-soaked socks, to buy some proper shoes.

When he brought the tray containing four cups of tea into the lounge, he saw his sister, daughter and wife all sitting together on the sofa.

They were looking at the photo albums from years ago.

Saying nothing, but beginning to well up, he left the lounge and went to heat up the food in the kitchen.

Soon it was time for bed. Despite having three bedrooms, Rose would have to make do with the sofa as the third room was now used for Post Office storage.

Prim felt like staying with her for a bit but realising that she could fall asleep within seconds, she went quickly to her room and lay on her bed next to Rufus.

There was one more job to do.

The Last Dream

As was now usual Prim found herself in the field. It was dark, as dark as it must have been if she had been still awake and walking around the fields around Little Grisly and with that thought she realised exactly what she was going to do in this dream and wondered whether, because she knew her dream's purpose, that it might fail.

Of course, these sorts of dreams were not standard, and she began to think about the other people who had such dreams, who helped others go either upstairs or downstairs and wondered if they ever met.

Perhaps Rose would know, perhaps Rose met these others. She simply had not had time to ask her before. At first it had all seemed rather outlandish, then came the realisation that it might all be true, things started to fit around other things and then there had been no time to sit and dwell on the whole grand saga of her family's history. It had been time only for action.

And she hoped that, if this dream worked well, she would not have any other of these dreams in her life time.

And she wondered what the actual time was and whether Barnaby Grudge, Private Grudge, First World War soldier and one of many millions to die, had finished his work along with Amy, Sadie and Lockie, and all was well around Little Grisly.

For a moment, and rather selfishly, she thought about the "what ifs" just in case they had not finished the task of re-burying all the members of the Percy family who had been resurrected by the power of the chain and whether she and her family would have to do some digging work too.

She immediately decided to stop thinking along those lines, after all what would be would be and she was concerned that by thinking of such stuff, her dream would end, she would awake, and the curse would remain, at least until she fell asleep again.

But she had remembered the chain and the fact that, despite being broken, they needed to somehow get rid of it, even if it was just chucking pieces into the stream, bin or even the crypt.

She thought about Barnaby again, how he had helped her, he had realised something and decided to change sides to her family rather than Lilith.

And now he wanted to go upstairs, and she wondered whether he had quite done enough to do so but decided that he must have done, after all, he had asked her to help him and, surely, he must have known in himself.

She thought it would be sad to say goodbye to him, but it had to be done, and he knew it.

She wondered whether, with the curse broken, she would ever see her Amy, Sadie and Lockie again.

She certainly hoped she would.

But, in her heart and her head, she knew that she wouldn't and that they probably deserved a long retirement from helping the Percy family.

Again, she put a stop to thinking of such things, so she could concentrate on the job in hand and wondered where her animal friends were, the ones who could talk in these dreams.

Looking around she noticed that the three of them, the dog, the fox and the horse were walking by her side and she felt silly that she had not noticed them and apologised.

"That is okay Prim," said the dog, "we thought you were deep in thought and did not want to disturb you."

"But, I should have realised you were here and said, hello. After all you have made me feel safe and welcome, and, this might be my last time here."

"We know that," said the fox, "well in this field anyway. One day, many years from now you will be waiting at the gate too, like this person."

And before Prim could even think or respond as to what the fox said, she had arrived at the gate, her three animal friends had disappeared, and there, waiting patiently was Barnaby Grudge, who, upon seeing Prim, stood to attention and saluted her.

"Thank you gladly ma'am for meeting me here. I can tell you that all tasks have now been completed and the crypt is back as it was."

"Thank you Barnaby, and are you ready now?"

"I should imagine so ma'am, well I am here so I shall say that I am."

And they walked away from the gate and through the field.

"I am sorry that I tried to kill you previously, I was not a very good soldier and, I suppose, not a very good or nice human being."

Prim stopped and looked at him. He was being brutally honest now.

"But you did something remarkable Barnaby, you changed, you realised your error, something Lady Elizabeth did not."

"No, she didn't did she, and we all thought she was the brightest. Still, I do feel a bit sorry for her."

Prim wasn't so sure whether she felt sorry for Lady Elizabeth but supposed in time that she would.

"Well here we are ma'am," said Barnaby, "best say my goodbye now and wish you all best. You are a right 'un I can tell you, I thought you were just some weedy little thing at first, but it turned out that you were made of strong stuff. It was you that got me thinking you know, whether I was right following the witch and maybe that I should think about a move."

And he saluted her again and Prim blushed.

"How do you know we are here?" Prim asked.

"Been here before. Before I was chucked out for what I did. Well, all that is now in the past. Cheerio ma'am and try and do something nice at Great Grisly Hall now all us residents have gone."

And Barnaby was right about being here and the usual flash of brilliant white enveloped the sky and blinded Prim for a second or two.

She did not hear any voices but instead woke up immediately in her bed, feeling exhausted but elated.

The curse of the Percy family was at an end.

Chapter Seventy-Seven

The last few damp days of Spring had decided to take a break and Prim rose to see that the sun had reclaimed the skies all to herself and, through the windows, there was a loving warmth.

She dressed and leaving her bedroom she checked the time and realised that the Post Office should be open but there was no sign that anyone else was up at all.

Prim entered her parent's room and her Dad was fast asleep and looked contented. Her mother, though, was awake and she looked at Prim and nodded, knowing full well what Prim was going to say.

"No work today Prim," Mum said, "I think the locals and visitors of Little Grisly can do without us for one day at the least. They probably heard us in the village last night anyway."

And she held out her hand to Prim's who took it and held it for a second quite firmly.

"Just going out before breakfast," Prim advised, remembering that, technically, she was still grounded but presumed that all that had now been forgotten.

"Have a nice time darling," said her Mum before turning around in bed to go back to sleep.

Prim sneaked a peak into the lounge and saw that Rose was also asleep.

They, we almost died yesterday. I think we all deserve a holiday.

And with that thought she remembered that she had been on holiday for almost two weeks and that she would return to school on Monday next.

That thought was quite a downer but, leaving the flat and walking out into the sun, she immediately felt happy again.

Yes, the curse had been broken, and the Earl would no longer haunt the fields around Little Grisly, but the most important point to Prim was that her family were back together again.

She skipped down the hill at this thought and went straight to St Hilda's to check whether everything was just as okay as Barnaby had told her it was.

The old lady who she had met only a day or so ago was busy inside talking to another old lady but still gave Prim a warm greeting.

Prim responded but rather than try and pretend what she was up to, went straight to the door of the crypt and noticed that the curtain had been neatly pulled across.

There was no point looking any further.

Instead, she listened to hear the old lady and she did not appear to be cross or angry or anything about the state of the church and Prim knew that everything here was fine.

Looking up she saw the stained-glass window of the hanging tree above the altar and simply smiled.

Prim left the church and began to walk towards the Swinging Witch and down to Great Grisly Hall.

But there was something.

Something missing.

People missing.

Amy, Sadie and Lockie.

They really have gone haven't they? They said their goodbye last night.

Oh, why could I have not said goodbye properly?

Why can't they still come down and be my friends?

If only just to say goodbye properly.

And her emotions got the better of her and tears fell down her face. She remembered when she first had a look around St Hilda's and that the three of them had stuck around in the churchyard and she went to see where they had stood.

She knew what she was going to find and within a minute or so had found a time worn, but still honeyed gravestone with their names on it.

And next door was one to their parents.

No wonder they came here. To be with their family

Except one of course.

And Prim thought whether Lilith should be buried with them, at the sight of her frightened face going back to hell but thought better of it.

For now, Prim was more interested in her friends, her best friends and the fact that she would never see them again.

Not in this lifetime anyway.

And she hoped that they would still want to play with her, even if she was a hundred years old.

Prim left and continued her journey to Great Grisly Hall, thinking all the way about them.

Outwardly nothing had changed to the exterior of her family's house. Inwardly, as she stood in the main hall and looked around nothing seemed to have changed too. The long table had been brought back, the paintings were all on show and that was that.

But, standing still, there was a feeling, definitely there was a silence, but the Hall had always had that. No, there was an emptiness about the place. Loved or loathed the residents had made the Hall feel "lived in" and now they had gone either upstairs or down, the Hall felt empty, hollow without them.

Prim looked around at the paintings and spied the Lady Angharad.

That could have been me.

She wondered whether she would ever dream again of her or anyone else connected to the past of this Hall.

She caught the eye of Lady Elizabeth and she wondered what was happening to her right now, several miles down below in the ground.

She saw Harry and winced at the thought that he would be with her.

Poor Harry.

He did not deserve what happened to him.

And she turned to the largest painting, that of the Earl and took off the horn from across her shoulder and placed it below his painting.

Imagine the stories I could tell with that horn?

And no-one would believe me.

We must start to think about the future.

What can we do with this place?

And Prim knew exactly what she wanted to do with this place.

Not a Post Office.

She knew exactly how to make this the Hall feel loved again, as it did in times gone by, even when the curse had been about.

And she would be its manager and run the Hotel with her parents and aunt.

And maybe she could get a real dog to play with Rufus.

She had something now to look forward to and she smiled.

She also smiled as she wondered how they were to ever pay for the all work that would have to be done to the Hall.

She thought about cooking and eating proper food for once, not the usual they ate at home, but fine dining, here at the Hotel and using vegetables and herbs grown in one of the gardens.

And she thought about lavender and decided that shrubs like that would never be allowed to grow anywhere near her Hall.

Prim decided that it was time to go back home and have breakfast. Then she could seriously think about what they could do with their ancestral home.

On the way back, she would pick some flowers to give to her Mum and aunt from the overgrown garden. In her pockets she realised she still had pieces of the chain and knew that the first thing to do once she got home would be to get rid of them fast.

And so, she left Great Grisly Hall and shut the main door behind her leaving the paintings, the long table and the small three-legged chair behind.

Printed in Great Britain
by Amazon

0222